W9-BDI-852

Praise for Marion Zimmer Bradley's
Previous *Sword & Sorceress* Anthologies

"The late Bradley's skill in choosing quality short stories is evident throughout this volume. Many characters and problems are so engrossing that readers will not wish the stories to end." —*Voya*

"Together with nineteen other tales, this latest collection featuring women who excel in their talents for magic and war presents a varied and entertaining sampler of current fantasy storytelling." —*Library Journal*

"Solid writing and an engaging range of themes . . . a series that is gaining in popularity." —*Booklist*

"Typical example of this anthology series—good to great stories emphasizing women/girls as strong females." —*Science Fiction Chronicle*

"A rich array of the best in fantasy short stories." —*Rave Reviews*

"Female warriors, witches, enchantresses make up this wonder-filled brew of horror and magic." —*Kliatt*

"Each tale is extremely well written, holding the reader in the grip of belief until the very end. A better collection of fine writing would be hard to find." —*Voya*

"A distinctive and quite vaired collection of stories. . . . we all should enjoy Marion Zimmer Bradley's latest collection of heroic fiction." —*Science Fiction Age*

SWORD AND SORCERESS XX

EDITED BY

Marion Zimmer Bradley

DAW BOOKS, INC.

DONALD A. WOLLHEIM, FOUNDER

375 Hudson Street, New York, NY 10014

ELIZABETH R. WOLLHEIM
SHEILA E. GILBERT
PUBLISHERS

www.dawbooks.com

Copyright © 2003 by Marion Zimmer Bradley
Literary Works Trust

All Rights Reserved.

DAW Book Collectors No. 1267.

DAW Books are distributed by the Penguin Group (USA)

All characters and events in this book are fictitious.
Any resemblance to persons living or dead is strictly
coincidental.

If you purchase this book without a cover you should be aware
that this book may have been stolen property and reported
as "unsold and destroyed" to the publisher. In such case neither
the author nor the publisher has received any payment for
this "stripped book."

The scanning, uploading and distribution of this book via the
Internet or via any other means without the permission of
the publisher is illegal and punishable by law. Please purchase
only authorized electronic editions, and do not participate in
or encourage electronic piracy of copyrighted materials. Your
support of the author's rights is appreciated.

First Printing, August 2003
1 2 3 4 5 6 7 8 9 10

DAW TRADEMARK REGISTERED
U.S. PAT. OFF. AND FOREIGN COUNTRIES
—MARCA REGISTRADA
HECHO EN U.S.A.

PRINTED IN THE U.S.A.

ACKNOWLEDGMENTS

Bread and Arrows © 2003 by Deborah J. Ross
Mermaid Offerings © 2003 by Linda J. Dunn
Blood Will Tell © 2003 by Dorothy J. Heydt
Mairi's Wine © 2003 by Mara Grey
The Mask of Medusa's Daughter © 2003 by Kathryn J. Brown
The Sorcerer of Rasston © 2003 by Patricia Duffy Novak
Legacy © 2003 by Lisa Deason
The Last Swan Princess © 2003 by Patricia Sayre McCoy
Swordtongue © 2003 by Anne Cutrell
Leaves of Iron © 2003 by Cynthia McQuillin
The Challenge © 2003 by Richard Calantropio
Celtic Beauty © 2003 by Winifred Phillips
Late Blooming © 2003 by Margaret L. Carter
Swords for Teeth, Mirrors for Eyes © 2003 by Charles M. Saplak
Shen's Daughter © 2003 by Mary Soon Lee
The Robber Girl, the Strangers, and Ole Lukoie © 2003 by Phyllis Ann Karr
Too in the Morning © 2003 by George Barr
The Song of the Stones © 2003 by Diana L. Paxson
Homily © 2003 by The Rev. C. Robbins Clark

CONTENTS

INTRODUCTION

Elisabeth Waters and Ann Sharp

The theme for this volume of the *Sword and Sorceress* series is finding your true self or your true path. In these stories the writers and characters attempt to answer the age-old questions: "Who am I?" and "What am I doing here?" Or, as people start asking when we're only toddlers, "What do you want to be when you grow up?"

Marion Zimmer Bradley originally wanted to be an opera singer. After she started to sell fiction professionally—in her teens—she still wanted to train for an operatic career, and planned to support her training with her writing. She wrote for every possible market for years before becoming soundly established as a science fiction and fantasy writer. Marion continued to sing for pleasure, and remained a lifelong opera enthusiast.

Lisa Waters never said, "When I grow up, I want to be Marion Zimmer Bradley's secretary." That happened by accident. When she was five, she wanted to be a ballerina. Unfortunately she had two major strikes against her: the wrong body type and no talent. By age seven she had become more realistic; she wanted to be a librarian. By her junior year in college, she had worked in one library or another for eleven straight years.

Ann Sharp wanted to join the Navy, but also had two strikes against her: the wrong body type and bad eyesight. She did have her own library card at the age of three and was turning out reams of dreadful prose at ten. This must have been the universe's way of preparing her to edit the Darkover newsletter.

Eventually both Ann and Lisa arrived in Marion's orbit. Marion worked constantly, and expected the same from everyone around her. Working for Marion was a tremendous education. Over the years she started a lot of people in successful writing careers; she even encouraged Lisa through her first novel. Looking at a shelf in a bookstore about a year after Marion's death, Ann and Lisa noticed that two adjacent authors with multiple titles were both people who had sold their first stories to her.

As it turned out, Marion wasn't finished encouraging aspiring writers. In October 2002 DAW decided on (a) *Sword and Sorceress XXI,* and (b) a new introduction to *Sword and Sorceress XX*—the original one having been written in the belief that this would be the last *Sword and Sorceress.* (Fortunately, unlike Marion, we're willing to use email, which makes cross-country collaboration possible, even easy. Marion used to say that she and her computer had a strange and wonderful relationship. We agree; the computer was strange and she was wonderful.)

Marion would doubtless be delighted to know that the series will continue—wherever she is, we're sure that her only regret is her inability to edit it herself. But she spent decades training the next generation, so there is hope that it will be done as she would have wished.

So enjoy the stories in this volume, and look forward to another one next year. Marion's legacy lives on.

BREAD AND ARROWS

Deborah J. Ross

Deborah is one of the many people who sold her first story to Marion. She has published numerous stories in *Sword and Sorceress, Marion Zimmer Bradley's Fantasy Magazine,* and the Darkover anthologies. At the time of Marion's death, she and Deborah were collaborating on a Darkover project, set during the Ages of Chaos, called the *Clingfire Trilogy.* The first book, *The Fall of Neskaya,* is out in paperback, and by the time this anthology is published, in summer 2003, I expect that the second book of the trilogy, *Zandru's Forge* will also be in print.

Marion was thrilled with what she saw of Deborah's work on the project, and Deborah just keeps getting better. It's a shame Marion won't be around when the books are published, but the rest of us can enjoy them for her.

Celine knelt in front of the brick-lined bread oven, her head and shoulders halfway inside the firepit. Her probing fingertips scraped against a cracked, unevenly heated floor tile. She took out her stone-wand, hoping she wouldn't have to dismantle the entire oven to make repairs. Nestled in a bucket of warm ashes, her salamander kept up an incessant grumble.

"Fire-go-out! World end!"

The string of bells on the front door of the bakery shop chimed gently, accompanied by the creaking hinge. Celine crawled backward out of the oven and clambered to her feet. Basalt stood just inside the opened half-door, feet spread apart as if braced against a storm, an expression of disapproval twisting his thin lips.

As if I didn't have enough troubles! First, my moon cycles, then this accursed oven, and now him!

Celine tucked a stray curl back under her widow's coif and tried to pretend Basalt was really here to buy bread. There were a few long-loaves left, arranged on their wooden racks like giant's matchsticks, plus the raspberry tart her friend Annelys had asked her to make for Herve's name-day and then not picked up. If Basalt would take the tart and leave, he could have it.

"Cold-cold-cold!" Fireling insisted. "Waiting here for-ever!"

"Salamander in a snit again?" He leaned on the counter with what he clearly imagined was an engaging leer.

"Did you want something?"

The leer deepened. "You know I do."

The curl of hair had unaccountably come loose again and Fireling's grumbling escalated to an outright whine.

"A long-loaf?" she asked. "Or this fine raspberry tart?"

"Just say yes. You're already the envy of half the maidens on Merchant Street."

"FIRE-GO-OUT!" Fireling yelped.

"Either buy something," Celine snapped, "or get out!"

With a sigh he handed over the sols for a long-loaf. She wasn't quick enough to snatch her hand back and so he caught it and kissed it. When she retreated at last to the back room, her temper was as foul as the salamander's.

Long past dark, with Fireling once again settled in a bed of gently glowing coals, Celine carried the raspberry tart down the narrow lanes to the inn owned by Annelys and her brother Herve. Throonish laughter filled the public room, with its low-beamed ceiling. The dwarfish caravaneers were, Celine saw at a glance, already half drunk. The inn's ale-imps squealed in protest from their barrels as they churned barley-malt mash into more of the tangy brew. Herve's half-wit son moved through the room, placidly refilling tankards. Annelys, holding a tray of bread and cheese aloft in each hand, cast Celine a despairing look and shouted above the din. Celine shook her head, *I can't hear you,* and made her way to the private living quarters. Two stools and a narrow table, set with cheese and a few apples, sat against the outer wall. Celine put the tart down and sank onto the nearest stool.

Herve followed her with a tankard, which he placed before her, grinning. "All the luck!" He angled his chin back toward the public room as he sliced off a hefty portion of the tart.

"Yes, you'll make a year's profits from just tonight," Celine said, grinning back. "Are you charging them double or triple? By the by, blessings on your name-day."

He planted a moist kiss on her cheek and hurried back to his customers. If Basalt had half his good nature, she might consider marrying him just to not have to work so hard.

What was she thinking? She'd already had one solid, decent husband. Oh, Jehan had meant to be kind, beating her less than another might and then only when he was drunk. The best thing and the worst thing he'd ever done for her was to leave her the bakery. So far, she'd managed to keep it going alone . . .

Annelys bustled in a short time later, flushed. "They'll be at it all night!"

"Yes," Celine said. Ale-warmth seeped through her tired body. "Herve and I already discussed how much profit you'll make."

Annelys took a slice of the tart. "Bless you! I haven't had a moment to eat. I was sure you'd sell it to someone else, I was so late."

"I almost did."

"Basalt?"

"I'd rather have splattered it across his face," Celine admitted.

"At least it's the shop he wants and not you."

Celine sighed and picked at a stray berry.

"What is it, my dear?" Annelys said.

"I don't know; I have been feeling tired with all the work. But Lys—my moon cycles, I've missed them twice now."

"Basalt?"

"Mother-of-God!" Celine sputtered.

Unspoken words hung between them. Instead of an unwanted pregnancy, did she face the wasting curse that had carried off Jehan's mother?

"Then you can do no better than to ask Old Magdalie. If anyone knows the truth of such matters, it's her," Annelys said, adding, "I'll go with you."

Close to midnight, Celine made her way through the hills above the town. Occasionally, she stumbled and sent a rain of pebbles down the rugged slope. Annelys hummed and strode along, surefooted as the goats who'd made the path. Once Celine too had walked these hills as if night-nixie magic guided her steps. Now her body had turned clumsy as her own dough.

Along the path, night dew coaxed wild sweet smells from the sleeping flowers. Here and there, a herder's hut or trollgate gave off flickering light. Goats shifted in their pastures. Celine inhaled, feeling memories stir. She remembered as a child lifting her arms on such a summer breeze, taking aim with the bow she'd carved and strung herself. She'd painted eagles and dragons on her bow, pretending to give it enchanted powers.

A willow branch, stripped to its pale core, became a milk-white steed to carry her on her adventures.

Where had those dreams gone? In the three years she'd been struggling to keep the bakery going, they had faded, as colorless as the petals of last summer's windrose. All too often, these days, she longed only to sleep.

"There!" Annelys pointed.

Celine, seeing the spark of yellow light, felt something lift within her. She would have the truth from Old Magdalie and know what she faced.

The hut fitted snug against the rocky hillside, running into the body of the earth. A cat came running to them, collar bells tinkling. Annelys bent to pick it up and stood aside.

Backlit, the wise woman came forward. "Is that little Celine? And Annelys of the merry laugh? Oh my dears, it has been too long since these eyes beheld you." With a firm grip, she pulled both young women inside.

Celine smiled despite herself to see how little Magdalie had changed over the years. The old woman still had the same shriveled sweetness, like a sun-dried elf, the same bright eyes, the same wisps of hair which, so like her own, would never obey the dictates of modest city dress. Magdalie's fingers, smooth and hard as carved wood, cupped her face and Celine felt the sting of tears.

"Tell me, child."

Celine sat beside the fire, burning with a strange golden light so unlike the smoldering embers of the herders and villagers. Words spilled out of her mouth, out of her heart. The long days of sameness, the beatings, the slow grinding days, the endless work.

At Magdalie's urging, Celine stretched out on the thin pallet. Those hard fingers touched her with wisdom and knowledge, gentle even when the insistent probing brought pain.

Celine closed her eyes and began to drift, as if she were a mote on a river woven from the sound of Magdalie's voice and her own breathing. Eddies and swirls caught her up, carried her along. She felt none of the heaviness that had sapped her strength these past months. How she longed to rest, to lie safe and cradled in her granddam's arms . . .

She awoke to the sound of her own name. Magdalie bent over her, one hand clasped in hers. Beyond, Annelys held the black cat in her arms, her brow furrowed.

"Have I—I must have fallen asleep." Celine struggled to sit up. "I didn't know I was so tired."

" 'Tis more than tired," Magdalie said. A strangeness in her voice stung Celine alert.

The world reeled in Celine's vision, but only for a moment. "My husband's mother died of the wasting curse, though she was a virtuous wife. I nursed her through her last days. I know what to expect. I will grow more tired with every passing moon and my body will wither away. There will be great pain."

"That can be eased."

"Can it?" Celine searched the wise woman's bright eyes for any hint of deception and found only kindness. Yes, she need have no fear of pain. And there would be no more struggle, no more unending days gnawing away at her spirit. No more Basalts.

"Is there nothing that can be done?" Annelys cried, as if the pain were her own.

"Nothing more I can do," Magdalie said, her eyes still fixed on Celine's. "There is something you can do, if you have the courage. Your death springs from your flesh, this much is true. But as a curse, its power is more than earthly, for the womb is the seat of birth as well as death. The old tales speak of a journey to the heart of the curse, a way to enter into its womb even as it has entered yours, to face whatever lies there. But this path is not for the irresolute. You will be tested in ways you cannot imagine."

"Tell us!" Annelys said.

"Do you wish this path?" Again, that piercing look. Celine hesitated.

"What's the problem?" Annelys demanded. "It's a chance!"

"Leave it alone, Celine said, getting to her feet. "Life and death are not all that different. Why choose one over the other?"

"Why? Why? Are you moon-mad?' Annelys followed on Celine's heels.

It seemed the easier thing to let Annelys rant, to spew her own fears into the sweet night air. They will lay me in the earth, and I will rest, Celine thought. Whatever sustained her during the climb now left her utterly. She was tired, so tired.

Hot white light poured into her eyes. Celine struggled upright, slowly recognizing her room in the attic above the bakery. Someone—Annelys—had opened the shutters wide. Laughing voices echoed from the street below. Breezes bore the promise of the day's heat.

"I should have been up hours ago . . ." Celine protested.

Annelys proceeded to haul Celine out of bed and into her overskirt and sabots. "It's Tourney Fair. Come on!"

Celine had intended to bake extra sweet twists to sell at the fair . . . How could she have forgotten? There was no point in trying to start the day's baking now, so with a sigh, Celine allowed herself to be led into the brightness. Annelys tucked Celine's arm in hers and they went along as sisters through the gathering throng that wended its way past the town gates, over the bridge with its mill and raft of shallow-bottomed

barges, over the range of gentle hills and out to the
great field. A miniature town had sprung up overnight,
with pavilions, shade screens, pole corrals for the
horses, flimsy booths, and carts. Tinkers and traders
called out their wares.

Celine knew many of the people gathered there,
either from the bakery or the inn. Strangers smiled
and waved, everyone on holiday. Annelys bought
lengths of striped ribbon, yellow for herself and blue
for Celine. Tying hers in the loose curl which had
escaped as usual from her widow's coif, Celine gazed
at the mountains that lay on the other side of the
town. How far away they seemed now.

Ryneld, the other public baker, had set up trays of
meat rolls and fruit bread, charging extra. He smiled
at Celine, once he realized she was not here to sell,
and offered her an apple bun. She was about to ask
where he'd found cinnabark so smooth on the tongue
when she noticed his gaze. Basalt stood a little way
apart, talking with a man in Duke's livery.

Celine eyed the other baker speculatively. He had
a son still young, but growing. Would he buy the bakery from her and run it with an extra apprentice as a
second heritage? Shaking her head, she set aside the
idea. He was not a man to try something new. And
what did it matter what happened to the bakery?

*Let Basalt have it, and every morning may he taste
Fireling's wrath!*

The thought of the temperamental salamander lightened her step. She and Annelys squeezed between the
onlookers to watch the contests. Men and a few
women, some in their masters' livery, sparred with
staff or wooden sword or shot at targets set into bales
of straw. Most used curved bows set with charms in
carved shell or wound with colored threads for luck.
In Tourney Fairs past, archery had been Celine's special pleasure. She'd even entered a round or two, al-

though her plain bow could not stand against the spells carved into a truly fine weapon.

Annelys clapped as the miller's son landed an arrow in the red zone. Celine, who had never much liked the miller's son, let her eyes wander toward the waiting archers. One man stepped away from the next group, drawing her attention. He alone wore neither livery nor ordinary clothing, but a long vest of studded black leather over crimson shirt and leggings. Even from half the length of the field, she felt his eyes lock onto hers. She became aware of the milky skin at the unbuckled neck of his vest, the midnight hair tumbling over the broad shoulders, the slow curve of the lips as if in recognition. She swayed on her feet.

"What is it, my dear?" Annelys asked.

"Nothing." Doubt swept away the moment. *He must have thought I twas someone else. It could not have been me such a man would want.*

And yet, her heart beat unaccountably fast when he stepped up to the line and dipped his bow in her direction in salute. Sun flashed on spiraling runes in silver wire as he took aim. His arrows went straight and true. The crowd cheered wildly.

Celine stood motionless as the victorious archer walked toward her. He bowed as if she were a great lady and not a widow with a shop. With sweet words he begged her pardon for his forwardness, asking only her name and the privilege of carrying her favor into the next round. While Annelys watched, open-mouthed, Celine gave him the ribbon from her hair, which he tied to a metal ring. His name, she found out, was Ian Archer, and that explained the odd lilting accent.

What was it Fireling chirped when she was warm and happy? Fire-burn-bright! World-ever-flame!

The salamander's joy filled her as she watched Ian Archer advance to the next round and the next. As if by magic, he always knew where she was standing, when she was looking at him. He would turn his head slightly, as if to say he was shooting just for her. All her life, it seemed, she had been waiting for something to happen to her, to carry her beyond the mountains, beyond the village, beyond the unceasing drudgery of the bakery, and here, on the eve of her taking leave of this life, he had come.

He went up to the dais where the duke and his lady presented him with a purse and a garland of lilies twisted into a golden circlet. Then the crowd closed around him, as if he had been no more than a dream. Afternoon shadows lengthened across the tourney fields as the last rounds began. Fair-goers streamed back to the town to continue their celebrations.

"Aye me, I'm late!" Annelys said with a happy sigh. "We'll be all night working. Did you ever see such archery? Did you see how he looked at you? Oh, you did!" She giggled and threw one arm around Celine's shoulders.

"I feel—so strange. Lys, do you think he bespelled me?" Celine's feet lagged, as if something invisible tugged at her, pulling her back toward the mountains.

"If he did, it's one of the best, the kind to keep your dreams warm all winter! Your cheeks are brighter than cherries! You don't think—the pain, is it still there?"

Celine dipped her head. But not for long. Now she had a reason to try Magdalie's path.

Magdalie had left the door wide open to the patterned starlight. In the hearth, embers dimmed and hushed, falling silently. Only whispers broke the stillness as Magdalie recited words so old that no one else now living had ever heard them spoken.

Once more, Celine lay on the pallet, her stomach still churning from Magdalie's concoction of herbs and ground resins. She clutched a talisman of intertwined hairs, one from the head of a crone who had died peacefully in her sleep, the other plucked living from her own head. This would serve as her guide for the inward journey. Returning to her body would be more difficult, Magdalie had warned her, for if she could not separate the hairs, or if she chose the one from the dead woman, she would wander lost between the worlds forever.

Dizziness crept over Celine, at first only the slightest sensation of whirling movement. She'd felt this way before, just as she was falling asleep. Only this time, instead of fading into unconsciousness, the vertigo intensified.

Celine tried to open her eyes, but could not move. She could not swallow, could not see, could not breathe. She could no longer hear her heartbeat or the rush of blood through her ears.

Suddenly, she found herself sitting up. Her body, naked, had become pale and translucent as glass. Below her lay a fleshy form, eyes closed in a tranquil face, breasts rising and falling gently. Her ghostly fingers held the talisman, now no longer two entwined hairs, but a glowing rod of braided metal. It tugged at her grasp, as if eager to be off.

Moving cautiously, she got to her feet, letting the rod draw her toward the open door. It pulled her down the path and straight for the steepest edge of the hill. But she did not go tumbling to her death on the rocky slopes below. She soared, spreading invisible wings across the sky.

The starlight intensified and with it came a sense of freedom, of leaving sorrow behind. Here she felt only peace, only stillness, and finally, as she grew quiet enough to hear it, the eternal, joyous song of the stars. A wordless song of delight filled her spirit even as the light filled her body.

By slow degrees, the light grew less brilliant and Celine became aware of a velvet darkness beneath her. By the time she touched the ground, she was once again solid flesh.

She landed with a jolt on a barren mud flat, clutching a tangle of greasy string in one hand. Wind howled through her ears. With an effort, she forced herself to her feet, looped the string around her neck for safekeeping, and began walking.

Celine had not gone more than a few paces when a flurry of ice pellets pelted her body. She gasped, doubling over and clutching her arms. Her skin burned with the sudden, biting cold.

Snow joined the hail. She hunkered down, hugging her knees to her chest. Her shivers grew more violent and then began to abate. Moments later, she lost all feeling in her fingers and toes. She knew from her childhood winters in the mountains what that meant. The end was not far off, but at least there would be no pain. Soon she would feel calm and warm as her body surrendered to the storm.

As Celine drew her arms hard against her body, her fingertips brushed the string around her neck—the talisman, the guide which was to lead her back to life. Instead it had brought her here to die.

I was ready to let go of living. Now, for the first time, I wanted something for myself, something more than work, and more work, men who want me only for what I can bring them—

It was so unfair, to have such a slim hope snatched from her.

I want a chance!

The string glowed between her fingers, by degrees warm and warmer. Her trembling slowed and then stopped. The storm passed as quickly as it had come, the snow rapidly melting. She knelt on a shallow, pebble-strewn cup before the entrance to a huge cavern.

She stood up, still holding the talisman. As she moved toward the cavern, it gave off a sweet yellow light. When she turned away from the cave, the light dimmed. A guide she had been promised; a guide she had been given. Her heart lifted.

She stepped over the threshold. The arching doorway of the cave was the same grayish stone as the mountainside, but inside the rock turned blood red. Another step, and she was caught, jerked forward as if the cave had sucked her into its belly.

Celine stood about halfway down a slope leading to a cavern so vast she could not see its borders. Stalactites hung above her, so distant they resembled dangling threads. On the rocky floor below lay a huge lump of stone.

Like a skull it was, distorted and leering, far less human than the Throonish dwarfs. It stood about twice the height of a man, and its gaping maw was large enough for her to pass within. Two blunted, downturned horns adorned the top of the skull, and the deep-set orbits were tilted downward, the better to watch her approach. Poison-yellow light flickered within the eye sockets. Glowing saliva dripped from the stone fangs.

Her feet froze to the path. The stone-skull sat in front of her, unmoving and pitiless. Any moment now, her courage would surely break, and she would turn and run. There was nothing this lump of rock could do to stop her. But if she did that, she realized, or even if she stood here forever, she would never return to the human world, never stroke Fireling's smooth hide nor smell the spice-buns she had made with her own hands, never travel beyond the mountains. Never laugh, never dream. Never see Ian Archer's slow smile.

All because she was afraid.

She had thought she had nothing to lose by undertaking this journey. Now, she saw as clearly as if engraved in letters of flame how much she risked.

As she passed beneath the teeth, a drop of saliva

spattered her shoulders. She screamed and clawed at
it, but went on. The interior of the stone-skull was
still and black. Not the wondrous, living dark of the
stars, but an utter absence of light and form. The
stone-skull, the red light of the cavern, even the glow
of the talisman, all vanished as if they had never been.

Slowly her fears seeped away. She felt warmer, as
if the darkness itself cradled her in loving arms. Her
knotted muscles relaxed. Her eyes focused on a filmy
wisp that suggested the lines of a kindly old face.
Closer and closer the image came, until Celine felt the
silken whisper of lips on brow, as she had often been
kissed as a child.

A well remembered voice murmured music to her
heart, "Celine my baby, Celine my love . . ."

It was not mere longing that put those words into
Celine's ears. She actually heard a voice—distorted
and breathy, a melding of every loving phrase she had
ever heard. She was a child curled in her granddam's
lap, pressed against the softness of her body, fingers
stroking her hair.

No drudgery, no worry, only peace . . .

She reached out, but her fingers grasped only air.
She stretched further and took a step, then another, all
the while finding only emptiness. There was nothing to
touch, nothing to hold on to.

"Celine . . ." The voice seemed less human now,
more like a twist of wind.

"No!" Celine screamed from the bottom of her
lungs. "Don't leave me!"

Then Celine was alone in the darkness. Loss, sharper
than the ice storm, swept through her. Wildly, she
sobbed that she could not bear it, that she would give
anything to be back in her granddam's arms . . .

Celine stood again in front of the stone-skull, only
now there was no light in the eye sockets and dull

gray chalk filled the mouth. She could not travel that path again.

She still held the talisman, but the hairs were no longer tightly entwined. As she looked down at them, they separated entirely. They looked identical, two strands of colorless filament.

It would be so easy to throw one down without thinking, hoping it would send her back to her grand-dam and this time she would stay with her forever. She could convince herself that she had tried, but luck had been against her. It wouldn't be her fault she'd guessed wrong.

There would be no guessing. She must choose with all her heart and soul. The uncertain tides of life . . . or the empty promises of the dark.

Celine crouched on the threshold to Magdalie's hut, sipping goat's milk from a horn cup. How thick and warm it was, with a tanginess that lingered on her tongue. One moment she felt weak as a baby, the next she wanted to dance. The heaviness, the unrelenting bone-deep tiredness of these last months, had lifted with the morning mist.

Here came Magdalie up the trail, mounted on Pierrot's donkey and using a willow switch freely to keep the beast moving. She helped Celine on the back of the sturdy beast, which sighed in resignation. The thick wool riding-pad looked as if it had been freshly brushed.

"Pierrot will come to collect him tonight," Magdalie said. She tied two cloth bags to the riding pad, one on either side of the donkey's rump. "Now, you will prepare these herbs as I told you, and take them faithfully and—"

"Yes, yes!" Celine laughed.

She let the donkey set its own pace, watching the tapering ears bob with each stride. The sun was well up, and she wondered how she had never noticed the intense blue of the sky, the bright green of grass and vine, the almost-black green of massed evergreen forest. Night-nixies had left strands of glowing dewdrops wherever shade lingered. A tangle of wildflowers, grasses, fragrant herbs, mosses, and rotting wood lined the narrow path. Birds sang as they swooped and darted across the sky. She sang with them.

As she neared the town, though, she grew quieter. She felt remarkably well, but this changed nothing. Bread still must be baked, a temperamental salamander to be appeased, Basalt to be reckoned with . . .

With the thought of Basalt came that of Ian Archer. She smiled.

The town sparkled in the noonday sun, pavilions and booths still standing for a last half-day of merriment and trade. A pair of half-grown boys darted toward her, calling.

"Mistress! We'll keep your donkey safe, only five sols!"

"You give me the five sols and I'll let you ride him," she called back.

"Oh, it's the baker lady." One of the boys broke off the chase, his face falling. "She's a hard one."

A hard one. Is that what people thought of her? Ah yes, she must have been, to have endured first Jehan and then widowhood.

I did not come back from the skull cave to do more of the same.

Celine left the donkey at the inn, happily munching oat hay in one of the stalls reserved for travelers' mounts. Annelys was at the farmer's market, restocking after the Throons and fair-goers had eaten out their pantries. Herve nodded at Celine, beaming. A good soul, a simple soul. She wanted to kiss the bald spot on his head, but it would embarrass him too much.

The bakery welcomed her like an old friend, sagging against its neighbors as if it were too tired to go on alone. And yet, they leaned on one another, each knowing its own place—bakery, butchery, green-grocer, wine shop—each filling the street with its own constellation of fragrances. From the back, she heard Fireling's plaintive whine.

"Fire-go-out! World end!"

No, the world wouldn't end, but she hurried to the back of the shop to ease the little animal's distress. Behind her, the string of bells chimed gently. She paused with one hand on the bellows, knowing that this time it was not Basalt.

"My lady." Eyes of green flecked with gold like a far-off sea regarded her with a twinkle. A pulse leapt in the hollow of his bared throat.

But now she saw the shadows beneath those eyes, the tiny lines, the tightness, the tracery of silver in the midnight hair. The black leather vest was worn raw in places, and the ring where he'd tied her token bore a tangle of faded threads.

"I have no bread to sell today, sir."

"I have not come to buy bread." It was just the sort of phrase Basalt might have used, had he been a bit more polished. In a rush, as if looking into a mirror, she knew what Ian Archer had seen in her.

Not her, Celine. Any lonely, overworked widow, starved for a bit of romance, would do. But he would leave in a day or three, taking his tourney prizes with him. On to another fair, another widow, and then another.

For a moment, she considered, for Ian Archer was not Basalt. He would pay in earnest coin with those eyes, that hair, that musical voice. Those arms were yet strong, those hands skilled, knuckles not yet swollen with joint-ill. And if he found a night's solace in her bed and offered illusion in recompense, what harm could there be in that?

On the freezing plain, in the cavern, within the stone-skull, everything had been so clean-edged, al-

most featureless. Even her emotions had been uncom-
plicated—hope, fear, love, loss. The outer world
wasn't like that. Weeds grew in the cracks of weath-
ered granite; dust fouled even the most carefully oiled
gears. People said one thing and did another, meant
well and yet brought sorrow.

While she was thinking, Ian Archer leaned on the
counter, face tilted away from her. He took in a deep
breath, released it in a sigh. The lines of his face and
body softened. She brought out a short loaf from the
last day's baking, one too stumpy for ready sale, and
offered it to him. The crust crackled as he tore a
piece off.

" 'Tis good bread." He paused in his chewing, eyes
thoughtful. "The flour is harder than we use in the
Isles."

"We call it frost-wheat," she said, accepting a mor-
sel in return. "It's a winter wheat, slow to ripen but
with good bones, or so the miller says when he asks
an extra sol for the grinding." Inside the shell of crust,
the bread was still tender and faintly fragrant, reminding her of fields of waving stalks lightly dusted
with snow. "But how does an archer come to know
of such things?"

"In the village where I grew up—oh, a handful of
cotts, not a grand place like this—my mother's family
made the bread, everything from running the water-
mill to the real baking. I had no sisters, just a handful
of rowdy brothers. We worked in the bakery from the
time we could stand. The smells here remind me . . .
I can almost feel the dough all silky in my hands . . .
but that was long ago."

"And the archery? You could not have come to
that late."

Dark brows tightened. "When the Boat-riders came
sweeping down from the north, we all of us stood to
the palisades. One day, I carried my father's bow."

And the luck-tokens carved into it had been real,

so that even a young boy shot straight and true. But the father did not.

Celine saw what happened in his face. *They burned the mill, the cotts. I alone, I was left to make my way in the world.* Sadness shot through her like one of Ian Archer's arrows. How had he managed to live with such a burden? She felt a strange kinship with this man who had no place, she who had one that held her in a merciless grip. Once she would have turned away with a few meaningless phrases, to remember him only on the loneliest of nights. Now, on this day of all days, the rich chaotic pattern of her life came clear.

"Ian Archer, Ian . . . Baker." Gently she laid one hand on his, as if he were her brother. "I have a proposition for you."

Tiny brass bells jingled from the gray mare's harness as Celine rode briskly down the road which would take her away from the village. The long black vest fit surprisingly well when laced to her shape, and the bowcase settled across her back as if it had always been there.

She'd left Ian Baker crouched over the firepit of the main oven, getting acquainted with the salamander. Fireling, after yowling her distress, had favored him with a flick of her slender tongue, just quick enough not to sear his skin. He'd laughed, a merrier sound by far than all his flattering words. When Basalt came by the shop, expecting an even more worn-down Celine . . . Ah, but she left that moment to Ian to relish.

Overhead, the sky grew warmer and brighter, quivering with light. Within its case, the bow hummed sweetly to her in its own language; she remembered how it had warmed under her touch, inviting her to string it, test it, draw out its power with her own.

"No more tourney-fairs for you, my beauty," she'd sung in her turn. "And no more endurance for me!"

Fire and moon! Dance through the air!

They were two of a kind, this enchanted thing and her. They needed only an adventure worthy of their mettle. And if one did not come to them . . . well, then they would go out and make it!

MERMAID OFFERINGS

Linda J. Dunn

Linda J. Dunn lives in Indiana with the usual assortment of allergen-producing cats. She is a computer specialist with the government, where she manages a network of PCs. At home she has a network of computers that are primarily Macs.

In her spare time, she has been digging up grass in her yard and replacing this with mulch and flowers. The result is that grass is becoming increasingly scarce and weeds are flourishing. As the backyard overlooks a small, man-made lake in the subdivision and neighbors are frequently fishing nearby, the story that appears in this anthology is the natural outgrowth of pausing during her gardening efforts to ask "what if?"

"You want me to butcher this and prepare it for the king's feast?" Freida asked before turning to stare again at the ugly fish in the garden pond. String-thin tentacles hung flat against the fish's head when it rose above the water to dance on its tail. The fish clapped its long, slender fins together, seal-like, and squealed a painful whistle before falling back into the water and swimming furiously around the pool again and again.

"Those who eat the flesh of mermaids will live forever," the earl said. "I cannot think of a finer meal to offer our king when he visits."

Freida studied her employer's expression, knowing well that the earl never joked. Yet how could she reconcile this ugly fish and a promise of immortality with the bedtime stories she'd heard of beautiful mermaids and drowned sailors?

The earl smiled, no doubt amused by her confusion. "My grandmother dined upon mermaid flesh," he said. "Pity she died at sea before we could learn if her story was true."

Freida looked back at the pond. She'd never quite forgotten her one glimpse of the youthful-looking countess whose body was never found. If eating the flesh of that ugly fish would make her as beautiful as Countess Karelia, Freida would gladly dive into the pond and eat it raw. Alas, she would probably only live overlong in a body few found attractive. Such things never were as simple as stories promised and wanting what you could not have only kept you from appreciating the attainable.

The mermaid swam facedown through the water and Freida peered closer, able now to see how a quick glance might trick a sailor into believing a half-woman, half-fish swam in the sea below the ship's deck. The ugly black tentacles on its head floated, hairlike, and the long, slender fins looked almost like arms moving through the water.

"Reminds me of an octopus sewn atop a human neck," said a voice she recognized too well. Eldric, the captain of the guards, had moved to her side when the earl walked away.

"Do you really think it necessary to stand guard over this?" Freida asked.

He shrugged. "Who knows? Those old legends of mermaids shedding their tails to walk upon the beaches at night just might be true."

"No," Freida said, shaking her head. "No sailor would ever be so drunk as to forget a face that ugly. We'd have heard stories in the tavern far different from the ones you're remembering."

"Those who drink overmuch find beauty where no others see it."

"Is that your excuse for flirting with the new serving wench?"

"I find youth and innocence attractive."

"What you really mean is that the lass is young and foolish enough to believe what you tell her."

"You're still holding what happened between us against me?"

"No," Freida said. "Against myself. When one lies down with dogs, one should expect to rise with fleas."

"I am not a dog."

"I've watched the male dogs in the courtyard," Freida said. "You need only shed your clothes and walk on all fours."

She turned away and strode back to the kitchen, determined to forget about the mermaid until it was time to prepare it for the banquet.

Alas, fate was not in favor of such forgetfulness. During the night, someone attempted to steal the mermaid.

Freida worked in the kitchen the next morning, listening to Eldric boast about the evening's adventures while Bess sliced vegetables and her boy stirred the fire. Finally, Freida could stand it no longer.

"Boy, you're stirring that fire to death. Go clean the garderobe or do something else useful." She turned to Bess next. "Listening to men's tall tales and fluttering your eyes at them is how you got that boy of yours. I do not need a helper with a swelling belly. Go fetch more vegetables."

Eldric watched them walk away and then turned to Freida with a smile. "I knew you would eventually send them away so we could be alone."

Freida picked up the nearest knife and pointed it at him. "If you think—"

"Put the knife down," Eldric said. "I am not seeking your affection again. I merely want you to come to the garden tonight and sit on the bench while we patrol the pond."

Freida laid down her knife, confused by his request. "Why? And what would be my gain from such an action? So help me, Eldric, if this is another one of your tricks—"

"No trickery," he said quickly. "I promise you will not regret honoring my request and that if you do this one thing, you will never be troubled by my presence again."

Freida laughed and turned back to her work. "Your promises are worthless, Eldric; but I will be there. Any opportunity to put an end to your annoying presence is one I cannot allow pass by."

She sat on the bench that night beneath a moonless sky, watching the guards around the pool and listening to the sound of frogs and crickets singing. Soft footsteps sounded in the distance and she turned to see a hooded figure approaching.

"You are the cook?" squeaked out a heavily accented voice.

"Yes," Freida said. "Are you seeking work?"

The hood shook and Freida wished she could see the face within the shadows. "I offer coin and riches to the one who can free my child."

"Child?"

The cloaked figure pulled back her hood and Freida stared into wide, unblinking eyes set into the flat face of the ugliest woman alive. Her face was so dark that it disappeared in the evening night and her hair hung in thick clumps that Freida suspected were tentacles.

"The legends are true," she said. "My daughter is young and cannot yet leave the water to walk among you. I beseech you, please, to free my daughter to return with me."

Freida glanced towards the pond and saw Eldric standing motionless, looking back at her. "He agreed to help?" Freida asked suspiciously.

The mermaid nodded. "I approached him last night, after I discovered that I could not steal back my child from this place. He said the only way to free my child is to take her from you, just as she is about to be— sacrificed to your gods."

"We're not—" Freida stopped, realizing that from their viewpoint, that was probably the closest they could come to understanding what humans were doing by offering a child as food to their king.

"I cannot," Freida said. "If the fish—your daughter— were to disappear, I would lose my place and possibly my life as well."

"I can bring gifts from the sea and fish to make a banquet fit for any god. I will give you pearls and gold coins. I will give you—"

"What are you giving him?" Freida asked, pointing at Eldric and growing certain why he was willing to help. He couldn't be doing this from the goodness of his heart, since he lacked one.

The mermaid held up a hand with three webbed fingers and thumb. "I gave him my smallest finger. It will grow back. Would you like one?"

Freida felt her stomach twist into a sharp knot and spin around several times. She shook her head and swallowed hard. Immortality. No wonder Eldric was willing to risk his post for this.

Freida opened her mouth to say "no" and heard the whistle-squeal of the fish in the pond again. This time, she listened with the realization that it was not a fish, but a small child crying for help. The mermaid before her clutched her chest and her eyes filled with tears.

"Please," she said. "She is so scared."

Freida hesitated a moment and in that second, she made up her mind. "My desires are different from

Eldric's. I need a fish of the same size and shape as your daughter and an octopus or two. You and your friends must also sacrifice twelve fingers, not just one. If you can do these things, then meet me the night before the banquet, beside the kitchen, with all that I have requested."

She glanced in Eldric's direction. "Do not trust that one overmuch," she said, nodding towards Eldric. "He has your gift now, and no longer has cause to assist. You would be wise to bribe him further with riches to insure your safe escape."

"I will do as you request," she said.

Freida brushed butter across the fish's tail while keeping a close eye on the bucket filled with sliced octopus tentacles. On the table nearby were twelve carefully disguised culinary delights that she told Bess were ladyfingers.

Bess did not understand; but did as Freida ordered and arranged them so there would be one for each guest of nobility dining with the king.

Twelve exactly. No immortality for Freida. Why would she want such a thing for herself? Eldric thought it a fine thing to run away with his riches, leaving the young serving wench behind with a swelling belly and no father for her unborn child.

He was too much a fool to realize he would spend an eternity wandering without friends or family. An immortal dare not live long in one place and must watch loved ones grow old and die, while they lived unchanging beneath the suspicious eye of those around them.

It would be many years before Eldric understood; but he had inflicted upon himself a punishment harsher than any she would have wished upon him.

The servants honored and respected her and the earl often paraded her before his guests to boast of her talents in the kitchen. She would not forfeit such a life for mere baubles easily lost to thieves and a lifetime of wandering from place to place with no true home.

She had no treasures from the mermaid, but she didn't need them because she was already rich in all that mattered. Besides, she had the one thing she'd wanted most from life in the last two years: Eldric was gone and he would never trouble her again.

BLOOD WILL TELL

Dorothy J. Heydt

Dorothy J. Heydt has been writing about the sorceress Cynthia ever since the first *Sword and Sorceress* anthology. By now, she needs only one or two more stories for the book she's planning, *The Witch of Syracuse*.

Dorothy lives in Berkeley with the usual assortment of cats.

It had been years since Cynthia had seen Neapolis. As the ship pulled up to the dock in the Neapolitan harbor at Puteoli, and the sailors made it fast, it seemed at first that nothing had changed: the drift of little houses up the hillsides, the smell of sulphur and fish, the chatter of seven flavors of the Koinë drowning out the cries of the gulls, the squat cone of Vesuvius smoking sullenly to the southwest.

But—

So many little fishing boats in harbor: it was a beautiful day, with just enough breeze to fill their sails well, why were they not out at sea? The war brewing between Rome and Carthage must be closer to open battle than she had realized.

The decks were full of people, milling like a nestful of ants stirred by a stick. A double line of Roman soldiers marched by, all dressed in hardened leather armor reinforced with shining bronze. The armorers had been busy.

The sailors hauled out the gangplank and seated its lower end on the deck. Cynthia shoulderd the bag that held her books and a few odds and ends, and turned toward the gangplank, but Demetrios blocked her way.

"I would like to have an answer before we go ashore," he said.

"I can't give you an answer, I shall have to think."

"You've been thinking for two days."

"If I give you an answer now it'll be *No*. Is that what you want? I must go to Awornos first, make an offering for the shade of my husband, ask for guidance if I can, before I think about marrying again."

Demetrios sighed. "All right."

And Demetrios, she reflected as she picked up the bag again, still thought she was talking about her first husband, poor old Demodoros who had died in the bean-field. He knew nothing about Komi, and she could see no reason to tell him that if she accepted his offer he would become her third husband, not her second. No one else remembered Komi now but his sister Enzaro, far away in Sicily, and . . .

And she stepped onto the deck, with Demetrios and the slaves behind her, and a voice shouted, ten voices, a hundred, raised in a tremendous cheer. Her breath stopped for a moment, but the clamor was not for her; the people were pointing behind her, out into the harbor. She turned to look. Something was moving slowly into the harbor, a ship, no, three ships, a big Punic warship flanked by two little Roman triremes that beside it looked hardly bigger than the fishing boats. For a moment Cynthia wondered who had captured whom; but presently she saw that the man standing at the big ship's prow was a Roman, waving a red military cloak like a flag. Someone had accomplished marvelous things.

There was no room for the big Punic ship to dock; the man in its prow leaped to the deck of a trireme and made his way to the dock. The people surrounded him, cheering him, trying to touch him, and he spread out his hands, shaking his head "no" in the Roman fashion; by the gods, the man was blushing.

The press of the crowd had swept Cynthia along till she could see the Roman officer clearly, and the world turned over. She knew the man.

The eagle's face she remembered had not softened, but the raven hair had touches of silver at the temples. Gaius Duilius Nepos, whose path had crossed hers off the Aeolian islands. He had seen her with Komi. This could be awkward.

No way of backing off, the crowd was packed as tightly as olives in a jar. Duilius turned his head and saw her, and his face lit up. "Cynthia!" he cried. "Another omen of good fortune. What brings you to Italy? Wait, I must speak to this gentleman. *Don't go away.*"

He turned back to talk to a man who must be the dockmaster, as their talk seemed to be all about where to put the captured ship. Glancing backward, Cynthia could see Demetrios and the slaves slowly making their way toward her.

A hand plucked at her sleeve. "Aren't you Cynthia, the witch of Syracuse?"

She turned. Oh, gods, it was that blue-eyed sailor who had been aboard Duilius' ship. Another who remembered Komi; crows take it, his whole crew might be around here somewhere. "Yes, I remember you. Are you still sailing for lord Duilius?"

"Not at present; my uncle left me his fishing boat and I've been sailing her up and down these waters, doing pretty well too. But it's not safe to go out any more, now these Punic wolves are abroad, everywhere between here and Sicily. Can you help us?"

"How can I help? If the courses of wars could be changed by witches, the whole history of the world would have been different."

"I don't need you to change the course of the war,"

the sailor said. "Only to help me hide my boat from those damned raiders."

Cynthia shrugged. "They're bigger than you are; you'll see their masts above the horizon before they see yours. Have one man on lookout, ready to give the alarm."

"They haven't *got* a mast, they move by oars. I have to wait till a ship's stern-piece rises into sight to tell whether she's Roman or Punic. By that time it's too late, their oars move them faster than the winds move me. Can't you cast some spell to warn me *before* those bloody pirates get above the horizon?"

Cynthia opened her mouth to say "no," but the word *bloody* had set something moving in her mind, like the first pebble that sets off a landslide.

To tell of a certain man, the direction in which he lies from thee, and how near, take a drop of his blood . . . It was one of the spells in one of the books; just at the moment she couldn't remember which.

. . . *and mix it into a gill of water with hyssop and brimstone and* . . .

But now Duilius put the dockmaster aside with a courteous word and stepped up to her other side. "Hail, Cynthia. The last time I met you, you saved my life; may this meeting prove as good an omen. What brings you to Italy?"

"Hail, Gaius Duilius. I've come to find a place called Awornos where, it's said, one can speak to the shades of the dead. Do you know where it lies?"

The Roman smiled. "I should, it's on my land. It's not far from here, and I shall give myself the pleasure of taking you there as soon as I have time. The capture of this ship is a stroke of luck we can't afford to waste. Rome yields to none in her skill in war on land, but at sea we are no better than raw recruits, and must learn the drill quickly.

"At present I command the Roman armies in Sicily;

I must return soon, but I wanted to see this ship safely delivered."

. . . and say these words . . .

They turned to admire the ship, now anchored in mid-harbor where nothing could run into it, with little rowing boats attending on it. Its decks were mottled with dark patches.

. . . and put it into a bottle, and whenever the man aforesaid shall be within ten leagues from thee . . .

"It's so big," Cynthia said. "I've seen them before, but not up close. How can it keep from falling apart?"

"Because of its shape," Demetrios said. "Its ratio of length to breadth is much lower. It's a trough, not a reed, and not so easily broken. It's slower than the old triremes, of course, but a ship like that isn't trying to outrun its enemies, it lumbers in and rams them. I still can't picture how your little Roman boats were able to take it, though I have some ideas."

. . . the bottle shall glow like a little sun, upon that side of it that faceth toward the said man.

Duilius turned toward him. "Oh, that's quickly told. We were transporting troops to Sicily in those little triremes. That ship pursued us too eagerly, and ran aground in shallow water. We boarded it and took it easily. You're a shipwright?"

"I studied shipbuilding in Alexandria," he said. "I studied everything. Eratosthenes was my teacher; he studies everything."

"This is my late husband's brother," Cynthia put in, "Demetrios son of Palamedes of Corinth."

Oh, gods, she had invented a different father's name for Komi, what had it been? Maybe Duilius wouldn't remember either. He said only, "Your husband's gone? I am sorry. May the earth lie light upon him," and turned back to Demetrios.

"Are you at liberty now? Would you accept a commission from the Senate and People of Rome?"

"I'm entirely at liberty, and I would consider a commission favorably," Demetrios said. "I came here to bring my brother's widow to Awornos; till she's done that I have no plans."

Duilius stood considering him, and Cynthia held her breath, imagining the Roman comparing tall, blond Demetrios and little, dark Komi in his mind. But he said only, "May it prove fortunate for all of us. Come, you shall stay in my house and we'll discuss it."

Demetrios collected his household with a glance and they made ready to follow Duilius. But the sailor tugged again at Cynthia's sleeve: "Lady, if the lord Duilius shows you favor, remember me."

"I don't know your name," she said, "but—"

"It's Antigonos."

"Antigonos, come see me at the house of lord Duilius tomorrow, or the day after. I think I may have an idea."

And, indeed, her head seemed ready to burst with the idea swelling inside it, she had conceived an idea and was now in labor with it, having no idea what kind of thing it might be. She looked at the ship again, its decks splashed with the blood of attackers and defenders. . . . *but it will also tell thee of the aforesaid man's blood kin, though shining not so brightly.*

And Cynthia, her idea safely born and swaddled in her mind, gave a great sigh of relief and followed after Duilius.

By the time they reached the house, Demetrios and Duilius had agreed that Demetrios would supervise the careful disassembly of the Punic ship, preparatory to building a new Roman fleet that could match it.

"Demetrios, I want something else," Cynthia said. "When you take apart the ship, I want every drop of blood from its decks, every crumb of blood I guess I should say, since it will have clotted and dried. Even if you have to pry the splinters off the wood to get it. Bring it to me in well sealed boxes, so that not a single fragment is lost."

"Very well," Demetrios said with a shrug. Duilius raised his brows, but he would never argue with the witch of Syracuse.

The house of Gaius Duilius was a young palace, with rooms winding around two sides of a small hill above the city proper. And this, the maid Rhodopë reported after gossiping with the house slaves, was only one of several houses Duilius owned, country villas and townhouses and a great mansion in Rome itself. Cynthia had a pair of rooms on the western side, looking out over the city to the sea; at the harbor's edge she could see, or imagined she could see, the tiny dot that was the captured Punic ship.

Rhodopë brought the gist of the war news to Cynthia before she could learn it from Duilius: the Roman armies besieging Agrigentum on Sicily had taken it, and were now spreading out over the rest of the island. Cynthia could only hope her friends there, Enzaro and Xenokleia and her family, would be safe. But then, the tyrant would be sure to bring his mother's household into a place of safety, even if she preferred to stay on her farm.

They joined Duilius for dinner, and he and Demetrios talked military and naval shop while Cynthia nursed her new-born idea.

Demetrios had sat up on the edge of the couch where he reclined at table, pushed his plate aside, and now seemed to be playing a strange game. His left elbow resting on the table, his wrist bent at a right angle, he raised his arm to the vertical and let it fall again so that his fingertips touched the tablecloth. "Got it," he said. "A portable gangplank, with a hinge *here* and a spike *here* for sticking into your opponents' deck. I'll have to work out the details. It'll make the ship top-heavy, I'll have to deal with that, but in the meantime, my lord Duilius, I suggest you have your soldiers train in crossing gangplanks, at a run, in full armor, without falling off. While they do that, I'll put a couple of the engineering team on the gangplank design while the rest work on the ship. With luck, they'll all be ready about the same time."

"And with the gods' favor, that will be soon enough," Duilius said.

"I may have something that will help too," Cynthia said. "I should be able to give you a report in a few days." And softly to Demetrios, in the Koinë, "I shall need that blood," and Demetrios said, "Tomorrow."

The next day the boxes started coming to Duilius' house, and the slaves brought them up to Cynthia's rooms, along with many earthenware plates with a cheap white glaze. A bronzesmith provided long pins and three pairs of tweezers. There was no way of telling one man's blood from another's, and Cynthia spent the day picking each tiny crumb apart from every other, and that night she dreamed she was the girl in the tale, set by a cruel mother-in-law to sort a roomful of mixed grain into its separate kinds, grain by grain.

Antigonos came to the house at evening on the following day, and Cynthia saw him in her workroom. What the builder had intended for a lady's parlor, suitable for pleasant conversation, had turned into a stillroom for authentic witches' brews. A row of braziers stood along one wall, supporting pots and kettles of copper and earthenware and bronze, and the air was filled with pungent fumes. The glassmakers of Puteoli had been raided for little bottles, perfume vials, teardrop amphorai and the like, and they lay everywhere—on tables, chairs, and sheltered areas of the floor.

"Antigonos," Cynthia greeted him, "give me a drop of your blood." And as the man took a step backward "Yes, it's for a spell, but none that will harm you. I've already tried it on myself and my maid and my brother-in-law." Antigonos rolled his eyes heavenward and held out his hand, and Cynthia pierced his finger with a pin and shook one drop of blood into a vial. She added a measure of stuff from one of her pots and stoppered the vial securely. "Now we need darkness," she said. "Come with me and you'll see a sight."

They stepped out onto the balcony outside Cynthia's bedchamber. It was already dark, and the little lights of the city shone like scattered fireflies. Cynthia spoke the words of activation, and the side of the vial nearest Antigonos began to glow; it lit up his astonished face.

"Now then," Cynthia said. "No, stay on that side, but look at me." She covered the side nearest Antigonos with her hand, and the light dimmed, but he could still see her face by the light that shone out of the vial's far side.

"It glows in every direction," she explained, "because in every direction there are men who are your blood kin."

"Actually, since my uncle died there aren't—" Antigonos began, but Cynthia cut him short.

"Men of this city," she said, "your distant kin, are enough to set off this much light. Now, suppose I have a drop of Punic blood in a vial? Whenever men of Panormos, or Lilybaion, or Carthage itself, come near, their kinsman's blood will glow in sympathy—and 'near' means several miles, further than you can see on shipboard.

"So I think, anyhow. I need to test it, Antigonos, at night and at sea, and there's no time like the present. Take me to your boat."

She wrapped up in her black stole and picked up a small chest. "These are the vials that haven't shone at all so far. Some shone brightly, some less so—my guess is that those were from Roman soldiers who bled, but survived, and these were from those who fell, but have surviving kinsmen in the city. But these that did nothing—maybe they are failures, or maybe they came from men whose kinsmen are all far away from here, ey? We'll find out."

"Where are we going?"

"Out of the harbor, as close to one of those Punic pirates as we dare. I trust they'll be out there. I have some favorable winds at my disposal."

She no longer had the flute of Palamedes, which had been lost somewhere in their travels, but she had a spell-song to sing that made the wind rise up at their backs and belly out their sails. Antigonos shrugged and commended himself to the gods, who were clearly on his side that night. It was well before midnight that Cynthia stopped humming her song and pointed to the horizon. There was a hulking shape on the horizon, dark against the stars.

Cynthia opened her box, and smiled. Some of the vials indeed were still dark, but most of them glowed with the soft light that said, "My kinsmen lie somewhere yonder." She plucked out the ones that were still dark, and wrapped them into a cloth and tucked them into one corner of the chest.

They had turned and gone a little distance from the ship, out of earshot at least, when the surface of the water began to heave, as if a great school of fish were beneath it. There was a light in the depths that rose, and burst out of the water, and Antigonos moaned and covered his eyes.

Again there was the strange ambiguity Cynthia had seen before, sometimes, in the appearance of the god. He might have been man-sized, standing breast-deep in the water on the little boat's port side, or immensely huge and far away. A crown of pearls was on his head, or maybe it was only the water droplets that fell glistening from his hair and beard. He held in his right hand the trident that marked him as lord of the sea.

"Hail, Neptune," Cynthia said. "Is it well with you?"

"Ah, it could be worse," the god said, and smiled, and all the choppy little waves fell calm. "You are doing me a service, Cynthia, though once again you don't know it. Rejoice for me. You, and others, are bringing me a new bride."

"Let me wish you happiness, lord," Cynthia said politely. "Do I know the fortunate lady?"

"No, but you shall." Neptune smiled again. "It's approaching midsumer, a propitious time for weddings," and sank again beneath the sea.

Antigonos was trembling violently. She patted his shoulder till he regained some of his calm. "What are you, lady, that the god of the sea speaks to you like an old friend?"

"Only a mortal," she said, "but one with unusual friends. Let's go."

When the boat was docked again, she pulled out one of the vials that had glowed at the nearness of the Punic ship and gave it to Antigonos. "If you go out by day, you'll need to look at this down in the hold, or under a black cloth. But this should tell you if men of Punic blood are nearby. One for you: the rest for the navy."

Sometimes the busiest days can be told in the fewest words. Under the eyes of Demetrios, the shipwrights of Puteoli took the Punic ship apart and measured all its pieces. Gaius Duilius went back to his command in Sicily. New ships by the dozens began taking shape on the shore, and in the hills above Neapolis, on raised platforms with oarports, men practiced rowing to the chant of the coxswain, two and three to an oar. Armed men, seasoned marines and ordinary Roman soldiers, practiced running two abreast over a four-foot-wide gangplank without falling off. Corvus, the Romans called it, the raven. Demetrios went twice to Ostia, the secondary port at the Tiber's mouth, to see to the preparations there and to report to the consul Gnaeus Cornelius Scipio, the commander of the fleet.

Cynthia stayed in her workroom, adding a crumb of dried blood to a gill of water, mixing with hyssop and brimstone, saying the words. Twice Antigonos took her out again to test the new vials. Once they were nearly caught by a Punic ship whose lookout saw the glow from the vials, but Cynthia called up a fog under whose cover they escaped.

Sometimes she went down to the shipyards to watch the big ships—quinqueremes, the Romans called them, "fivers"—take shape. Each team had a master who knew what he was about and a crew of apprentices who were learning by doing. But there were dozens of men who sat by the side, patiently making thousands of treenails to be pegged into the growing hulls, or sharpening an endless procession of dulled plane-irons and adzes. As one ship slid down the beach into the water, ready for provisioning, men behind it dragged the keel-timbers into place for the next. In this way nearly one hundred ships were built in sixty days.

Some of the new ships were set to patrolling the Italian coast against pirate raids; others sailed to Messina for supplies. Most of them, before setting forth, were visited by a figure wrapped in a dark stole, who left a glass vial in the hands of captain or mate. Consul Scipio came to Puteoli to inspect the work, and Cynthia tried to get an interview with him, but his secretary told her he was a very busy man who might have time to talk to her after the war ended. She shrugged and went back to her workroom.

Again it was Rhodopë, some days before midsummer, who brought her the news that was all over the harbor and the city: Scipio had taken a fleet of seventeen ships and, while supposedly on his way to Sicily, had attacked the Punic city of Lipara, in the Aeolian islands. A Punic fleet of twenty ships had taken the Roman ships and Scipio himself, whose fate was currently unknown.

Cynthia shook her head. Quite possibly this would have happened even if she had been able to give

Scipio one or more of her vials. "What happens now?
Do they send for the other consul? I don't know his
name, but they always have two, don't they?"

"Lady, the other consul is lord Duilius, and the trib-
une here has sent the fastest ship he has to Sicily, to
tell him."

Cynthia struck her head with the heel of her hand.
"I've had my head among the pots too long. Come,
let's go get some air."

Two days later Duilius was back in Neapolis, gathering every Roman ship that could be spared from shore
patrol. He did not come home even to sleep, and like
Scipio was surrounded by aides, heralds, and officers
who would not make way for the likes of the witch of
Syracuse. She managed to learn, not through Rhodopë
but through Antigonos, that the fleet would set off at
dawn the next day.

"Which is the flagship, on which Duilius himself will
be sailing?" she asked him. "If you don't know, find
out. I have to be on it."

"You've gone mad," he said.

"Do it."

So it was that in the early hours before dawn, as
the rowers began to make their way aboard ship, the
first three made up five, with Antigonos and Cynthia
in their midst. Deep in the hull, where boxes of hard-
baked bread and amphorae of water lay for the rowers' needs, they built a hiding place for her, cramped,
but no smaller than the linen basket in which she had
escaped from Alexandria. One of the rowers was a
friend of Antigonos, who had promised the other two
inexpressible disaster if they should tell the secret.

"May the gods be with you, lady," Antigonos whispered. "I feel as if I should come along, but—"

"No, your task is to get out in your boat, once this
fleet departs," Cynthia said, "and watch the vial I gave
you. If we are defeated, and the Punic fleet ap-

proaches, you must sail back to Neapolis and give the alarm."

"I will." Antigonos picked his way back between the oar-benches and climbed out of the ship as the rest of the rowers began to climb in.

Cynthia let several hours pass before she ventured out of her hiding place. She had time, even, to consider whether she was doing the right thing. Romans had killed her father and poor old Demodoros, whose face she could no longer remember.

She could remember Komi's face very well, however, whom Tanit and her Punic ships had slain. She rested her head on her knees and let the tears prickle her eyelids. She remembered Aretë, too, the young goddess Virtue or Excellence, who had said Komi was one of hers . . . and the Romans, too, temples of virtues and honor she had called them. If it came to Romans against Phoenicians, then, or to Rome against Carthage, she knew where she would stand.

And, judging that enough time had passed, she got up and made her way among the startled rowers and went to confront Gaius Duilius.

She found him on deck among his soldiers, looking up at the heavy iron spike of the raven, high overhead against the mast that held it. The Roman seemed neither surprised nor angry to see her there, but only shook his head Roman-fashion, the opposite of the Hellenic. She showed him her remaining vials, and he said only, "May the omen be favorable a third time. When we pause at evening, to take our bearings, I'll have them distributed among the other ships."

The following day, the fleet approached Sicily; Cynthia crouched in a little shelter on deck, watching the light flicker in her remaining vial. The further they sailed south toward the Straits of Messina, the more the light seemed to concentrate toward the southwest. Finally she emerged from the darkness and told Duilius, "They appear to be over that way, not so much toward the Straits. What lies in that direction?"

Duilius' navigator squinted at the pale shapes of the Peloritans ahead, and turned to look at the darker shapes of the Aeolians behind. "If the mountains are there, and the islands are there, then that would be Cape Mylai. A good place to shelter a fleet, my lord, I suppose they could be there." And Duilius thought for a long moment, and gave the order to change course.

Slowly the Peloritans rose higher above the horizon; gradually the vial grew brighter, till she could see it glowing in the shade of her cupped hand. "They'll see us coming before we see them," the navigator said, "with these raven things as tall as masts." And Duilius said, "But we know where they are already." So they went on.

The mastless Punic warships popped up over the horizon without warning, scattering across the water like ducks on a pond, making for the Roman fleet. "Look at them," Duilius said. "They have not even bothered to keep in formation, they think we are easy targets. Pass the signal: no ship is to lower its raven until its target is well within range."

The leading Punic ships bore in among the Roman ships, each seeking a target to ram. Under the deck, the voice of the coxswain rose in a rhythmic chant, and Duilius' ship turned in place as half the rowers pulled forward and the other half backed, turned to face its attacker, not quite prow to prow. The Punic ship's painted eyes glared fiercely above its bronze-sheathed ram. Three sailors held the pulley rope that controlled the raven, their eyes on the raised arm of Gaius Duilius. Closer the attacker came, closer, and Duilius brought down his arm like a sword-stroke. The raven fell, just to starboard of the low prow, and sunk into the portside deck of the Punic ship. Oars thrashed uselessly; confused shouts went up. The Roman soldiers formed a column of two abreast and ran along the raven's plank into the enemy's midst. The first two held their shields before them; the following pairs held theirs to the sides, to guard against attack as they came on board. The Carthagenians began to scream. Gaius Duilius drew his sword and followed. Cynthia, after a few moments, turned away.

All across the water, the ravens held Roman ships to Punic ships in a deadly embrace. Further away, Cynthia could see the remaining Punic ships moving in—and seeing the fate of their companions—backing, putting round, turning to flee. The vial in her hands glowed like the sun with Punic blood, and she took it back to the shelter and hid there with it till all was over and the vial grew dim again as the wrecked ships sank and the spilled blood washed away into the sea. Then she came out again to find Duilius.

He stood, unhurt, with his hands before his face, making a prayer of thanks to Neptune and the patron gods of Rome. She let him be. She threaded her way between awed soldiers who paused from binding their wounds, hammering out dents in their bronze armor, to stare as she went by. From the prow she could see the water of the sea, calm again now, and the distant line of Cape Mylai; no ship in sight but the Roman ships.

Then far to the west something rose from the water: Neptune again, tremendous in size, his crown of pearls gleaming, his robes glistening, wading knee-deep with his right hand outstretched, his face radiant with joy. Cynthia turned. There, where Italy and all Europe made no more than an imagined line against the horizon, marked by cloudbanks bright under the westering sun, another tremendous figure came to meet him. A woman's shape, long hair flowing, armed and armored, with a long spear in the crook of her arm. She met Neptune in the midst of the ships and gave him her hand. The light swelled unbearably, and Cynthia too covered her face with her hands and offered prayers of good fortune, for she had seen the wedding of the Roman nation, which made her mistress of the sea.

As they returned to Neapolis the following day, Gaius Duilius drew her aside, out of earshot of his men. "I promised Demetrios," he said, "that if this trick of his worked I would see to it that he got Roman citizenship; that is, I shall adopt him. I have four sons, all brilliant young men; now I shall have five."

"My respectful congratulations, my lord," Cynthia said. "He will bring you further honor."

"He said—forgive me if I speak plainly—that he hopes to marry you. Have you given him an answer?"

"Not yet. I still have to go to Awornos, and consult with the shades there."

"As I promised, I'll take you there myself, tomorrow or the next day. May you find answers to all your questions there, and an answer for Demetrios too. I would be happy to call you my daughter-in-law."

The fleet returned to Neapolis at dusk. The harbor of Puteoli flickered with the light of lamps and torches, and the people were thick on the docks waiting to welcome Duilius and his victorious fleet. They had brought a litter to take Duilius into the town, where a committee of senators was waiting to greet him. Soldiers and sailors poured down the gangplanks to mingle with the crowd, and Cynthia went ashore in their wake, her darkened vial in her bodice, wrapped in her black stole. But someone caught her arm.

"Are you Cynthia? Please come with me, my son is very sick." And as she blinked and stepped back, "You *are* Cynthia, aren't you? The witch of Syracuse?"

"I was," she said. "Now I think I am the witch of Rome. Lead the way."

MAIRI'S WINE
Mara Grey

Mara Grey has a deep interest in Celtic languages, music, and stories that started when she discovered a passion for the Celtic harp twenty years ago. She has performed professionally and given harp lessons, but she is presently concentrating on integrating her music with her lifelong intimate relationship with nature—she has worked as a gardener and written several books about gardening.

At present she is writing stories that rise out of a mixture of Celtic worldview and personal experience. Mara lives with her son, daughter, and cat in a ramshackle house surrounded by gardens on ten acres of land north of Seattle.

Ràs stepped out of the hill and stretched, slowly, first one arm up to the sun, then the other. She drew a deep breath and closed her eyes. Yes, there was the scent of may-tree blossom, and the apple-scent of wet eglantine leaves and underneath them, the earthiness of soil.

The sunlight was warm on her face and that was best of all. She smiled. This was worth the fight to win her freedom to go out as she chose. Well, not a fight, exactly. After all, the Fair Folk were only her foster-family. It had, however, taken numerous presents of her own making, weavings and carvings mostly, to win their agreement. And that had taken time she'd rather have spent sparring with Meana, the most respected warrior in the *sìdhean*.

She looked hard at a clump of white-trunked birch

to her left, frowned, then walked over and tapped one with her finger.

"What are you doing here, Father?"

The tree blurred and melted into the form of a fair-haired, bearded man dressed in the same soft yellow tunic, leather jacket, and britches as she was herself.

"Coming with me this time, are you?" His voice was deep, with bell-like overtones. A persuasive voice, she thought, and steeled herself against it.

"No. I'd like to be human for a while. Why not? Since no one will tell me who my mother's people are, I'll wander." She drew her sword. "I may not be the best warrior in the *sìdhean,* but I'm good enough to make my way. out here."

He laughed. "Yes, I'm sure you are. In fact, I think both you and your opponents will be much surprised." He reached out and touched her pale hair. "Those who raised you . . . they call you Ràs ni Bheithe, don't they? Fury, daughter of Birch. They see more clearly than you do. Much as you wish otherwise, you'll come to me for training in the end."

She gave him a tight smile, then turned and started walking down the hill. After a few moments, she called back over her shoulder to him, "Even you might find a century dull, Father. Don't wait."

A few days later, she left the forest, sighting a scattering of houses across a small moor. As she came closer, she saw cattle and sheep, with a few figures drifting among them. She slowed her pace to a saunter, signaling her peacefulness. They would think her a man, of course, in these clothes, and she didn't want them running for bows and swords.

A small boy's yell brought heads out of windows and from behind doors as she neared the settlement. She saw a stout gray-haired woman standing in front of one house and walked up to her. With her straight back and the way she stood her ground as others joined her, she must be someone respected, one of the leaders.

"Madainn mhath." Ràs kept her voice low and courteous. "Good morning. Blessings on all gathered here."

The woman smiled. "Blessings on you yourself. Would you like oatcakes and fresh milk?" She gestured toward the door with her hand. "Come in."

Everyone, from toddlers to a thin old woman bent over a stick, crowded in behind them, obviously excited by having a stranger in their midst. The inside was no more than the usual dirt-floored, soot-smeared room, but Ràs was impressed with the dignity of the owner. This woman knew she had no reason to bow to anyone. A woman worth knowing.

"I am Anna ni Donnachadh," she said, "and this is my daughter, Mairi."

A brown-haired girl stepped out of the press of people and smiled. "Welcome. My mother and I are fortunate to have you in our house."

Ràs suddenly felt grubby and worn. Just seventeen, perhaps, Mairi was as graceful and well proportioned as a deer, and as lovely as one of the wildflowers that dotted the fields. *I'm only twenty,* she thought, *but did I ever look like this?*

Anna's eyes twinkled. "The flower of the town, such as it is, my Mairi. Not even I could have matched her when I was young. But there are other gifts in the world than beauty."

Ràs met her eyes squarely, then nodded. "Such as sight, perhaps?"

"Among others." The woman turned and said a few words to another gray-haired woman, who brought a pitcher of milk and the promised oatcakes. Then she placed them on a small table and motioned for the guest to sit.

"A long walk you've had, I'm sure. Eat now, and tell us what you wish of your journey." There was a murmur from the rest. "We don't get many travelers, you see, and we've all heard about everything that's happened here many times over. It would be a treat to hear new tales."

Ràs took a bite of an oatcake and smiled at her. "These are excellent. New-made, are they?" The woman nodded. "Of course I'll add a few stories to the pot as well as bits about my fortunately uneventful travels. Let's see, I did meet a pack of wolves yesterday, but they didn't seem to notice me. Rude, wasn't it?"

She saw bodies lean toward her as the room turned quiet. And what am I going to tell them? she thought wryly. That I walked out of a hill of the Fair Folk a few days ago? Never mind. I've been outside enough to make it up. And stories I have, stories they've certainly never heard. I could get lodging for a week on three of them alone, the ones that take more than one night's telling.

She looked around and thought, yes, I could stay here. I wouldn't mind at all. Then she began. "I came over Beinn Gharbhach last week and . . ."

There was a shout in the distance, then more, closer. Ràs put down the shuttle and stood up from the loom with relief. She was glad to help, of course, and the past few weeks in Anna's house had passed quickly, but it wasn't her sort of work.

Mairi's face lightened and she jumped up from her spinning. "It's Alasdair, Mother, I'm sure of it. It wouldn't take him much longer to get back from Baile Lainn."

Then she looked at the warrior-woman and blushed. "We're going to get married, you see. He left the morning you came."

Anna turned from the fire where she'd just set some oatcakes to bake. "Go along, then." She put on a mock frown and sighed heavily. "I won't get much work from you the rest of the day, I'm sure, but make sure you card the rest of that bag of wool by tomorrow night."

A few seconds later, Mairi was gone. Anna glanced sharply at Ràs, then laughed and said, "We deserve a rest, ourselves. You do a fine job at the weaving, girl, but I can tell your heart isn't in it." Then she got the pitcher of milk out of the corner. "And some of the old baking needs to be eaten up, as well."

Ràs stood up and stretched. "Thank you. I have to admit that I usually spend more time in sword-sparring than loom-work. What's Alasdair like?" Then she smiled. "Perhaps what I'd really like to know is whether or not he deserves such a sweet-natured girl. I don't think I've heard her say a mean word since I got here."

"Oh, he's good enough. Perhaps a bit too quick to take offense and a bit too slow to ask pardon for his own mistakes." Anna suddenly looked older, the lines in her face deeper. "I'll miss her, even if she is only a few miles away."

During the silence that followed, Ràs realized that she missed no one, not even her foster-mother, Sorla. She'd never felt the obvious closeness shared by Anna and Mairi with anyone in the *sìdhean*. They'd fed her and taught her and left her alone to wander. Even the few humans they kept to make things for them usually ignored her. What did it feel like, being loved like this?

"Ah, well," Anna sighed. "Soon there'll be grandchildren running in and out."

A few moments later, Mairi danced into the room, breathless, followed by a black-haired young man with a broad grin on his face. "Mother, look, he's brought wine for the wedding! And a yellow silk scarf for me!"

Perhaps, Ràs thought, watching, *they love each other because they're human. But wolves love their pups, at least I think they do. How do I understand this? Would the human half of me love a child, or a man?* Then she remembered her manners and stood up.

"Alasdair, this is Ràs," Mairi said, laughing. "I think she'd probably rather fight than weave, but she's helping us get the cloth done for my new cloak."

His eyes shone. "A swordswoman? We could have a match this evening, perhaps."

"I would be pleased." She realized that she liked this young man, liked his impulsiveness and his quick, graceful movements. And no one else had offered to fight her. Yes, it was likely that he did deserve Mairi.

Everything was ready for the wedding tomorrow. Alasdair and a few of his friends were off with their bows getting deer for the feast. The bottles of wine occupied a place of honor in Anna's house, next to the growing pile of bread she and the neighbors had baked. And, of course, there was whiskey and beer, besides.

"Where's Mairi, do you know? I haven't seen her all afternoon." Anna's face was red from the heat of the fire and her hands were covered with ashes.

Ràs shook her head. She was hemming the wedding dress, her fingers remembering the fine stitches one of the human women had taught her when she was only five. It was tedious work, but she enjoyed listening to the gossip that flew back and forth across the room.

"I think she went over to the river to wash," another young woman said. "There's a pool down below the waterfall that's more fun to swim in than the upper ones. But she's been more than a while at it. Perhaps I should go see if she's all right."

"Yes. Go on. We can finish without you." Anna bit her lip, then looked at the warrior-woman, her eyes suddenly wide and afraid. "Would you go with her?" Then she sat down, heavily.

"Of course." Puzzled, Ràs put on her sword and left, following Mairi's friend. Then the cold hit her stomach and she started running. "Come on. We need to find her right away."

The girl's body was still warm, her damp hair and skin showing that she'd already washed, then dressed. Her shift and overdress, however, had been ripped and pulled into a tangle of cloth around her neck. Blood had spread from the knife wounds in her chest and pooled around her body.

Ràs stood up, feeling numb, unable to think. The other girl's sobs mixed with the ordinary rushing noise of the river, the wind in the trees. There was even sun warm on her face. How could this happen? How could anything so cruel happen in the middle of such happiness as there had been this day?

Teeth clenched, she searched both sides of the river for any sign of the murderer, but there were no more than there would have been if a hawk or a vulture had dropped from the sky. Hid his trail in the shallows, probably, and who knows where they'd find it?

After straightening Mairi's clothes out as best she could, she picked her up in her arms. "Come on," She said, more harshly than she meant to. "We can't help Anna by delaying the blow."

Alasdair poured the wine he'd bought for the wedding into glasses set around the coffin. His skin was grayish and his face looked like it had been carved from granite, but he'd refused to let anyone else arrange the wake and funeral.

He'd made Anna drink a quart of whiskey, though she'd never said a word, not wept or screamed or even cried. "Mairi's my wife," he said, "and I'll bury her well before I mourn. And I'll care for you as I would my own mother. You'll not want for anything, I promise you." Now she sat in the corner, her eyes dull, her mouth a thin line.

Ràs watched him and approved, but she felt more

a stranger than ever. *What right do I have here, a spectator to their grief and anger? I feel it, myself, but I knew Mairi such a short while. And is this part of loving, too, the terrible hole left when they're gone?* She closed her eyes, trying to ignore it for a while, trying to think of swallows and may-blossoms, of living things.

Alasdair lifted a glass to the villagers massed around him. "Come, friends, and drink to my wife, though we never had time to say the vows. Bless her now, as you would have blessed us at our wedding."

Then he lifted a bottle. "This is the last of the wine that I brought, and I swear to you that it will be drunk on the day the beast who killed her dies. We will share it then, as we share this portion now, in celebration of a gentle, generous-hearted, beautiful woman. I swear to you that we will share it when we can give her spirit the peace of revenge!"

Troubled, the warrior-woman heard his vow and wondered how he'd fulfill it. An oath was a heavy thing to bear for years without hope of rest. They'd searched, of course, and found nothing at all. Oh, there was a well traveled path downstream, but twenty or thirty horses had passed there recently. Any sign was lost in the confusion.

She knew that she didn't share their limitations, that she had other resources, some she'd never explored. Could she use them now? Did she want to use them?

Yes, she decided finally. *Yes, I'll do whatever needs to be done to help Alasdair drink this wine and have his revenge. Then we both can go on.*

"Father," she said, stepping into the clump of birch. "I want to talk to you." There was enough moonlight to show her the grass and the gracefully drooping branches, but little else. The midnight stillness was heavy, almost watchful.

She waited a moment, then repeated her request. She was starting to wonder if she would have to go looking for him, when a white owl glided down, blurred, and became the man she knew as her father. She wondered now what the word would have meant if she'd been fully human.

Before he could say anything, she put a hand on his arm and said, "I have to find out something, a thing beyond human knowledge. A friend of mine was murdered, and I'm going help avenge that death. Now will you help me without pulling me into your world the way you always want to?"

He was silent for a moment. "Why is it you think I'm so different from them?" He grabbed her wrist as she leaned forward and started to protest. "Yes, I can change shape. Yes, I stay young for centuries. But my people were once the same as them. We simply looked farther, tried more ways of being in this world."

He gestured toward the cluster of houses. "Do you think they don't long for power? That they wouldn't give half a lifetime to know what it feels like to be an owl or a hawk? Do you?"

"I don't know, and right now I don't care. All I want is to know who killed Mairi. Tell me that and then we'll talk about it." Her voice was low and intense.

"All right. Get the man who was going to marry her and meet me where she was killed at dawn." He smiled as her eyes widened with surprise. "Oh, yes, hearing thoughts is another of my talents. Useful, too. Are you sure you don't . . ."

But she was already walking away.

The two of them picked their way through the brush and tree trunks as the clouds overhead turned from darkness to gray, arriving where Mairi's body had lain just as their edges turned pink and gold. Ràs silently cursed her father for his showmanship. Why couldn't the old fox simply tell her the name of the man and let her go?

"Will you tell me now what this is about?" Alasdair's voice was tight, each word curt. "And why you pulled me out of bed in the darkness without telling me any more than that I had to come for Mairi's sake? Of course I'd come. You knew that. Now explain yourself."

She put her hand on her sword and pointed to a fallen log. "Just sit and keep quiet. I've asked for help to find the murderer, and all you need to do, I think, is watch."

He reached for his own sword, then walked over, sat down, and looked at the ground, his face hard.

Suddenly tired, she pushed her hair back from her face. "Look, Alasdair, you have every right to avenge her and I have none. But there's an advantage I have. I don't want to explain it. For Mairi's sake, will you just wait and watch what happens here?"

"All right." Then he looked up at her and gave a short, humorless laugh. "What else could I do for her? My vow to butcher him like a boar in November is as empty as my stomach right now. Which way do I go, east or west or even down to the sea? Tell me and I'll be gone, but right now I feel as helpless as a calf tied to a post, bawling for its mother."

"I know. That's why I asked . . . someone . . . to help us."

"And that's why I'm here."

Alasdair's eyes widened as the pale-haired figure flared up from the surface of the ground to become solid and ordinary in front of him.

The birch-man glanced at his daughter. "All right, it is a bit dramatic, but it saves explanations, doesn't it?"

"Just tell us what we need to know." She knew she sounded surly, but why flatter him? Then the thought occurred to her that perhaps, just perhaps, she was jealous of his talents. She frowned and brought her mind back to their problem. "You wanted us at dawn and here we are. What kind of an answer do you have?"

After giving her a sly smile, he threw out his arms to the trees around them, then turned to address them, one by one. The language he used was liquid, sonorous, slipping tantalizingly into her mind, as if she should know it. She wondered if Alasdair felt the same, or if it was part of her heritage.

After a few moments, he dropped his arms, listened for a moment, then said to them over his shoulder, "They remember. They will put the man's face into your minds if you wish."

Ràs and Alasdair looked at each other. He looked calmer than she'd expected. Perhaps the stories he'd heard around the fire all his life had prepared him for uncanny events. He spoke first, "Yes. Yes, of course."

She sighed. "All right. Tell them we wish it."

"Close your eyes and think of nothing. When you see the man clearly, open them."

At first she saw only blackness, but gradually, slowly, a point of light broadened and stretched into the figure of a black-haired man in an embroidered white tunic with a red cloak around his shoulders and a circlet of gold on his head. He held a bloodied dagger in his left hand and he was laughing.

'Oh, by the Nine Powers of wind and sky!" Alasdair gasped. "It's the foreigners' earl, the one from the castle down by the ford." He jerked a dagger out of his belt and pulled out his sword. "I'll gut him like a fish, I'll tie his entrails in knots, I'll . . ."

"You'll do nothing," the fair-haired man interrupted. "You'd never get to him and you wouldn't live an hour after you tried. Give your blood-vow to this woman and I'll help her accomplish it. Otherwise your Mairi's death will always remain a pitiful stain on your people's memory. Give it!"

Alasdair looked from one to the other, a surly, trapped expression on his face. "All right," he said at last, "I give her leave to seek vengeance for my wife. But if you fail, I'll hunt you down as I would have hunted him, I swear it!" Then he turned and walked away.

As Ràs opened her mouth to speak, her father put his hand out and touched her cheek. "And now, daughter, you will learn the shape-changing ways of the most ancient people in this land, of my people, for they offer the only path you can take."

She closed her eyes and stood still a moment, fighting the impulse to attack him, the impulse to run. But he had her trapped like a hare in a noose. This was something she was bound to accomplish, she wanted to accomplish, and he was right. There was no other path she could take but the one of power accepted, explored, and used.

"All right," she said finally, then her eyes blazed at him. "Show me quickly, now."

Fooling the earl's men was so easy that she felt as if she were cheating. Perhaps she was. Who would be prepared for danger from a bird?

The castle was on a small hillock surrounded by marsh and winding channels. The river itself skirted one edge, its sluggish current both a barrier to invasion and a highway to the sea. It stank of greed and rotting dung and she had to steel herself to enter it.

She waited until it was almost sunset, for she wanted to catch the earl asleep. Then she stepped out from under the trees and thought herself into the shape of a swallow, the one that seemed easiest for her to catch with her mind. During the week that her father had trained her, though, she had sometimes felt some sort of tree-shape tugging at her attention. Later, perhaps.

She darted around the stone walls until she saw an unoccupied room, then flew in and folded her wings next to an embroidered hanging. Then, slowly, for her swallow-feet were awkward, she walked behind it and settled herself to wait.

She wouldn't have admitted it to her father, but she enjoyed the new sensations she'd found through his teaching. Tumbling out of a window to swoop and slide and skim over a lake. Looking down onto a meadow then flashing past a thousand flowers. Turning so quickly that thought could hardly keep up with her wings. Everything was new, an exciting game to play. How could she have lived without it?

There were shouts and laughter from downstairs, the dining hall probably. Then they ended and she heard feet tramping back and forth, smothered giggles and low voices. Then these, too, stopped. When everything was quiet, she flew out and up to the window sill. Now which was the earl's room?

She looked into eight windows before she found the one that was obviously his, larger and more richly furnished than any other, with two torches lit by the door. She thought herself into her own shape and crept closer. Yes, that was his face, though the lines of it were softened by sleep. Would she ever be able to forget it?

His sword was lying on the floor, within arm's reach, a heavy, brass-hilted broadsword very different from her own. The swords of the *sìdhean* were more delicate, but stronger and less likely to crack under great pressure. And, she had to admit, more suited to a woman's arm. Still, this one would do.

A girl lay on his other side, half covered by the blanket. Too bad. She'd probably scream and Ràs had wanted this to be an execution, not a battle. And yet she didn't want to kill him before he knew what was happening and why.

She took up the sword and pressed the point against his throat. His eyes opened and he moved one arm, then froze.

"What do you want?" he whispered.

"Cover the girl with the blanket and tell her to keep quiet, then go over to the window. Slowly, or I'll just kill you now."

The girl yawned and then sighed a little as he covered her. Then he stood up and glared at his captor. "I'll . . ."

"Too loud. I'm the one with the sword. Quiet." And she pressed the point against his chest.

"I'm related to the king himself." he hissed. "You can't do this. I don't know how you got in here, but if you even scratch me your head will rot on a pike outside my gate. You'll never get away. Never!"

"I'll go the same way I came, but that's not important. Do you remember the girl you raped and murdered a week ago?"

He stepped back, his eyes staring, and she leaned forward. "Yes, I see you do. You thought no one would ever know, and no one could ever touch you, with your guard and your relative the king." Then she raised the point to touch his throat again. "But I'm a witch. I flew in here and I'll fly out. I used my powers to track you down and there is no escape. Do you understand?"

He nodded and closed his eyes, as if waiting. And with a prayer for the peace of Mairi's soul, she drove the sword into his chest.

Alasdair caught Ràs' eye as he poured the last of the wine into glasses held in outstretched hands and nodded slightly. She gave him a small smile and nodded back.

She'd told him what had happened, of course, for he had a right to know, but had sworn him to secrecy. A wonder, everyone said of the earl's mysterious death, and him a cruel brute who treated his people like slaves. No one asked Alasdair any questions, however, when he asked them to gather by Mairi's grave. Everyone, even the children, stood in silence as he opened the last bottle he'd brought from Baile Lainn.

After the last few drops were poured onto the mound of fresh earth, he lifted his glass and said, "To my wife, to Mairi, may her spirit cross the black river of death in peace."

Anna, her back straight as a young girl's, stood beside him. After taking a sip, she poured the rest of wine onto the grave, then turned and left without a word. Everyone followed her, muttering and whispering now among themselves.

The warrior-woman walked over to Alasdair, who was looking off in to the distance, and put her hand on his arm. "It's over," she said. "Now it's time to go home."

"Yes," he said without looking at her. "She's gone and I am here. It's time to go back to living." Then he turned his head suddenly to meet her eyes. "Are you staying? You're welcome, of course. I know Anna still needs help. But you seem like you're slipping away, even while you're standing here."

She saw the shadow of awe in his eyes and sighed. "Yes, I'm leaving, not today, but soon. You know I'm not completely human. How could I pretend to be what I'm not?" As she spoke, she realized that this was what she had feared most, that there would never be any place for her, anywhere.

But he straightened up, grinned, and put his arm around her. "Don't be daft. You're as human as I am. And if there's a bit more to you than that, so what? You go off and learn how to change yourself into fire or sparrows or rabbits if you need to. But come back. You'll have a place by the fire any night you choose."

Feeling suddenly lighter, she said with mock severity, "The only reason I'm coming back, young man, is to keep you in training. You take your sword out of its sheath every day, even if it's only to split a straw. And get the other men to join you. It's disgraceful, the sloppy way you all swing. And furthermore . . ."

And they walked away without looking back.

THE MASK OF MEDUSA'S DAUGHTER

Kathryn J. Brown

Kathryn J. Brown lives on Seattle's Capitol Hill with her agent/editor/husband, two stuffed tapirs, and several hundred rubber stamps. She's undertaking the Culinary Arts Program at Seattle Central Community College, and has been "nearly finished" with her first novel, tentatively titled *Dark Fire,* for several years.

"The Mask of Medusa's Daughter" is her third published short story. The others, "Seasons and Stone" and "Dark Queen," appeared in *Pirate Writings* and *Marion Zimmer Bradley's Fantasy Magazine*, respectively.

Of this story, she says, "My husband pointed out that there is no sorceress, and the only sword mentioned gets left behind. Still, I think it's in keeping with the spirit of the anthology."

Calli stomped into her chamber and flung the curtain shut behind her. Shoving back her hood, she tore off her mask and hurled it into the darkness. A sliver of daylight pierced the gloom as her mask bounced off the sack she'd hung over the room's narrow window, then hit the floor with a dull clank. Groaning, she slumped onto the bed, burying her face in her hands.

Her face—no matter what she did, everything always came down to her face. With her fingertips, Calli traced the jutting arch of her nose and pressed at the softness of her lips. Her face felt just like the faces she saw on everyone else—until she reached the top of her forehead, where a tangle of writhing, eyeless snakes took the place of hair. The snakes were definitely different. Yet even their presence didn't explain what happened to people who saw her unmasked. People looked at snakes all the time without turning to stone.

If she studied her reflection, she supposed, that might answer some questions. But she'd never dared to look, unable to face the monster she might see. Only Andras—stone already, or, at least, bronze—had seen her face and survived to share his observations. He said she looked beautiful. But Calli was familiar with beauty, and she knew that beauty didn't turn people and animals, even insects, into exquisitely detailed sculptures. Besides, Andras' judgment wasn't always what it should be, as demonstrated by the mess he'd gotten himself into.

That thought thrust Calli to her feet. She couldn't sit around feeling sorry for herself. She had to help Andras. Since her offer to ransom him had failed, and King Turannos kept him too heavily guarded to rescue by stealth or force, that meant yet another debate.

Calli shut her eyes and imagined walking through the royal garden to the place where she met with King Turannos. All she had to do was remove her mask—dialogue over. But the thought of the sudden silence, followed by the thumps of stone birds and butterflies fallen to the ground, wrenched her stomach. Even the image of King Turannos as a silent statue gave her only brief, guilty satisfaction. She'd vowed not to use her face to destroy living things, and she wouldn't.

So, as pointless as it seemed to exhaust another afternoon locked in verbal wrestling with King Turannos, it also seemed to be the only reasonable course of action. At least she'd get to see Andras. With a sigh, Calli donned her mask and pulled her hood back over her head. Then, throwing aside the curtain, she strode from her chamber in the porters' lodge, past the courtyard altar, to the gate of King Turannos' garden.

As usual, neither of the regular spearmen gave her a second glance, but the new guard captain again blocked her way. Calli drew a deep breath, ready to renew her argument that, even though he personally had never seen her before, and even though he didn't trust someone who wouldn't reveal her face, he should at least ask someone, anyone, before denying her entrance. But, before she could speak, he proclaimed, "King Turannos expects you. Do not be late again."

Calli's hands curled into fists as she fought the urge to show the new guard captain her face. Instead, she brushed past him into King Turannos' garden.

Inside, the garden's beauty washed away her anger like a cleansing wave. Her eyes, accustomed to darkness since her childhood underground, couldn't make out details beyond arm's length, but she could see the colors bursting all around. She could smell the sun-baked fragrance of flower petals resting on the path, and she could hear the songs of birds. "So different," Calli whispered to herself. "So different from the darkness."

She understood why Andras had wanted to come here. She even understood why he'd slipped off one of the gloves that normally hid his hands, to run his fingers over the blossoms of an olive tree. She just wished that sunlight hadn't glinted quite so oddly off his metallic skin, catching the eyes of King Turannos.

King Turannos, it turned out, was a passionate collector of beauty. As soon as he'd seen Andras, he'd ordered his soldiers to seize him. Calli had petitioned King Turannos in his garden every day of the fortnight since.

Now she knew her way, navigating as much by scent as by sight. Calli found King Turannos in his usual spot, seated on a stone bench beneath an arbor of blossoming grape vines. Andras stood displayed beside him.

King Turannos smiled at her. A handsome man, graced by an athletic build and eyes that gleamed with merciless intelligence, he actually seemed to enjoy their daily debates. No matter how many times Calli's arguments ran over familiar ground, he answered her with fresh vigor.

"Welcome, Calligenia," he greeted her. "What do you think of my garden this afternoon?"

"It's beautiful," Calli replied, "as always." The question had become a ritual between them, and she barely heard the answer she gave. Instead, she reached out to Andras.

When she and Andras traveled together, he always wore high boots, long gloves, and a hooded cloak more enveloping than her own. But King Turannos had stripped Andras of his concealments, exposing his bronze features for all to see. Calli touched Andras' ear, then the sculpted hair forever pushed behind it, and took comfort in his familiar textures. Squeezing his arm, she asked, "Are you still all right?"

Andras nodded. "I'm surviving." But his voice sounded tired, his usual cheer eroded by the weariness of captivity.

"He's amazing," King Turannos declared, "isn't he?" His words reminded Calli of his presence, and she stepped away from Andras. It bothered her when King Turannos talked about Andras as if he were an inanimate object just because Andras was different. She wondered what King Turannos' reaction would be if he knew what lay beneath her mask and hood? Would he address himself then, as if she, too, no longer existed?

"I wish," King Turannos continued, "that you'd tell me how you came to own him."

"I don't own him," Calli corrected, though such distinctions seemed to slide off King Turannos. "He's my friend. Please release him."

King Turannos stared at Andras. "A living statue! Made of bronze, no less. If there was any way I might acquire others like him, I might consider letting you have this one back . . ."

"There are no others," Calli assured him. "And there never will be." Andras was unique—a gift to her, from the gods, to keep her from exacting the retribution they so richly deserved for helping Perseus murder her mother. It ate at Calli, sometimes, that she'd settled for any peace offering at all. True, she'd been too young to remember when her mother had fallen to Hermes' sickle. And it was wonderful to have Andras in her life, a companion she could enjoy without having to worry about what might happen if her mask slipped. Still, she worried that she'd been appeased too easily. The gods deserved to be punished for what they'd done. But, by the time they'd offered her Andras, she'd grown sick of the killing, sick of the lives turned cold and hard by the sight of her. So, she'd accepted Andras and vowed never again to use her face to destroy any living thing—an oath she usually felt glad to keep.

King Turannos tugged at his beard. "Surely, you could at least tell me—"

"No. Even if I knew how to make more like him, I wouldn't tell you. Nothing intelligent deserves to be created just to live its life as less than a slave."

"Not a slave," King Turannos protested, "an honored guest."

"An honored guest who has to go where you tell him to go, and do what you tell him to do?"

"Beauty owes a debt to the world. The gods wouldn't create it if they didn't mean for it to be seen."

Calli stared past King Turannos toward a grove of trees, their white blossoms blurred together like waves of foam. "And ugliness?" she asked. "What debt does ugliness owe?"

King Turannos dismissed her question with a wave of his hand. "Ugliness is a useless thing. A punishment." His gaze went back to Andras. "But beauty sings to men's souls. It heals and inspires. Beauty is the heart of all goodness."

"And so I," Calli murmured, too softly for King Turannos to hear, "must be the root of all evil." The weight of her clothes in the heat of the garden suddenly seemed too much to bear. She wanted the conversation to end.

Ready to make her official plea for the day, Calli knelt before King Turannos. "You are the king of this city. You have the power to do as you choose, but not the power to make your choice right. Not even the gods have that power. So, again, I ask you to release Andras."

She waited. Sometimes, if she'd managed to talk King Turannos into a corner during their debate, he left her on her knees for a long time. Usually, however, he let her rise after a moment, gave her a few coins—as if she was nothing more than a flute-girl—and invited her to return the next day.

"I applaud your persistence, Calligenia," he announced, leaving her kneeling. "And I commend your true appreciation of my garden. So I've decided to give you a chance to win back your magical statue."

The patronizing tone of King Turannos' voice, and his reference to Andras as nothing more than an enchanted trinket, made Calli bite her lip. She struggled against the temptation to stand up, take off her mask, and explain to the stone king exactly why she didn't have to win back someone who wasn't rightfully owned. But the thought of killing still sickened her and she'd given her promise to the gods. Besides, she felt a bit afraid to expose her face within King Turannos' garden, as if the sight of her might so affront its beauty that the trees and flowers would uproot themselves and attack her. So she remained kneeling and only asked, "Win him back? How?"

"By now, I imagine, you've become acquainted with my city. Do you know the temple of Persephone?"

Calli nodded. It was a small temple, alone on a hill at the outskirts of the city. She'd walked past it several times. She felt a kinship with Persephone, reluctant queen of the underworld. Persephone was someone who surely understood how it felt to live in darkness. "I'm familiar with it."

"It has come to my attention that the priests there are guarding some great secret. Something powerful beyond imaginging. I want you to get it for me, and bring it to my garden."

"And you'll free Andras?"

"I think it would be a fair trade. You may rise, Calligenia."

Calli stood. It felt good to have something to do besides spending the afternoon on her knees, then pacing the city like a penned wolf. "This secret," she pressed, "how will I know it?"

"I'm sure you'll solve that problem when you come to it." King Turannos extended his hand to her. "Let me give you my blessing."

Calli stepped back. "Thank you. However, I prefer to succeed or fail without the blessings of kings." Or, she added silently, the blessings of gods.

Moving to Andras, Calli brushed her fingers across his face. "Next time," she chided fondly, "keep your gloves on." Andras smiled, and she once more marveled at how easily he moved his bronze lips. Wishing she could smile too, Calli turned and left.

Late that night, Calli set out for Persephone's temple. However, when she reached the circuit of stones that marked the border of its sanctuary, she hesitated, again questioning her decision to bring her sword despite the prohibition against violence on sacred land. Part of her didn't want to honor the gods by respecting their laws. After all, they'd been open enough to violence when they'd helped Perseus murder her mother.

But, as she stared across the darkened grounds, Calli felt her anger fade. Persephone had played no role in Medusa's death. Why blame her, just because she was a goddess? Calli reached beneath her cloak, pulled her sword out of its sheath and set it beside the stones. Then she stepped over the boundary onto hallowed ground.

Unlike King Turannos' garden, the soil around Persephone's temple was rocky and barren. A lamp, set on a pedestal by the sacrifice pit, cast its light eerily through the branches of stunted trees. Calli stole through the shadows, circling around behind the pedestal, her ears straining for any sounds of approach. But whoever kept the lamp lit must have been off performing other duties.

Calli knelt and peered into the pit, immediately shoving her hands against the ground to steady herself as the stench of blood assailed her. Something small and terrified seemed to cry out within her. She felt the forgotten memory of her tiny hands pushing at the vastness of her mother's body, unable to understand why her mother wouldn't move or answer her cries. She remembered the reek of blood.

Holding her breath, Calli forced herself to finish examining the sacrifice pit, but it seemed to be just that—a pit. She jerked to her feet and staggered a few paces away, gasping for air. When she'd regained her breath, she crept toward the low, rounded, tomblike shape of the temple itself.

Inside the temple there was no lamp, but Calli moved through shadows as easily as if they were sunbeams. She knew darkness. After her mother had

been murdered, her Gorgon aunts, Sthenno and Eury-
ale, had taken her down into deep caves to be raised
where neither the eyes of mortals nor the eyes of gods
could penetrate. She'd lived in absolute blackness for
years, before the desire to avenge her mother had
finally driven her into the light.

Calli circled the temple hall twice, but found nothing that might hide whatever she'd come to find. No
door, obvious or concealed, led to another part of the
temple, and the hall was nearly empty, just support
columns and a statue of Persephone on a tall platform
less than a pace from the back wall. Frustration welled
up inside her, and she pounded a column. Nothing!
Could King Turannos have been wrong? So help her,
if she had to go crawling back to him one more
time . . .

Why did her dealings with people have to be so
infuriating? She tried to be reasonable, but her mask,
and the sense that she was different, seemed to turn
people against her. Her aunts had warned her that it
wouldn't be easy to live outside the caves of her childhood. They'd told her that she'd never be accepted by
those who lived in the light, that she'd be shunned
and harassed, maybe even stalked and murdered like
her mother. She was a creature of darkness, and in
darkness she should remain. Calli reached up and
touched the cold, hard lines of her mask. What was
she? Where did she belong?

At a loss for what to do next, Calli drew back her
hood enough to let the tongues of her hair-snakes
taste the air. As they licked at the darkness, a new
smell came to her—incense. She froze, expecting some
priest to emerge from the shadows with a bowl of
burnt offerings, but nothing moved in the darkness.
She heard no sound but the thudding of her own
heart.

Breathing deeply, Calli relaxed enough to follow the

scent of incense to the raised statue of Persephone. It seemed strongest there, despite the absence of anything that could cause it.

Calli's skin prickled. Was something trying to warn her? The gods were usually busy with various concerns, and couldn't constantly watch over each of their temples, but perhaps she'd picked exactly the wrong night for her raid.

Pulling her hood forward, Calli shook her head. If she'd attracted the attention of Persephone, it was too late to back out now. She might as well press on. Then, at least, she'd deserve whatever punishment was flung down upon her.

In search of some clue or compartment, Calli ran her fingers over the sides of the shoulder-high platform, tracing the carvings that told the story of Persephone. On the left side, simple pictures depicted Persephone's childhood with her mother, Demeter, goddess of crops and weather. The front showed Persephone's abduction by Hades, and the fateful six pomegranate seeds she'd eaten while in his domain. The right side concluded her story with the confrontation between Demeter and Hades, and their compromise— Persephone would spend six months of every year with her mother, but also six months in the underworld with Hades, a month for each pomegrante seed she'd eaten. And so winter came into being, the product of Demeter's grief during the six months she spent separated from her daughter.

Calli's fingers lingered on the third scene. She'd seen winter. Not the winter of coastal cities like this, where winter meant a slight chill in the air. She'd seen winter in the mountains. Winter that killed everything it touched. She remembered plodding through the snow and ice, feeling that she alone understood the depth of Demeter's sorrow.

A belated shiver brought Calli back to the darkened temple and the task at hand. She reached around to the back of the platform, wondering if there was some epilogue to the story, or if the artisan hadn't bothered to carve any images on the side of the platform that faced the back wall. But her hand found neither carvings nor blank stone—only empty space.

The platform had no back side. It was hollow. Pressing her back against the wall, Calli squeezed behind the platform. She sensed that, somehow, its dark inner void was larger than the structure itself. Warily, she set one foot inside, down onto the top step of a descending flight of stone stairs.

As Calli peered into the blackness, no sound rose from below, but she could smell the incense even without using the tongues of her hair-snakes. Cautiously, keeping one hand against a wall and the other in front of her, she followed the scent downward. The staircase spiraled into the depths until light flickered around the last turn and the steps ended in a natural cavern. A lamp, set on a pedestal in the cavern's center, illuminated the mouths of two tunnels. More lamplight shone from one shaft, but the smell of incense seemed to waft from the other. Since the scent had guided her this far, she decided to follow it farther.

Calli crept along the unlit tunnel, probing the darkness with her hands. As her fingers slid against the cold, damp rock of the cave walls, she thought of Andras' bronze skin and his daily cycles of temperature— night-cooled, sun-warmed. She wondered what he was doing now. She imagined King Turannos parading him before some late night guests, expounding to them how his garden alone was worthy of Andras' beauty.

Maybe King Turannos was right. How could she condemn Andras to a lifetime of looking at her when he could spend that lifetime surrounded by trees and flowers? Beauty was a reward, ugliness a punishment, and Andras had done nothing to deserve punishment.

Glimmers of light danced ahead as Calli approached the portal of a large, circular chamber. Lamps were mounted on sconces around the wall and an elaborate wooden box sat on a pedestal in the center of the room, surrounded by bowls of smoldering incense. Her heart leapt. King Turannos' secret must be inside that box. She could take it, find her way out, and return to the palace. Then Andras could decide for himself what he wanted to do.

Calli slipped into the chamber. First, she examined the room's wall and inspected the pedestal, searching for anything odd that might suggest a trap. Finding nothing suspicious, she then reached for the box. Just as she touched it, a cold wind surged up from the floor, shrieking like something awakened from the dead. She crouched as it whipped around the room, extinguishing the lamps. Then, in darkness, she waited until the wind died away and nothing else moved. Slowly, she stood. Just some freakish cave draft, she told herself, repeating the thought several times until she began to believe it. Again, she reached for the box.

"Patience, Calligenia," a woman's voice counseled from somewhere in the dark. "All things in time."

Calli spun around, grabbing for her sword before she remembered leaving it outside. "Who are you?" she demanded, unable to see anything in the total blackness. "What are you?"

"What do you think?"

Calli sniffed the air, but the odor of incense overwhelmed everything. She couldn't hear any breath or heartbeat but her own. "A priestess," she guessed, trying not to let her voice sound hopeful.

"Let's just say I serve Persephone somewhat more directly than that," the voice laughed.

As Calli considered the implications, she became fearfully glad she hadn't been able to draw her sword. "King Turannos—" she started to explain.

"We know about Turannos," the voice cut Calli off.

"Don't worry, he'll get his secret. May it teach him something about taking things that aren't his." The wind stirred again, its chill fingers caressing the edges of her mask. "I'm more concerned about you."

"Me?"

"It's time you faced certain truths. Take the box and follow the sound of my voice."

Too frightened to protest, Calli swept her hand through the darkness until it brushed against wood.

"Take it," the voice repeated.

Calli lifted the box and waited for further instructions. None came. Just as she began to wonder if she'd dreamed the voice or fallen victim to some magical ward, a soft sound touched her ears. It was singing, melodic but too quiet for her to make out any of the words. Something forgotten stirred in the depths of her memory, bringing her comfort and sadness at the same time, a flash of something loved and lost forever. Her mouth opened, trying to shape a name, but the memories dissolved before she could speak. Repressing a shudder, she forced herself to follow the song.

It led Calli back to within sight of the cavern she'd first descended into. Then, just beyond the reach of the lamplight, the singing stopped and the voice spoke again. "Now. You must do exactly as I tell you. Walk into the light and open the box. Don't look back. Do you understand? Whatever happens, do not look back."

Calli hesitated. She wanted to enter the cavern, away from the chill wind and familiar singing, but that meant stepping past whatever had led her this far. Going on meant turning her back on whatever still lurked in the shadows. Held captive by her fears, she stood frozen.

"You're afraid to go forward," the voice sympathized, "but if you don't, you'll stay in darkness forever."

Calli grimaced, angry at herself for being foolish, and at the voice for observing her foolishness. Pushing her fears aside, she strode into the cavern.

"Now open the box."

Calli eyed the stairs, just a few paces away. She could bolt, run up the steps, and flee the temple. Perhaps Persephone would forget about her. "If I do this," Calli pressed, "do you promise that Andras will be set free?"

"Your bargain with Turannos has already been kept. If you care only about Andras' freedom, you may leave now. If you care about your own freedom, open the box."

Calli stepped closer to the lamp on the pedestal. For a moment, she stood there, shifting the box in her hands. Then she opened it. Inside, a flat circle of brightly polished metal glinted up at her, reflecting the details of her shape.

"Take off your mask."

"What?"

"You can't hide from yourself forever."

Calli's fingers shook as they touched the edge of her mask. Could she live with knowing? If she looked at her face and saw a monster, would she irrevocably become that monster, for all time? Would she ever again be able to take off her mask around Andras if she actually knew what he saw? "I can't," she whispered. "What if I belong to darkness?"

"Be brave, Calligenia," the voice reassured her. "Have the courage to see yourself as you truly are."

Calli bit her lip and lifted her mask, bracing herself for the horrible visage she would see. But all that showed in the mirror was bright white light. "I don't understand."

"I said that you would see yourself as you truly are. Now you have. Whatever your face looks like, however beautiful or ugly, you've seen your soul. That's what matters."

"Light," Calli marveled softly.

"Darkness and light are all that really exist. A face—anyone's face—is just the mask they wear over it. And contrary to Turannos' presumptions, an ugly mask does not always conceal a soul condemned to darkness."

Calli caressed her reflection, hardly able to believe it. "Light," she repeated.

"Yes. Now you know." The voice grew fainter, as if it was fading away. "I hope it makes your burden a little easier. Lead a good life, Calli. My child."

Memories of a lullaby, sung to her when she was younger than young, flooded into Calli and the box dropped from her hands. She barely heard the polished metal disk skitter across the cave floor. "Mother?" Her whole body fought to turn around, but, at the last moment, she remembered her mother's instructions about looking back. Frozen, Calli screamed until it echoed off the cave walls. "Mother?!"

But nothing answered her.

Dawn hung over the city as Calli trudged back to King Turannos' palace. Her body ached, and her mind felt as murky and haunted as the caverns under Persephone's temple. It didn't occur to her to wonder what prize her quest had won for King Turannos until she felt the air grow cold around her. Pulling her cloak tightly about her body, she climbed the steps to the palace's entrance hall and strode past the porters' lodge into the atrium. King Turannos' soldiers were gone and, beyond the gate they normally guarded, snow drifted down over the brittle, brown remains of his garden. Calli understood now. Winter—the grief of Demeter—was the secret power of Persephone's temple.

Calli found King Turannos beneath the skeleton of his arbor, hunched over on his stone bench, his face buried in his hands. He didn't answer when she asked if Andras could leave, but she doubted he had the strength to renege on his bargain.

After a short search, Calli located Andras in a grove of olive trees, toying with the icicles frozen on their branches. His bronze body glistened with frost.

"We can go now," she told him.

He turned toward her and smiled. "I guessed as much. Thank you, Calli."

"Andras?" she asked. "My face? What does it look like?"

Her question seemed to puzzle him, so Calli poured out her night's tale. When she'd finished, she expected him to look as surprised as she felt, but Andras only chuckled, shaking his head.

"I never really noticed your face, Calli. All I ever saw was your soul." Gently, he touched the cheek of her mask. "From the first time I looked at you, all I ever saw was light."

Calli closed her eyes. "Thank you," she whispered, partially to him, but mostly to her mother. Her face had never been her choice. But now she knew that her life was.

"So," Andras asked, "where do we go from here?"

Into darkness or into light, her path was her own. Calli opened her eyes as she answered him. "Anywhere. Anywhere we want."

THE SORCERER OF RASSTON

Patricia Duffy Novak

Patricia Duffy Novak lives in Alabama, with her husband, Jim, her daughter, Sylvia, and an assortment of cats and dogs. She has sold a number of short stories to Mrs. Bradley: for this anthology series, for *Marion Zimmer Bradley's Fantasy Magazine*, and for the Darkover anthology series. She has also sold to *Realms of Fantasy* and *Adventures of Sword and Sorcery*.

Garrin Windson, a main character in this story, has also appeared in stories published in *Marion Zimmer Bradley's Fantasy Magazine*.

From the top of a small rise, Lauren watched the dark-haired man poke at the fire-pit in her camp, setting sparks flashing in the dawn mist. The fellow wore the rough leathers of a mountain man, with his dark hair in the characteristic queue, but he was taller and leaner than most of his kind. Over his shoulder, she could make out the hilt of a two-handed sword.

When Lauren had climbed this hill to check the road, she'd left the bulk of her belongings, and her horse, below. The animal grazed placidly where she'd staked it, apparently unconcerned by the stranger—and he with it. He kept his attention on the fire-pit. An odd interest, Lauren thought, for a thief.

As a wizard of the White path, Lauren had only limited skills in magical attacks, but she'd learned to compensate for that lack. From its carrying case on her back, she drew a small crossbow and loaded it. She didn't relish this interruption of her journey to

Rasston, where a serious problem needed her investigation. Still, she should be able to dispatch this annoyance quickly.

Finger on the trigger, she stalked down the hill, into the stranger's view.

"You there!"

The man looked up at her, then spread his hands before him. He was a clean-shaven, good-looking fellow in his early twenties, not the usual scruffy camp scavenger.

Keeping her aim on him, she edged closer. "Don't move."

There was no menace in his expression as he waited silently. His eyes were vivid blue, rare coloring even among the light-eyed mountain people. There was something familiar about the man, now that Lauren saw him closely. But she couldn't quite match the resemblance to anyone she knew. "State your business."

He shrugged slightly, keeping his hands extended. "Sean the Bard at your service, ma'am. I'm trying to find a live coal. Easier than starting my own fire."

A plausible explanation, Lauren thought, except morning was usually the time to bank fires, not light then. And why did he look so familiar? She stared at his face, thinking those eyes should not be easy to forget.

"May I put my hands down please?" His vowels, she noted, were nasal, giving his speech the customary mountain twang. She glanced at his horse, which was grazing farther up the valley, and saw among the saddle packs a triangular outline that looked like a harp case. He seemed to be exactly what he claimed.

She considered for a moment, then lowered her bow. "All right, but no sudden moves."

"Thank you, dear lady. An arrow through the throat would do little to improve my signing. Although the other bards might thank you." He gave a smile that made his blue eyes crinkle. "Are you traveling my way? I'm heading to Rasston and would be happy for company on the road."

She almost accepted his offer. But then he tilted his head, glancing at her obliquely, and his identity came to her in a flash.

Garrin Windson. An awkward boy at Wizards' Keep, all knees and elbows, his face covered with pimples, his hair short and unruly, but the same blue eyes—and the same self-conscious turn of head. She'd been a novice mage, studying for journeyman status, and he a first-year apprentice.

Her heart hammered as she recalled the tales she'd heard of the man that boy had become, accusations, never proven, of heinous crimes: murder, treason, betrayal. They said he'd tried to steal power from one of the wizard Masters. Worse, they said he'd destroyed an entire village to pay back the rough treatment he'd received as an unwanted, half-blooded bastard child.

She brought her crossbow level again. The man's wizard powers, drawn from the strong Blue path, were reported to be enormous, more than a match for a simple quarrel. Still, the weapon gave her courage. "What are you really doing here, Mr. Windson?"

At the sound of his name, the cheerfulness fell from the man like a mask. "So you do recognize me."

Only a trace of the mountain twang remained. He had spoken with a mountaineer's accent when she'd known him as a boy, but the years he'd spent in the lowlands had flattened his speech.

"Yes, I remember you, although you've changed greatly."

He shrugged. "I knew you at once. Not that I needed to see your face for that." He pointed at the fire-pit. "You left traces of White magic in the fire. You might as well have signed your name."

"So that's what you were doing there."

He nodded. "I've been tracking you."

Her stomach tightened. Rogue mage, reviled by

most of his fellows, he could have no honest business with her. "What do you want?"

"Master Fen sent me news that you were going to Rasston, to hunt the sorcerer. He told me to travel with you."

Lauren felt her face flush with annoyance. Fen, the senior White Master on the Wizards' Council, was a well meaning old man, but at times he could be meddlesome. Of all the Master wizards in Alworyn, he alone had defended this Garrin Windson, claiming the young man not guilty of the crimes laid at his feet. Fen's support had pretended Windson from being imprisoned, and had kept him a nominal member of the Wizards of the Four Ways, but the younger man had since had almost no dealings with the rest of the Order. He'd become an army scout, Lauren had been told, working the border for the king. Little news of him had come her way in the last few years.

She looked at the man before her, all hard lines and angles. Certainly, he was a more powerful wizard than she—perhaps the most powerful wizard who'd ever lived. But she didn't want, or need, his help. "Do you always do what Fen says?"

"I do." Windson's tone held a depth of conviction that surprised Lauren.

"And if I were to tell you to leave me alone?"

"Then I would follow you." The same unwavering conviction in his voice.

Lauren sighed and let her crossbow drop, useless against him anyway, and the weight of it was a strain on her arm. "Why did you tell me you were a bard?"

Windson's mouth thinned, making him look menacing enough to match the rumors Lauren had heard. "Sean the Bard is the name I'm known by in these parts. I thought it would be easier to persuade you to travel with me if you didn't know who I really was."

She couldn't deny the truth of his assessment. The bard he'd claimed to be had seemed a harmless, pleasant man. Now she knew the truth, but could think of no way to get rid of her unwanted companion. If she would not stay with him, he would track her, and she had little hope of losing him along trails that were unfamiliar to her.

Windson kicked a stone, sending it clinking down the valley. "I'm also tracking this killer. I was on my way to Rasston when Fen's message found me. Perhaps together we'll have some luck."

His expression told a different story than his lips. Arrogant, like so many of the male wizards, he clearly believed her incapable of taking care of herself. She ached to slap the condescension from his features, mighty Blue wizard or no.

"Perhaps," she said, holding back her irritation, certain that an outburst would do no good. And equally certain that no matter what happened in Rasston, Windson would claim all the glory, just like any other man. Lauren turned and began to gather her belongings, all the while cursing Fen for sending this unwanted protector.

Garrin, too, cursed Fen. He rode in silence a few horse-lengths ahead of Lauren along a winding mountain path. The sun, nearing zenith, had burned off the mist and taken the chill from the air. It might have been a pleasant morning's journey, Garrin thought, were it not for the woman behind him. The expression on her face when she'd said his name had told him exactly what she thought of him—not that he'd expected any different, given the stories that circulated among his so-called peers.

Garrin's back was stiff with tension, and he had an ache along his jaw. But Fen had asked this favor, and he could not in conscience refuse it. He owed Fen a debt of gratitude he could never hope to repay. Without Fen, he might have lost his sanity, if not his life, when the charges of treason and murder were first

brought against him. Only Fen had believed him,
helped him. If Fen asked something, Garrin would do
it, his own personal feelings be damned.

But what in the five hells was a White wizard doing
tracking a sorcerer? Better by far if she had just stayed
in the lowlands, where she belonged, and left this
problem to him. She'd likely only get in his way.

Garrin forced himself to think of something else.
The scenery was certainly pretty along this stretch of
road, streams tumbling through rocky canyons, layers
of awakening vegetation, and a wash of golden light.
He tried to focus on that, rather than the woman behind him, who was no doubt wishing she could throw
a dagger at his back.

About an hour past noon, Garrin stopped at a small
clearing beside a stream. He pulled a sack from his
canticle bag, and let the horse loose to graze and
drink. Lauren followed suit, then stood with her gaze
fixed on the distance, her lips pursed.

"Here." He held out the sack.

She reached into it, then screamed and jumped
backward, staring at the fleshy object in her hand.

Garrin watched her, reading the horror in her eyes
as her gaze moved from her hand to his face. "Dried
apricot," he said crisply. "What do you think it is?
An ear from my latest victim?"

A flush colored her face, betraying the accuracy of
his guess. He snorted. "You shouldn't believe everything you hear. I haven't killed anyone in weeks."

Her face had returned to its normal color. "You're
joking, I assume."

"No. About three weeks ago, I killed two people
near Charliehold. I buried the bodies at a crossroad
near an inn, but I left their ears alone."

The apricot fell from her hand. "Are you confessing
to murder?"

Garrin let out a sigh, already tiring of the game. "I

killed two sorcerers who'd kidnaped a child. I got there in time to save the child. The king sent me a medal for it."

Her expression didn't soften much. "Then why didn't you say that? Why did you lead me on with that talk of killing people? Are you always so unpleasant?"

"No, not always." He shrugged. "But most people don't scream when I offer them fruit." He took out an apricot, popped it into his mouth, chewed, and swallowed.

Her cheeks pinkened. "That was silly of me."

As close to an apology as he was going to get. He nodded, accepting it. "Why are you chasing this sorcerer anyway? Fen didn't say."

She glanced away and then back at him, tilting her chin in a pose of defiance. "I dreamed about the killer. And I dreamed that I could find him and stop him. I don't expect you to believe me. Almost no one has. Except Fen," she added in a grudging tone. "He urged me to leave at once."

"Well, that makes sense." Garrin pushed an errant strand of hair from his face. "Fen has true dreams like that sometimes himself."

Lauren's eyes lit in surprise. Fen seldom spoke of his talent, Garrin knew. Years ago, he'd told Garrin it was one of the rarer gifts of the White path. And this woman was a White wizard as well. Perhaps she did have some value, after all, and could provide some help in finding the killer.

"I suppose that's why Fen asked me to guard you," Garrin said. "To be sure you stayed safe while you tracked this killer."

"You think I need you a guard?"

Garrin raised a brow. "White magic is nearly useless against sorcery."

"I have my bow."

"Phhht." Garrin didn't even try to hide his contempt.

He gestured at the horses, who were chomping the lush spring grass. "We better go. It's a long ride to Rasston and I'd like to arrive before dark."

Lauren's face had tightened, but she merely nodded, then went to get her horse.

By the time they arrived in Rasston, the sun had already begun to set. The town was fairly good-sized for a mountain village, Lauren noted, with dozens of houses, a mill, and several stores. The inn was a rather ramshackle building with oilskin windows and a thatched roof. Several hogs wandered loose in the yard and rooted in the ditches beside the road.

A man of about forty, with dark brown hair poking out from a battered cap, sat on the porch of the inn, watching as she and Windson dismounted and approached. He raised a hand in greeting. "Sean!" he called to Windson, not bothering to rise.

Windson's expression changed swiftly, becoming a mask of jovial goodwill, much like the one Lauren had seen that morning. "How are you, Jeb? The master will be wanting me to play tonight, won't he?"

The man shrugged. "The master died a few months back. A cousin of his came from Undertown to take over, but I reckon she'll be glad of a musician, so long as you'll work for tips. Custom has been slow of late. We've had some trouble lately. Likely you've not heard or you'd not have come. Been ten killings in the last fortnight. People are afraid to go out after dark. You'll draw a little crowd, maybe, but not the usual."

Windson's brows quirked up. "Is that so? My bad luck, it seems." His mountain accent, Lauren noticed, had returned in force. He was really quite a good actor, she decided. She almost could believe he was not the same man, so different did the affable bard seem from the bad-tempered wizard.

The man Windson called Jeb gestured at Lauren. "Who's your lady friend there, Sean?"

"We met on the road," Windson answered. "Name of Lauren, isn't it?" He looked at her expectantly.

"Yes."

"Are you needing a room, ma'am?"

Lauren appreciated the lack of questions about her business. From what she'd heard, the mountain folk seldom pressed for intimacy where none was offered. "Yes, please. I don't know how long I'll be here. At least a night."

"Got plenty of empty rooms," the man said. "I'll tell Mistress Arla you're here and send the boy to take care of your things." He doffed his cap, then ambled into the inn.

"Where do you sleep?" Lauren asked Windson, as she watched him unload his packs and harp.

"In the front room, on the floor. It's free to musicians."

"But you're not really a—"

He shot her a quelling look, and she bit off her sentence just as a boy came out the door. "Show Miss Lauren a good room, Yule," Windson said to the lad. "I can take care of her horse."

"Aye, Sean." The boy grinned and unhooked her saddlebags. "This way, miss."

He led her into the inn, which was every bit as shabby on the inside as the out. Oil lamps cast feeble light, and the interior was gloomy. Perhaps it was better this way, Lauren thought, with the dark hiding most of the dirt. As her eyes adjusted to the low light, Lauren saw that the inn had two patrons, men who sat silently together, near the cold hearth, sipping at tankards of ale. A woman stood behind the bar. Young, not particularly attractive, with square features and a heavy brow.

The woman smiled at Lauren. "Welcome. Not much

of a place, but it's all I have." She came around the bar and gestured at the lad. "Go on, Yule, see to the horses. I don't pay you to stand and gawk."

The boy put down Lauren's bags and scuttled away. Arla picked up Lauren's things and started walking. As Lauren followed the woman through a back door and along a corridor, she found herself ill at ease. Something bothered her about the inn, beyond the dust and grime, but she couldn't say what. Imagination, probably, brought on by too much time thinking about the Rasston sorcerer.

The inn's mistress took her to a small room at the end of the corridor. The bed creaked as Arla set her saddlebags on it, the mattress sagging under the weight.

"Won't have much noise to disturb you, ma'am." The woman gave a quick smile. "You're the only one staying the night, besides that harpist who just showed up. He's quite a musician, Jeb says. Seems you might have a treat if you'll come to the common room this evening."

"Thank you, I believe I will," Lauren said. It was not her custom to frequent common rooms alone, but if she wanted to learn about the sorcerer, she'd need to talk to the locals. "I hear you've been having some trouble in these parts."

"Trouble?" The inn's mistress frowned. "There's always trouble, ma'am. Sometimes worse than others is all."

She turned and left before Lauren could comment. Not surprising she didn't want to talk about the killings, Lauren thought. Probably afraid she'd scare away her only guest.

Lauren went to the door, pulled in the latch string, then leaning her back against it, she released a quick pulse of cleaning White magic and grinned as the worst of the dirt vanished. One advantage of her chosen Path was that she seldom had to wield a mop.

*   *   *

An hour into his performance, Garrin rose and stretched, putting aside his harp to take a long pull on his mug of warm and rather flat ale. Custom had not been as bad as Jeb had predicted. A bit shy of his usual crowd in a town this size, but the new innkeeper, Arla she said her name was, did a brisk enough traffic in ale and wine. The patrons, he had noticed, arrived in groups of two or more, and left the same way. No one, other than Lauren, had come into the room alone.

The White wizard, dressed in clean pants and tunic, sat rather stiffly at a table by herself, nursing a glass of pale wine. Ale in hand, Garrin meandered through the maze of tables and, not waiting to be invited, plopped down near her. "Any tunes you'd care to hear, ma'am?"

Her expression was blank as she met his gaze. "I have no preferences."

"Is the music not to your liking then?" He effected a pout and was rewarded with a smile, quickly replaced by a frown.

"Oh, you play and sing quite well. And I'm sure you know it." She leaned forward, dropping her voice. "How do you do that? It's almost like you become another man. I swear there have been times tonight I've forgotten who you really are."

Garrin took a sip of his ale, nasty stuff, but he was thirsty. "There are times I wish I could forget. Perhaps the bard is closer to the truth than the wizard. I don't really know."

She gave no answer, but instead studied him with her cool, gray eyes. Eyes that reminded him, in way, of Fen's. Was she reading his character, the way Fen said he could? And if so, what did she see? He forced a smile that he knew would look completely genuine to anyone who observed it, then spoke in a fairly loud tone as he rose. "Well, ma'am, thank you for the pleasure."

She thrust a coin at him, the customary tip for a musician. He grinned and pocketed it. Then he walked through the crowd, stopping to chat with the customers. The subject of the murders came up a few times, but Garrin learned nothing he'd not read in scouting reports. People simply turned up dead, with most of their blood drained away. The last killing had been two nights ago, and the corpse was already buried. No hope of getting any residual magic traces from the body. Even if he dug it up, too much time had elapsed. He might have to wait until the killer struck again before learning anything. A sad way to go on, but perhaps the only one. He sighed as he returned to his spot near the bar.

Lauren didn't learn anything, either. She didn't really know what she'd expected; her dreams had given her no hint as to how to proceed once she got to Rasston. All she'd known was that she must go. Now she felt foolish, especially with Garrin Windson here to observe her failure.

He was certainly an excellent musician; she'd give him that. His rendering of some of the old, tragic ballads nearly brought tears to her eyes, but well before midnight, she'd had enough of sitting in the common room, nursing her drink. And she certainly had no interest in having any more conversations with Windson. Fen might like him, but she didn't. She put her money down for her wine, then went to her room.

"Well, that was better business than we've had in a month." Arla grinned at Garrin as she spilled the money box on the counter. Her teeth were small and even, only lightly stained. "If you've not earned a fair night's work in tips, I'll throw in the difference. I'd like you to come back."

Garrin shook his head. "Your customers were generous."

Arla clinked the coins into neat piles. "I heard you asking about the killings."

Garrin shrugged. "Thought it might have the makings of a good song."

"I could show you where the bodies were found. It's late, but there's a moon."

Garrin considered. He was certain he'd find no traces of sorcery at the sites, but perhaps he'd glean something from the pattern of slayings. Besides, he was restless, and the walk might do him good. "I'd like that."

He waited while Arla counted her coins and locked up the money. Finished with her task, she hitched a cloak around her shoulders and smiled. "Come along then."

Garrin put his harp aside and followed her from the room.

Lauren woke in the dark, every nerve on edge. She'd had her dream again, and this time she'd also seen a hooded figure. A woman by the shape and dress. Danger fluttered about the woman, as solid as a cloak. The next victim? Something told Lauren that the murderous sorcerer would strike tonight, and this woman would somehow be involved.

Lauren's head ached with tension as she pulled on her boots and dress. With no conscious plan of where she was going, she picked up her bow, left her room, and crept along the lightless corridor. Walking into the tap room, she gave a low call. "Garrin?"

No one answered. The fire had burned to embers, leaving the room lit with only a slight red glow. She raised her hand and released a flux of clear white light. The room was empty.

Where could he have gone? An urgency grew inside her. Something whispered a warning, saying she must find him right away. With a churning dread, she recalled the details of the crimes he was accused of committing.

They said he'd used sorcery to destroy that town. Could he be the Rasston sorcerer? Could his story of being sent by Fen to watch her be a lie?

The thought made her blood freeze. Facing an ordinary sorcerer would be difficult enough for a White wizard, but how could she defeat Garrin Windson?

But on the other hand, how could she not try? She'd taken an oath to protect the citizens of Alworyn from magical threat. Dying was better than oath breaking, in her mind.

She eased herself from the inn, into the clear, cool night. The moon hung low and bright in the black sky, but she tuned out the images sent by her eyes. Another image grew, a man and a woman in a mortal meeting along a moonlit path. Now she could see that the man in her mind's eye was clearly Garrin Windson.

Her pace quickened, taking her into the woods.

"Here's where the last one was found." Arla pointed to a patch of ground next to the narrow roadway.

Garrin knelt, turning his back to the innkeeper. Dewy grass wet the knees of his trousers. The ground he examined was bare of anything else, unfortunately; no traces of sorcery remained. He started to rise, but before he could get off his knees, a sharp pain pierced his back. Then something wet and warm ran down his side.

He staggered upward, twisting to see Arla. A bloody dagger hung from her hands. Purple light rose about her. Garrin's stomach turned. "Sorcery," he whispered.

"Trusting simpleton," she hissed. "Now I have your blood." She brought the dagger to her lips, kissed it. Garrin felt the impact of that touch, a shiver that hit his soul.

Cursing himself for a fool, he dropped to the

ground, clutching at the bloody gash in his side. He'd let down his guard because he hadn't believed a woman could be capable of such bloody murders. Deception, yes, or poisoning, but not this kind of crime. Not for a moment had he suspected Arla. The throbbing in his back told him how badly he had misjudged.

Did she know who he really was? He didn't think so. If she did, she wouldn't take time to gloat. Her spell wove lazily around him, chains of purple fed by the blood oozing from his back. Pain clutched at him, making it hard for him to concentrate.

He needed a strong blast to break her spell, but if he tried and failed, she would learn the real nature of the man she had captured. And if he failed to defeat her with his blast, she could use his own drawing of power against him, draining his wizard power and taking it for her own. No one would be able to stop her then. All of Alworyn would lay vulnerable before her. Could he risk it?

He hesitated, weighing his possibility of success. All the while her spell wove tighter around him, until all his chances were gone. He would die here in Rasston, he realized. His own fault.

Garrin stared into her night-darkened eyes. No glimmer of compassion lit their depths. She was a monster who enjoyed the murders she committed. Her knife fell again, slashing him across the arm. He screamed, and Arla laughed, her voice ringing out in the stillness.

A moment later the laugh caught in her throat, and she fell next to Garrin, the shaft of an arrow emerging from her back. From the placement of the arrow and Arla's lack of motion, he gathered it had pierced her heart.

Lauren stepped from the shadows, holding her crossbow in one hand. She looked down at Garrin, but he couldn't see her eyes. "How badly are you hurt?"

"I think I'm dying." The grass beneath him was warm and sticky, and his limbs had started to turn cold.

With her free hand, Lauren released a pulse of white, healing energy. "You won't die tonight," she said. "White mages are useful for some things after all."

He felt his ripped skin knit together, the pain in his arm and back subsiding to a dull ache. He pointed at Arla's body. "I was an idiot. I let her trap me."

"I saw." She raised her hand again, releasing another pulse of energy. "Now, sleep and let me work."

He closed his eyes.

At false dawn, Windson woke. The spell Lauren had cast was not meant to keep him unconscious long. She sat on the grass beside him, where she'd kept watch over him through the night. A few feet away, the body of the fallen sorceress lay in death's rigidity. Lauren had never killed a human being before. It had been surprisingly easy, no more than a touch of her finger on the trigger, no different than shooting a target.

Still pale from loss of blood, Windson looked up at Lauren with wide, wondering eyes. "It was me," he said. "Fen wanted you to protect me, not the other way around." He started to laugh, then groaned in pain.

"You'll be sore and weak for a while," Lauren said. "White magic is a poor substitute for true healing. But you'll be all right, by and by."

"You saved my life," Windson said. "Have you thought of that? You've rescued the most hated man in Alworyn. Few will thank you for that. Except Fen."

Lauren shrugged. "I took an oath to protect all citizens of Alworyn from magical threats. I did what I had to do."

"And that's all?" His strange blue eyes caught the first light of dawn.

"Does it matter?" She knew what he wanted from her, vindication, acceptance, but she couldn't give it. Too many questions lay unanswered, such as the fate of his poor, doomed town.

"No," he said. "I suppose not."

To her surprise, he rose on his own power. His strength of will, she thought, must be enormous, but then the strength of will of a man who could keep on living under the circumstances of his life must be no small thing. He took one last look at her and then began tramping along the forest road, heading toward the inn. A bend in the road soon took him from her sight.

Lauren rose and stood silently, watching the sun rise through the trees. A long journey lay before her. A long journey, alone, but at the end of that journey she'd find warmth and acceptance, a hero's welcome for what she'd done. They would sing songs to her at Wizards' Keep and raise glasses in her honor.

Everything she set out to do in Rasston she had done. The honor she wanted was hers. Why then did she feel only a dull ache inside? It was Windson, she realized. It had been so easy to see him as the sorcerer. She had said nothing of her suspicions, but the shadow of her judgment lay over her like a pall.

She bent to retrieve her bow. If she walked slowly enough, Windson would be gone before she got back to the village, and she wouldn't have to face his questioning eyes again. Nothing should detain him at the inn. His business in Rasston was finished, now that the sorceress was dead. And he would know she didn't need his protection anymore. But then, she never had.

LEGACY

Lisa Deason

Lisa Deason's short fiction has appeared in multiple volumes of *Sword and Sorceress,* as well as *Marion Zimmer Bradley's Fantasy Magazine,* and *Such a Pretty Face.* She is an active member of SFWA and, like everybody else, is working on a novel.

Lisa says, "It's been my particular honor for Mrs. Bradley to call me 'one of her own.' She bought the very first story I ever sent out back in 1991 and, in the years since, I've enjoyed her witty comments on many others. I'll miss those comments and I will certainly miss her."

The man fell dead at Serenity's feet as she struggled to draw the violently shaking sword from the scabbard on her back.

The piercing *all-clear* whistle wafted through the heavy afternoon air and she released Legacy's ornate, golden hilt.

"Reni? You okay?" her dark-skinned friend Mykos asked, his hands still aglow from the mage-bolt he had just thrown.

"I'm not hurt," she said, thinking, *I'm twenty-three, muscled, and in good shape. So why am I acting like some fragile damsel needing to be rescued?*

The black carriage behind her creaked and she turned, expecting Princess Anja to ask about the swift—and swiftly contained—attack. But it was not the red-haired Anja who pushed aside the shutter.

It was like looking in a mirror and seeing her own reflection twenty-five years hence. Serenity didn't fear

104

streaks of gray in her thick, dark hair or creases and lines advancing across her smooth skin. It would terrify her, however, to see such cold, brittle anger radiating from her own blue eyes.

Serenity walked away under the pretext of reporting to the watch captain. But she felt that unyielding gaze on her spine like a hundred tiny pinpricks, bleeding her to death, drop by drop.

The plains stretched in all directions, a rolling expanse gilded silver by the diffuse moonlight. Serenity wiped away the moisture condensing on her black leather gear as she gazed out into the chill, dense night.

Princess Anja made the trip to the Shalstaic hot springs four times a year to enjoy their restorative power, despite the somewhat perilous trip it took to get there. The journey going had been relatively easy. Coming back, they had already been attacked twice and were not yet halfway to Kiora.

I hate these plains, Serenity thought. *When the fog comes in, bandits could stroll right up to you and you wouldn't know it until you bumped into them.*

Muted laughter wafted through the damp air. She glanced back at the soldiers' tent where those off duty were gathered to escape the weather. The princess had her own tent, a much more spacious one set within a ring of guardsmembers. Serenity herself was stationed on the outermost perimeter.

"And that was when the *other* fifty bandits came through the pass," a clear alto voice said. "Though one look at my sword, covered in the blood of their foul kinsmen, sent them running . . ."

The words drifted away. Serenity shifted Legacy's heavy burden on her back, striving to control her annoyance.

Does she have to tell that story to every soldier from here to the edge of infinity?

She could have taken comfort if it had been an

exaggeration. But, until the injury that ended her career, Merriment duShayne really *had* been that good.

Guardswoman Ceelie Larragan approached, calling, "If you hurry, you can catch the end of Captain duShayne's story."

"I've heard it before."

"Oh, of course," the blonde said. "How lucky you are!"

Serenity chose not to reply to that. Instead, as she strode away, she said, "Your shift should be quiet. There's been no movement so far."

Usually she would have gone to the soldiers' tent for a mug of hot, bittersweet *kaida* and camaraderie.

Not tonight, though. I never should have applied to become one of Princess Anja's personal guards. When I was a regular guardswoman, at least I didn't have to be around her *every day.*

So she went past the soldiers' tent to a smaller one beyond it and rattled the door flap. " 'Lo, Mykos. You home?"

The flap obligingly lifted free of her hand and she entered.

Mykos sat at a tiny desk, studying a huge, leatherbound tome.

"Am I disturbing you?" she asked.

"Never. Not in the mood for old war stories?"

She snorted loudly.

He shook his head, sending his shoulder-length black braids dancing. "She casts a tall shadow, hm? Especially in the same profession."

"There's always a duShayne in the Royal Guard. I'm Merriment duShayne's only child."

A sparkle appeared in his rich brown eyes. "I've always wondered why your mother never changed her name to something more . . . intimidating?"

The corner of her mouth twitched. "It's a family superstitition: the gentler the name, the more ferocious the child. The custom's been passed down for ten generations, right along with Legacy."

She unsheathed the sword, holding it so that the table lantern highlighted every golden swirl. The crossguard flared like brilliant wings, shimmering with diamond-dust, and the center was dominated by a giant emerald. The blade itself shone like a silver flame.

"It's a beauty," Mykos said. "Is it enchanted?"

She thought of Legacy's inexplicable shaking. "Why would you ask that?" she said carefully.

"It has that feel, though I'd have to test it to be sure."

"The duShaynes would never use an enchanted weapon. We don't even dare to be born mage-gifted."

"Too bad," he said. "You don't know what you're missing."

And that, she thought, *is the story of my life.*

The next morning, Serenity stood in the soldiers' tent, her spine locked like a metal rod.

Merriment sat on a low bench, deliberately leaving her at attention. Her black, military-style skirt was tailored to make it impossible to tell that one of her legs was a wooden replacement from mid-calf down. She looked, as always, ready to take on an army.

"Draw your sword," she commanded.

Serenity obeyed, hoping fervently it wouldn't start quivering. But Legacy held steady in its "present" grip, turned across her waist with two fingers on her left hand balanced on the flat near the tip. She fully expected the elder duShayne to smack her with it.

But Merriment didn't accept the blade.

"Well," she said in cool tone. "I was beginning to wonder if you knew *how* to draw it. I don't think I've seen it in your hand since we left the hot springs."

Serenity didn't respond, her gaze fixed on the tent wall. The light winked off the impressive display of medals affixed to the front of Merriment's black vest. Serenity blinked, momentarily blinded.

"I don't understand you," Merriment finally said.

"You've got the skills, I've made sure of that. So why did I see you get your skin saved by a mage?" Disdain dripped from the word.

"There was a problem with my gear, ma'am."

"And it won't happen again?"

"No, ma'am." *I hope,* she added silently.

"Then I expect to see you handling yourself like a duShayne, understood? Don't you forget that it's your responsibility to uphold our legacy."

How could I forget? "Yes, ma'am."

"Sheathe your weapon."

Legacy slid home in a single, smooth motion.

"Dismissed."

Serenity gave a crisp salute, then left the tent. A tall blonde woman with a green band on her left wrist crossed in front of her, nodding amicably.

A chill went down Serenity's spine, like an evil premonition. *Healer Danise is just here as a precaution. She hasn't even had to bandage so much as a scrape so far.*

The uncomfortable feeling refused to be banished by simple logic.

I'm a duShayne. I'm not afraid of a fight.

But her heart was beating noticeably faster in her chest.

Fog rolled in not long after the caravan got in motion, limiting visibility to a handful of feet in any direction. Serenity rode slowly behind the princess' carriage, her cloak pulled tight against the dampness.

Unease skittered along her nerves. The fog muted the thumps of the hoofbeats and the soft squeaks of the carriage wheels. She scanned the thick, white banks around her with the growing certainty that bandits were silently advancing beyond her sight.

Legacy rattled nervously in its scabbard. She unsheathed it quickly, before it became impossible.

Movement, to the left.

A man on foot roared out of the fog's cover next to her. Serenity's gelding reared so steeply she feared he was going over. She disentangled herself from the stirrups and leapt free, landing in a crouch.

The battle was engaged in a heartbeat. Serenity's breath tore raggedly from her throat. *It's just like sparring,* she told herself, trying to stave off the panic rising within her.

Legacy quivered, shining in the dim light as though lit from within. The physical differences between it and the bandit's plain blade were as obvious as those between a regal queen and a ratty beggar.

But the great sword seemed to be trying to escape her grip, as if to run and hide. Soon, Serenity's entire body was vibrating from the struggle to simply hold on to her sword.

The bandit was far from a trained swordsman and the fight should have been skewed heavily in Serenity's favor. Yet she was losing ground, barely parrying his brutal, unskilled thrusts.

A hard swipe knocked Legacy to the grass at her side, where it flopped pitifully like a fish out of water. She did an acrobatic jump-and-roll to take herself away from the bandit's sword while bringing her in reach of her own. She came back up, her shuddering blade in hand again, expecting to find the man charging at her.

Instead, he was racing for the princess' carriage.

Mother will get him before he can hurt Anja, she thought as she gave chase. *That's why she rides with her, as a last defense.*

A few feet before he made it to the carriage door, Ceelie appeared out of nowhere in his path. With a tremendous overhead swing, her sword came down and caught his. The sudden change of direction knocked him flat on his back with a bone-jarring thud. A sharp thrust through his torso finished him.

Serenity skidded to a halt, jaw sightly agape at the

other guardswoman's sheer efficiency. Legacy trembled, its hilt cold against her palm.

"Such an impressive display deserves to be rewarded," Merriment said. "Not only by the princess, as you will be when we reach Kiora, but by a fellow soldier who understands how much skill it takes for heroics to look so effortless. As the senior member here of the Royal Guard, that pleasure falls to me."

Serenity shifted her weight, afraid that Legacy was going to begin clattering loudly in its sheath as she stood amidst the gathered guardsmembers. The day was bright for the moment and visibility was excellent as the caravan paused for the impromptu ceremony.

Merriment was at the front, looking official and imposing. Princess Anja smiled at her side, her hair shining like a red flame in the sun. Ceelie faced them both, eyes radiant and spine so stiff it looked painful.

"There's only one adequate reward I can think of for a time like this," Merriment went on and Ceelie managed somehow to straighten even more.

The elder duShayne unpinned a large red and gold medal from the mass she wore. "This is the Star of Valor, given to me when I saved the queen's life over twenty years ago. Guardswoman Ceelie Larragan, I now award it to you."

Ceelie looked as though she had been expecting something else entirely, but covered quickly as Merriment limped forward and pinned the medal to her dark tunic. The guardsmembers applauded.

As Merriment looked out over the small crowd, Serenity averted her gaze. Yet she still felt the scorn in her mother's eyes, even if she didn't see it.

Legacy trembled once, like a small, wounded animal.

"You said you could test it. Would you?"

Mykos arched a dark brow in surprise as Serenity

laid Legacy on the desk. "Sure, but why? You said it wasn't enchanted."

She had decided not to tell him about Legacy's peculiar problem just yet. If it *wasn't* enchanted and the shaking was actually all in her head, she didn't want to risk word getting out. And if the fault was Legacy's, then she hoped Mykos would know how to remedy it quietly and no one would ever be the wiser. "It doesn't hurt to check," she said.

He clearly knew there was more to it than that, but all he said was, "It'll take a few hours. Stop by in the morning."

Serenity jolted awake, her instincts screaming. She rolled from her cramped cot, weaving her way through the handful of sleeping guardswomen, and out of the tent.

The night seemed calm and, after a moment, she began to wonder if she had imagined the trouble. But the sense of danger remained and she had been in the swordfighting trade too long to dismiss that feeling offhandedly.

Despite the late hour, there was a flicker of lantern light visible inside Mykos' tent and she headed that way.

"Mykos?" she called softly. "You awake?"

She heard an odd noise and pushed the flap back. Then she breathed a horrified curse and shouted for Healer Danise.

Mykos was sprawled on the floor, unmoving, and Serenity hurried to him. His gray tunic was so bloodstained she couldn't even determine his injuries.

Danise came in, looking sleep-rumpled but competent, and motioned her back. Serenity complied and stumbled over Legacy half-hidden on the ground behind Mykos' desk.

The legendary sword was bloodied from tip to tang.

In shock, she then noticed the book on the desk and read the gold-leaf letters on the cover.

Enchanted Weapons and Their Inherent Dangers.

Several hours after sunrise, Serenity sat in the soldiers' tent. Legacy, now wiped clean, rode quietly in the scabbard on her back. Fellow guardsmembers bustled about, securing the camp for Princess Anja's safety.

"Guardswoman duShayne, report!"

She automatically jumped to attention and her mother limped slowly in front of her, her icy eyes flashing fire.

"There was evidence that someone crawled out the back of the tent," she said. "So presumably you weren't the one who tried to kill Mage Mykos."

"Correct, ma'am."

"Then how did your sword come to be used in this attack?"

Serenity, aware of all the eyes and ears directed her way, chose her words carefully. "Mage Mykos was examining it at my request."

Merriment's foridable gaze narrowed. "For what?"

To see if it's enchanted and that's why it shakes every time I try to use it, she thought. Aloud, however, she said, "It was personal, ma'am."

"You were going to get Legacy enchanted, weren't you?" the elder duShayne demanded. "How *dare* you tamper with this blade? What, did you want it to shoot bolts of mage-energy so you won't have to engage in honest combat?"

"I *didn't*—" Serenity began hotly, but Merriment cut her off.

"I don't want to hear it. Dismissed!"

Serenity spun on her heel, nearly crashing into Ceelie, and mumbled an apology as she hurried away.

She went to the healer's tent, where Danise allowed her to peek in at Mykos. He was asleep, pale beneath his dark skin, and crisscrossed with a multitude of bandages.

"Is he going to live?" Serenity asked.

"He lost a lot of blood, but the injuries weren't as severe as they first appeared. Almost clumsy, in fact. I'd say you showed up before the final blow was delivered."

Healer Danise patted her shoulder kindly. "I've given him some *sona,* so he'll sleep for a while. He should be as good as new in few days."

The caravan finally moved off the plains and onto the path leading through the Avida Mountains before stopping for the night. The massive mountains provided some shelter against attacks, though their many connected caves created a multitude of hiding places they had to be wary of.

Serenity was sitting alone in the soldiers' tent when Ceelie walked up, carrying two mugs of *kaida.* "May I join you?"

Serenity didn't feel like making conversation but nonetheless said, "Sure."

Ceelie sat a mug before her and Serenity inclined her head.

She drained half of the mug in one gulp, the rush of bittersweet heat making her head swim.

Ceelie cradled her mug and stared contemplatively into the amber liquid. Serenity was glad that the other guardswoman didn't seem inclined to talk.

She waited for the heat of the *kaida* to recede, but instead it strengthened, gathering behind her eyes.

"Guardswoman?" Ceelie said. "Are you all right?"

Serenity tried to respond, but her tongue felt thick and foreign. Darkness swelled up through the heat and overtook her with a great, unstoppable crash.

She came to in dizzying waves, silver light stabbing at her eyes, with her wrists bound tightly behind her back. In a few moments, her vision steadied and she realized she must be in one of the mountain caves.

Then she saw Legacy hovering several feet above the ground in a shaft of moonlight.

"What's going on here?" she asked, unnerved.

Legacy moved slowly through the air, but it was no longer an eerie apparition—she could see a hand on the hilt.

This isn't the work of bandits, she thought. *I'm no one they would kidnap for profit. So who . . . ?*

The moonlight glinted chest-high on the barely decipherable silhouette. Suddenly, she knew.

"Why are you doing this, Ceelie?" she asked flatly.

"Celestial," the other said.

"What?"

"My name is Celestial, just like the third duShayne to carry Legacy. You really are the disgrace of the bunch, you know. So incompetent."

Serenity struggled to sit up, her mind whirling. "Is that why you cut Mykos like that?" she asked slowly. "You were trying to frame me?"

Ceelie chuckled. "Everyone knows how good I am. I can kill with one sword-thrust. A clumsy murder would certainly look more like your style, wouldn't it?"

"Why, Ceelie? Why are you doing this? What is it you want?"

"It's *Celestial,*" she said through gritted teeth. "And I want what the original Celestial received."

Serenity quickly scanned her memory for something usual about her many-times removed grandmother. Like all of the celebrated duShaynes—up until herself, of course—Celestial duShayne had a long list of distinguished accomplishments.

"Pathetic," Ceelie snarled after a few minutes. "Let me tell you your own history, then."

She began to pace. "Humility duShayne never bore a living child. Wen she was in her forties, she took her student, the best swordswoman of her generation, and formally made her her heir. Celestial Westikan then became . . ."

"Celestial duShayne," Serenity finished. "I'd forgotten."

No wonder she looked disappointed when Mother gave her the Star of Valor, she thought incredulously. *She was expecting to be made a duShayne and given Legacy!*

"This isn't going to work," she said. "My mother's not going to set me aside and take another heir, even if I disappear."

Ceelie stopped. The white crescent of her teeth slashed through the shadows of her face. "You're not going to simply disappear," she said. "You're going to kill the princess. I, alas, will come upon you too late to save her. I'll try to take you alive but . . . You were crazed, out of your mind. It's a tragedy, really. I'm sure Captain duShayne will be distraught for a while, but she'll have another daughter before too long. A daughter she can be proud of."

She believes what she's saying, Serenity thought, hearing the note of fanaticism in the blonde woman's voice.

"The problem with that," she said, "is that I'm not going to kill the princess."

"Don't worry," Ceelie purred. "I'll take care of it for you."

Legacy's point dipped to Serenity's right and she saw the outline of a body and a glint of long, red hair.

"Anja," she breathed.

"I have nothing against her," Ceelie said. "I like her, actually. But she's the one you have to kill. No one else, not even your precious mage friend, would be enough."

"How did you even get her here?" Serenity asked, stalling. Almost imperceptibly, she began rocking from side to side, gently working her bound hands underneath her.

"I had a busy day. I visited Healer Danise first, checking in on poor Mykos and helping myself to as much *sona* as I could without her noticing. Then I delivered mugs of *kaida* all around. I told the princess and Captain duShayne that they were from you. That way, when Captain duShayne wakes up, she'll believe you're the one who drugged everybody."

Serenity's hands were now firmly beneath her, the rope cutting cruelly into her flesh. She had also been pulling her legs into position, digging her heels into the hard rock.

"Then finally, *finally*," Ceelie went on, "this beautiful sword will once more be in the hands of a true swordswoman."

She held Legacy up to the moonlight, admiring the way the silver illumination ran the length of the bright blade to the golden crossguard, then pooled in the deep heart of the emerald.

By the time Ceelie tore her infatuated gaze away from Legacy, Serenity had already shoved down on her heels as hard as she could. Her body popped through the loop of her arms, then she rolled into a reverse somersault, coming up on her feet. Her hands were still bound but were now at least in front of her.

"No! You're not interfering with my plans!" Ceelie barked, heading for the unconscious princess.

Serenity made the most prodigious leap of her life and crashed bodily into the other woman. They both sprawled to the ground, grappling for Legacy.

Ceelie planted the sole of her boot into Serenity's breastbone and pushed. Serenity sailed backwards, landing near the princess. Ceelie loomed over them, raising Legacy.

Terrified and angry, Serenity threw herself over Anja's defenseless form.

"It doesn't matter which order you die in," Ceelie growled, but something seemed to be distracting her.

Serenity then detected a faint glow radiating from Legacy. *That means it's also shaking. Is it responding to my emotions?*

"Legacy won't bite me!" she shrieked, pumping her chaotic feelings into the words. "I'm a duShayne by blood and by right. She's served my family for ten generations, the honored sword of honored swordswomen. And now, *she's MINE!*"

Ceelie staggered back, making an inarticulate noise deep in her throat. Legacy shuddered so furiously that it created a low, droning buzz.

Serenity got her feet under her and strode across the cave. Ceelie took a swing at her, but her arms were so agitated by the sword's motions that the hilt slipped free of her hands. It landed crossways at Serenity's feet, as if presenting itself.

Ceelie didn't dive after it. Instead, she drew her own sword as Serenity retrieved Legacy.

Even with her wrists bound, Legacy's hilt felt good and right in her hands for the first time. *She really is mine,* she thought and the blade flared a brilliant silver.

Ceelie howled a war cry and came at her with a powerful overhead swing.

Legacy seemed to float in Serenity's grip, as light as air. The great sword wafted up to meet the other and, at the moment of impact, it rang out a clear, triumphant note.

And Ceelie's sword *shattered.*

Legacy swung around, seeming to guide Serenity rather than being guided. It would be an easy thing to strike the killing blow, the easiest—and perhaps the most deserved—kill of her soldiering career.

Yet she forced the blade to stop, the razor-sharp edge hanging a breath away from the other's unprotected throat.

"Can't do it?" Ceelie asked derisively. "A *real* duShayne—"

Legacy moved again, the flat rapping smartly over he left ear. The blonde's eyes rolled up and she crumpled in mid-sentence.

"What do you know about being a duShayne?" Serenity said. "And besides, I won't let you die on Legacy's blade. You don't deserve the honor."

Serenity rode ahead of the princess' carriage as the procession wound its way out of the deep shadows of the Avida Mountains. Towards the rear of the caravan, Ceelie was in one of the pack wagons, under arrest and heading for a trial.

Hoofbeats approached and Serenity glanced back, then straightened, startled. Her mother rarely rode anymore; her replacement leg didn't conform to sitting a-saddle very well.

"May I speak with you?" Merriment asked.

"Of course, ma'am," Serenity said formally.

"I had an interesting conversation with your mage friend." She gestured at Mykos riding ahead of them. "He said that after he woke he told you that Legacy isn't enchanted."

Serenity nodded.

"Legacy's just a sword, Reni." he had said. *"The power if yours."*

"How can that be? I'm not a mage."

"Yes, you are. A minor one, I suspect, which is how you've unknowingly kept it suppressed. But mage-energy won't hide forever. It works its way out and, for you, it focused on your sword. Legacy must have always felt strange and unnatural to you. So your frustrated mage-gift made Legacy do strange and unnatural things."

"I'm mage-gifted, Mother," Serenity said.

"The duShaynes are swordfighters, not mages," the older woman immediately countered.

"When we get to Kiora, I'm resigning my commission."

"There's no need to do something drastic," Merriment said. "If you want to receive instruction on your . . . mage-gift—" the words stuck in her throat "—then do it around your Guard duties. You saved Princess Anja's life; you're sure to got a promotion."

"It doesn't matter. I've made my decision."

An edge crept into Merriment's tone. "There's always been a duShayne in the Royal Guard."

Serenity sighed. The tall mountains were casting shadows so deep that they seemed to be riding through a pool of darkness.

In more ways than one.

"I've tried to carry our legacy, Mother, and I'm not talking about the sword. It should be obvious by now, though, that I'm not a very good swordfighter."

"Surely you don't think being a *mage* is—"

"I don't know," she interrupted firmly. "This is new to me, too. Maybe I'll find I don't want to be a mage, either, but I have to explore this. I have to find out if there's more to me than just being a second-rate swordswoman hiding behind her family's name."

"Serenity!"

"Don't worry, though. I'll leave Legacy with you. You shouldn't have any trouble finding a new heir to carry it."

Through the murky illumination, she was surprised to see tears gleam in Merriment's icy blue eyes.

"I don't ever want to hear you talk like that again! You're my heir, always and forever. If I've acted disappointed, it's only because I want you to reach the potential I *know* is in you."

"I thought you'd be glad to have someone more deserving carry Legacy," Serenity said softly.

"You're the one who deserves to carry Legacy, Ren. I've never questioned that. And if I've made you question it . . . then I've been wrong."

Merriment extended a hand across the short physical span and the much larger emotional one between them. "Will you forgive me?"

Legacy rattled in its sheath, but this time not out of fear or anger. "I'll forgive you, if you'll forgive me," Serenity said and clasped Merriment's hand.

The caravan finally emerged from between the mountains. Mother and daughter smiled at each other, riding out of the darkness and into the dazzling sunlight.

THE LAST SWAN PRINCESS

Patricia Sayre McCoy

Not much has changed since Patricia's last bio, in *Sword and Sorceress XII*. She still has the same husband, same twin sister, and same job. She has more rejection slips, but not enough to stop her from sending stories out. She says "It won't be the same, though, with Mrs. Bradley gone. She was the first editor I sent anything to, and her encouraging reply, even though she didn't buy my story, made me bold enough to try again. She bought the second story I sent her (the second story I sent anyone), and I'll always be grateful to her for that. Mrs. Bradley's encouragement of new authors through her anthologies and magazine is hard to measure, as she seemed the most open to new writers. Getting her first letter that began 'Dear Author' was a thrill beyond belief, and I am sorry that future new authors won't have the thrill that I had."

Seven swans there were on that great lake, high in the mountains. They disappeared with the setting sun and returned with the morning star. Each shone as if of pearl and opal, and each wore a silver crown set with pale gems. Once a year, on Midwinter's Day, they were princesses again, for the shortest day of the year. It was said that if one could find the pass called the Devil's Gorge and climb the mountain while the sun still lit the sky of their twentieth year, they could be freed and remain human.

This year, as they flew to the lake in answer to the spell, one swan lagged behind. Although all were white and strong, she was the whitest, whiter than the

121

fresh snow in the ice lands of the north. Bigger than her sisters, too, her strong wings carried her far closer to the stars and sun than her sisters could ever go. This day, she flew beind the others, constantly turning her head back, looking behind at the dark form far behind. A black swan followed, too small to keep up with her, even when she flew slowly. He could not hope to match the speed of her or her sisters ahead; they flew on wild wings to their transforming. Reluctantly, she caught up with them as the pull of the witch's spell became too strong to ignore. She cried out at losing the black one, but had no choice but to fly on.

So it was in the first year of Tsar Dmitri the Fair that the seven swans returned to the great lake at sunrise and put off their feathery robes and stood forth as princesses again. Robed in white silk with silver embroidery, they shone in the rising sun as it glittered off the lake.

"Oh, my sisters," cried Anna, the eldest. "How tired I am of this swan life. Curses on that miserable witch who enchanted us!"

"Yes," agreed the next oldest, Olga. "How long has it been since we were bespelled? Our brother is now Tsar and he was then but a new-born child."

"Yes, but remember, the witch still lives," warned Marya. "And remember her spell? How can our brother call us by our right names and free us when he has never seen us?"

"And do we want him to?" whispered Sofia, the youngest. But no one heard her.

"Look sisters!" one of them cried and pointed towards the pass. Silhouetted against the rising sun was the dark figure of a mounted warrior, the banner on his lance fluttering in the breeze. As the sun broke over the mountains, the banner blew clear. It was the golden serpent on green, sign of the Tsar. Dmitri had come.

Suddenly the wind rose, a cold blast that broke the lance and nearly toppled the horse. The princesses could see the rider struggling with his mount, vainly trying to hold him steady on the narrow trail. The wind gusted stronger and dust filled the air, obscuring their sight. The dreadful scream of a terror-stricken horse filled the air and when the dust died down, the horse and rider were gone and Ratha the witch stood before them.

All but Sofia drew back, sobbing. She alone continued to watch the pass. Ratha turned towards her.

"You will not find him," she cackled. "Better men than he have died in the Devil's Gorge."

"He is our brother," Sofia replied. "He will come."

Anna then came to her and seized her arm. "Come away, Sofia. Beware the witch's evil powers."

Sofia shook her off. "Dmitri will come," she repeated. "Someone should be here to greet him."

Ratha cackled again, her evil laughter echoing in the gorge. Sofia finally let Anna draw her back beside the lake with the others, but her eyes never left the pass. The day wore on, mists burning off in the pale winter sun. Gradually the shadows lengthened until only the mountain peak remained lit.

"So, Highnesses," Ratha said, coming over the black sand towards the princesses, "it is nightfall and your brother has not come. You are swans forever now."

Sofia's heart leaped, but before she could say anything, a breathless voice broke the stillness.

"Not so, evil one." it said. "I am here and one rock on the summit is still lit. You gave me until the last night of the shortest day of the twentieth year faded to come to the lake. I am here and the rock still shines."

Dmitri leaped down from the broken rocks framing the gorge.

"How did you survive the demon wind?" Ratha demanded.

Dmitri laughed and held up a small vial. "Tears of the Holy Mother, from the cathedral, and a blessing from the priest. Alas, my horse was not so lucky." His face clouded. "He was a good steed, loyal and brave. You owe me for his life."

Ratha spat. "That for your horse. And the Holy Mother. Water won't save you now!" But Sofia noticed she kept far away from the vial.

"I've come for my sisters." Dmitri said.

"Hah," Ratha sneered. "Have you, my prince? Well, that's not so easy. Do you know them?

"I would know my sisters anywhere." He replied. "Those who know such things say we look alike."

"That you do, my prince, that you do. Come and see."

Raising her voice, she called out. "Come here, Highnesses! Here is one who says he is your brother and knows you. Let him see. Introduce yourselves." She laughed wildly as the wind rose again and blew her laughter across the lake.

Seven princesses came at her call, each exactly like the other. Dmitri looked from face to face, desperate to see each detail in the quickly fading light. But in the haze all he could see was the light winking off their jeweled robes. Each princess stepped forward and said her name, and he stared hard, trying to see some difference between them, but alas, there was nothing to see. Even their ages were the same, by Ratha's evil spell. Despair filled his eyes as he frantically looked from one to another. He could not tell them apart.

Sofia had stayed back as long as she could. She had a magical jewel, a christening gift from her mother, that would grant the holder his or her heart's desire. She knew it would grant Dmitri the knowledge to tell them apart if he truly wanted it, but she was not sure she wanted him to succeed. She hated being human, for then she was too tall and off balance, her feet hurt from walking, and she couldn't fly. All her strength and agility in the sky were lost to her on the ground. She couldn't even glide gracefully as her sisters could, rather, she lurched and shuffled, unable to coordinate her legs, knees, and feet. The heavy hem of her robe didn't help her either. It was always in her way, tripping her each time she turned around.

But finally the witch beckoned to her. She saw Ratha grinning wickedly and knew she had an awful fate in mind for Dmitri. Sighing, she stepped forward and repeated her name. As she turned back to join her sisters, she dropped the jewel in his hand. Ratha could not see in the dark and Dmitri quickly caught it and hid it.

"Now my prince," Ratha said. "You have met them. Tomorrow they will return here and take their human forms one last time. If you can call each one by her name, they will be free from my spell. If you make one mistake, swans they remain. And if you make a mistake, I will kill you. Go, princesses. Return with the sun."

Quickly the princesses bowed to Dmitri and flung their feather robes around their shoulders and flew across the lake, calling mournfully. Dmitri alone remained with the witch.

Ratha threw back her head and howled a deafening spell. As if in answer, a whirlwind appeared to carry her away. Riding the wind as one would ride a horse, she flew above Dmitri shouting, "Tomorrow, my prince. One mistake and they are swans and you are dead!"

With the first hint of dawn the swans returnd. Dmitri rose stiffly from his shelter by the rocks and joined them on the beach. One by one they glided to shore and turned into women. He watched them intently, hoping to see some difference he had missed last evening. But they all looked as alike as before; each tall, slender, and pale, with fine robes and silver crowns.

Casting his eyes around for the witch, he drew the

jewel from his sleeve and examined it. It was a small
blue gem, shaped like a sphere. He had never seen it,
but he remembered his nurse telling him of his mother's favorite jewel. She had hung it around the neck
of her youngest daughter, who loved it too. He had
never heard that the gem was magical, but his sister
must have given it to him hoping it was.

The wind began to howl again and the princesses
turned to look back across the lake in terror. All but
one. She pointed to the jewel and put her hand to her
eye as if to look at something in it. Dmitri shook his
head, puzzled. She repeated the gesture again and
then turned away as Ratha landed. Dmitri looked at
the gem again and suddenly nodded. Folding his hand
around it, he hid it so no one but he could see it. His
sister must believe it was magical.

"Come, Highnesses," Ratha called. "Turn about,
dance now. No clues for your handsome brother!"

Sadly they did so, changing places again and again
until no one could remember who had been where.
Even if they had given Dmitri clues, they were useless now.

Then the princesses lined up and Ratha took
Dmitri's hand. She smiled an evil smile and bowed.

"Good morning, Highness," she said. "Here are
your sisters. Name them!"

Dmitri knelt on the sands a moment, head bowed,
hands clasped. Hidden from the witch, the blue jewel
glowed faintly and small pictures appeared. Dmitri
watched as they scrolled past. The first one showed a
young queen, lying in a royal chamber, a newborn
baby at her breast. Behind her in the window, fire-
works exploded as the country celebrated the birth of
their Tsar's first child. "Anna" chimed in his ear. The
next picture showed an older child, barely big enough
to hold the young one on the chair with her. "Elena"
the voice said. And so it went. When the pictures

ended, Dmitri drew the holy vial from his tabard, kissed it, and rose.

"I am ready," he said steadily.

Slowly he walked past them, pausing at each princess for many moments. Hidden in his hand, he kept one eye on the jewel and the other on his sisters. He held his breath, but as he passed one princess, the jewel showed him a frayed thread in her collar.

"Anna," the voice repeated. Elena had one pearl slightly darker than the others, Marya had a pale freckle on her cheek. And so it went. Ludmilla had a broken nail on the little finger of her right hand, one of Vasilissa's diamonds was a bit yellow, Olga had one strand of golden hair among her black tresses, and Sofia had a small bump in her nose, invisible unless pointed out. Triumphantly, Dmitri named them all. Ratha stared.

"This is impossible!" she hissed. "You were helped somehow. Do it again!"

Three times she made him repeat the test and each time he named each one correctly, remembering what he had seen and heard before. At last Ratha could no longer deny the truth. Gnashing her iron teeth, she vanished in a fiery cloud. The princesses rushed over to their brother, laughing and crying.

"We're free, we're free!" they said, kissing him, dancing around him and stopping to kiss him again.

Finally Dmitri raised his hand. "Beautiful sisters, while I would like nothing better than to talk and dance with you for days, we are still high in the mountains in the winter. I have horses waiting for all of us beyond the gorge, but we must leave now if we are to leave at all. The coldest part of winter now approaches.

They took one last look at the dark lake and then turned away. As one, they hurried across the black sands to the Devil's Gorge. Days later, after many adventures that do not come into this story, they arrived at the golden palace of the Tsar.

There the princesses settled into their new lives and lived several years in love and contentment with their brother and each other. Anna and Olga married kings from the far western lands and had several children each. Marya married a khan from the south and was the mother of a fine boy, and Elena was to marry a great chieftain of the north. Two fine princes of the Rus were courting Ludmilla and Vasilissa and betrothals were expected any day. Only Sofia was left without a husband.

"I am sorry, my sister," Dmitri said having just come from a council session. "There just isn't any other ruler you can marry. A royal princess cannot marry anyone else. But you can stay here with me. You know that I love you."

"I know, dear brother," Sofia said. "But you have a wife and children too. I cannot demand all of your love. And I do not want a husband. I do not understand this human life yet. I was a swan most of my life."

Dmitri nodded. "Yes, you were only three years old when you were enchanted. Even our next youngest sister was already twelve. But you are human now. I thought that was what you wanted. You helped me break Ratha's spell."

"Of course I did," Sofia replied. "I knew my sisters did not want to be swans forever. I don't know what I wanted. But now I know what being a princess means. These heavy robes weigh me down, the food is too rich, and I have nothing to do."

Dmitri sighed. He knew the weight of protocol the court had developed. If it weighed heavily on him, how much more would it weigh on his youngest sister, the princess without a place?

"What can I do, sister?" he asked.

Sofia shook her head, eyes filled with tears. "There is nothing you can do. I want to be free. I remember the long nights of summer, the white nights when the sun never left the sky and we flew long into the twilight with other swans. It was peaceful and so beautiful. We were free, brother. Free of princes, children, courts. Even the witch had no power over us then."

If she also remembered the black swan she did not say.

Dmitri sadly shook his head. That kind of freedom he couldn't give her. Sofia brushed past him and was gone. Dusk found her in her room, a carved chest opened beside her, and her swan feather robe in her lap. Tears fell on it, brighter than diamonds.

As the sun set across the land, the shadows of the church domes spread across the city, and she heard, far off, the call of the wild swans returning to the lakes and ponds of the north with the summer. Suddenly, with a sharp cry, she flung herself at the window, leaning out most alarmingly, in time to see the last of the swans pass overhead. One of them was black and a glint of gold shone from his head. She buried her head in the swan robe and cried.

She heard a knock on her door and when she called, Vasilissa entered.

"Dmitri told me what you said. I remembered mother's jewel," she said. "It grants one's heart's desire. If you recall, Dmitri returned it to you when you came here. Use it and be free."

Sofia returned to her chest and took out the box the jewel was kept in. In her hand, the gem warmed. Startled, she looked at it closer. She had thought its magic had been used up by Dmitri, but apparently that was not true. Leaning closer, she saw pictures in the jewel. She was just able to make out small figures in it. One was the black swan she had seen flying overhead. As she watched, it touched down and shed its skin and stood revealed as a dark man. On his head he wore a golden crown and his robes were embroidered with jet and black pearls.

Sofia's eyes were wide. Another enchanted swan! He could teach her. How could she find him? She looked closer, trying to see something she could recognize. Alas, though she had traveled far as a swan, she had hardly left the city as a human. Places looked too different from a swan's sight and she saw nothing she knew. Still she peered again and again into the gem until it grew too dark to see. She lit a light, but when she returned to the jewel it was dark.

She wept herself to sleep, wrapped in her swan robe.

In her dreams, she flew to the dark man's land and they flew all the night together, dipping and soaring for hours. She awoke the next morning with only a dim memory of her dream, but she knew in her heart that there was a man who could give her her heart's desire. All she had to do was find him. But all she remembered was the black swan and she didn't know who he was as a man.

Days and weeks passed as Sofia tried to find the identity of the black swan. A black swan was not a noble's emblem, nor the symbol of any country anyone in the realm knew about. The wise women she asked knew nothing. Even the Gypsies were unsure. Finally one day, an old washerwoman came to court, asking for the youngest princess.

Though her maids and waiting women were horrified, Sofia ordered the old women brought to her. She received the old woman in her sitting room, where tea and cakes were served. After the old woman had eaten her fill, Sofia waved the servants out.

Leaning forward and taking one thin, frail hand in hers, she asked, "What do you have to tell me, Grandmother?"

"I have heard that you are looking for tales of a black swan, Highness," she replied. "I know a story about one. He is a prince and an enchanter, and is said to live far to the south where even the stars are different. He visits the northlands for a few days in early summer when he goes to the northern seas in search of black pearls for his robes."

Sofia's eyes glowed. This sounded promising. "Where exactly in the north does he go for the pearls, Grandmother?"

"To the lost sea of Duv, the story says," the old woman replied. "All the stories agree on that. But no one knows where the Sea of Duv is, nor do the stories agree on how to get there, save that it is far to the north, beyond all human dwellings."

Sofia's eyes glowed. This sounded promising indeed! The old woman looked at her and said hurriedly, "It is a dangerous place, Highness. Not a place for a gently bred princess."

Sofia was too excited to listen and she wasn't a gently bred princesses in any case. She had grown up a swan. Lordly birds, they went where they pleased and only the great eagles were braver. After sending the old woman on her way with enough gold to keep her in luxury for the rest of her life, Sofia went in search of her brother.

"I forbid it!" Dmitri shoutd when she asked permission to go in search of the Sea of Duv. "I will send woodsmen to this sea of yours but you will not go there yourself."

Argue and threaten as she would, Sofia could not change his mind. That evening, when her sisters joined them for dinner, they agreed with him too. Finally Sofia left the table in tears. But Dmitri was satisfied. He was certain he had made his wishes clear. His sister was not to risk herself on such a journey. To be certain she could not slip out, he gave orders to the guards and grooms that she was not to leave the palace grounds alone, and no horse was to be saddled for her unless he approved it.

Sofia flew into a rage when she found out. But there was nothing she could do about the guards and grooms. Retiring to her room she leaned out her window, hoping for a glimpse of the black swan. She took the mysterious jewel from her chest and examined it again. She remembered when she was little, her last human memory as a child, that she believed she could hear her mother speaking to her through the gem. Remembering the sweet voice, she whispered "Can you help me find the black swan?"

A clear voice sounded in her ear. "Yes."

"Can you help me escape the palace?"

"You must become a swan and fly free."

"How can I become a swan again?" Sofia asked. "I've put on my swan robe before and nothing happened."

"That is because you do not know the spell," her mother's voice replied. "But I can make you a swan. Put your robe across your shoulders."

"Wait!" Sofia gasped. "Can you teach me the spell?

"No," the voice said. "You cannot work my magic. You need other magics. You are a swan at heart and I was human. But I can help you find your teacher.

"Now put your robe on. Take me with you when you go. Carry me in your mouth and drop me when you reach the Sea of Duv."

Sofia rushed to her chest and pulled out the swan robe. Throwing it on, she returned to the window. She heard faint chanting, in a language she almost knew, but it was too faint to understand or remember.

A light flared and she was transformed into a swan of purest white. Picking up the sphere-shaped jewel in her beak was difficult, but she finally grasped it tightly and flew into the night.

The rising sun found her far to the north of Tsar Dmitri's palace. Gliding to a halt on the smooth waters of a small lake, she carefully placed the jewel in a hollow on the rocky shore. It shone pure blue, like the summer sky, in the new light of day. Her lesser swan's hearing was unable to hear even the loudest sound from the jewel, but suddenly she was human again, standing on the shore with her swan robe lying beside her.

Picking up the jewel, she asked, "Where are we?"

"Far north," the voice said. The borders of your brother's kingdom are so far away that they do not even know his name here. But we have twice as far to go to reach the Sea of Duv."

Sofia sighed with weariness. So far! She'd had no idea that the world was so large, even for a swan. Setting her shoulders, she began gathering driftwood for a fire. Spring was still cold this far north.

Three nights later, she came to the dark waters of the Sea of Duv. Cold, strong winds blew from the northern ice, straining her swan's wings, and the waves broke on steep, fir-covered shores. Struggling against the bitter winds, she searched for a place to land. Lower and lower she flew, wings aching with weariness, until she barely cleared the whitecaps. At last, in despair, she cast herself onto the sea. Strong legs thrusting against the waves, she forced herself towards the rocky shore.

At last she felt the rock beneath her feet. Staggering ashore with her last strength, she spat the jewel onto the rocks, where its bright glow faded as its power died, and fell beside it in a swoon. When she awoke, she was human again and dim sunlight fell on her face. Beside her stood a strange man dressed in a black feathered robe. The black swan.

"I thought I'd be too late to find you!" she gasped.

"Find me?" he repeated. "Why were you seeking me?

Sofia thought for a minute. Why was she seeking him? To learn the swan magic, certainly, but there was more than that. She was strangely drawn to him, even at her first glimpse of him following her to the mountain lake. Swans mated for life, she remembered. Did he remember her in that way?

He was waiting patiently for her answer, so she told him part of her reasons for seeking him. "I want to be a swan again. I have no place as the youngest princess."

"Is that all?" he asked. "You came all this way for that?"

"All? How can you say that? You who have also known the freedom of the skies? What can compare to that in this body?"

He nodded as she continued, "Teach me how to change. I can only change now with the help of the gem."

He looked at her slowly for a long time. Returning his look, Sofia began to be afraid. Who was he really? She didn't even know his name. He could be a cruel sorcerer for all she knew. And she had asked his help. What would he ask in return?

"What will you give me if I teach you?" he asked finally. "Everything has its price."

Sofia bowed her head. "I have nothing to give you," she replied. "Gold and gems you can get for yourself, I know. You are a prince yourself, they say, so land and titles will not tempt you. What else is there?"

He smiled. "I think you know, Princess. Why else did you come so far? Fly with me a season and that will be payment enough."

"But I . . ."

"Just fly, Princess," he said, raising one hand to forestall her protests. "That's all I want now. A companion who knows the glory of flight and the prison of the ground. I have never met anyone like me before."

"My sisters and I were swans for twenty years," Sofia said.

"Yes, I saw you. I tried to join you, but you were too swift and strong for me, and I could not keep up. I saw you leave with your brother and knew you would never come back. But I never forgot you and I never met another enchanted swan. I have been lonely for many years."

"Why haven't you taught someone your magic to become a swan too?" Sofia asked.

He shook his head. "I never met anyone who wanted to be a swan. Not even to accompany me." He smiled slightly. "I must confess, I thought at least one or two of the single maidens my ministers kept shoving at me would have agreed to try it. Just to be noticed."

Sofia laughed. "You sound pleased that they didn't."

"Perhaps. Shall we go now? It's cold here by the shore."

"Very well," she said. "I'm Sofia, Princess Sofia, that is. I keep forgetting my title."

He bowed. "I am Prince Srinam and I cannot forget it. Too many people keep reminding me of it."

"Well, I will not."

So saying, she climbed to her feet and followed him into the fir grove to a small glade. Casting his cloak around his shoulders, he turned sunwise, and a black swan with a golden crown stood in his place. Turning again, he was a man.

"That is all?" Sofia asked suspiciously. "You just throw your cloak on, twirl and turn? No spells, nothing."

"It's how I do it," Srinam replied. "There is one thing more though. You must will the change with all your heart. No part of you must hesitate. Then feel your swan-self. It is still there, in your heart. Feel it, will it and become a swan."

Days passed and the seasons turned toward summer. While Srinam flew in the deep blue skies above, Sofia struggled on the ground, willing her heart to burst if only she could become a swan once more.

Finally, one fine day in late summer, Srinam approached her.

"I must leave here soon," he said. "I have been away from my lands too long. My borders were not peaceful when I left and I fear war after the harvest. If you cannot change, I must go without you."

Sofia wept to see him gliding above her, so soon to leave. She had found her place with him, she thought, and could not believe he would leave her. Yet she knew a ruler's duties and he very well might leave her if he had to. Once more she tried the swan change. This time as soon as thoughts of her sisters and Dmitri entered her mind, she replaced them with the pain of losing the black swan, of never being a swan again, but forever the last princess, the one without a place. Terror nearly broke her heart, but beyond terror was a glorious light. Suddenly, Princess Sofia vanished and a great white swan with a silver crown stood in her place. Trumpeting, she launched herself skyward as Srinam soared down to meet her. They danced the day away in the skies, swooping and soaring far out over the dark sea. From that day on, there were two crowned swans in the skies above the Sea of Duv.

Three days later, they left the Sea of Duv and flew south. On the first day of autumn, two crowned swans, one black, one white, circled the Tsar's palace, calling in human voices for the princesses and the Tsar. Guards and ladies streamed in from all over the palace as the swans landed in the courtyard, Sofia transforming as Dmitri and Anna rushed to take their sister in their arms.

"Sofia!" Anna cried. "We thought we had lost you forever."

"I wasn't lost," she replied, tears of gladness running down her cheeks. "I was finding myself, my swan self. Dmitri, promise me you will never lock me away again."

Dmitri hung his head, "I promise, sister. I do not

want you to flee again. But where are your manners? Who is the black swan with you?"

"Prince Srinam of Duv and the Pearl Island," she replied, beckoning him forward as he changed. "He taught me the swan magic. And I am going with him when he leaves for the south . . . I promised him a season."

Dmitri looked stricken. "Are you going away so soon? After you've been away so long? And who is this Prince of Duv? I have never heard of him."

"Dmitri," Anna reproved. "We drove her away once, now let her be. She is a swan, she can fly where ever she wishes. You cannot stop her."

So saying, Anna took Sofia in one arm and Srinam in the other and led them into the palace, now blazing with lights in celebration of the last princess' return.

And when the storms threatened and Prince Srinam could stay no longer, Sofia went with him on his long journey southwards.

"Dmitri," she said before she left. "I will return to see you and my sisters. You do not have to imprison me."

"No more locks, sister," Dmitri promised.

"Yes, Sofia," Anna said. "You will always be free. We should have realized that you were different from the rest of us. We were humans transformed into swans, but you were always a swan. Fly far, sister, but remember that we love you. Come back to us as you can."

With that, Sofia and Srinam launched themselves into the cold, clear air. Long after they were out of sight, their wild trumpeting could be heard above that of the common swans that were also winging their way south. And every midsummer's day, two crowned swans return to the Tsar's palace and the Tsar and princesses once again welcome the return of their youngest sister, the Swan Princess.

SWORDTONGUE

Anne Cutrell

Quite a bit has changed for Anne Cutrell since she was first published in *Sword and Sorceress XIV*. She graduated with a B.S. in architecture and has worked for several years in that field. She lived in Maryland and Washington, D.C., then moved to Colorado. She's planning to go back to school for her master's degree, which will doubtless delay the completion of any of the several novels she has started.

Dalia woke in strange room. She didn't remember going to sleep there and couldn't imagine why she wasn't in her own room. Her right side felt strange. Actually, it didn't feel anything at all, and that was strange. She looked down and saw her whole right arm was swathed in a white bandage. At the movement of her head, she realized that the right side of her face was bandaged as well.

She tried to remember what had happened. All that came to mind was the sensation of incredible heat and the smell of smoke. Her throat constricted at the memory. She felt an unexplained terror and she drew in breath to cry out. The air seared her throat and lungs as if she were breathing in fire itself. She exploded in a fit of coughing.

The door opened and a concerned-looking woman in green came in. She took a glass from the side table and pressed the rim of it to Dalia's lips. Dalia sipped hesitantly, then drank more deeply and the cool drink flowed down her throat, easing the inflammation.

"Who?" Dalia croaked and was astonished to find her voice raw and sore.

"I am called Jaleen," the woman said with a smile. "I am a healer."

A beautiful blue and green stone in a pin at her throat caught Dalia's eye.

"A Melanir healer," Dalia observed.

"Yes."

"What happened?" Dalia asked, almost afraid to find out.

Jaleen put a cool hand on her forehead and smoothed back her hair.

"Your mother's inn caught fire and burned to the ground."

She saw Dalia's stricken expression and hastened to soothe her. "Don't worry, your family is safe and well.

"There were unusually few injuries, considering the size and intensity of the fire. A few had minor burns and one boy broke his leg jumping out of the second story window. You had the worst burns, but even those are not as bad as what could have happened. You will retain use of all your limbs, your throat and right eye should return to normal, and with some help, your scars should not be as bad as they might be."

Dalia was silent a moment, trying to remember.

"Why me?" she asked, her unbandaged eye watering.

Jaleen chose to understand this as a request for more information, not an esoteric question about the nature of destiny and luck in the world.

"You were leaving the burning building when a hysterical woman grabbed you and begged you to save her baby. You went back in and found the child in a room on the second floor, but on your way back out you were struck by a falling beam. Your father and another man were able to get you out before the building collapsed."

Now tears were running down Dalia's face as her memory returned.

"It was so dark," she cried in her hoarse voice. "It was so dark, but it was the middle of the day. The smoke was so thick I couldn't see. I couldn't breathe. I was carrying the child and I heard a crack above me. I looked up and saw the beam on fire and coming down on me. I tried to protect the baby." Dalia's right arm rose from beneath the covers, as if she were reliving the experience.

Sobs shook her damaged body and set off another bout of coughing. Jaleen held her shoulders and pressed the glass to her lips once more.

When the sobs had subsided somewhat, Jaleen put aside the glass and said, "You know what I am, which means you won't think it strange if I ask you to look into my waterstone for a moment."

Dalia's eyes went back to the stone at Jaleen's throat. The swirled blue and green seemed to undulate and sparkle, like the surface of a wind-stirred lake. The apparent movement was mesmerizing. As her thoughts grew fuzzy and her eyes began to close, she realized that Jaleen was humming a song. From the tides that were pulling at Dalia's mind, one thought rose to the surface.

"The baby?" she asked hazily.

"She will be fine; she just inhaled too much smoke."

Dalia smiled in relief and slipped under the waves of sleep.

"What? You're crazy!" Dalia threw up her arms to emphasize her point, even though her right arm was still stiff.

"Look, it's for your own good," the man in front of her said calmly. "It's not save to defy the Elements and you've obviously been marked."

"A scar on my shoulder does *not* mark me for service to Fire! I don't even *want* to be a warrior!"

The man braced himself against the corner of his desk and ran a hand through his short, graying hair. "I'd like to point out that I have much more experience in this than you do. A flame shaped scar, surrounded by healthy skin, most certainly *is* a mark of Fire! Fire is the warrior's element! It must have known what It was doing when It marked you."

Dalia sighed and sat down in a hard chair opposite him. "I can't imagine why. I've never even thought about being a warrior."

The man smiled wryly. "I don't know why either. My only thought is that you've never tried it, so maybe you'll like it when you have."

Dalia shook her head disbelievingly. "I don't like violence. I never have."

The man shrugged. "Just try it. Enter the Tsyrath school and see how your first year goes. Maybe you'll like being a warrior. Or maybe we'll understand better what Fire intends."

Dalia sighed again. "All right, Ghermot, but I don't think it's going to work," she sid dubiously.

"Come on, think positively," Ghermot said, reaching out with his right hand. A firestone ring glimmered on his ring finger, marking him as a Tsyrath warrior himself.

Dalia met his right hand with her own gloved one, gloved to hide the burn scars. Her face had escaped heavy scarring, but her entire right arm, except for an area of unblemished skin surrounding that blasted mark on her shoulder, was puckered by scars.

She would try what he proposed.

Six months later, Dalia was instructed to attend her own progress review. Ghermot, as headmaster of the school, was present, as were her instructors. Her tactics and strategy instructor could not praise her enough. She was at the top of her class. The opposite was true in her weapons class. In drills, her form was excellent, but she remained unable to turn her skills to fighting with an opponent, even when the exercise was with padded weapons. She would flinch away from any attack, and her well practiced counter-attacks would fall apart. The instructor sat down, shaking her head, concluding that Dalia was "hopeless."

Ghermot looked at Dalia.

"I have tried," she said with a frown. "Give me credit for that."

"There is also your discipline problem," he reminded her. "Your theory and history instructors gave you high marks, but you often argue with them."

Dalia opened her mouth in astonishment. "Of course I argued!" she exclaimed and stood up. "That's the point of education! To learn to think!

"And it wasn't an argument until they refused to listen to my points," she muttered as she sat back down again.

Ghermot waited a moment to see if she would continue, then said, "I have also been approached quite a few times by instructors who have broken up loud and vigorous arguments between you and other students. That you have managed to avoid them turning into physical fights in a warrior school is quite admirable."

Dalia's mouth quirked upward at this last statement, but she managed to suppress it into a stern look again.

Ghermot continued, "I have had reports that you get into arguments at the marketplace as well. Is this true?"

Dalia looked straight back at him.

"Yes," she replied evenly, "but they had it coming to them. They were trying to cheat people out of their hard-earned money with blatant lies."

"Have you ever considered that's what merchants do?" Ghermot asked.

Dalia scowled. "Well, they shouldn't! Just last week, Helram, the cloth merchant, tried to sell rot-weakened cloth to a poor old woman! Anything she would have made out of that cloth would have been useless! There should be some limits to the size of the lies they tell!"

Ghermot raised his eyebrows at her vehemence, but kept silent.

Dalia's weapons master spoke. "Regardless of Dalia's argumentativeness and ability to stay out of physical danger, she cannot continue on in her weapons studies until she masters the ones already at hand. She is, admittedly, a very good archer, but I have my doubts about even those skills being turned on a person when needed. I cannot allow her into the intermediate classes."

Dalia rose from her chair. "I agree that I should not advance in the weapons classes. If I had my way, I wouldn't be studying them at all."

She turned to Ghermot.

"This whole thing was an experiment from the beginning. I have never claimed to be a warrior. I simply cannot overcome my aversion to violence.

"But," she continued in stronger voice, one unmarked by the smoke damage of six months before, "I do admit that I look forward to my history, theory, and strategy classes. Let me continue in these at least. You yourself said that I have been marked for something. I don't know what it is, but perhaps it includes instruction in rhetoric."

"I agree," Ghermot said with a sigh. "Fire knows what you are marked to do, but the least we can do is continue to train you, at whatever level you can attain. Please do continue with the weapons classes at the beginner level. Perhaps there will be some breakthrough."

Dalia looked dubious, but as all her instructors agreed with this statement, she acquiesced.

A year later, Dalia had still not advanced beyond beginners level in her weapons class. She merely did the drills for exercise now. The instructors no longer required her to train with other students. In her other classes, however, she had advanced past all the school's usual curriculum and was continuing on her own, with the occasional guidance from her most respected instructors.

She had fallen asleep over a book she was reading for her paper on "A Study and Comparison of Honorable Practices in War," when she was wakened by the smell of smoke.

Strangely, she wasn't alarmed by this, merely curious. She followed the scent down several dimly lit hallways, until she reached a section of the school she had never entered before. The scent lead her down some stairs and into a strange room. Torches affixed at each corner revealed beautiful murals painted on each of the five walls. The door to enter, of course, occupied one of walls. Painted on the wall immediately to the left of the door was a healer, wearing a robe of deep green and blue, rising from a lake. On the wall to the left of that, there was a magician robed in white and silver standing in the clouds, hands sparkling with light and feet suspended in midair. Continuing to the left, a painted warrior draped in a heavy cloak of deep red reached for the handle of a door set in a wall of flame. And finally, coming full circle, on the fifth wall was painted a brown-robed scholar reading in the shadow of a beautifully striated bluff. The ceiling was painted in swirls of gold and silver. Faces seemed to look down out of the swirls, but when she looked again, they were gone.

Dalia's eyes returned to the painting of the warrior at the door. Something about the door seemed so real. She walked toward it and, as she got closer, it seemed more and more as if it *was* real. It seemed so real that when she got within arm's length of the wall, she automatically reached for the handle. And was astonished when cool metal met her hand.

The door swung open effortlessly, revealing a darkness beyond. In the distance, she could see a flickering light. Dalia hesitated. Shouldn't she be in her room, sleeping? She looked into the impenetrable dark again, the light beckoning. She hesitated a moment longer, but something drew her forward.

Once Dalia had passed through the door, the light grew brighter and brighter, until the darkness was banished and she saw that she stood in the town marketplace. The sound had grown with the light, and now raucous calls from the hawkers filled the air.

She looked around the market, a question niggling at her brain. Wasn't it the middle of the night?

The question left her head a moment later when she spotted a situation that prompted an automatic reaction.

A portly man, flanked by two beefy, blank-faced men, seemed to be harassing an old man at his tiny stall. She plowed forward through the crowd, arriving at the conflict just before the portly man reached out to shake the old man by his tunic.

"Sir!" she exclaimed. "What do you think you are doing? What gives you the right to accost an elderly gentleman in his place of business?"

The portly man drew back, looking Dalia over in amazement. His eyes scanned behind her and noted she was alone. He puffed out his chest, like a conceited rooster.

"Young lady," his double chins folded upon themselves as he looked down his nose at her, "I am a representative of the king."

Dalia raised her eyebrows.

More folds appeared between the man's mouth and neck as he pulled his chin in even further and reached up to grasp the lapels of his coat with both hands. Not coincidentally, this move revealed the king's seal on his finger.

Dalia raised her own chin.

"What is your business with this man?" She gestured at the poor man—a farmer, she now noticed.

"I am attempting to collect the king's taxes."

"And that requires attacking a defenseless citizen?"

The tax collector blew his breath out his nostrils, obviously reaching the end of his patience.

"This man is not willing to pay his taxes. I am authorized by the king to extract those taxes by any means possible. Allowing this man to escape his duty would set a very bad precedent."

The tax collector snickered slightly. "He offers to pay half what he owes and claims he cannot pay more."

Dalia inclined her head. "Indeed. And how much does he owe?" She had some thought of paying the other half herself. The tax collector's next words froze her hands at her belt pouch.

"Twenty gold filia."

Dalia's mouth dropped open and she had to force her voice to normal levels before she said, "*Twenty?!*"

She was so stunned that she was, for once, silenced. The tax collector took the opportunity to expound on the subject.

"Every year, it is every man and woman's duty to put forward a portion of his or her income toward taxes. It is these taxes that support . . ."

"Excuse me," Dalia interrupted in an outraged voice, "but I believe you said 'a portion of his income.' Twenty gold filia must comprise more than two-thirds of this man's annual income! He cannot live on the remainder!

"Look at his stall! Two planks supported at either end by a barrel! He has not even a cover to keep off the rain or sun! How can he possibly make enough money to be placed in the twenty gold fila bracket?"

The tax collector shrugged his shoulders. "I am not the one," he said, "who makes those decisions. I merely *collect* the taxes."

Dalia's eyes narrowed as a thought struck her.

"You know, I have a suspicion," she said. "A suspicion that this man is not in the twenty gold filia bracket at all. If you were to move him up a bracket or two, and then gave over the original sum to the crown, while keeping the surplus, who would be the wiser?"

The tax collector looked a bit alarmed at this statement, but managed to keep his composure. "How preposterous! I am a king's man!" he protested.

"For example," Dalia continued, this time addressing the crowd that had begun to take notice of the argument. "For example, let us say that this old farmer's actual taxes were ten gold filia, a sum that he can pay and still live, and the tax collector claims that he owes twenty. The tax collector collects this amount, or whatever he can get out of the farmer, and then gives ten to the king. He is now richer by ten gold filia! Just by squeezing it out of this man's blood!"

The gathered crowd began to mutter threateningly.

The tax collector gulped and began to back closer to his guards.

Dalia looked at the guards and had another thought. "Is this why you have guards paid by your own hand rather than the king's own soldiers as is your right?"

The crowd responded to this by pressing in toward the tax collector and his guards, who began to look nervous.

A tingling sensation swept over Dalia, and when her vision cleared, the scene had changed somewhat.

The tax collector was gone and in his place was a huge salamander. The crowd and guards ran back, seeking shelter from the unbearable heat that emanated from it. It was ten feet tall at the shoulder and sixty feet from nose to tail.

Dalia's first impulse was to run, but as she turned, she noticed that the old farmer, who had so recently escaped the clutches of the tax collector, could not. The salamander's tail had curved around, blocking his escape. Its hot breath seared Dalia as its head turned to faced her.

"What Dalia? Not running? Are you going to attack me with your needle and pin?" The roaring of the salamander's voice sounded like a forest fire.

Dalia stepped forward, but something heavy clanked and dragged at her leg. She looked down and found that she was dressed in armor, and a sword weighed on her left hip, while a long knife was strapped to her right. She held a shield in her right hand.

She threw aside the shield and unbuckled the sword belt, dropping it on the ground. She stripped the gauntlets from her hands and stepped forward, reaching out, both hands bare.

"I have already faced you," she said defiantly. "See the marks of your teeth on my skin?"

She shed the armor, piece by piece, finally leaving only her aketon, the padded doublet that protected her from the mail.

"I faced you once before unarmed and saved an innocent. I will do so once again." She strode forward, ducking under the salamander's twitching tail to stand beside the cowering farmer.

As she had passed the farmer's stall, she had picked up a bucket of well water and brought it with her.

The salamander's laughter was even more terrifying than its voice. "Will you put me out with that thimbleful of water?" it asked.

"No," Dalia said, then she turned to the farmer and doused him with the bucket.

The farmer stared at her, water dripping from his straggly beard.

"Go, fool!" Dalia exclaimed. "It cannot set you alight now! Cover your face with your sleeve and *go!*"

The farmer did as he was bid, ducking under the

undulating tail of the salamander and running to safety.

"Very clever." The salamander grinned at her, its sharp teeth like white flames. "But now you will have to rescue yourself as well."

Dalia grinned back. "I need no protection from you. You are a creature of Fire and so am I. We are siblings, you and I."

The salamander's tongue slipped in and out as it thought for a moment.

"Prove it," it said, with a hint of triumph, but also curiosity.

"Very well," Dalia said. "Put your face near me."

The salamander did as she asked, moving its head down to her level. Dalia tried not to flinch away from the stifling heat.

"Now, if I can touch you and come away uninjured, will you ackowledge our kinship?"

The salamander nodded, sending scorching waves of air over her.

Dalia pulled back the sleeve on her right hand and looked at the salamander's sleek nose. It was scaled, not with ordinary hard plates, but with small flames. She reached forward, using her right hand because if she failed, she certainly didn't want to lose her only good hand. Memories of her ordeal at the inn flew up like sparks. She doused those thoughts as best she could till only steam remained.

She put out both hands, feeling the blistering heat, but finally believing Ghermot's assertion that she had been chosen by Fire. If this test, for that was all it could be, didn't confirm that, she didn't know what could.

Her hands touched the dry, slippery surface of the salamander's nose and she stroked it soothingly.

The salamander's tongue flicked in and out and it closed its eyes in ecstasy. It cuddled closer, pressing up against her hands. Dalia laughed and scratched harder. She noticed, with a corner of her mind, that not even her clothes were being singed.

Dalia laughed again, and found her voice echoing in a stone chamber that suddenly appeared around her. Whether the chamber was transported to her or the reverse, she was unsure. It was a similar chamber to the one she had left at the beginning—five walls all painted with murals, except that these were much more ornate and held multiple images. The salamander was gone, as was the marketplace.

Instead, five people stood waiting to one side. One of them was Ghermot, dressed in mail and armor overlaid with a bright red surcoat. He smiled at her and came forward, arms open and inviting.

She smiled back and stepped into to his embrace. A moment later she stepped back again and found she was wiping tears from her face. She grinned at Ghermot to let him know she was all right.

He grinned back and she could see his eyes were watery too. Then he turned to his companions, his hand upon Dalia's shoulder.

He cleared his throat and said, "I would like to present the newest Tsyrath warrior, Dalia Swordtongue."

Dalia started at the new name he had given her. She glanced up at his face, but he had begun to introduce the names of the others.

"This," he pointed to the handsome older man in blue and green, "is Melanir healer Doab Watertouch."

"Next," his hand moved to the petite woman in dark brown robes, tied with a straggling piece of rope, "is Iria Bookstone, Torant scholar."

"And this," he turnd to a very tall, stout man in a white gown spangled on the sleeves with silver beads, "is Alahri wizard Robard Cloudhead."

Ghermot turned to Dalia and said in an undertone, "These are the headmasters of the other schools."

Dalia bowed to them and all bowed back, smiling.

Ghermot then turned to the tall, elegant woman resplendent in cloth-of-gold. He bowed to her and Dalia followed his example. The woman bowed back.

"I, my dear," she said in a kind voice, "am Laran, agreed upon by all the Elements to be a representative of Spirit."

The gentleness with which she spoke made Dalia want to embrace her, and had this not been such a ceremonious moment, she would have.

Ghermot broke the spell by speaking.

"We observed that you passed the Test. Most unusual methods for a Tsyrath." He smiled at her. "But, we already knew that you were unusual. Do you have an idea what Fire has in mind for you now?"

Dalia looked down at her hands and saw a firestone ring glittering on her damaged right hand. She lifted it up to look more closely into the stone. Reds, oranges, and golds flickered within, like a banked fire. She looked up questioningly at Ghermot.

"The firestone is a focus for your control over the power of Fire, not a source of that power," he answered her unasked question.

Dalia looked into the stone again.

"Yes, I do have an idea. I think that there are vulnerable people who need an advocate to speak for them. Words are just as effective as swords for correcting wrongs in the world. I think the first thing I will do is take a look at the king's tax system."

Ghermot smiled at this.

"I can see I have named you well, Swordtongue."

LEAVES OF IRON

Cynthia McQuillin

Cindy was been a member of MZB's household for years, but even before that, she was selling stories to her. Cindy has had stories published in both *Sword and Sorceress* and in *Marion Zimmer Bradley's Fantasy Magazine,* as well as a variety of other markets. She is multi-talented; she and her partner, Dr. Jane Robinson, have performed as the singing duo "Midlife Crisis" in addition to their own individual singing and songwriting careers.

Tally stumbled into the cairn more by accident than by design as she fled the attack on Tibor's Forge. One moment she had been crashing through the moonlit brush beneath autumn-sparse trees, and the next she was plunged into stony darkness. She pressed her back firmly against the reassuring strength of the stone walls, and held her breath for the span of a dozen heartbeats, listening hard for sounds of pursuit. But nothing out of the ordinary disturbed the chill, clear night and she sank down to crouch just inside the well camouflaged entrance with a barely audible prayer of thanks.

As her eyes adjusted to the dimly lit chamber, she realized it was no ordinary burial mound she had stumbled upon, but something far more grand. How odd that the people of Tibor's Forge had never suspected such a monument lay so near their village. But perhaps Dama Brit had known and simply never said; the old magic-worker kept many secrets. Tally winced at the thought of her mentor, who even now might be a helpless prisoner of the troll band that had overcome their strongest smiths with ease.

It had been so long since anything or anyone had threatened the good people of Tibor's Forge that they had been taken completely unaware when the raid began. No troll had even been seen thereabouts for at least fifty years. Only she and Dama Brit had been awake to hear their approach; but the magic-worker's fine house stood at the edge of the wood far from any other, so there had been no chance to warn even their nearest neighbor.

"Go to the woods and hide," Brit had commanded, though Tally begged to stay and help with whatever magic her mistress might be planning to loose. The gods only knew what help a half-trained apprentice might be, but her heart ached at the thought of leaving her mistress to face danger alone.

"Go!" Brit had insisted. "I can't do what I must with you underfoot."

"Dama . . ." Tally had begun, knowing how childish her objections would sound.

"No, child, do as I say. If this night goes ill, someone must remain free to spread word of the attack and fetch aid from Turner's Bend or Latinor when daylight comes. Besides, I'll be better able to focus if I know you're safe away."

Dama Brit had always protected and defended Tally, right from the day, twenty years earlier, when they had first found her, a naked squalling babe, abandoned at Headman Vilran's door. His wife, Solan, had decried her as a changeling, demanding she be left to her fate in the woods. But Dama Brit had intervened, speaking of a dream she'd had that night. Her dream familiar had warned her that just such a child would come, and that the girl must be nurtured and cherished, for she would one day save them all.

The Dama's word carried more weight than Solan's, so Tally had been spared and fostered to the Brinallens, who had no daughter. The couple, though grateful enough for another strong back and an extra pair of hands, were hardly loving, and Tally had expected to end her days no better than a servant in their house. But when her cycles began, to her surprise, Dama Brit once more intervened in her life, claiming Tally as her apprentice.

She had indeed proved to have a gift for magic. But like so much else about her, the power she wielded proved to be clumsy and capricious. Her spells were as like to break as to mend, and her gift for mind-speech worked most often when she didn't want or need it.

"Be patient," Dama Brit had said. "Great talent takes time to master." But it seemed now that time had run out. Tally choked back a sob as she remembered the screams of terror and rage that had accompanied her flight from the village.

She had caught glimpses of the huge shambling figures moving with single-minded purpose toward the center of the village as she slipped into the trees. But she had sensed the deep slow power of earth in their movements and their thoughts, feeling something almost like kinship with the brutish, elemental creatures. Her stomach clenched at that traitorous thought, but it was true. For all her appearance of humanity, Tally had felt closer, in that one instant, to the monstrously alien beings who attacked her home than she ever had to the people who had raised her. And that realization disturbed her more than anything else.

Shaking off the shroud of memory, Tally rose to examine the chamber. Something rolled away from her foot. Stooping to feel for it, she discovered the remnants of a torch. Though she saw well enough in ordinary darkness, light would be useful if she were to explore further. Digging out the flint she carried in her belt pouch, she struck spark after spark until the ancient wood reluctantly took flame.

The torch must have lain for a very long time in the cold damp chamber, for it smoked horribly and smelled faintly of mildew and dust. Holding it aloft she saw that the chamber was one of massive proportions and that a doorway toward the rear led into an even larger room. Curiosity momentarily overriding caution, she stepped through the opening to discover what appeared to be a reception hall with yet another doorway at its rear.

This she ignored, her attention being drawn to the long stone dais that dominated the room. At its center was set a huge seat carved from a single mass of the clearest, most delicately colored rose quartz crystal she had ever seen. Even laden with dust, it glowed softly in the flickering torchlight. Four more seats of less elaborate design and less extraordinary stones were ranged on either side—marble and citrine to the left; agate and quartz to the right.

As enthralled as she was by the beauty of the rose quartz throne, what drew her was the figure seated there. Some ancient and powerful magical force hummed to life as she stepped up onto the time-worn granite of the dais to examine it; the volume of the power-song it broadcast nearly drowned the warm, soothing chime of the crystal as she approached.

Clothed in regal splendor, the remains of some long-dead mage or potentate seemed to meet her gaze with an imperious stare. But it must have been a trick of the light, for upon closer inspection she saw that what really sat upon the crystal throne was a skeleton in rags, held intact by bits of leathery sinew. But as she stared, that other, grander image once again overlaid the reality, then faded entirely.

Such an air of antiquity and power clung to the place and to the throne's occupant that Tally couldn't help wondering if she had stumbled into one of the entrances to the Faerie Realm so often spoken of in legend. A shiver ran up her spine at the thought. But the skeletal remains were far too broad and substantial to have been one of the slender, soulless tricksters of elven kind, and too tall, for they were closer to human height.

In truth, from her brief vision and the broad-shouldered, heavy-boned frame, she thought that lordly creature might have carried flesh very much like her own if she had stood a third again as tall. And she was very tall and broad for a human girl, besting the height of every man in the village. What sat here in final repose had been no lord or lady of humankind or any other race of being she knew. Even so the figure drew her.

Without thinking, she reached to touch it. But as her fingers brushed the massive breast bone, whatever trick of time had preserved it was broken, and the remains collapsed in upon themselves, sending up a cloud of dust and a clatter of sound like a sudden hail storm. Tally jumped away, nearly knocking herself off the dais.

When her heart had resumed its normal pace and she could breathe again, she stepped back to examine the pile of now mostly disjointed bones, noticing a soft metallic gleam among the tangle. Upon closer examination, she discovered a strand of dark gold beads caught among the ribs.

The necklace was heavy and fairly long—finely veined leaves alternating with rune-carved disks. Though the fine metal workers in Forge were among the best in the realm, she had never seen workmanship to rival this, and the metal was strange, oily and coarse to the touch. It was definitely not discolored gold or ancient brass as she had first thought.

As she held the torch nearer for a better look, her hand once again reached out of its own accord. It was the necklace itself that drew her. The energy pulse of the obviously spell-worked metal was deep, strong, and cold, but the sensation was not unpleasant as it caressed the edge of her consciousness, becoming all she could feel, all she could hear. She desired the magic of the rune charm, so perfectly wedded with the pulse of the metal, as she had never desired anything before.

Pyrite, the beads sang as she hefted it, crystalline iron wrenched living from its ageless bed of stone and oxidized by the air, then shaped by the hands of a master carver—not forged as she had first thought—and spelled by a true master of magic. The two, working in concert, had set the elements of earth and magic together with a mighty purpose so alien that Tally could hardly guess at it.

How long had it lain hidden in the dark, waiting for her to find it and carry it once more into the world? Years certainly, but the waiting was ended and, as she slipped the cold strand over her head and settled it beneath her jerkin and blouse, she felt complete for the first time in her life.

Tally hardly remembered her return to the deserted village, but now she stood before the empty forges of the metalworkers, open-walled hall trembling with what seemed more anticipation than fear. The fires had been banked for the night long before the attack, and glowed with a sinister hue. She had seen no one as she searched the length of the village from Dama Brit's house, which was sealed inviolate by spells Tally would find difficult to defy, to the crafter's fair at the opposite end. And yet, quiet as everything seemed, she sensed the presence of others moving all around her.

A sound—like footsteps heard through a dream—drew her attention to the wood, which lay a hundred yards or so beyond Forge hall. There were flickers of movement all along its edge. She peered hard at the shadow pools beneath the tangle of branches, until figures began at last to coalesce in the moonlight.

There were a dozen in all, slender men and women with skin like pearl and eyes like black glass. They came toward the hall, moving slowly, but without caution, examining Tally as boldly as they did their surroundings.

They don't know I can see them, she realized with a start, when they began passing comments back and forth in a strange sibilant tongue that she did not know yet somehow understood. *It must be the necklace, allowing me to see and understand them!* How else could she have pierced the faerie glamour? Even Dama Brit didn't possess that trick for all her learned years.

"What are you doing here?" she demanded, looking directly into the eyes of the dark-haired elven male who stood nearest.

Surprised, he paused to examine her, but showed no other sign of dismay.

"Come, you may as well answer me," she said, "for I see and hear you as well as you see me. Don't bother to pretend I don't." When he continued to eye her in silence, frustration made her add, somewhat less politely, "I don't have all night. Just tell me what you want or go! This is no place for your kind."

"Nor for yours, halfling. Yet here you stand making demands of your betters," he replied in a voice as chill and sharp as the autumn air, adding more thoughtfully, "We had believed those of the first blood long gone from this world. And what is this I sense?" Moving with inhuman grace and speed he placed his palm a hair's breadth above where the necklace of leaves and disks lay hidden beneath her clothing.

Compelled by his gaze, which pierced her with its beauty when he turned the full intensity of it upon her, Tally slowly drew the heavy beads from their resting place. The power spelled into the crystalline matrix of raw iron rose to match the elf lord's own as it swung free in the moonlight, releasing Tally from his compulsion. With a gasp, she clutched the beads protectively to her.

"Saaa," his breath hissed out in wonder and dismay. "These are strange days indeed that see Cierulan and Bane's handiwork once more unearthed and in the hands of such as you. We had thought that piece destroyed a thousand years past."

"It's mine now!" Tally cried as he leaned forward to examine it more closely.

"Foolish girl." He laughed then—not a pleasant sound. "We have no use for such a thing. It is iron, which is no faerie metal. You must know that if you have been taught any magic at all."

"If iron truly is elves-bane as legend says, I would keep my distance," she said, swinging the heavy beads in his direction.

He laughed again, stepping just far enough away that she didn't graze him.

"It is cold iron such as your people forge that may harm my kind, not the living metal you hold. You truly are as young and ignorant as you appear, and nearly as helpless," he said dismissively, turning to go.

"Wait!" she cried, catching his arm. "I need help. The trolls have taken everyone from Forge. The gods only know what they'll do with them."

"Their fate is of no matter to me."

"Then why did you come?" she cried, a sudden wave of desperation making her sound as childish as he obviously thought her to be.

"In hopes of catching some of the stone-heads unaware. We thought to pick off some few while they were busy with your people. But, alas, as you can see, your folk put up precious little resistance and the business was done too quickly."

"You might still catch them if you hurry," she offered hopefully. "They haven't more than an hour's start, and must go slowly with prisoners to shepherd."

"We are too few these days to face a war band in

full force, prisoners or no," he replied, unimpressed. "It is better to bide our time and pick them off in twos and threes when we may without risk. Unnaturally long as our lives may be, we still die far too easily, and for our kind—soulless as we are—death is forever."

"At least help me find their lair," Tally begged. "It will be well hidden and I don't know where to look. And think. You have said those of my kind are rare. Someday I may grow into the power I possess and be able to repay your help in kind."

"If you live so long." But his scornful reply was interrupted by the slight, fair-haired woman who stood nearby following their conversation.

"I'll come with you," she said.

"I forbid it!" he hissed, ire making his delicate features fierce.

"*You* may do as you please, my lord," the woman returned in a sweet but taunting tone, "and *I* will do as I please. And it pleases me to see how this halfling maid fares on her quest." She grinned at Tally then, showing the tips of perfectly white, delicately pointed teeth.

"You go too far! But you are right, I can not command you, even for love. But be wary what you choose, for there is more danger here than you know."

"Danger . . . phaw!" She cried explosively. "I am bored nearly to death with doing the safe and reasonable thing. I refuse to cringe in shadows anymore, hiding from the world I love for the promise of a few more years. No matter what you or the others say, this is not living."

"If your mind is set, then go!" He paused before storming away to hiss, "But if you are fortunate enough to return, be sure you bring no danger with you, or I shall see you dead by my own hand, daughter of mine or no!"

*　　*　　*

Sereph, which is what Tally had chosen to call the elf woman since she would not reveal her true name, had proved an excellent tracker. Shortly after sunrise she had discovered the entrance to the trolls' cavern stronghold at the base of the foothills some quarter day's journey from Forge. It was so well disguised that even if the trail hadn't been carefully obliterated by the rear guard, Tally would have walked right past it in broad daylight.

The two sat watching the entrance from the cover of a dense thicket at the edge of the wood. The stronghold was spelled to remain sealed till nightfall, so there was little to do but wait.

"Why can't *I* see the entrance?" Tally demanded in frustration, squinting at what appeared to be a solid rock wall. "If the necklace allows me to pierce the elven glamour it should have worked on anything a troll might contrive."

"Sometimes a firm grasp of the obvious is more useful than all the cleverness in the world, halfling," Sereph chided. The amusement in her tone was teasing rather than derisive, but Tally still found it annoying.

"My name is Tally," she snapped. The elf might be tireless and impervious to minor aches and pains but *she* had missed a night's sleep and was footsore and aching from their long, fast-paced journey. "I'm sick of being referred to as a halfling, like some kind of mongrel dog. What is it that I'm supposed to be half of anyway, *and* what obvious thing am I missing?"

"I didn't meant to offend," the elf replied, looking very nearly contrite. "But the young can be so very blind."

"Just answer my questions."

"Very well. The obvious thing you missed is that trolls don't cast glamours. Their skill lies in knowing the ways and working of stone. The necklace is spelled to enhance perception and understanding between un-

like creatures, so it would be of no help. If you look
closely, you'll see that the cleverness with which the
trail and entrance have been disguised is a matter of
knowing how stone and earth should look, and understanding the ways they may be altered."

"And the matter of my parentage?" Tally sullenly
demanded.

"What do you know of legends?"

"Dama Brit made me study all she knew, though I
never found them of any particular interest or use,"
Tally admitted, with a shrug. "Is there one in particular I should know?"

"Try Giants in the Earth," Sereph said, eyeing
Tally speculatively.

"The first people from whom all other peoples are
descended?" Tally returned her look with one of
puzzlement, then remembered the cairn with its massive chairs and skeletal inhabitant. "But surely *that*
tale *is* a myth. How could such unlike creatures as
elves, trolls, and humans be descended from the
same stock?"

"Magic!" Sereph replied. "The most powerful magic
left in the world pales before that which the first ones
wielded like gods.

"Creation, destruction, transformation—nothing was
outside their scope, and that proved to be their undo-
ing in the end. Though the rest of my race may rail
against the slow death of our kind as their magic seeps
from the world, I believe there is a rightness to it.
We've tampered too long and too much with nature;
it's only fit she should reclaim her own."

"But to lose magic completely!" Tally was at once
saddened and horrified by the prospect.

"Never fear that, Tally," the elf said, deliberately
using her name. "The natural world holds her own
magic—in the rhythm of the tides and the slow procession of the seasons. Life itself *is* magic, the very best
kind."

"So," Tally said, doggedly returning to the point, "you're saying that I'm the daughter of one of these first ones?"

"My best guess is you were sired by the last of the original line on some human woman, though there's no guessing to what purpose. But I think you know more than you're admitting . . ."

After a moment's pause to consider, Tally began her tale, describing the throne room and its lone inhabitant in detail as well as all she had seen and felt.

"I doubt it was mere chance that sent you running in the direction of the cairn or drew you to take the necklace," Sereph commented, when Tally was done.

"Do you think the cairn was my father's grave?" Tally whispered, her skin growing suddenly cold.

"More likely the entrance to one of their subterranean cities, a presence hall where they could receive reports or tribute from their thralls. The first ones always preferred to dwell in the depths of the earth, where they could bask in the elemental forces from which they drew both life and power."

"How did they come to create the other races?" Tally asked, leaning forward intently as the elf woman spoke.

"That's a sad story and one I fear we are all doomed to repeat, for powerful as they were, the first ones were blinded by their obsession. It wasn't until they'd sacrificed nearly everything in pursuit of the magics they so desired to control that they saw the folly of what they'd done. They seldom mated, so they were never many, and though they could prolong life with their arts, they were not immortal. To salvage what they could, the handful that remained used their own seed and eggs to create new and diverse versions of themselves. But even in this they proved hopelessly vain and self-serving, creating slaves instead of equals or heirs.

"Humans were created to farm, hunt, and toil in the sunlight world the first ones themselves disdained, providing food and tools for all the others as well as themselves. So that they would never covet the power in the earth, the first ones made them fear the dark.

"The trolls they created by wedding their own flesh with the earth they so loved. Slow of thought, but strong and persistent, they were set to quarry stone and mine the metals and rare elements the first ones required for their experiments. To keep them docile and dependent trolls were made to fear the sun.

"And lastly, they created elven kind as companions, and to oversee both men and trolls, as well as to assist them in their magical work. In their search for true immortality and ever greater sources of magical power, the first ones discovered other realms. But the few who remained were loath to risk themselves, so elves were sent to explore these unknown realms and there found freedom!"

"In the Faerie Realm, which you have made your own," Tally said, finally making sense of much she had earlier failed to understand. "Did you then turn on your creators and destroy them?"

"There was no need," Sereph said. "In escaping, we had sealed their fate. Without us to keep the others in line, they simply lost control. The humans, always willful and curious, followed their instincts. Spreading into new territory, they diversified in every way imaginable and for all the shortness of their life span, their drive to survive has allowed them to out-breed both of their longer-lived cousins. It is they who will inherit the world when everyone else has gone."

"If your fate truly is sealed as you say," Tally quietly asked, "why bother with the trolls? And why do they prey upon humans?"

"Bad blood, I expect," Sereph replied, with a shrug. "Elves accept humans as lesser if somewhat amusing kin because of our superficial likeness. But they see trolls as hulking, brutish caricatures of themselves, an abomination to be wiped from the face of the world. What the trolls think, no one knows. As to why they attacked your village . . . They're not quick or skilled in anything but stonecraft, so they need slaves who can bear the light of day to hunt and grow food for them. For this they need human stock.

"But we have a long night ahead of us," she said, before Tally could ask anything else, "and we've already gone too long without rest, so I suggest we try to sleep through the day. We'll be safe until dark."

"As you say," Tally agreed with a yawn, all at once feeling her own exhaustion. She found a spot with some cover and a thick enough carpet of moss to offer a cushion to her aching bones, wrapped her thick woolen cloak securely around her, and lay down to sleep.

They woke an hour or two before nightfall, which gave them time to forage for food and scout. By full dark they had uncovered half a dozen side entrances, one of which showed no sign of recent use.

"This one's probably our best bet," Sereph said, eyeing the deceptively small entrance speculatively. "Trolls may be slow thinkers, but they aren't stupid; there may be deadfalls or traps, and I'd just as soon not go in the front entrance if we can help it."

"My gut says this is the one, too," Tally agreed, wiping her face on her sleeve. "I'll take the lead; with the necklace my senses are heightened tenfold."

Sereph nodded and gestured her inside.

It seemed to Tally they had been inching cautiously through the dark for hours by the time they finally found the captives, though Sereph assured her barely an hour had passed since they had entered the twisting uneven tunnels. The odor that rose from below was nearly overpowering as they came out onto a ledge overlooking the recessed cavern. The smell of human excrement and blood mingled with that of rotting foodstuffs and fear.

"Gods!" Tally swore under her breath, nearly gagging. "How can you bear it?" she demanded of the elf who stood calmly surveying the space below, seemingly unaffected.

"Different sensibilities, I expect," Sereph replied. "Look, over there to the far right. Is that your Dama Brit, the one in the green and blue embroidered robes?"

"Where?" Tally gasped, following the direction Sereph pointed. "Yes, gods be praised! I never had much luck with mind-speak, but maybe with the help of the necklace I can reach her."

Closing her eyes, Tally drew a deep calming breath then, carefully forming a picture of Dama Brit's face in her mind, she sent her thought-voice into the darkness."

Dama, I'm here!

Where? came Brit's quick, sure reply.

Above and to your left.

Are you alone?

No, but only one is with me. An elf woman.

It will have to do, came Dama Brit's weary reply.

Her mentor was uninjured though frustrated and afraid, so much the necklace had shown Tally. But she hadn't a clue what to do next. Most of the villagers were huddled near the cavern walls, but she saw none of their hulking captors.

"Where are the trolls?" she murmured aloud, looking at Sereph, who apparently saw as well as she by the magical phosphorescence of the cavern walls.

"Humans are blind in the dark, so there's no need to guard them. Anyone desperate enough, or brave enough, to try feeling their way out will be easily caught and killed. A very practical way to weed out the troublemakers."

"You don't have to sound so impressed," Tally muttered, then silently she sent an edited version of what Sereph had said to Dama Brit.

No one is to do anything till I tell you, she finished.

As you say, came the terse reply. As Tally watched, Dama Brit began feeling her way from person to person, pausing a moment to speak to each, before moving on.

"I'm going to scout the main entrance," Tally murmured to Sereph. "It's the only place we've seen large enough to get everyone out with any speed. If I'm gone too long, get as many out as you can the way we came."

Once through the long, open, and well trodden tunnel that led from the cavern to the main entrance, Tally was amazed to find that area as seemingly free of trolls as the cavern of the captives had been. The concealing rock that had blocked the entrance before was rolled partly aside and pale moonlight lit the good-sized storage area within. Everything the trolls had looted the night before was stacked along the walls.

"I don't know why," she told Sereph upon returning, "but they seem to have gone out and left the front door open."

"It's probably a trap," the elf maid returned, nonchalantly.

"Very likely, but in my experience humans would rather go down fighting than wait meekly in the dark, and once we're outside we might have a chance."

Stealing down to the cavern below, the two gathered Dama Brit, Headman Vilran, and Forge Master Anders to help organize the rest. As Tally had expected, her plan, chancy as it was, found no dissenters. She led the way, with Dama Brit, Anders, and Vilran keeping the central group moving and Sereph bringing up the rear.

Even with the light-spells Dama Brit and Tally were able to produce, and the will-o-the-wisp faerie glow Sereph called up to help guide them, it was slow going, and Tally was sure the sound of their passage, which

was magnified by her own paranoia, would bring the
trolls from wherever they had vanished. But they
reached the storage room unimpeded.

The entrance stood a good third of the way open
as Tally remembered, leaving room for three or four
people to slip out at a time. But as she surveyed the
bare stretch of ground that lay between the entrance
and the comparative safety of the wood, an unpleasant
prickle of warning arose at the base of her skull. No
sooner had the bulk of their party exited the cave then
the trap was sprung.

"Oh, no!" Tally groaned, suddenly sensing troll
thought all around as huge, lumbering figures began
emerging from the trees.

A scream from within confirmed her fear that retreat was futile. The trolls must somehow have known
she and Sereph had penetrated their defenses and
planned to help the villagers escape. She saw her error
now, for it was only when they moved to some purpose that the trolls' thoughts were distinguishable
from the long, slow dream-song of stone. Patient and
unmoving as they waited to spring their trap, they had
been invisible, even to Tally's magically heightened
senses.

"Wait!" she cried, in desperation. The spell-fire she
had summoned flared brightly as she pulled the necklace of pyrite leaves and rune-disks from hiding, to
hold it aloft. "I am a daughter of the first ones, whose
blood we all share, and a true heir to the power of
Cierulan and Bane, and I command you to stop!"

To her amazement, the trolls halted their advance,
shuffling uncertainly back and forth as they muttered
among themselves. To the human ear their language
sounded like the grating and groaning of stones.

Can it be that one has come at last? she heard the
words in her mind as the necklace translated. *She com-
mands the Leaves of Iron,* another added. Then more

wistfully a female voice murmured, *To be abandoned, uncared for, and without purpose, no more.*

No more, no more. They all took up the murmuring chant, moving towards her with shy uncertain steps, like children afraid of being rebuffed.

"It's all right, let them come," Tally commanded, when Anders and the other smiths moved to protect her. "I'm in no danger."

"She speaks truly!" Sereph added pushing past them to stand beside Tally. The trolls gasped and shied back to see an elf in their midst.

"It's all right," Tally said again, this time more softly to reassure the hulking figures that crouched around her like a pack of awkward hounds. "She's a friend and will not harm you. Is there one among you with human speech?"

"All understand," replied a female, with an odd crumbling look about her that spoke of great age. "I, Gron, speak best."

"Good, Gron," Tally said, motioning her forward. "You come and stand by me to speak for your people. Master Anders, Headman Vilran, you will speak for the people of Forge."

She paused then to take a deep breath and organize what she would say.

"We are all children of the same blood, though of very different gifts and needs. We should not hate and kill one another; this weakens us all, depriving us not only of our lives and property, but of the benefit we might derive from working together in cooperation, as we were always meant to do."

Muttered expressions of distrust and age-old prejudice arose from both sides, which she quelled with a look.

"Don't be a fool!" she growled at the Forge Master, when he turned away with a curse. "You need metal for your forge, good iron, tin, nickel, and zinc. And the fine-metalsmiths need silver, gold, and copper as well as gemstones, which must be mined at great cost and hardship by men who despise and fear the mines. And what about quarried stone for your builders and artisans?" she turned to demand of Vilran.

"And your people, Gron," she said turning her attention to the trolls. "You need the food humans raise, and the tools they forge to work your quarries and mines."

Gron's nod was mirrored by all her fellows.

"How make work?" the troll asked, glancing sidelong at the villagers. "No trust here."

"I believe I can be of service," Sereph said, before Tally could reply. "If both sides agree to a peaceful trade relationship, I can organize things and act as a mediator and go-between."

"Are you sure?" Tally whispered. "This could be a lifetime commitment."

"Better than moldering away in safety or retreating from the world entirely as so many of my kind have done," Sereph breathed in return. "It's what we elves were created for after all. Besides, this is the most fun I've had in years."

"Will that suit you all?" Tally asked aloud.

"We're willing to try," came the humans' reply, but the trolls seemed less certain, muttering among themselves as they glanced unhappily at the elf.

"We have hunted and hurt them too long for trust to come easily," Sereph softly said. "I can stand as surety for the people of Forge, but you must offer *them* something else."

Fingering the pyrite necklace, Tally looked from one anxious heavy-browed face to another. There she saw not only the fear, hurt, and need of a thousand years of abuse and misunderstanding, but also hope, as new and tenuous as the first leaves of spring.

"If you will not trust them, then trust me," she said

at last. "I will stand bond for their good faith and stay with you for as long as you wish it."

"Protect and guide?" Gron murmured, a sound like grating sand, as she held out a plaintive hand.

"To guide and protect," Tally affirmed, taking the rough hand in her own, "for as long as I shall live."

As if a signal had been given, the trolls came one by one, to touch her with gentle wondering fingers, then withdrew back into their cavern.

Gron, the last to retreat said, "Free to go," motioning to the villagers who stood staring in awe at the once shy, clumsy girl they thought they had known. "What they not carry, we bring later."

"Thank you. Tell your folk we will meet in one month's time to make terms and formalize our agreement." Tally said.

"Good. Will need time to think and talk," Gron said, patting Tally's shoulder before following the other trolls inside.

With a sigh, Tally turned her attention to the Headman and Forge Master, saying, "Sereph will lead you home. And," she added to the elf, "you'd better let your people know the trolls are no longer fair game. For good or ill, they're under my protection, and I suspect that protection might someday be more than any of us bargained for."

She hefted the necklace meaningfully, then slipped it once more beneath her clothing. As Sereph nodded and stepped aside to speak with Vilran and Anders, Dama Brit's familiar figure came striding toward their little group.

"I couldn't be more proud if you were the daughter of my flesh and not just of my spirit," the old magic-worker declared, suddenly embracing her. Such displays were rare and Tally was touched.

"Thank you," she murmured, not quite comfortable with the unexpected intimacy.

"In one momentous night, you have not only mastered your talent, but have discovered your true self and fulfilled the destiny I dreamed for you."

"Perhaps," Tally said, stepping away from the Dama's embrace, seeing the old woman as she truly was for the first time in her life. "But your dream hasn't proved as true as you believe. In your vision my destiny was to save the people of Tibor's Forge; but in reality, it was to free us all from the tyranny of unwarranted hatred, fear, and prejudice, and to restore—in as much as it may be restored—the bond that was broken between us."

"Yes, of course, child," Dama Brit replied, "that is important, too. But there is so much more—"

"I must go now, my people are waiting," Tally suddenly said, unable to bear Dama Brit's uncomprehending yet beneficent expression any longer. "May the gods guide and keep us all."

With one last wave to Sereph and a heartfelt sigh of trepidation, she turned her back on the villagers who had raised her, yet never truly known her, and walked into the troll caverns to join those who anxiously awaited her within.

THE CHALLENGE

Richard Calantropio

Richard Calantropio lives with his wife, Mary Ann, daughter Deborah, three dogs, numerous birds, and, because he is a volunteer with a wildlife rescue organization, the occasional raccoon, opossum, squirrel, or hawk.

He studied music at the San Francisco Conservatory, and he still dabbles in some composition at home. He has also studied screenwriting at the University of California Santa Cruz Extension campus. By day he works as a field technician for a large electronics firm, by night he takes on his secret identity: the writer. He says that he grew up believing that fantasy, science fiction, and horror were the only food and drink anyone really needed, which made it inevitable that he would eventually start writing in those genres. His first sale was to *Marion Zimmer Bradley's Fantasy Magazine.* This is his second.

"You mustn't accept, Mother. It's a trick, it has to be," Safiyah pursued the argument she had begun in the council chamber. "I've seen her with the Shikan-Tzee and everyone knows the river trolls are all backstabbing smugglers and pirates. This—this—" she gestured toward the short woman in black robes standing in the doorway.

Her mother, Aiesha, hung the amulet of First Bow of the Two Rivers in its place of honor on the wall. "Is this true, Mazi? Have you been consorting with the outlaw trolls?" she asked the older woman.

Mazi shook her head. "It was only Sahak, the boatman. Short and ugly, yes, but as human as you or I."

Safiyah turned on Mazi. "A boatman? You expect

us to believe you met a boatman in the middle of the night?"

"Safiyah!" her mother cut her off. "Think. Before you cross a line you are not ready to cross." She stepped out of her slippers and pulled on high desert boots of soft suede. "Mazi is Second Bow, you will show proper respect."

Safiyah thought her mother looked worn down by the four hour council meeting, yet she persisted. "Why are you doing this? You've never been a slave to the old ways."

"The valley has never been confronted with a pestilence like the shaking sickness before either," her mother said in exasperation. "When the land is in dire peril, a chieftain does what she must. This blessed land between the rivers is all we have. Outside there is only desert." She put on a hooded cloak of desert tan. "Besides, I have already accepted. The council has studied it and it is a proper challenge, conforming to law and custom. The creature is on the old lists."

"A creature that turns flesh to stone? A creature that doesn't exist?"

Her mother strapped on her long knife and smiled. "Safi, you really must live longer than sixteen seasons before you profess to know everything."

Mazi smirked, her tone dripping disdain. "The bir naween would do well to emulate our chieftain's regard for tradition."

Bir naween, "crippled bird." The years fell away and Safiyah was six again, on the street, hungry and hurt, scratching for bare existence, enduring the taunts and—

She whirled, her single long braid swinging around to slap on her breast. "Toad!" Her hand flew to the handle of her long knife.

She was quick, but Mazi moved like a viper. She yanked Safiyah's head down by her braid. Safiyah froze, feeling the prick of Mazi's blade under her chin.

"Curious," Mazi said. "I see but two ribbons in your

braid, bir naween, yet you would draw steel on a Second Bow with five. Incredibly brave. Or stupid." She twisted the braid around her hand. Safiyah winced.

"Mazi!" Aiesha's shout brought her up short. "Now it is you who cross the line."

She flung Safiyah's braid away with contempt. "Pah! Scurry back under your mother's wing, chick, if you ever discover who she was."

"Both of you, this quarreling does no one credit. Safiyah, you will go to the mews. Jess and hood Scree, I wish to take him with me."

"But—"

Aiesha's voice softened. "Now, Safi," she said, brushing her daughter's cheek with her fingertips. "Please. Then you can comb and braid my hair and we will make our farewells."

Safiyah left. The limp that had drawn Mazi's scorn made her feel awkward and grotesque. She leaned against the closed door, eyes burning with tears, and heard her mother's voice drop ominously.

"Safi is young, you do not have that excuse. In deference to your title, I will remind you once and only once. Safiyah is my daughter by choice and I love her no less for not having borne her myself. Do you understand—my daughter? Second Bow or not, if you ever insult her again—" Mazi broke in with a hasty apology. Safiyah hurried to ready her mother's hawk for travel.

It was late afternoon when she stood in the forecourt with her mother. Three of Mazi's Wolves—the name of her band—were to act as escort.

"Must you travel with them?" The dour Wolves in their black cloaks sat their camels with insolent ease.

"The Hawks won't be back from the hunt for days. Your own Lions are all novices. Would you have me go alone?"

"I would not have you go at all."

"Safi, you see enemies everywhere, but your greatest enemy is yourself. In truth, with your mind and your spirit, you can be anything you wish to be."

"You know what I wish."

"Which is why I persuaded them to admit you as a novice. Keep in mind, though, that what the land needs now is healing." They had hugged and she was gone.

The evening breeze from the river was cool and restful, but Safiyah did not sleep. Instead, she lay on her back watching a small spider on the ceiling.

I wonder if it knows I'm watching it, she thought as the spider followed its meandering path. She pounded her pillow, but it still felt like a week-old loaf of bread.

Mazi had dredged up a law written by a mad queen two hundred years ago; a law unspoken and ignored, until now. The notion that a chieftain could somehow heal the land by slaying a mythical creature in single combat made no sense. Why couldn't her mother see that?

The shaking sickness had come to the countryside only half a season ago, inflicting horrible lingering death. Farms went unworked, healers at all the gates checked everyone, turning away any that showed signs of the disease.

Healers, fah! she thought. *If only they could really—*

A muffled clink from the courtyard brought her fully awake. She watched a stumpy figure leaving the city by the huntress gate. One glimpse was as good as falling over her. It was Mazi. Safiyah threw on her cloak, strapping on her long knife as she went out the door.

Outside the city, she watched Mazi climb the trail leading up the canyon to the cave of the fire wizards. That was not good. The caves were cursed, forbidden, no one visited them anymore. The clouds momentarily uncovered the moon, bathing the canyon in an eldritch light. Safiyah felt afraid. Not of wizards, they were all long dead, but for her mother, alone on the desert with Mazi's Wolves.

A lantern's yellow light spilled across the path ahead and Mazi ducked to enter a low opening. Safiyah crept up and hid behind a thorn shrub.

Mazi was speaking and Safiyah heard a slow, grunting reply.

"Hunh, so this is the best place you could find for a meet? It, hunh, gives me the creeps."

"Hah!" Mazi barked. "A quaking troll, now I've seen it all. I thought your kind were nerveless. Are you sure you don't have the shaking sickness?"

"Hunh!" he grunted. "Don't speak of such things, especially, hunh, in this place. You'll call the accursed plague to us."

There was an odd, gasping sound that Safiyah couldn't identify. Then she realized Mazi was laughing.

"Superstitious lout," she finally continued with a snort. "First a dead wizard's cave frightens you and then you think to ward off the shaking sickness by waving a lucky charm." She laughed her wheezy laugh again. "By all the demons, I needed that." Her voice hardened. "Fool of a troll. We meet here because we were seen together and I will not make that mistake again."

"Hunh! Who saw?" the troll grunted with alarm. "Not the witch queen, Aiesha!"

"Chieftain, you idiot. No, only some lame fool of a novice. And it has all been taken care of. Now, have you done what was agreed upon?"

"Hunh, the crate is in your warehouse at the docks, but your witch sisters have already told you that or we would not be here now, hunh. And what you want with such a creature is something I would not care to say, hunh."

"Keep it that way or I might think your tongue needs shortening."

Safiyah heard the clink of coins being counted.

"You have your pay. Wait here a while after I have gone. Then make your way back to your boat. And douse that lantern."

"I am no witch, hunh, I cannot see in the dark."

"By the stars, even a novice—very well, but keep it covered."

The troll's low rumbling went on. "Hunh, I can't say it's been a pleasure, but if ever you might need—"

"Let me be perfectly clear. Our business is concluded, yes? Good. So there is no reason for us to ever see each other again. If we do meet again, I will have to kill you. Do we understand each other now?" There was the soft ringing of a long knife leaving its scabbard. "And if you do not immediately remove your grubby little hand from that toothpick in your boot, I will remove it for you." Silence. "Excellent."

Safiyah held her breath as Mazi came out and made her way down the path. She slid her own knife from its sheath and settled in. Waiting was something a huntress did very well.

And she *was* a huntress. Huntresses did everything together; they found food, kept watch for enemies. Her mother was wrong in thinking the hunting bands throwbacks to the old days. As to healers, pah! Pessaries, poultices, purges, bloodletting! She had no aptitude for such things. Besides, they could stitch up a scratch maybe, but anything else was beyond them. Her own crooked foot was proof of that.

Naturally the shaking disease had them completely baffled. The fools drained so much blood the patient grew weak and had no way to fight the disease. No, what was needed was something to stop the tremors so the victim could eat, drink, hold food in his belly, strengthen his body to fight the disease. But what could—

She heard a footfall and the squat form of a troll slunk out of the cave carrying a lantern. She stepped up behind him and laid her knife across his grimy throat.

"I am Safiyah, huntress of the sixth rank," she lied in her lowest voice. "You will answer my questions or forfeit your life."

A low grunt escaped him and he dropped his lantern in surprise. "Hunh, everyone wants to slice up a troll. What is it with you witches? Do you all thirst for troll blood?"

"Shut up and listen. You were paid by Mazi. What for? Speak."

"Shut up, listen, speak. Hunh, which is it? It is enough to confuse poor troll brains. All I did was transport some cargo up from the south is all."

She pressed the knife. "What manner of cargo?"

"I don't know, and that's the truth."

She drew the knife a fraction.

"Wait, wait! The man I acquired it from, he was one of the tree peoples, he warned me not to open the crate. Hunh, hunh. Said it had food and water to last the journey. There were two, hunh, hunh, small air holes at one end—but he said not to look in them or I'd regret it."

She drew the knife again. "And?"

"Yes! Yes. Hunh. You're right there, you're right, hunh, 'course I looked. Wouldn't be much of a businessman if I didn't, right?" The troll chuckled. "Had to know what I was sellin'. Tell you this though, one look was enough, hunh. Thank the river gods that the thing was, hunh, facin' away from me or I'd be a troll in some human's garden, I venture."

"Explain."

"Silly witch, I'd be turned to stone of course. It was a basilisk for sure, hunh, hunh. Yes, yes, a basilisk."

"You lie!"

"Hunh! Say what you will about us, but a river troll's word is his word. It was, hunh, just as the legends say, ten feet long, all scales and claws."

She tried to sort it all out. Her grip relaxed only a fraction, but it was enough for the wily troll.

"Whooooof!" the breath exploded from her as he drove a horny elbow back under her ribcage. Spinning clear, he snatched a short dagger from his boot. She was down on one knee struggling for breath. He tossed the knife from hand to hand with casual ease.

"Hunh! A little wet behind the ears for a sixth-ranker aren't you? Old Mazi'd have my ears tacked to a board by now."

He moved in, making short, probing slashes. She scrambled to her feet and parried. Once, twice. He was good, only her longer blade kept him at bay.

He grew bold and pressed in. She felt her back against the wall. Her foot slipped. She caught herself, dropping her knife.

A gap-toothed grin split his face. "Hunh, you're lame! You must be the one—"

He never finished. She braced herself against the rock and drove both feet into his mid-section. He doubled over, staggering backward toward the edge.

"Watch out!" she sprang toward him, reaching out. Too late. He straightened, arms windmilling, and went over the edge with a scream cut short by the rocks below.

She looked down at his sprawled form. She hadn't meant it to happen. She only wanted to question him. She retrieved her long knife and for the first time it felt heavy around her waist. A living basilisk. She would have to warn her mother, but first she must speak with her band, if they would listen.

Safiyah sat in the saddle sipping sweet mint tea and tossing the crumbs of a barley cake to the doves pecking about in the low scrub. The river with its lush farmlands were far behind her and the sun, rising over the Haf'Zahir, the Heart of Fire, splashed the gray landscape with deceptively welcoming hues of rose and gold-tinged lavender. From here to the Pillars of the Sky there was only stone and sand, sky and sun.

She rinsed her hands and made a small libation as her camel shifted impatiently beneath her. She spread her arms wide and turned her face to the sky. "Haf'Zahir, in fear do I enter your great emptiness. As the smallest of insects will I cross your vast face. Have mercy. Let she who watches, watch over me. Let she who listens, hear me. Mother and father of the two rivers lead my mother and I safely home from this wilderness."

"Hut, hut." She tapped the camel's flank and entered the desert. She thought of the spider on her ceiling. The sun was already hot.

The next morning she picked up a trail and for several hours followed the track of three camels among the boulders at the base of some low hills. Something wasn't right, her mother's group had four camels. Turning a bend in a dry streambed, she came upon three of Mazi's Wolves.

Strewn about like so many toppled statues, they lay frozen where they fell. Hands reaching, mouths open in silent screams. She dismounted and stepped cautiously among them. Thankfully, her mother was not there. Tentatively, she touched one of the huntresses. Hard, cold, like stone, but not stone. The camels were the same.

It had been dreadfully fast. Knives were gripped unused in stony fingers. Rough planks scattered among the bodies told the story. She saw where a camel stumbled. The crate had fallen, struck a boulder there, and shattered open. In seconds, three fourth-rank huntresses had died without striking a blow.

She cupped her hands to her mouth. "Mother!" she called to all four directions, but the hot wind carried no reply. She knelt and examined the tracks of the fearsome beast. Loose grains of sand tumbled from the still sharp outlines. They were new, very new, less than an hour old perhaps. They followed the stream bed. Climbing the bank, she unslung her bow and nocked an arrow. Tracking was the one time her limp was no disadvantage. It slowed her down, kept her cautious.

"Scree-a-w-w!" Safiyah's heart nearly flew out her mouth as Scree landed on a nearby boulder.

"Stupid bird!" she hissed.

He puffed, rattled his feathers, and screeched again. He had bonded to Aiesha at hatching and was devoted to her. He wouldn't stray far.

"Where?" Safiyah said to the preening hawk. "Go to Aiesha. Aiesha. Go now!" she commanded. Scree blinked and took off. Not far ahead, he began the lazy circling common to his kind. She hurried toward the spot.

In the streambed below the circling Scree, Safiyah found them. The scene was no less terrible for being a familiar one. Three more Wolves and four camels lay in disarray, petrified like the others. Then she saw the basilisk. At least ten feet long, its scales shimmering in the clear air. It stood motionless, only the slow heaving of its flanks betraying the fact that it was alive. *Thankfully it faces away from me,* she thought. Then she saw why.

Aiesha sat petrified, her back to the bank, staring into the face of the creature. She was unmoving and statuelike as the others. Her knife was raised, frozen in the act of a throw that surely would have been the beast's death if she had completed it.

Safiyah's vision blurred as her eyes filled. Too late, she was too late. She choked back a sob. Her grief was replaced by rage. She drew back her bowstring in a fury and let fly.

There was a twang followed by a soft thud as the arrow buried itself in the ground a foot from the beast. It turned, claws kicking up a shower of sand. She drew her knife and with a wail, charged down the embankment in a hobbling run.

"You killed my mother!" She glimpsed a snaking tongue, flashing teeth. Closer. Its jaws gaped. Closer, she had to get closer. Its eyes blazed. She still had thirty feet to cover. Something was spraying—

Steel flashed through the air like summer lightning and the creature was pinned to the ground by a long knife through its head.

"Safi, stop! Listen to me! Don't move." Aiesha was shouting. Safiyah stopped in astonishment. She was alive! "Don't touch it! Don't get any of its venom on you. Come quickly, but stay clear of the venom on the ground."

Safiyah ran to her. "Mother? You're—I mean you're not—" Aiesha struggled unsuccessfully to stand.

"Turned to stone? No, Safi, thanks to your magnificent charge, but it was a near thing. I couldn't hold my arm up much longer."

"I don't understand. How—"

"We were breaking camp when the creature attacked without warning. It came out of nowhere. A camel slammed into me, threw me into the wall. I was dazed—I couldn't move—where could such a beast have come from?"

"Mazi. It escaped before its time. It killed three others of the Wolf band."

"It does not surprise me. It was quicker than anything I've ever seen. I must have blacked out, that's probably what saved me."

"Let me have a look at that ankle." Safiyah cut away Aiesha's boot with smooth, careful movements and gently probed the bruised flesh with sensitive fingers.

"I discovered that its vision is poor in bright light, but it sees motion extremely well. I moved like a snail. It took forever to work my knife into throwing position—"

"Hold still."

"Sorry. But when I finally got my knife raised, it had inched so close that I feared it would spray me even as I threw."

With a few deft slashes Safiyah cut several strips from the hem of her cloak. "Not broken, but it'll need binding." She wrapped the ankle tightly.

"You do that very well," her mother said. "Anyway, I could only hope it would turn away. Which it finally did, thanks to you."

Safiyah examined her work. The taut, precise wrapping gave her satisfaction. "Here, see if you can stand now. Lean on me."

"Much better," she said, taking a tentative step. "I think I can manage."

"Ho!" a voice called out. "It seems we have two crippled birds now."

Mazi looked down from the embankment flanked by the remaining four of her band. They kept their bowstrings taut and the gleaming arrows left no doubt as to their intended targets.

"Why, Mazi?" Aiesha asked.

"Why indeed," Mazi said. "In four seasons you must yield First Bow. Did you think I would meekly step aside for this crippled fosterling you groomed as successor? She has no respect for the old ways. She is not even fit to be a huntress, let alone a chieftain. She has no honor."

"Honor? Is there honor in treason?" Aiesha asked. "Why not just stab me in the back?"

Mazi shrugged. "As you well know, that would not be as easy as you make it sound. Besides, for you to be killed in the city would have raised questions."

"And yet, your plan unravels like a cheap carpet, Toad, so what are you to do now?" Safiyah taunted.

Mazi laughed, that same wheezing sound that Safiyah had heard at the caves. "What am I to do, she asks. You are truly remarkable, chick. True, the loss of six of my band is regrettable, but I adapt. The remaining four will accomplish what needs to be done. And recovering my gold is some compensation. Thank you for dispatching the troll, by the way."

"You knew? Then why—"

"Because I knew that you would try to warn mother, then I could have you both. I admit I did not plan it that way, but one must always be ready to take advantage of what Providence offers." She glanced at her bowmen. "Enough talk. My sisters grow weary."

"Wait!" shouted Safiyah. "Wolves, listen, the punishment for treason is banishment. The punishment for assassination is death. Don't listen to Mazi."

Mazi smirked. "You're forgetting, there is no punishment when no crime is proven."

"Have you heard enough, my sisters?" Safiyah continued shouting. "Do you hear this toad prepare to do murder?"

"We hear," a new voice called and one by one the nine novices rose from the boulders around them, arrows aimed at Mazi's small group.

"What—how did—" Mazi was spluttering.

"Before I left, I told them the Second Bow had contrived a test. They were to become your shadow. To follow you and your people wherever you went. If they remained undetected, they would earn their third ribbon, but if they were seen, it meant demotion." She turned to her mother. "I think they earned their ribbon, don't you?"

"Indeed," said Aiesha, impressed.

"Oh, and by the way," said Safiyah as Mazi and her band were led away, "I *did* plan it that way."

"So the creature was only a venomous reptile from the southern jungles then?" asked Safiyah after Mazi's trial.

"Yes, if 'only' is the right word to use. It's quite a terror. Its venom acts almost instantly, though it becomes harmless once it dries."

"Mother, I've been thinking about that. What if only a very small amount, say a drop, were mixed with a quantity of water to weaken its potency? Might it stop the tremors of the shaking sickness without killing?"

Her mother looked at her in astonishment. "Why, Safi, it never occurred to me. Do you think—of course—I shall have the healers look into it."

"I think I should like to research it myself. Let me do it, Mother."

"It would mean traveling to the southern jungles. What of your training?"

"I've been thinking about that too. Would you be very disappointed if I did not become a huntress?" She unbelted her long knife and handed it to her mother. "I'm afraid I'll never be very good at it."

Her mother smiled and took the knife. "How could I be disappointed? I think you will be a truly powerful healer. As to becoming a huntress, as far as I'm concerned, you've already earned your ribbon."

CELTIC BEAUTY

Winifred Phillips

Winifred Phillips is the author of more than a dozen fantasy, science fiction, and horror stories for National Public Radio's *Radio Tales* series and she has won the American Women in Radio and Television Gracie Award for outstanding achievement for her work. Information about the series is available at www.radiotales.com.

This is her first sale to *Sword and Sorceress,* although she has sold a story to *Marion Zimmer Bradley's Fantasy Magazine.* It appeared in issue 13, Summer 1991.

Leborcham could not help watching the king with an undercurrent of contempt in her eyes. He feasted upon the meal with the same self-absorbed abandon with which he feasted upon the adoration of everyone around him, and it disgusted her. She knew if he turned slightly and met her eyes, he would see her hard expression, and immediately expel her from the table. *If he would just turn my way for a moment, I might be free of his wretched company,* she thought, letting out a long breath. She looked over her shoulder to seek out the man who hosted the feast, a celebration in honor of King Conchobar mac Nessa, ruler of Ulster. It was obvious that the king prized this little lordling, and it wasn't hard to see why. The lord had given a long speech in praise of the king, going on and on about the wealth and glory of the kingdom of Ulster. He said something about it being a "golden age," guarded by the "noble warriors" of the Red Branch. However, the lordling had now gone. She cast a quick glance at the "noble" warriors around the table, then regretted it instantly. *How can they continue to talk with that much food hanging out of their mouths?* she thought, looking conscientiously down at the tabletop.

She had to concede, at least to herself, that the king had done well. Ulster province now stretched far into the south, and Conchobar mac Nessa, for all his faults, enjoyed power that rivaled all of the rulers who came before him. Moreover, he'd earned the respect of Cathbad of the Druids, which was no small accomplishment. She turned her gaze to Cathbad. The old wizard wore a dour expression, but that was perfectly normal. His long, stone-gray beard masked his face and gave his appearance an air of mystery. The hem of his luxurious white robe spread out on the floor around his feet, and the effect produced was quite grand. If he hadn't rolled up his sleeves so that they might not be stained with gravy, he might have been an impressive sight.

Cathbad sat at the king's left. Leborcham sat at his right, and it was a place of honor, she knew, even if she didn't feel particularly honored to sit there. It could not be said that the king respected her. No, more accurately, he *feared* her. If Cathbad could be regarded as an astrologer and magician, then Leborcham could only be called a mystic—inherently sorcerous—a dreamer and a seer. She possessed the three Gifts of Inspiration: the sleep of prophecy, the trance of visions, and the power of the word. As an ollamh—the highest rank of the poetic class—she had the power to glorify the deserving with praise and, on the converse side, she had the right to obliterate the unworthy with satire. So the king had every right to fear her. If it were not for this fear, Leborcham knew that she would not be sitting at the king's side.

He detested her.

A rustle of movement in the feasting hall interrupted her train of thought, and she turned to watch the wine bearers rush around the table in answer to the impatient shouts from the "noble" warriors of the Red Branch. Then a clatter to her left drew her attention to the king. Conchobar had decided to use the shoulders of the Druid as leverage in his effort to stand, forcing poor old Cathbad to clutch the edge of the table in surprise, grunting under the weight of the king and—ah!—stained his sleeves after all! Leborcham disguised her laughter by coughing, covering her face with her hands. Finally, King Conchobar regained his feet, leaned heavily against Cathbad, raised his goblet, and proclaimed in a loud, sloppy voice, "We have tonight enjoyed the froos—" He paused, regrouped. "The fruits of our labors, for as warriors we have ensured the safety of all that we possess. It is our right . . ." He trailed off for a moment, his eyes wandering the now silent chamber.

Where is he going with this? wondered Leborcham.

"It is our right . . ." he continued, ". . . to reap the harvest we have sown . . . to enjoy the bounty around us . . . for all that we see is ours. The goddess of sovereignty has bequeathed to me the land and all that it offers, and as a generous leader, I lay my wealth and my holdings before you . . ." He stretched out his free hand in a delirium of magnanimous self-glorification, splattering wine from his goblet upon the table as he did so. "Men of the Red Branch," he said, his voice rising to a near bellow, "Let us drink to our fair land, to our women and our duns, for surely to own things of such great beauty is what it means to be truly blessed!"

Immediately, Leborcham shot a startled look at the Druid and was not surprised to see the same astonished expression on his normally stolid face as he returned her gaze. The room had erupted in cheers, so Leborcham didn't bother to speak, instead mouthing *What has he done?*

Cathbad shook his head in perplexity, his lips moving to form the words *He cannot know.*

She rose slowly to her feet, looking upward, toward the ceiling, and she could feel in the way her blood flowed through her veins that something was about to happen. The room still thundered in cheers and laughter, but the king turned his eyes for the first time to Leborcham, and the color drained out of his face. "What . . . ?" he said, but his words were drowned by the noise.

And then a sound erupted over the hall—so loud that it drowned the tumult of the crowd, rattling cups and plates and forcing the legs of the feasting table to tremble and throb against the cold stone floor. Every voice in that chamber fell dead silent at once, but the absence of their voices was like the cessation of a whisper against the shrieking terror of the sound that shattered the air. Like the wail of a woman in mourning it rose in pitch and volume, but like the sound of a lightning strike it seemed to sizzle the air and pound into the floor under their feet with the violence of nature unleashed. The torches mounted against the wall guttered as a chill gust swept through the room, and the king ducked his head sharply, his hands flying up to protect his head from an unseen menace, his mouth opening and closing, opening and closing, obviously shouting, without a hope of being heard.

Then, as suddenly as it had begun, the sound died away.

". . . *happening, what is happening?!*" shouted the king in the now silent hall.

Happening, what is happening? answered back the corridors beyond the chamber, echoing the king's terror with perfect accuracy.

All eyes turned to the king.

Conchobar flushed in embarrassment, rounding abruptly on Leborcham. "You did that!" he shouted in a clear voice. The terror had obviously sobered him

"I saw you! You stood before it began! You knew it would come!"

Anger erupted in Leborcham like fire. "No, you have done this! You have invoked the goddess of sovereignty, and claimed that the land which is hers belongs to you! Do you not know that you are just a caretaker? Now you have offended her! We have heard her scream of sorrow!"

Conchobar shook his head in annoyance. "Nonsense," he replied, "You do not know what—"

The rest of his sentence was lost as the high-pitched wail sounded again. This time, the warriors of Ulster clapped their hands over their ears. Leborcham saw the wide-eyed fear in the eyes of the king. The sound died away, and no one spoke.

Leborcham took a breath to speak, but was interrupted by the gray-bearded Druid. "I must disagree with Leborcham," he said quickly, in a reasonable voice. "This cry is not a reproach, my king, but a warning: an omen of future doom." He turned decisively, at once the master of the moment. "Where is the lord of this manor?"

At once, a servant stepped forward, and informed Cathbad that his lord was busy attending to his wife, who was with child.

Cathbad frowned. "Bring this woman to me at once."

Leborcham turned on Cathbad. "Old man, leave her alone, or you will upset her, and bring her early to her time." The Druid shrugged, unconcerned. Leborcham felt the juices of her stomach beginning to simmer with bile. "I tell you, Druid, this unearthly cry we have heard tonight is not a mere warning! It is a reproach, for our king has claimed that his joy comes only from a thing of beauty that he owns, and beauty must be cherished for its own sake. The goddess is the owner of all, and we are her caretakers. I fear that the future of Ulster will depend on our king's enlightenment in this matter." She let her voice drop to a steely whisper. "You think only of pacifying the king's fear—you know I am right. The king must offer apology to the goddess, as quickly as he can. You do him a disservice to council him wrongly."

Cathbad took a step toward her, his dark eyes narrowing in silent fury. Leborcham felt a tight smile spread across her features. *Do you want to fight me, old man?* she asked with her eyes. *Do you really want to test your luck?*

The king took that moment to loudly clear his throat. A young woman stood under the entranceway of the chamber, supported by her lord and attended by two maidens. This obviously was the lady of the fortress. King Conchobar rose to his feet upon seeing the pale, dark-haired lady, who was clearly heavy with child. "Come closer, good woman, and let my Druid speak with you."

Reluctantly, Leborcham stepped aside, allowed Cathbad to approach the dark-haired young woman. He laid hands upon the lady's swollen belly, lowered his head in an impressive manner. Silence hung over the company. Leborcham felt herself holding her breath. For all the Druid's faults, he was a true wizard, and even when she knew his interpretations were wrong, she recognized his power. Cathbad closed his eyes, and spoke in a low voice. "The cry we have heard tonight," he began, "The cry was a mighty omen, for it was the spirit of this unborn child that shrieked from within the womb."

Again, there was silence, as Cathbad strove to read the signs of the future. Leborcham listened in fascination as the Druid spoke again. "The child you bear will gaze upon the world with eyes like emeralds. Her yellow hair will gleam as gold. Like the purest marble will be her flawless features, her cheeks will glow with color, her lips will be as red as the berries of spring. Her beauty will shine like a blinding light that transfixes the lords and chieftains of Emain Macha, but much conflict and slaughter will come of it. I see death in the future, because of this unbearable loveliness. The child will be a curse of beauty that will level bloody destruction upon the kingdom of Ulster."

The room erupted in a great roar of voices. Fear and frenzy surged through the hall. In utter disgust, Leborcham heard cries to the effect that the child should be killed upon her birth. Pushing her way to Cathbad's side, she shouted in his ear, "Damn you, old man, don't you ever think before you speak?"

Cathbad turned quickly to the dark-haired lady, who had paled in horror, her fingers pressed against her cheeks. Cathbad reached out to her, and was just in time to catch her as she swooned.

"Enough!" cried King Conchobar.

A hush fell over the hall.

The silence remained as the lord of the dun supported his wife past the hostile, staring eyes and into the safety of the corridor beyond.

Conchobar met Leborcham's eyes for a long moment. "Here is my decision," he said, his eyes pinned on hers. "The child will live."

Protest and outrage rang throughout the hall. Leborcham let out a relieved breath. The king had seen reason. He would make reparations to the goddess for his arrogance, and all would be well. Leborcham watched with a rare feeling of warmth for her king as Conchobar waved his protesting warriors into silence. "The child will live, I say! But hear me, everyone. This child is mine!"

Leborcham took in a harsh breath, in shock. The king still stared at her, and there was something in that gaze that reminded her of a defiant little boy. Then Conchobar let his focus swing across the faces of his warriors. "This child is mine, and will be mine for as long as I live. I will keep her as I keep my treasures, locked away and safe from thieves." He leveled a

pointed look at each of the men around the table.
"She will live to serve me, and when she is a woman,
she will become one of my companions." He turned
back to Leborcham, and a cool smile touched his lips.
"This beauty will belong to me, I tell you, and I will
ensure that she never beholds another man. No power,
mortal or otherwise, will keep me from what is mine.
Do you understand me?"

The king swept the room with his eyes, saw that he
had been understood. Then he turned once again to
the gray-bearded Druid, lowered his voice slightly, and
asked, "The child will be a woman of incomparable
loveliness, you say?"

"But cursed, my king," Cathbad answered in a dull
voice, keeping his head lowered.

Conchobar shrugged, unconcerned. "Not if she is
kept hidden."

Leborcham felt herself setting her teeth. She took
a step toward the king, spoke in a clear, loud voice,
so that her words rang throughout the hall, "If you
must keep this child, then I will hide her for you!"

"Out of the question," Conchobar snapped, impatiently. "The child is mine, I will keep her where she
may serve me best."

"No, you will give the child to me, so that I may
hide her until she is grown," Leborcham proclaimed,
formally, so that all might witness her words. Then,
she leaned across the table, and whispered in the
king's ear. "If you do not, then I will weave a story
about you in which you perform every act of coward-
ice known to man. You will become a laughingstock."

"You wouldn't—!" the king hissed.

"Would you care to take the chance?" answered
Leborcham. "You will find yourself scorned by everyone you meet. I promise you, I will do this, if you do
not give the child to me."

He measured her determination with a long, as-
sessing stare, then his face twisted in a grimace.

"Aach," he grunted, "all right, all right, the child will be yours, until she is grown. But then, you will bring her back to me," his voice dropped in menace, "or I will have your head on a pike."

"Done." Leborcham answered.

Derdriu knew the story of her birth well. Her guardian had not kept secrets from her, not even when the truth was hard and unforgiving. Derdriu knew the curse of her birth, knew that prophecy foretold how she would become a plague upon the warriors of the Red Branch. But after so many years, the story held little weight in her mind. It didn't seem real. The cottage in which she lived with Leborcham—that was real. The music, the art, the poetry that Leborcham taught her—real as well. The hours spent in the practice of needlework were more real to her than any story, even a dour and terrible story such as the one surrounding her birth. And Derdriu knew the power of stories, for her guardian was a great poet, and had taught her much of the storyteller's art. Still, she could never imagine herself as cursed, even if a Druid had said it was so.

Leborcham had made sure that Derdriu knew the story of the curse as soon as she was old enough to understand. But now she was nearly of age, and Leborcham did not speak of the curse anymore. For that, Derdriu was grateful.

King Conchobar had visited them many times over the years. He came with the attitude of a charioteer gloating over a prized horse. Derdriu knew that the king loved her, in a way. He thought she was beautiful. He valued her hair, called it a "veil of gold." He said that her eyes were like the meadow grass, wet with dew. He thought he was courting her, but it was impossible for him to court someone whom he believed was already his, and Derdriu felt the hypocrisy behind every honey-coated word he said. She hated him. But he was right. She belonged to him, and it didn't matter whether he showered her with praise, like a queen, or scorned her, like a peasant. It wouldn't change the fact that she belonged to him.

Soon, Conchobar would claim his prize, and take Derdriu to him as an amusing toy with which to while away his time. Derdriu tried to keep busy, to maintain a cheerful outlook, if only for the benefit of her foster-mother, who with each passing day grew more and more solemn. Then, one winter morning, Derdriu and Leborcham stood in the crisp air outside their cottage door, watching their servant prepare a rabbit for that night's dinner. Derdriu was tired—her cheerfulness had disappeared, and she found herself broaching a subject she never thought to raise again. "Tell me again what the Druid said, about the curse."

Leborcham looked startled for a moment, then sighed. "He said that your beauty will drive men to kill each other."

Derdriu closed her eyes. "I don't understand it."

"Nor should you," answered Leborcham, and Derdriu could hear the bitterness in her tone. "I don't believe you are cursed. I believe that the king carries the curse within him, and whatever doom waits for him, he will bring upon himself."

"I don't want to go with him," Derdriu murmured.

"I know," answered Leborcham, with a strange expression on her face. "If you had your choice, my beloved Derdriu, who would you choose to be your husband?"

Derdriu stared across the snow for a long moment, surprised by the question. She'd never been asked what she wanted. Taking a moment to think, she watched their servant prepare the meat of the rabbit for roasting. A black bird swooped down out of the sky and skittered across the snow, crying out in a loud, hungry screech. Derdriu spoke slowly. "Do you see the blood of the rabbit running upon the snow, and

the raven that dips its beak into it? In my mind, I see
a young man, with hair like the feathers of the raven,
cheeks flushed and ruddy like blood, and skin as pure
as the snow. I can see him so clearly in my mind, it
is as if we had met before. But that is not possible,
for I have seen no men but Conchobar. What does
it mean?"

Leborcham smiled. "It means that you have been a
good pupil, my Derdriu. I have taught you all I know
of the Gifts of Inspiration, and you have learned so
well that now you have had a vision that is true. The
man you speak of is named Naoise, and he lives not
far from here. I will take you to him, if you wish it."

"But, the king will be angry—" Derdriu began.

Leborcham cut her off. "The king is of no conse-
quence."

"But he threatened you with death—" Derdriu protested.

"I know, I know." Leborcham waved a hand. "Perhaps it is time I saw some of the world, traveled beyond the realm of Ulster. I am tired of this place, I
will find some other land in which to practice my art.
Do not worry for me, you must think of yourself."
Her words were stern. "Choose. You must choose
now, there will be no better time. Will you go to find
the man you have seen in your mind? Or will you
stay, and submit to Conchobar as his slave?"

Derdriu could feel the tears welling behind her eyes,
and her hands trembled, but her voice was firm. "I
will go and find the man I see when I close my eyes."

"Come, then." Leborcham took Derdriu by the
hand, and led her across the snow, into the depths of
the wood.

Naoise was a son of Uisliu—one of the members of
the Red Branch, and Naoise himself was a great warrior. But beyond his strength on the battlefield, Naoise
was best known for his sweet voice when he called his

father's cattle home from the lands surrounding their fortress. In the wintertime, Naoise would sing in the days of Oimelc—when the lambs were born, for it was believed that the ewes gave two thirds more milk when his melody floated over the rampart walls. Leborcham had heard the tales of the boy when she went to the village, and had seen him herself on the forest paths, singing and strolling along without a care in the world. This was a boy who'd never known bonds, had never experienced the restriction of his liberty. It was strange that Derdriu's vision had led her to a boy like Naoise, but Leborcham would not argue against a vision, no matter where it led.

It was the ringing song of Naoise son of Uisliu that guided Derdriu and Leborcham as they crossed the wood and finally drew them to a clearing, where they could clearly see the black-haired boy standing on one of the rampart mounds of his father's dun. The sun dipped in the sky behind him as he wove a warm, rich melody with his strong voice. He was not tall, but he had broad shoulders, and a handsome face with pale features and flushed cheeks. Leborcham smiled. *If I were thirty years younger* . . . she thought.

Derdriu whispered, "He is so like my vision! What should I do?"

"Speak with him," Leborcham answered, shaking herself from her reverie. "You will know if your destiny lies at his side. But," she added in a stern voice, "do not let him speak of curses, or deny you out of fear."

Derdriu stood, hesitantly, and walked slowly toward the black-haired boy. Leborcham noticed that her delicate feet barely left a mark in the crusted snow. She was like a woman of the Faerie—a vision from the Otherworld. Leborcham found herself thinking of the curse, then she quickly dismissed the thought from her mind. *What will come, will come,* she told herself, watching her foster-daughter make her way slowly to the boy's side. Derdriu held the folds of her dress in her slender fingers, but watched Naoise only from the corner of her eye, so that she could see merely a fraction of his awe and astonishment. *As well he should be astonished,* thought Leborcham, then listened as Derdriu spoke in a hushed voice. "I have heard your song echo across the wood, son of Uisliu."

He stammered for a brief instant, then managed words. "My voice today brings me something much more lovely than has ever before come at my call."

Good, good, thought Leborcham.

Naoise paused, searching for words. "And yet, somehow, I knew that you would."

Derdriu raised her eyes, and met his.

The moment was kinetic.

They are meant for one another, thought Leborcham, and her heart swelled in happiness.

The boy looked at Derdriu closely, and then his expression darkened. "You are Derdriu! You can be no other. I should not even be speaking with you. You are cursed."

Derdriu's breath caught in her throat, and tears spilled across her cheeks.

Leborcham felt herself tense, fought the urge to charge forward, seize the boy by his shoulders, and shake him.

But then Derdriu surprised both Leborcham and Naoise by leaping toward him in sudden fury and seizing both of his ears, squeezing them so that Naoise let out a pained cry. "Shame!" Derdriu's eyes burned. "How can you look at me, and say such things? There is a curse, indeed, but it is your own idiocy, and I will make sure that all of Ulster knows of it if you deny me now!"

Leborcham stifled a cry of triumph. Derdriu had learned her lessons well!

Naoise stammered for a moment, taken completely aback by Derdriu's outburst. Then he bowed his head in shame, and said, "I am sorry, but the king will come for us if we pledge ourselves to each other. We will both die."

Time to step in, Leborcham thought, and stepped out from between the trees. "No, you will not."

Naoise jumped at the intrusion, but Derdriu laid a reassuring hand upon his arm. Leborcham ignored his reaction, continued. "If you are brave enough, you will survive to enjoy each other. In the land of Connachta you will find sanctuary from King Conchobar and the warriors of the Red Branch." She turned to her foster-daughter. "Will you go?"

It took only a moment for Derdriu to make the decision. She nodded, then looked to Naoise, who had eyes only for her lovely face. He gave one sharp nod, and Leborcham was touched by the devotion in his gaze. *He will make a fine husband for my dear girl,* thought Leborcham. She sighed, partly in relief, partly in resignation. "Then let it be so."

That night, as the stars wheeled over the land of Emain Macha, King Conchobar of Ulster walked along the ramparts of his dun, sleepless and troubled. For seven nights, he had been rudely awakened by the same disturbing dream. In the dream, he saw himself standing on the sacred plain of Temair, where great inaugurations were conducted. He was dressed as if he were to be crowned high king, but a woman stood before him, shrouded in a dark cloak, and other than this mysterious figure, he was alone on the plain. When he turned to the woman of his dream and removed the cloak from about her face, he saw that her features were those of the lovely Derdriu, and that she held a crown in her hands. But at the same time, Conchobar knew that this woman only shared Derdriu's appearance. In truth, she was the goddess of sovereignty, who watched over the kings of the isle. So each night in his dreams, Conchobar would reach to take the crown from her hands, and each night, it would disintegrate into dust that scattered in the wind. "Shame, Conchobar," said the woman in his dream—the woman whose appearance was that of the lovely Derdriu. "The land of Ulster has been given a great gift of beauty, but your selfish greed robs your people of this gift. It is not for you to possess every treasure, Conchobar. You have forgotten your duty as king." And with these words, Conchobar would awaken from his nightmare, and would sleep no more.

Now, as King Conchobar paced alongside the ramparts of his fortress in the dead of night, he heard a low voice at his side. "You are troubled, my lord?"

"Cathbad!!" exclaimed the king, catching sight of the Druid's heavily lined face in the spectral light of the midnight stars. "Don't startle me like that! You've shortened my years!"

"My apologies," answered Cathbad the Druid. His long white robes rustled in the dark, and his silver-gray beard shone lustrous and fine in the moonlight. He spoke with utmost gravity in his manner. "I have beheld a dire prophecy in the heavens, my lord, and I must now tell you what the stars have shown me."

King Conchobar felt as if an icy hand were squeezing his heart, but he forced himself to speak calmly. "Tell me, then. What have you seen?"

The Druid turned his eyes to the stars. His words were grave. "The greatest of the sons of Uisliu has betrayed you."

"Naoise?" Conchobar asked in disbelief. "Naoise—betrayed me?"

"The stars do not lie," Cathbad intoned. "Naoise has stolen the heart of the fairest maiden in all the isle. He has besought the help of his two brothers, and together the three sons of Uisliu have carried away the cursed beauty known as Derdriu."

In that moment, the king remembered his dream, remembered the goddess of sovereignty warning him that his greed would rob Ulster of a great gift of beauty. But then the memory was overwhelmed by his anger—his wounded pride. "I am betrayed! By my honor, I will revenge! I will mount an army, and tear the land apart to find her! I will hunt her and the sons of Uisliu to the ends of the earth, and beyond, before I let her go! She is mine!"

"But remember the curse, my king," Cathbad warned. "Blood will be shed because of Derdriu's beauty, she will be the cause of much suffering—"

But King Conchobar listened no longer. "Assemble the warriors of the Red Branch! Ready my chariot! We ride tonight!"

The next morning, far to the southeast, beyond the kingdom of Ulster, where the rugged mountains rose high into misty peaks, Queen Maeve looked out over the land of Connachta from her vantage point high atop the walls of her fortress. The sun rose over the river Brea, and the shimmering light glinted in her eyes. The breeze cooled her face as she stood upon the ramparts, with a willowy girl in a dark cloak at her side, and watched a company of chariots approaching. "Tell me, Fedelm," she said, "what do you see coming from out of the north?"

The girl of the Scots turned her impassive gaze upon the approaching chariots. "They are people of Ulster, my queen," she said. She spoke with absolute certainty. "Three brothers and a beautiful maiden. They are fleeing their homeland."

The queen turned her lovely face to the crisp breeze. Her pale hair blanketed her shoulders in strong waves, and as she watched the chariots approach, her steely blue eyes narrowed. "Use your inner sight and tell me. What do these Ulstermen want here in my lands?"

"Sanctuary," answered the prophetess. "Protection from King Conchobar and the warriors of the Red Branch."

Queen Maeve raised her brow, spoke thoughtfully. "Of course, it would be so. I know Conchobar, he is a stubborn fool, and he drives anything of true worth away from him. If these people come to us for sanctuary, then we must carefully consider the tenacity of their pursuer. Conchobar will not sit idly by; be assured that he will chase these refugees to my door, in which case we may be forced to defend them. What do you think, my friend? Should we take them in, or send them away?"

"The maiden who rides with them is much desired by King Conchobar, and he chases these Ulstermen even as we speak," said the prophetess, closing her eyes and crossing her hands over her face in the traditional posture of the seer. "And yet, this hour is an auspicious one, my queen. If you give these people sanctuary, you will appease the goddess of sovereignty, and the land will be blessed."

"Is this true?" A pleased smile touched the lips of Queen Maeve. "Then let it be so. We are not friends of King Conchobar or the land of Ulster, we owe him no loyalty. Let these refugees enter."

As her chariot drove through the entranceway to the hill-rath of Connachta, Derdriu looked up, and for a brief instant imagined that she saw on the top of the ramparts a flash of sun glinting against yellow hair, bleached with lime as was customary among the rich and powerful. But the vision was too brief to be trusted. So Derdriu and the sons of Uisliu rode their chariots past the fortress walls and were led across the courtyard.

Derdriu walked slightly ahead of Naoise, keeping her eyes defiantly ahead, fiercely ignoring the staring eyes of the men who had gathered to gawk and point at her. Since she left her cottage in the woods of Ulster, she had encountered many who looked at her with that same naked desire, and the more she saw these stares, the more she understood what Conchobar's Druid had called the "curse of beauty." It was easy to become contemptuous of these men—of their undisguised craving for something that only she could bestow upon them. She saw her own power in their suppliant stares, but could feel nothing but disgust, for them and for herself. The whole thing was base, and she wanted no part of it.

The queen's steward led Derdriu and the sons of Uisliu into the center of the royal house, where existed the apartment of Queen Maeve. Derdriu, Naoise, and his brothers shared a moment of awed silence, and they exhaled together, taking in their surroundings.

Derdriu walked slowly between the immense copper pillars, her eyes transfixed by the bronze ornamentation on the walls and the silver moldings that rose to the crossbeams high over her head. Everything glittered. The entire room was encrusted in riches. Naoise turned to his brothers who walked behind them and attempted, in vain, to sound unimpressed. "This must be a rich country, that can afford such spectacle."

"Indeed!"

The voice came from behind them. They turned.

The queen swept into the room—a powerful presence, dressed in dusky red, moving with the grace of a dancer and the power of a warrior. In her wake followed a retinue of servants that scattered themselves about the chamber like seeds blown in the wind, drawing aside the curtains to let in the air, bringing in jugs of wine and platters of cheese, fretting over every immaculate detail of the lavish room. Queen Maeve ignored them, her attention focused on her guests. "So wealthy is my kingdom that your King Conchobar grinds his teeth in envy." Her eyes glittered, and the smile she offered was less than warm. Then Maeve's eyes fixed on Derdriu's face, and a long silence settled over the room, broken only by the crackling of the huge fireplace as the queen studied the maiden who had come to seek sanctuary in her land. Derdriu shifted her weight, uncomfortably. "Ah, yes," murmured the queen, "I see why Conchobar might chase you to the ends of the earth. What is your name?"

"Derdriu," she answered, slowly.

Queen Maeve nodded. "Come, Derdriu, do you play fidchell?"

Queen Maeve crossed to a gilded table next to the fire, where a playing board with gold and silver pieces waited to be used. Derdriu followed her, hesitantly, her voice hushed in confusion. "Yes, my teacher Leborcham instructed me in the game, but my queen, there isn't time, the king of Ulster follows close at our heels . . ."

Queen Maeve seemed not to hear Derdriu's warning. "You know the game, then? Good! Good!" Maeve sat at the table and gestured at the playing board. "Now look, you see the many pieces at your disposal. Which will you move first?"

At that moment, from outside the royal apartments, Derdriu heard shouts, and the clatter of weapons raised as the warriors of Connachta ran across the courtyard. In panic, Derdriu shot a quick look at Naoise, who let out a hissing breath, and exchanged glances with his brothers before turning to the queen. "I fear that King Conchobar is outside your manor walls, Queen Maeve. My brothers and I must join your warriors to protect the fort."

Queen Maeve shrugged. "Do what you will. My army is quite capable of protecting this fortress, and this is not a battle worthy of my attention, for there are no lands or titles to be gained. But if you must join my warriors, then do so. Now, Derdriu, I am waiting for your first move," said the queen, folding her slender fingers and sitting back in her chair.

Derdriu felt her throat tighten as she watched Naoise and his brothers race out of the apartment.

She could not see the battle beyond the fortress walls, but she could hear the cries of the fallen, and the shouts of the aggressors as they advanced. Her blood chilled as she listened, and when she could bear it no longer, she blurted, "How can you play a game, when there is bloodshed beyond your walls?"

The queen's expression became very serious. "Isn't that what you are doing? Playing a game?" She tilted her head slightly, her eyes boring into Derdriu's face. "Are you not manipulating your king?" She pursed her lips. "Why else would you flee your land with a low-born soldier? A woman such as yourself could have the richest lord in all the isle. So, are you not using these warriors of Ulster to drive your king into marriage?"

Derdriu stared, in abject shock—the concept to which the queen had given voice appalled her, and she could find no response to equal her revulsion. But finally, she was able to manage words. "My heart is given to Naoise. I . . ." she hesitated, then said, "I could never use him. I love him."

The queen frowned, tilted her head thoughtfully, and it was clear that at that moment she was considering the possibility that Derdriu was telling the truth. Derdriu remained silent. The expression of perplexity on the queen's face deepened. "I suspect that we share much in common, Derdriu. We both are highly prized for our appearance." She paused. "You should be more ambitious, Derdriu, you can do much better than this common soldier; your beauty gives you the freedom to choose the best match, control your own destiny. You could own everything that comes before your eyes. This devotion to the childish concept of romantic love is a weakness that holds you back."

Derdriu took in a deep breath, let it out. She reached to the playing board, picked up the golden pawn, and turned it in her fingers. "This is a beautiful object, but it is also cold. If it were made of wood, it

would be warmer to the touch." She put it back down
on the playing board. "But then, if it were made of
wood, it wouldn't be as decorative."

"What do you mean?" snapped the queen, impatiently.

Derdriu felt the truth of the "curse of beauty" fall
into place in her mind as she spoke. "King Conchobar
wishes to own me, like this trinket. He would surround
me with riches, like what I can see in this room. He
would adore me. But his adoration would be cold, and
the riches he offered would be cold, and I would be
cold as well. He would think he owned a prize. Perhaps, if I chose to see this from your perspective, I
would own a king . . . I would own him. But don't
you understand?" Her voice overflowed with passion
as she rose to her feet. "I don't want to own anyone!"
With a violent sweep of her hand, she upended the
fidchell board and sent the glittering pieces flying
across the floor. "This isn't a game! I love Naoise, and
now he is on the battlefield, and he might die! We
must do something!!"

Queen Maeve stood so quickly that her chair fell
back with a loud thump against the floor.

Derdriu met the furious gaze of the queen. Derdriu
trembled inwardly, but not for an instant did she let
her fear show.

Then the queen lowered her eyes, gazing absently
at the fidchell pieces as they rolled aimlessly on the
floor, and at length a change came over her, a less-
ening of anger, replaced by a contemplative expression. She absently raised a foot and halted the slow
rolling progress of the silver pawn with a booted toe.
Then she said, "Follow me," and turning abruptly,
swept out of the room.

Derdriu struggled to keep up with the queen as she
strode through the apartment and into the courtyard.
Together, they climbed the rough-hewn stairs that as-
cended to the fortress walls, where they could see that

the battle between the warriors of Connachta and King Conchobar's men had reddened the ground with blood. The clatter deafened Derdriu as she frantically scanned the mass of struggling, writhing bodies, looking for a crop of black hair and a familiar, red-cheeked face.

"Naoise!" Derdriu shouted involuntarily as she saw him. He faced King Conchobar himself, and they struggled against each other in a great clash of swords. Their grunts and cries echoed across the field. In panic, she turned to the queen. "Please, you must do something!"

"And indeed I will," the queen answered. In a lightning instant, she seized Derdriu by the shoulders and drew a dagger from a sheath at her waist, holding its glittering edge against Derdriu's neck as she shouted, "Conchobar, I have what you want! The fighting will stop now, or I will kill her!"

In the silence that followed as the men below lowered their swords, Derdriu held her breath in shock, not daring to move.

Maeve shouted, "Send the sons of Uisliu into the fort unharmed! Do it, or the lovely Derdriu will spill her blood on these stone walls!"

The king of Ulster looked up at the queen of Connachta, saw the terror in Derdriu's eyes and the hard determination in the stance of the queen, and slowly lowered his sword. The warriors of the Red Branch followed his lead. Derdriu watched as Naoise and his two brothers walked back into the fortress unmolested by the men of Ulster. All this occurred in perfect silence.

As the last of the brothers of Uisliu crossed through the fortress doors, Queen Maeve turned to Derdriu and whispered, "Go down and join them. In the courtyard you will find a tall woman in a cloak—she is called Fedelm—tell her I order her to lead you out of Connachta and across the sea to her homeland in the

Isle of the Scots, where you will be safe. I will hold off Conchobar and the Red Branch until you are gone."

Derdriu watched as the queen quickly sheathed her dagger, and realized the queen's clever ruse with a burst of joy. She opened her mouth to offer thanks, but the queen shook her head impatiently. "Do not thank me. I hope your love brings you joy, Derdriu— you seek riches of a different sort, and I will not stand in your way. We are alike, you and I. Yours is a noble heart, like mine. The only difference between us are the eyes through which we see the world." The queen gripped Derdriu's shoulder tightly, then stood back and spoke in a harsh voice, as if barking a command. "Now, go!"

That night as the sun set over the battlefield of Connachta, Conchobar was informed that his lovely prize had escaped, and that Queen Maeve and her warriors had made that possible. Derdriu and the sons of Uisliu had set sail with a woman of the Scots to guide them, and were now far from his reach. Conchobar and his men had fought from the glow of dawn to the setting of the sun, and the reason for their battle had long since fled.

King Conchobar would have ground his teeth and raised his fists in rage if he had not felt such embarrassment and shame. Because of Conchobar's avarice, the entire isle had lost a great gift of beauty. He thought again of his dream of the goddess of sovereignty, of her warning to him that he had forgotten his duty as king, and then Conchobar mac Nessa called back his warriors from the battlefield of Connachta, and returned in shame and disgrace to Ulster.

As Derdriu stood on the deck of the ship and looked out upon the sea, the wind fluttering her skirts and rushing over her cheeks, she thought of the land of Alba in the realm of the Scots, where she and her future husband would find their home. She thought of the life they would share together, the happiness they already knew in each other's arms, and then she breathed in the salty air, feeling for the first time in her life as if she were truly, finally free.

LATE BLOOMING

Margaret L. Carter

Margaret L. Carter started selling to MZB for her Darkover anthologies many years ago. She also had a story published in *Sword and Sorceress V.* She has a Ph.D. in English and has written or edited several books on the supernatural in literature. She specializes in vampires, and she edits a semiannual fanzine, *The Vampire's Crypt.*

Her first novel, *Shadow of the Beast,* a werewolf story, was published in 1998. She also had a vampire novel, *Dark Changeling,* published electronically in 1999. Both novels were set in Annapolis, where she has lived for over a decade. It must be a relief; her husband is a captain in the U.S. Navy, and there was a period when they moved back and forth between the east and west coasts every year or two. They have four sons, and three grandchildren—probably more by the time this anthology is printed.

Margaret says that her immediate goal as a writer is to continue publishing novels in the sub-genre of paranormal romance.

The air in the forest clearing shimmered like water, and sounded with a noise like a distant thunderclap. The shock of unleashed magic rippled through Miri. She straightened up, a mushroom clutched in her hand.

It came from back there. From home.

She knew at once that the wave of energy meant danger. The only mage presently at the manor, her Aunt Katwin, wouldn't have cast a spell of such shattering force for practice.

Aunt Katwin had ordered Miri out of the workroom

in exasperation, after Miri had reduced another beaker to fragments the size of gravel while trying to enchant a potion. *To keep me out of trouble,* Miri thought. *I'm not good for anything else.* She communed with plants and sensed their qualities, but that talent gave small consolation to a family who had hoped for another powerful mage like the rest of her mother's kin. At the age of sixteen, Miri still showed ineptitude in every other branch of spellcraft she'd tried. So once again she'd been banished to the woods to gather mushrooms for dinner, leaving Aunt Katwin in peace to pore over the latest rare codex she'd bought at auction.

Dropping a red-spotted fungus into her basket, Miri rubbed the center of her back and listened. No more unnatural sounds. No rotten-fruit scent of evil sorcery—but then she wasn't close enough to pick up such a taint. Her mother or brother might possess the required sensitivity. They were away from home though, attending the duke's court with her father.

Miri brushed off the knees of her trousers and started back to the manor. She walked lightly, listening with ears and mage-sense for any hint of a threatening presence. Underbrush drew away from her footsteps to clear a path, a phenomenon so natural to her that she hardly noticed it anymore. Closer to the house, she tiptoed from tree to tree, clinging to their trunks as if they could protect her. Her skin began to tingle. Her forehead became clammy with nervous sweat.

When the trees thinned, she paused to reconnoiter. Now she caught a whiff of the overripe-fruit aroma she associated with malignant magic. A hand pressed to the bark of a spindly pine brought her an image of what it had "seen" within the past hour: A column of men armed with bows and short swords snaking through the forest toward the manor. Their blue livery looked familiar to Miri, but for the moment she couldn't place it.

The crack of a twig banished the vision and snapped her back to the present. Not twenty paces away, a brown-bearded man dressed in that same blue tunic stood and gaped at her.

She stared back, frozen for an instant. When he drew his sword, she backed away from him.

"Who are you, girl? Come along quietly, and I won't hurt you."

Miri turned and dashed for the forest's depths. The man raced after. With her chest already aching, she cast a glance over her shoulder. He steadily gained on her.

She blundered into a tree. The collision delayed her long enough for the man to close within sword's reach. The tip of the sword grazed her forearm. Again she broke into a run, lurching over the bumpy ground while her blood dripped onto the moss.

Help—please— She wasn't sure to whom or what she prayed, but at that moment a tree root bulged out of the sod and tripped her pursuer.

He landed with a grunt, then spat a curse and struggled to rise. Miri cried out a command at the limb just above him. A branch the size of his arm split off and fell on his head. Again he crumpled to the ground.

Almost as startled as he must have been, she crept close to look down at the armsman. *I didn't know I could do that!* The man didn't move. Unconscious, but for how long?

She fingered the small knife at her belt, intended for slicing tough plant stalks. *I should cut his throat, so he can't warn anyone I'm loose out here.* But she couldn't make herself do that. Instead, she willed a tangle of vines to entwine his legs and arms. Unsure whether a shout would carry from here to the manor, she forced herself to stuff leaves into his open mouth.

Allowed a closer look at his tunic, she remembered the significance of that shade of blue and the lightning-bolt badge on the chest. The man served Lord Alvar, their nearest neighbor; his clan, also mage-gifted, had a long-standing rivalry with hers. *Why are they here? Why did they choose to attack now?*

Because most of her family was away, of course; what did Alvar hope to gain, though? Since her grandparents' day, the competition had remained professional and social, never violent. Her father employed guardsmen to defend against pillaging outlaws, not his fellow barons.

I must get help. Despair settled upon her at the thought of the two hours' walk to the closest village where she could find a mount, followed by a full day's ride to her family's nearest ally. And no guarantee that a neighboring baron, however sympathetic, would offer any substantial aid. Meanwhile, what would Alvar's people do to Aunt Katwin, not to mention the surviving servants and armsmen?

Fighting for air in shuddering gasps, Miri thought, *Very well, that's a poor plan. I'll have to take on the invaders myself.* The notion almost shocked the breath out of her all over again. Yet she had instinctively made that tree into a weapon, in a way she hadn't imagined possible. She clutched the oozing cut on her arm. *My blood—and my fear—somehow they unleashed a new level of power.* With the enemy ignorant of her whereabouts, she might have a chance to rescue her aunt, if no one else. After binding the wound with a strip torn from her shirttail, she headed for home.

No other scouts or sentries intercepted her in the next few minutes. At the verge of the cleared land surrounding the manor, she knelt to press her palms to the earth. Closing her eyes, she sent a questing thought through the entangled roots of the grass.

Her inward sight showed her three of her father's guards sprawled lifeless on the ground. *Dead?* She breathed hard to dispel the dizziness that swept over her. No, their hearts still beat. Alvar must have magically stunned them. Even as she watched, two of his henchmen stepped out of the house to drag the unconscious guards inside. That he'd refrained from outright slaughter gave Miri some comfort. Her aunt might still be unharmed.

How could she get close enough to find out, without being caught? Though not a fortified keep, her family's estate had the basic protections against attack. One such precaution was the flat openness of the lawn surrounding the manor. No concealing shrubbery, nothing but thick grass—

Her talent easily coaxed vegetables and flowering plants to grow faster than normal. Never as fast as this emergency required, but, then, she'd never had reason to try. Pressing harder against the earth, she commanded a nearby patch of grass into unnatural vitality. A sensation like a rush of wind swept over her. The greensward burst upward like a fountain to half her own height, waving in the breeze like a stand of wheat.

After a momentary surge of dizziness faded, she circled around the perimeter to the rear of the house. She peered between the trees, past several outbuildings, to survey the stone wall. Alvar had set no guards here. Why should he, with no doors on this side and no windows on the ground floor? Why would he expect an attack at all? With a silent prayer that none of his people kept watch from those windows, Miri whispered the growth spell again.

A gust of wind blew across the field. In its wake the grass shot up and spread like flame in the dry season. Pain stabbed through her head, but the sensation vanished within seconds.

She stretched out on her stomach and crawled into the tall weeds, reciting a cantrip to make them arch over her instead of clearing a path. Now, if anyone glanced in this direction, they wouldn't see her gradual approach. Sweaty and itchy, she wiggled like a snake toward the building. Every few seconds, she paused to reach through the roots for information on her surroundings. No one came out to investigate. After what felt like an hour of creeping, she lay against the back wall of the manor. She panted, rubbed her cramped legs, and considered what to do next. Flowering vines adorned the lowest level but were constantly trimmed to keep them from climbing the stones. A single word from Miri urged them up the wall to her aunt's window. With their tendrils wrapped around her fingers, she extended her senses along the vines to Aunt Katwin's bedchamber. The spoiled-fruit smell surged over her.

The door was shut, with only two people in the room. Aunt Katwin, still in gray trousers and work tunic, sat tied to one of the two heavy, oaken chairs near the window. Lord Alvar, a stocky, blond man with a square-trimmed beard, lounged in the other. "Shall we try again, Katwin?" he said. "Where is the Codex of Marcionus?" Miri recognized the title of the tome her aunt had acquired at the recent wizards' auction.

The bound woman's plump bosom swelled with indrawn breath. Alvar raised one hand. "Don't even think of it. A single word resembling a spell, and I'll strike you mute again."

"You might as well," said Aunt Katwin, "because you won't get an answer from me. What is the point of this outrageous invasion? My bid topped yours, and I purchased the Codex fairly. It's happened before, and next time you may win the contest."

Alvar folded his arms. "This time is different. That book belonged to my great-grandfather, before it was stolen."

"Oh? And who did he steal it from?"

The wizard frowned but didn't raise his voice. "The Codex has special value for me."

"That's why you made that ridiculously extravagant offer to buy it."

He nodded. "And you refused, so here we are. I made sure your sister and brother-in-law wouldn't be home to interfere. Your nephew went with them, I know. What about the girl?"

"She's gone to attend the duke, too."

"I don't need a truth spell to let me know you're lying," Alvar said with an unpleasant smile.

"Why would I bother?" She moved her head from side to side, apparently trying to dislodge a lock of gray hair that had escaped her headband to dangle over her forehead. "Miri couldn't help you. She has no power worth mentioning."

Huddled in the overgrown grass at the base of the wall, Miri swallowed her anger at this remark. Though she knew Aunt Katwin was trying to protect her, she also knew the truth of the statement.

"She must have some talent," Alvar said, "given her parentage, mage gift on both sides."

Aunt Katwin tried to shrug but was stopped by the hemp rope around her arms. "Some measure of plant-sense. At birth she tested as having strong magic. It must have been a mistake, because we've never seen any sign of it. I've tried introducing her to every branch of magic I know." Her voice took on an acidic tone. "But your spies must have told you all this."

"Yes, I've heard rumors. Is that why you haven't apprenticed her to a plant mage—still hoping to uncover that mysterious gift? It must be humiliating, with all the other flamboyant talents in your bloodline."

"We may be reduced to making a good marriage for her, in hopes that the gift may surface in her children. Not that any of this concerns you, Alvar."

"Speaking of marriage, I'm prepared to offer for

you again. We could share the power of the Codex
and forget all this squabbling." That smile again. Miri
wished she were close enough to slap him.

Aunt Katwin twitched her shoulders. "Hah! I turned
you down twenty years ago, and I haven't changed my
mind yet."

Miri hadn't known that bit of family history. *So
that's part of why he has such a grudge against us.*

Alvar emitted a long sigh. "Very well, let's stop
wasting time. I know you have the Codex under locks,
wards, and a concealment spell. Shall I start tearing
the house apart or just force the information from
your mind?"

"I'd like to see you try."

Miri knew that without the specific cantrip to coun-
teract the concealment spell, searchers could blunder
around for days before finding the chest that held her
aunt's rare magical texts, if they found it at all. She
also knew that Aunt Katwin's power most likely
equaled Alvar's.

So did he, obviously. "True, overriding your shields
might well drain my reserves. Then I'll just bring one
of the housemaids up here and see how much of her
pain you can stand. No physical harm done, of course.
But you still won't like it, will you?"

Nausea made a lump in Miri's throat. She choked
it down. Enough listening; she had to act. With a murmured phrase, she enlarged the vine to the thickness
of a tree branch. Now it formed a sturdy natural
ladder. A tug reassured her that the tendrils were
firmly anchored. She climbed, arms aching, to just
below the second-floor window.

From within, she heard Alvar still arguing with her
aunt. Miri ignored the cramps in her fingers and cast
her mage-sense through that wing of the manor, using
the wooden ceiling beams as a conduit. She found no
one else nearby. Alvar must have had the servants
and guardsmen locked up. Across the corridor from

Aunt Katwin's suite, Miri banged a door with a mental shove.

Alvar sprang from the chair and looked toward the noise. "Blast it, what's going on?" he opened the door and stepped into the hall.

Emboldened by the success of her trick, Miri made another door slam, around the corner.

"Who's there?" Alvar marched down the hall, shouting for his guards.

Shaking from the exertion, Miri dragged herself into the bedroom. Aunt Katwin gasped but didn't cry out. Rather than trying to force her numb fingers to slice at the rope with her knife, Miri concentrated on the hemp fibers to make the strands pull apart. The rope pooled on the floor like an uncoiling snake.

She helped Aunt Katwin stand up. The older woman massaged the rope marks on her arms. "Miri, how in the world—" she whispered. "Never mind, we'd better get moving."

She leaned on Miri as they started toward the open door. At that moment Miri heard Alvar's returning strides and a clatter of boots on the stairway. She urged Aunt Katwin into the corner between bed and wardrobe, then turned to face the man who stalked into the room. One of Alvar's men crowded in beside him.

"I thought I sensed something—" Diverted by Miri's presence, the wizard stopped to glare at her rather than casting a fresh spell at Aunt Katwin. "So you've been here all along. How did you—never mind." He waved his guardsman toward Aunt Katwin. "If the lady tries to speak, silence her."

The guard, hand on his sword hilt, shoved past Miri toward her aunt. With a rush of heat through her veins, Miri leaped into his path. Anger made the pulse hammer in her temples. She screamed a high-pitched syllable. A wooden post broke off from the bedstead, flew across the room, and rammed into the guard's head. He toppled heavily onto the floor. Miri leaned on the wardrobe to keep from falling herself, light-headed at the sight of the man's blood.

Alvar stared at her. "No power? Girl, I've been seriously misinformed about you. If you can kill with a single word, I'm sure you can tell me where that book is." He reached for her.

Kill? He's dead? Miri struggled against the panic that threatened to drown her wits. She backed up and shouted a phrase that leaped into her mind from some unknown layer of memory. One of the heavy wooden chairs skidded across the floor at the intruder. Alvar whirled in astonishment. The chair struck him in the back of the knees, and he collapsed into it.

Terrified that he would catch his breath to pro-nounce a spell, Miri shrieked another cryptic word. The rope spiraled up from the floor to whip around him, momentarily trapping him in the chair and, more important, encircling his neck. The loop pulled so tight that he could do no more than gulp for air.

At the same time, the arms and legs of the chair cracked open. Branches burst forth and twined around Alvar. Seconds later, he sat in the middle of a thorny cage.

Aunt Katwin staggered to the bed, her hand on her chest. "I've never seen anything like this—never. I've met a few plant mages, and I've never heard of one who could bring dead wood to life."

Miri stared at Alvar, whose face turned redder by the second. "What are we going to do with him?"

"For one thing," her aunt said, "don't kill him, too." She grabbed a handkerchief from the drawer of her bedside table and jammed it into Alvar's mouth. "Release the rope, quickly."

With a shuddering sigh, Miri relaxed the loop. Her aunt used the length of rope to tie the gag in place. "Now you won't be casting any hostile spells while we talk this over."

Alvar scowled at her.

"Suppose we refer this quarrel to the duke?" she said. "What do you imagine he'll think about your conduct, when his wizard casts truth spells on all of us to get the full story?"

A sound like a growl rumbled behind the gag.

"Or you might give your sworn word not to repeat this assault in any form, and the duke won't need to hear about it. Just remember what will happen if you break that promise. We'll leave you to think it over."

She led Miri into the adjacent sitting room. Miri collapsed on the sofa, her head on her aunt's shoulder. Sobs shook her body. "I killed a man—"

"Hush, dear, it was self-defense."

"I could have killed Alvar—wasn't thinking—"

Aunt Katwin held her close until her breathing quieted. "You did remarkably well, child. What you need is training. If plant magic can be that powerful—well, it's time we found you a master or mistress in your own sphere."

Miri rubbed her eyes. "You want to send me away?"

"For your own benefit and the honor of the family. Any wizard with similar gifts would be proud to take you as an apprentice."

SWORDS FOR TEETH, MIRRORS FOR EYES

Charles M. Saplak

Charles M. Saplak has sold over one hundred stories to small press and professional publications. This story takes place in the same alternate history as his story "Spider's Offer," which appeared in *Sword and Sorceress XIII*.

When he's not writing or working Charles enjoys woodworking, gardening, birdwatching, and playing with his children Charlene and Marshall.

"Bethnia! Here!" My master, the warrior Dahazendtre, growled, not looking up as she sat brooding, opening and closing her hands, staring into our meager fire.

I snapped myself from my reverie and took my place before her.

"I would be alone, girl. Take the gifts to the others. Approach only if they welcome you. Stay away from me until just after the sun rises tomorrow. Wait outside camp at that time, be quiet, and only come into camp when I call. Understand?"

I nodded and bowed. Her behavior was not eccentric; the task she faced on the morrow required concentration, balance, and meditation. The Ritual of the Dragon's Tooth demanded that everything for her, both around her and within, be just so.

Springtime lay on the land of Daerkeveid, although there above the timberline on the Mountain of Oldest

Fire, home of the Ancient Dragon, springtime was a relative term.

Frost still glazed stones and scrub brush where it had written itself in the shadows. In the distance some wailwrens called plaintively, and smoke from Dahazendtre's meager fire (meager because anything larger would have seemed disrespectful to the immense *wuhrhmenn* that slumbered inside the rocks beneath us) curled into the sky. The day was clear and bright, so much so that I could see distant patterns on the countryside—the villages and cultivated lands of the Protectorate of Daerkeveid. I even imagined that when the mists parted enough I could see the towers of Castle Glaurrensterrn, although surely if I saw it at all it was as the merest speck, a vision residing more in a young girl's hopes—or in my ideals—than in the sight of my seventeen-year-old eyes.

Somewhere in that castle silent priests would still be sitting vigil beside the lifeless body of the potentate, Gkhull, that withered politician who even when he lived was referred to most politely as the Stopgap King. He had died unexpectedly, and as his power had only been grumblingly recognized at best—a sort of grudging compromise—there were now numerous factions with vested interests, each with a different idea of how the power should be shared (and many with the idea that it shouldn't be shared at all). It was nearly ten years since King Roekus, the last real king, and his family had been murdered on the road to Tyrrannia.

In all of Daerkeveid there were only three knights considered worthy of a dragon's tooth, a ritual that had fallen into disuse, or perhaps had been enshrouded in the mists of secrecy and legend.

And thus was my master, Dahazendtre, brooding into her fire. Second to none in courage, never matched in battle, she knew that she could become one of the few so honored, and so position herself as a possible ascendant to the throne. The dukes and courtiers and barons and ceremonial knights were petty people, and the Knight's Guild felt that a warrior, a *real* warrior, would be needed to impose peace on the land.

Thus had many people whispered into her ear, and now we were on the side of the mountain, and she was waiting to make her attempt for the dragon's tooth.

"Then go!" she said.

I gathered the gifts to which she had had referred— hard breads made from some dark Kavonian grain; small pouches of salt; leather bags of a dark, bitter, strong wine; and, without saying good-bye, set out.

The first camp to be visited was that of Wissagalos, a knight I knew by reputation only. I hadn't seen her at the Warrior's Lodge three miles or so down the slope of the mountain. She had been here for a better part of a week, preparing for her turn at the dragon. Thus the demands of *ouhunous* would make my errand much more difficult than common sense would dictate. Wissagalos, as most senior knight, had rights to the first attempt at a dragon's tooth and so had the uppermost place at the summit, while my master was third. I would need to pass the camp of Ambiraas, a warrior from the southern border, who had taken his place between us as second in line.

Wissagalos had camped on a small plateau—only thirty feet or so across, little more than a ledge actually, located a half mile or so farther up the mountain, where the air seemed noticeably thinner and colder. She had a small lean-to constructed, with her fire-pit beside it. As I approached their camp I whistled tunelessly but loudly, knowing that to come upon a knight unannounced and unexpected could mean facing weapons, and I had no desire to face the point of an arrow held back by anyone as preoccupied as was my own master.

Wissagalos' page met me about thirty yards or so away from the lean-to.

"Well met," the girl said, holding up her right hand.

I nodded. She wasn't a very impressive thing, so far as I could see. She was small-boned, and short for her age, which I judged by her figure and face to be about twelve or thirteen. I doubted that she could carry enough equipment for a knight, although Dahazendtre had often told me to never judge an opponent—or an ally—by size.

I held up my bundle.

"Bread and salt," I said. "My master, the warrior Dahazendtre, respectfully offers these tokens to your master, the warrior Wissagalos."

"Wissagalos accepts," she said, without looking back. "And she invites you to present them yourself."

Very gracious of her master, and very unexpected. She was preparing to face the dragon, yet had time to offer courtesy to a lowly page, and in fact the page of a potential rival?

I followed the girl to the lean-to, and as we walked she said to me, "My name is Pearrenz—yours?"

"Bethnia," I hissed, but I didn't want to be distracted, wishing to represent my master and myself well before Wissagalos.

The old warrior wasn't at all what I had imagined. She was lean, with a thickly wrinkled face like soft leather. She slouched before the fire like a person with no pride, and stared into the flames as if watching momentous events unfold there. She was scarred, like most knights, but the scars were all faded. Her hands were knobby and spotted, and the left hand was missing a finger. In that left hand she held an arrow, and in her right she held a dagger in a scabbard.

I held out my packages.

Wissagalos smiled, and gestured with the fletched end of the arrow for me to sit down.

"Open the gifts and share," she said.

I took a place on the ground on the opposite side of the fire, and Pearrenz sat at Wissagalos' right hand. I unwrapped the bread, and as I did so Wissagalos offered me the scabbarded knife. I withdrew it—its blade was of the rare metal which is more shiny than white gold, yet harder than iron. It was double-edged; one side was serrated, the other straight. Its bone handle was carved like a coiled serpent, with a carved disk that looked like both a moon and like an eye adorning the crosspiece. I felt a little self-conscious using such a fine weapon to carve the bread, but Wissagalos seemed completely at ease.

"I take it your master is well?" she said.

"Yes."

"Did she mention that we served together, more than twenty years ago, in the battles against the Unnaturals to the south?"

I hadn't heard Dahazendtre speak of it, but the fact was recorded in quite a few histories. I told her that.

"I am glad to see her in the position she is in today," Wissagalos continued. "She deserves a tooth; at least to my eyes she deserves it. Of course, one has to last a long time in order to get the chance, which we both have done."

I was uncomfortable saying anything. Although having a tooth didn't automatically qualify anyone for anything, we all knew the situation. We were silent for a while, chewing the bread sprinkled with some salt. Wissagalos allowed me to drink of the wine first, and if she did so because she feared poison, she managed to do so with such grace and good cheer that I would have felt bad not to drink. I hoped to make her think the wine wouldn't bother me, but it was so bitter and burning that after my first swallow I had to clear my throat a bit and blink back a few small tears. Wissagalos then bade me to pass the pouch to Pearrenz, who took far too large a swallow, then grimaced and made a rasping sound.

"Perhaps I should keep the wine for myself, while you and Pearrenz share water," Wissagalos said, chuckling, and thereafter she kept the pouch, occasionally taking small sips and smacking her lips.

We all were silent for a few moments.

"I trust your journey here was pleasant?" Wissagalos said. "At least as pleasant as travel can be for a page, carrying the load."

"It was," I said, then had nothing else to say. Inside I was bursting with things to talk about—how my master brooded, the tense moments back in the lodge when she had declared her intention to vie for a tooth, the hundred and one opinions I'd heard these past few days on who would be a good regent for the land and who would not—things that would never have been proper to discuss with these two rivals.

Perhaps Wissagalos sensed my discomfort. "I feel like talking," she said. "Perhaps you two infants have questions for me, an old woman who knows little?"

I probably could have asked a thousand questions, but Pearrenz started.

"Are you afraid about tomorrow?" she said.

I'm not sure if I gasped or not. I could never have imagined myself asking Dahazendtre such a question. This page–knight relationship was liberal indeed . . .

But Wissagalos seemed to take no offense, and actually cocked her wrinkled head to one side and furrowed her brow, as if she were considering the question and examining herself within in order to provide an answer.

"Afraid?" she said after half a minute. "No, not much afraid at all. This, I believe, is due as much to age as to courage. All the dragon could do would be to kill me, and at my age the prospect of death isn't so frightening."

"What is the dragon like?" Pearrenz continued.

Wissagalos shook her head, her gray hair stirring in the breeze. "I have no way of knowing. I've never seen it before. The Ritual of the Tooth is like death in this respect; no one who has ever gone through it has described it for those who have not. It was never something that the survivors bragged of. Most who have tried didn't survive, and, it is said, many survivors have left the mountain and dropped their weapons as they walked, never to be heard from again."

"In the One True Tongue, 'Derkhonn' means 'The Monster with the Evil Eye,'" Pearrenz piped up, and I wondered, *How did she know that?* I wanted to say something similarly impressive, but could think of nothing but the wet nurse singsong—

In Ealdefuer,
A dragon lies—
Swords for teeth,
Mirrors for eyes.

"This is so," Wissagalos replied to Pearrenz's comment. "Just as our land is called the Dragon's View, and the Royal Castle, Glaurrensterrn, is 'The Place That Returns the Dragon's Stare.'"

"Why haven't more knights tried for the tooth?" I asked.

Wissagalos shrugged. "So few have had the right combination of—honor—credentials—in a word, *ouhunous.* Ambiraas, with his victories against impossible odds, or the noble Dahazendtre with her devotion to duty—or my own meager self, with my longevity in the face of the Eternal Spider that weaves lives and epochs into an Infinite Web in a Cave of Darkness. And of those who have the opportunity, some might ask themselves, 'Why should I?' The distinction means little outside our own narrow circle of sword handlers, and in ordinary times the favor of sword handlers is worth less than a belly's worth of black bread."

"Is that why you've waited so long?" Pearrenz asked.

Wissagalos stared into the fire for a full minute before answering. When she finally spoke her voice was quiet and even.

"I've never needed the respect of others—until now. But every person is guided both by her own spirit, as well as by the times in which she lives. Times are different now. I need to do this. I need what I might gain."

"Will you be in line for the crown?" Pearrenz asked.

Again Wissagalos shrugged, but her gesture, if I could read so much into the movement of her old bones, was not so much carefree or resigned as it was suggestive of one shouldering a burden. As she answered she stared at Pearrenz with an expression difficult for me to interpret.

"Perhaps there is much else to be gained. Guidance. Reassurance. Courage . . . for difficult tasks ahead."

Later, as the sun approached the far horizon and the wind strengthened and the chill of the evening air grew another row of teeth, Wissagalos stood and stretched and yawned.

"It will be dusk soon, young Bethnia—do you plan to also honor the camp of Ambirras this evening? It would be good for you to be back at your camp before night falls. And could you please take this child with you so she stirs not and keeps me awake? One rule I've tried to live by is to always get a full night's sleep before any day which may be my last alive."

So Pearrenz and I walked back down the mountainside to Ambiraas' camp.

I rather enjoyed her company. Although her master was above mine, Pearrenz herself was far less experienced than I, and younger to boot. Being a page, particularly one to such a woman as Dahazendtre, in the difficult situation she was in, placed a strain on me which was eased somewhat by having a younger girl to talk to.

When she heard that I had been to Castle Glaurrensterrn, she envied me that.

When I heard that she had spent two years of her life with a Meisterilein priest, two years with a physician, and two years with a blind tomeweaver, I envied her learning—and I told her so.

"Wissagalos is likable," I said, struggling to find allowable words that would let me say that I truly respected her master, and wished her well.

"She is wonderful to me," Pearrenz said, nodding. "I never knew my family. Wissagalos said that no one could say for sure what kind of people I come from, and whenever she sees a beggar or an Unwanted, or when we see a fine duchess and duke in the distance, she points them out and says they could be my family. I've been treated well."

A part of me, the childish part, wanted to grab her hands and dance and say, "Oh, friend Pearrenz, one of us may be in the castle serving the Queen of Daerkeveid within a year!" but that girlish part of me was small and quiet beside the part of dignity and duty.

We were met outside the camp of Ambiraas by a tall youth, not far from full manhood, at least in stature. He regarded us coolly as he leaned against a stout walking stick.

"I'm Earrf, second to Ambiraas, Daerkeveid's greatest warrior. I've served him and fought by his side on occasion. State your business."

I held my pouch aloft.

"I serve the master knight Dahazendtre, and my companion serves the Master Wissagalos. We bring gifts and respects for your master Ambirra. My name—since you have introduced yourself—is Bethnia, and my companion's name is Pearrenz."

"Gifts," Earrf said, sniffing. "So you figure it's not

too early to curry favors with the next King of Daerkeveid."

I bit my tongue. It wouldn't do for me to trade insults with a boor—his master, in the arcane calculus of *ouhunous,* was currently favored over mine.

Pearrenz, rightly or wrongly, felt no such constraints.

"Mind your manners, page," she snapped. "These gifts are freely offered, and currying favor with Ambiraas would be like sharing witticisms with an ape."

Earrf clenched his teeth and stepped forward to loom over Pearrenz. "Do everyone a favor, little girl, and convince that old granny you work for to get out of the way. Even if she survives the dragon she won't live long enough to do Daerkeveid any good. She'll catch a cold within a year and be the Stopgap Queen, and next season when the stars are again right, we'll have to do all of this again. Meanwhile, the borders will have shrunk a piece at a time, every day, until Unnaturals and outlanders walk our streets and Daerkeveid is nothing more than a memory."

"And would Ambirraas be much better?" Pearrenz snapped. "The warrior who's never lost a battle—nor taken a prisoner?"

Earrf sneered. "How disappointed your master will be when she finds that the dragon tooth can't be used to replace any of hers, which are all gone."

One thing I'll give to Pearrenz: she didn't waste any time searching her mind for a witty rejoinder. After Earrf made his remark about Wissagalos's teeth, Pearrenz immediately bared hers, clenched her fists, and rushed straight at the young man who was twice her size.

Fencing lessons from Dahazendtre had taught me a tiny bit about reflexes and preparedness. Still, I barely had time to snag the young girl around the waist and keep her from running straight into Earrf, who had raised the stick and was ready and eager to brain her.

Pearrenz squirmed and jumped in my grip. "Let me go!" she hissed.

"He's twice your size," I said through gritted teeth. "He'll skull-crack you, especially since you're blind with anger."

"Oh, let the kitten go," Earrf smirked. "They never learn anything until they're spanked, you know."

That set her to thrashing around even more violently, and his comments made a part of me want to let her go, even to help her, but instead I just held her more tightly and grimaced into her ear, "We've come bearing gifts and no matter what he says to us you have to be polite. Anything else is a disgrace to our masters!"

At that point Pearrenz stopped squirming. I was glad that she was seeing reason, but as I set her down and turned around I could see that my reasoning had nothing to do with her behavior.

On a rock seven feet high, about fifteen feet down the path, a figure stood. He was a huge man, at least six feet tall. He wore leather leggings and sleeves, and a long vest that appeared to be leather reinforced with metal ribs and rings and plates. He carried a longbow and wore a quiver across his back. His face was darkened by sunlight, crossed with scars. His hair was like the stiff bristles on a pig, and had receded away from his face. His moustache and beard accentuated a fierce frown.

His eyes were dark and cold, his expression stony.

Ambiraas.

"Visitors, master," Earrf said, bowing. I noticed the look in Earrf's eyes as he spoke to Ambiraas. It was subtle, but unmistakable. It was an element that, to the way of thinking of many people, should not exist between servant and master.

Fear.

Ambiraas, with one tip of the bow he held, gestured us forward.

Earrf, subdued now, waved us along the path toward his master.

Pearrenz and I walked along the path to stand looking up at Ambiraas. He made no indication that he would come down from the rock.

"My master, the warrior Dahazendtre, sends these gifts," I said, holding out my pouches.

Ambiraas nodded slightly. "And your companion?" he said, nodding toward Pearrenz.

"I serve Wissagalos," she said.

"Are you her only servant present?" Ambiraas asked.

"I am," Pearrenz answered. If she was intimidated at all, she didn't show it.

"And how long have you served warriors?" Ambiraas continued.

One year," Pearrenz said.

Ambiraas nodded at that. "And when does your esteemed master plan to make her try for the dragon's tooth?"

"With the first light, as soon as the cave can be entered," Pearrenz said.

"And what weapons does she plan to take?" Ambiraas pressed.

I glanced at her. She was ready to answer, but a subtle change came over her, like the hush which drops over a forest when a large predator cat creeps through it.

"I do not know, Warrior Ambiraas," Pearrenz said, her tone shifted; formal, no longer defiant.

Perhaps Ambiraas sensed the shift as readily as did I.

"And *your* master," he said to me. "Her plans for tomorrow?"

I maintained my gaze. "She shares not her plans with me, save that tomorrow she will try for a tooth."

Ambiraas regarded me, knowing that I was evading,

yet knowing that he couldn't compel any more out of me.

"Earrf will accept your gifts," he said, then turned and clambered down the rock, then headed back along the path to his own camp. We had been dismissed.

I turned the pouches over to Earrf without comment and gently took Pearrenz's arm, moving back along the path. No one said anything, although the glances that passed between those two were both fiery and chilling.

The sun was close to the horizon as we moved back toward the main pathway of the mountain. In the sky, night was shaking its cape of darkness. Soon, soon, all would be decided.

I looked back. Earrf stood where we had left him, and was certain that we were watching, as he very pointedly poured the wine out onto the black bread that he had tossed onto the ground.

It was an odd moment—surrounded by great people and being involved in historic events I may have been, but somehow watching him do that suggested to me just how much the world was changing, and it made me sad.

Pearrenz and I walked together a way, not saying much of anything really, then reached a point where she would continue up to her camp and I would walk downward to mine.

"Well parted," I said, then headed back toward my own camp.

My bedroll was where I left it outside of camp, and I was eager to lie down after a day crossing the heights, walking through that thin air. I relied on my own internal clock and the expectation that I would awakened by the cold air so that I could be ready when Dahazendtre called the next morning.

At that point I would not have been surprised, the night before the dragon's cave would open on the mountain of legend, I would not have been surprised to receive a night full of dreams of ancient *wuhrhmenns* and *derkhonns* with razor teeth and bloody beards, of dead kings and sweeping battles, of the clangor of knights' swords and the cheers of fancy courtiers from castellated towers, of musical processions through labyrinthine streets, but the fact of the matter is the ground was hard and the air was cold, and my mind was only able to conjure a very few worried conundrums of who would be king or queen and who would not and what it would mean, and then I was sound asleep.

"Bethnia," my master was calling. Something in her tone made me pull myself a little harder from the land of sleep. An edge in her voice; neither anger nor impatience, a sort of urgency.

I blinked back the darkness and threw off my bedroll. I felt soggy.

"Bethnia," Dahazendtre called again, wandering through my field of vision like a ghost. I rubbed my eyes and attempted to make things clearer, but could not.

"Bethnia!" Dahazendtre called.

Rising to my feet, I realized why I had such a hard time seeing. During the course of the night a thick fog had enwrapped the mountain. I could see clearly no more than fifteen feet in any direction. The sun was not visible. It felt as if the demigods had drawn a curtain of mist around us all the better to isolate this little play of human destinies.

I gathered up my bedroll and made my way toward Dahazendtre's shadow.

"Here, Master," I called. I had no idea how late it was. Could there be any greater embarrassment than for a page to oversleep on the day her master faces an ordeal?

Through the mists we approached each other, her

shape resolving itself as she neared. Soon enough I could see her, dew darkening the cloth of her ceremonial jerkin, glistening on her skin.

"I've received a signal, Bethnia—from up there." She gestured as she spoke, pointing to the top of the mountain. "We're needed, girl. Something unexpected has happened."

"Are you still to try for the dragon's tooth, Master? Have Wissagalos and Ambiraas already tried?"

The mists swirled about her, giving her voice when she finally answered a distant, weakened quality.

"Wissagalos is dead."

Earff led us to a narrow pass at the top of the mountain, about half a mile from the entrance to the dragon's cave. It was a place where one had to traverse a thin ledge that wound up a sheer rock face. Anyone walking there had to be extremely careful, although it didn't seem to be a place beyond the skill or agility of Wissagalos. It was a place where one would be exposed, in plain sight of anyone hiding in the rocks below or above.

Ambiraas, his face slick with perspiration, stood at the top of the pass, glowering down at Pearrenz, fifty feet below him, struggling with something. Presently I could see that Pearrenz had descended the rock walls to retrieve the lifeless body of Wissagalos.

I made my way down to help her. Earff stayed behind to rig up a rope anchored around a tall stone.

My master went to speak to Ambiraas. I tried to steal every glance I could at the two knights, to read what I could in their postures, expressions, gestures. I could almost hear Dahazendtre asking Ambiraas the obvious questions—*how did he come to find her body, what did he think had happened?*

"Words are sharper than knives," they say, and I don't know what words passed between the two. I could see Dahazendtre leaning forward, her shoulders squared, her hands above her waist—everything short of accusatory. Ambiraas stood with his head back, his face like stone, his arms crossed—everything short of flat denial.

But the intricate spectacle of the knights' confrontation was not my main business. Pearrenz's face was awash with freely flowing tears. Wissagalos was no heavier than a bundle of sticks, but she was plastered in amongst sharp rocks, blood staining one breast of her cloak, and forming drying rivulets on her face and neck.

I was ready to not only help but to supervise the younger page in the task of retrieving the body, but it did not turn out that way.

She supervised me. Even though her tears continued to flow and her voice was a croaking whisper she told me not to let Wissagalos' arms drag as we carried her; she chided me if I failed to keep her head above her feet; she ignored the shouted instructions from Earrf above us to secure Wissagalos' body into a bowline made in the end of the rope so it could be hoisted.

Instead, at Pearrenz's direction, we two held Wissagalos tucked under my right arm and Pearrenz's left, each of us using the other hand to clutch the rope and walk slowly up the rock face while Earff, Ambiraas, and Dahazendtre carefully heaved us upward. More dangerous, yes, more difficult, certainly, but a method which best served *ouhunous*.

When we had regained the ledge I found it necessary to sprawl on all fours while I struggled to regain my breath. Pearrenz, still crying, sat beside me, cradling the bloodied head of her dead master.

Earrf coiled up the ropes, eyeing Ambiraas and Dahazendtre.

My master looked down at the face of the older woman, pain and regret apparent in her gaze. She had come to the mountain to save the country, not to see old allies die.

Ambiraas, for his part, continued to look like stone.

"I'll waste no time heading into the cave, Dahazendtre. Within two hours or so you can take your place trying for a tooth."

He said this matter-of-factly, as if the dead warrior there at his feet was nothing more than an unpleasant circumstance. Watching him I could well understand how and why he had gained his reputation as a ruthless, dispassionate warrior.

He turned on his heel, gestured to Earff to follow, and made his way back along the ledge toward his camp.

"Bethnia, aid her," Dahazendtre said, glowering as she watched Ambiraas walk away. Her expression may have reflected her feelings toward him, or perhaps toward the mountain and the dragon, or perhaps toward the entire situation. Or perhaps, toward something inside herself—it was not my place to know for sure.

I had to show Pearrenz many of things involved in the construction of a proper pyre. As cold as it was in the mountains, the work brought sweat to my skin. (On a day when the future of the kingdom would be decided I started by being ordered to the most common labor!)

We gathered stones to build a ring around the pyre; the best stones were those between ten and twenty pounds. Most of the stones at that level of the mountain were exposed, but were scattered amidst other stones too large to move. We sweated and puffed through most of the morning.

I showed her how to build the lower course with enough gaps, so that the pyre could serve as a chimney for an updraft. Once we had an oval of stones about eighteen inches high we filled it with dry scrub. The wood there was exceptionally well suited: dry from the constant winds, resinous evergreen things with thickly knotted branches.

I didn't actually arrange Wissagalos' body, leaving most of that to Pearrenz. It was not squeamishness on my part, but propriety.

I instructed Pearrenz to lay out the woman in her finest, but it turned out she had no finest, wearing what was comfortable and easy to carry. Pearrenz arranged the woman's clothes as neatly as possible, the largest bloodstain very visible on her left shoulder and breast, the smallest spots hardly noticeable on the other places she had cut or torn when she had fallen.

I asked for her armor and weapons, but she carried no armor and had gone off to meet the dragon carrying only her shiny knife with the bone handle, which had not been found. As for the arrows she carried, she owned no bow, preferring not to hunt and claiming not to need a bow for self-defense. The arrows were only used for pointing when she gave Pearrenz her lessons, the young girl explained, tearfully. These arrows we wrapped in the old woman's faded hands, which we laid on her chest.

Pearrenz held the torch and placed it to the scrub brush, as I told her, at the body's waist, from its southern side. I gave her a chance to say whatever prayers to the gods she wished to say, and then watched as, with unfought tears streaming down her face, she touched the fire to the wood.

Later, as Wissagalos' face had peeled back within the flame to reveal a blackening skull that grinned at the sky, we stood watching her smoke rise (breathing some of it in as the wind shifted). By the time the sun had risen and chased the mists from our mountainside, Pearrenz had stopped crying.

"Come on," I told her, softly. "I'll help gather your things. I know that Dahazendtre will let you travel with us. You mustn't worry, you know. We'll take care of you."

Pearrenz answered with an even voice. Something in her tone surprised me.

"Should a page be assisting a knight who is delivering a message, and the knight should die before that message is delivered, what should be the page's duty?" she asked.

"To deliver that message, if possible," I answered.

"And if a page were traveling with a knight to join a battle, and the knight should die before reaching that battle?" she asked.

"The page should continue toward the battle," I answered. "Pearrenz, we've all heard these campfire stories. 'The Steadfast Little Soldier,' and such . . ."

"And if a knight is sworn to protect a life, and the knight should die doing so, and the page lives on, what is the duty of that page?" she asked, not letting me elaborate beyond my answers. I realized that her tone was like something I might expect from Wissagalos, sitting there, asking questions.

"What are you building to with these questions, Pearrenz? What are you wanting to say to me?"

Then she looked me in the eyes and spoke.

"I will do what my master set out to do. I will go into the Cave of Oldest Fire, and there attain a dragon's tooth."

Why I followed her, I can't easily explain. Certainly I was curious. Perhaps I hoped to convince her to stop her foolish quest and turn back. She had no chance at all, or so I felt. Also, I probably felt some desire to protect her. In any event, before long we stood at the mouth of the cave, she ahead of me, pausing only for a moment.

"You can still stop this," I said. "Go only a little way in and then come back. Come back as soon as you feel anything strange. Just toss a stone in as far as you can, then let's go away from here. Any of these things will fulfill the demands of *ouhunous*."

"Try to understand, Bethnia," she said over her shoulder. "There are times when *ouhunous* leads us, but other times, we ourselves, by our actions, define *ouhunous*."

Her words, taken alone, recounted here, may have contained a kernel of truth to be examined and debated over campfires and around banquet tables. But on that misty morning near the summit of Ealdefuer, with the smoke from her master's pyre still clinging to us, her words were not as important as the way she said them, so that as she walked forward into the darkness of the cave entrance, I followed.

The cave entrance was small, and could have easily been mistaken for a shallow wrinkle in the mountain's face. Nothing distinguished it save for the inscription crudely scratched onto the rock beside the cave:

NONE
WHO
ENTER
RETURN

When I read those words I thought of Wissagalos, and I could picture her chuckling and shrugging. She had said that dying wasn't a daunting prospect for one her age.

But I was much, much younger.

At the back of the entrance was a thin sliver of emptiness, an opening through which we insinuated ourselves, turning sidewise as we did so.

We had traded the mist-laden day for a darkness so thick I felt that I was breathing it in, tasting it.

The sliver of diffuse light grew smaller and smaller behind us, replaced by the sickly glow from the cave walls. Every rustle of our clothing, every wheeze of our breath, the drumming of our hearts—all were reflected back to us by the rock chamber. The air was a disturbing tapestry of smells: dust, decay, dampness, and—intertwined in all—hints of reptilian musk and of charred substances.

Pearrenz pushed ahead, not saying a word. The place demanded silence and respect. For my part, I was gripped by a gut feeling that the chambers through which we walked were surely much larger than the outside of the mountain that contained them. Whether this was due to some natural illusion or to the supernatural characteristics of the place, I couldn't say.

As we moved onward, me reaching forward to rest my fingertips lightly on Pearrenz's back and so not become lost, the sense of isolation became worse and worse. There in the darkness the outside world was so far removed as if to be an illusion, a fading dream, and I was letting this child lead me out of the world, out of the flow of time.

This reverie was interrupted when Pearrenz kicked something on the ground, stumbled, and almost fell.

"Look," she said, gesturing in the dim glow from the rock walls.

At her feet lay a skeleton.

Crumbling leather and dust-laden armor lay intertwined with the dry bones. The skull grimaced up at us. A medium-length iron sword in a style I didn't immediately recognize was encased in the ribs, but I couldn't tell just by looking how it had come to be there, whether it had been sent there to end the poor wretch's lifetime, or whether it had fallen into that position as the years caused the bones to settle.

Pearrenz ignored the bony grinner at her feet and hissed back at me, "Come on . . . this is the way."

And how she sensed this I couldn't say. To me the passages inside the mountain were a jumble. It was as if she had developed a more acute sensitivity to our surroundings. At one point we were squeezing through a jumble of limestone stalagmites and Pearrenz suddenly froze, causing me to press against her all the harder.

"Not this way," she whispered. She then bent down and found a pebble, then tossed it forward to the place we would have been. I waited one second, two seconds, three, four, five, then heard it clatter far below us, echoing like rocky laughter as it fell.

"Back," Pearrenz whispered, and as we moved back we realized that the limestone stalagmites here had a subtle but undeniable slant to them, so they had made our passage toward the fall easier, and had we not been two girls in our youth, had we been men, especially men in armor, or carrying weapons, our movement away from the pit would have been blocked.

We traveled further on, me clinging to the hem of Pearrenz's jacket. We soon encountered a chamber in which the ambient light seemed clouded, and I learned why as we walked through it. It was strung floor to ceiling, wall to wall, stalactite to stalagmite with cobwebs. Although I'm not by nature squeamish, these webs swaying in the darkness caressed my skin like ghostly fingers, and recalled for me Wissagalos' words about the Eternal Spider laboring in the Cave of Darkness.

To make matters worse, the chamber of cobwebs was evidently a node in the network of tunnels that crisscrossed the insides of the mountain. Several passages led out of the chamber. Was the dragon's cave also a maze? Had the skeleton we had passed earlier been a tomb raider or a quester who had died within twenty feet of the cave entrance, perhaps unable to find his way out after encountering the dragon, or perhaps never having found the dragon at all?

Did a similar fate await us, the two pages who had foolishly presumed that *ouhunous* demanded they subject themselves to the ultimate ordeal?

The very thought of it was like a physical pressure tightening around my chest, pressing down upon my shoulders.

"See here, Bethnia," Pearrenz whispered, pointing up to an elaborate snare of webs that swayed slightly above our heads. "It moves."

She moved her hand around above her head.

"Warm air, from there," she said, pointing to one of the openings in the chamber wall. "That's the way."

Although I felt with all my heart that she led me toward an ill-considered fate, again I followed.

The breeze that she perceived led us onward, and whether we traveled for miles or for a few feet, whether we spent hours or minutes, I could not say.

Presently the wan light from the cave walls brightened slightly, and we moved toward yet another chamber.

Pearrenz led me into a place that was littered with what I at first took to be oddly streaked, triangular stones. The floor was shin-deep with them.

This chamber, although still dimmer than most starry nights, was more brightly lit than any passage we had yet encountered. A jagged horizontal fissure, about shoulder high, ran across one wall, and through this glowed a warm orange, oddly pulsating light.

And the source of that light. . . .

It was fate that one such as I should attain only the barest glimpse of the dragon.

But of course I was preoccupied at that point with what was at my feet, the odd, triangular stones. All were smooth, but they were easily kicked around, and so could not have been as heavy as normal stones of that size. Besides, they were far too regular in shape and texture. Puzzling. . . .

"What are these things, Pearrenz?" I whispered.

As I spoke I picked one up. Its texture was too uniform. It was a base color of light gray, inscribed with fine black lines in random streaks and squiggles. Despite the random nature of the markings, in the dim light I had the fleeting impression that if one were sufficiently wise, the surface could be read as one might read a history parchment.

"Its life," Pearrenz whispered back. There was something odd within her voice.

I looked up—Pearrenz was silhouetted against the horizontal fissure. She stood still, and her face, illuminated by the orange glow, was moved to an expression of wonder.

"Its life . . ." she continued, and I realized that when she was saying "its life" she was referring to the life of an actual being, one that she saw before her.

"Don't you see it, Bethnia? It has lived forever . . . it's a part of this mountain. These are its scales. Inside it is a fire, from the stone of the mountain itself, and it slowly grows, and sheds these, and these become stone again . . ."

She stepped forward and raised her hands, slowly, respectfully. She moved toward the chamber opening, toward the light.

I tried to follow, to go where she went, to see what she saw, but for me there was only a glimpse. And yet what I saw through that fissure in the stone will stay with me all my life.

Closest to us, I could make out a massive arm, folded back upon itself, each section as great as a horse. The arm ended in a clawed hand that lay flat upon the stone floor, its fingers each as large as a full-grown man. Each finger ended in a nail, a shard of black crystal as big as a man's head.

The shoulder and back of the thing receded away from my vision, but as the bulk of its form retreated from shade to shadow to darkness, I still had the unsettling impression that its shoulder was a small hill, its back a looming cliff.

It was all covered with interlocking scales such as

those at our feet, but while those we walked on were gray and lifeless, the scales still attached to the dragon possessed infinite colors. The shells of jewel-like beetles; the wings of huge, delicate flies; the plumes of forest-dwelling birds; the scales of slender fish from icy seas—all of these things can present miniature living rainbows, and all of these were shamed by the color of the dragon's scales.

And its face . . .

Its face . . .

Drawn toward the wondrous sight, I moved toward the crawlspace, toward the chamber of the dragon.

"Come back here, missy," someone said with a scratchy voice as thin, dry fingers wrapped about my wrist.

I whirled about, and at first could see no one in the dim light.

Behind me, Pearrenz moved forward and clambered through the fissure.

I felt as if I was being clutched at by a ghost but could not cry out for help.

"Who told you you were worthy?" the voice continued. As I watched, a pile of dead scales slid against each other, forming a mockery of a human shape, with chest, legs, arms, and a flat triangular head.

"You don't belong here," the head said with a voice as gritty as the grinding of glass. "I can smell that you don't belong. You're not a knight. Could something so low as you come in to try for a tooth? If something so low as you were to look into the master's eyes you'd melt. You'd explode. You'd fry and leave two boots full of grease behind."

"No, she's not a knight," said a voice from behind me, a voice twice as scratchy as the first.

I turned to face my second enemy. As I turned I could glimpse Pearrenz in the Dragon's Chamber, standing before its face . . .

A second scale-beast stood before me, and it

reached out with a lightning-quick hand to grab my free wrist.

"This is a knight," the second creature said, reaching down into the scales at our feet with its free hand, scrabbling around, then plucking up a nearly intact skeleton, this one wearing a rusted helmet and a chain around its neck.

"Now this fellow has been here for nearly four hundred years, keeping us company. Now he was a proper knight, and see how far he got? Now why, little Bethnia, vain Bethnia, proper Bethnia, loyal Bethnia, why do you think yourself more deserving of seeing the dragon than he had been?"

As the creature spoke it shook the skeleton, and the skull toppled off, clattering back onto the floor of scales.

Where the skull rolled to a stop, a third creature formed itself and arose, holding the skull before it as it did so.

"Look at me, I'm a knight, I'm a knight, oh no, I fell to pieces," it said. Then it cackled, the most hideous sound I've ever heard, a sound that made my flesh crawl.

The eye sockets in the skull it was holding looked sad.

"Bethnia has come to stay with us," the first scale creature said, tugging at my wrist.

"But she shouldn't stay here in one piece, like Sir Grinzalot over there. She should really get the feel of the place, and to do that you've got to be at pieces with yourself," the second one said, tugging at my other wrist.

"Arrogant little girl," the third said. "Let's make her at home. Start with the arms. But first, make a wish."

Then all three cackled, and again my skin crawled.

Each of them had a grip that was stronger than any human opponent, stronger than any rope, any chain. I tried to set my feet to get leverage, but the scales slid and shifted beneath my feet, and they had me stretched to my maximum arm span in a second. I felt grinding in each shoulder, and the sound set them to cackling again.

And then Pearrenz crawled back through the fissure in the wall.

The three scale creatures looked up at her, and one gasped. The other two probably would have gasped also, or shrieked, but they hadn't time enough to do so.

She held something before her, not as a weapon, not as a ceremonial thing, but as a suddenly revealed secret, a source of light, something that was *hers,* a thing that emitted a warm glow of light.

A dragon's tooth.

And before that light, the scale creatures collapsed and fell at our feet, clattering as they did so.

I looked to Pearrenz, gasping for breath as I did so. "Thank you," I huffed. "you've saved me for sure."

She didn't answer.

She still held the tooth, and she offered me her hand, offered to lead me out, but she said not a word, and there was no recognition in her eyes.

She was as one dead.

Our journey back through the passages of the mountain was silent, didn't seem to take long, and was uneventful.

And presently we emerged into the light, into a changed world.

The setting sun cast mile-long shadows across the landscape of Daerkeveid as we approached Pearrenz's camp. The remains of Wissagalos' pyre were completely gone, the ashes scattered in the wind, nothing left but an oval of blackened stones and a dark spot on the ground where she had been. It occurred to me that from that high point of the world, the wind would take her ashes to every place in the world, perhaps traveling farther than she had even in her long life.

Pearrenz only looked at the spot for a moment, not even stopping as she walked. She still hadn't spoken, so I was certain that her mind had been addled somehow, or that she was in shock from her experience in the cave.

I gathered up a few things—they had brought very little—and put them in a bundle that I offered Pearrenz, but she ignored me, clutching the tooth as she did.

We continued down the mountain, and before long came to Ambirraas' camp. When we were still forty yards away or so I spotted Ambirraas staring at his fire, while his belongings danced about in the wind, and his tent flapped wildly about, staked to the ground at only one corner.

Seeing his camp in such disarray, I was alarmed, sensing that something evil and irreversible had happened.

"Come on," I said, tugging at Pearrenz's sleeve, pulling her into a half-hearted run.

Before long we were close enough to the camp that I could see what was really happening.

It was my master Dahazendtre who sat there by the fire.

Ambirraas lay stretched out dead, a knife in his chest.

Something in the way Dahazendtre slouched, in the way she swung her head to stare at us as we approached, something in her eyes spoke of utter defeat. A thousand fears raced through my mind.

Had she been wounded in a fight with Ambirraas? Or worse still, had she been unable to approach the dragon's lair without my help? Even as I considered that I realized it was a vanity on my part, that more likely she had tried to go on, but had been stopped, or perhaps had looked for Pearrenz and me, and missed her chance.

I despaired! All of the dreams and ambitions of the day before had fallen apart.

And yet, there were my duties.

Duties . . .

I knelt before Dahazendtre.

"Forgive me, Master, for I have failed you. As I try to earn your trust again, let me help you. Were you injured in your fight with Ambirraas?"

She turned to look at me. "Fight? There's been no fight here—or at least none in which I've been involved. Ambirraas was like that when I found him, as I came back down the mountain."

"Then who could have done this?" I asked. Even as I said it I noticed the handle of the knife between Ambirraas' clutching fingers. It was the braided serpent carved in bone—Wissagalos' dagger.

"Claws of Werra!" I cursed. "Wissagalos' ghost was here. She did this!"

Dahazendtre rolled her eyes. "Girl, don't walk past three simple explanations in order to find a strange one. And besides, ghosts don't carry knives, do they? Take a look at the way his hand is around that handle. He holds it tightly which means that he was holding it when he died. Deathgrip. But see how his palm faces up? I don't think he was trying to pull out a knife someone else had stuck in. I think he put that knife in himself."

"Why would he do such a thing? Because he tried for a tooth and failed?" I asked.

"No," Dahazendtre said, shaking her head. "I think it was *because he got his tooth*. He'd killed Wissagalos because she was ahead of him; he normally wouldn't have stolen anything, but that knife is a thing called *steel*, such a rare blade that he couldn't resist. And after he had been to the dragon he couldn't live any longer, and he used her knife to take his own life. There was something that happened to him in the gaining of the tooth. Something he saw there—something hard for me to explain . . .

"In any event, that useless Earrf was here going through Ambirraas' things when I came down the mountain, not even bothering to prepare a proper pyre for his master, suicide or no, leaving him for the buzzards. Earrf took whatever he could carry, the little ghoul. He was probably too superstitious to take the steel knife from his dying master's chest, although maybe he was working his way toward that when I interrupted him."

"Where is the tooth that Ambirraas gained?" I asked.

"I do think that Earrf crept away with it," Dahazendtre said. "If that is so he's just purchased himself the most poisonous segment of luck any young man could wish for."

My master was silent for a moment, looking into the distance. Then she looked at me with her doleful, dull eyes, and spoke to me with words that were far more harsh in implication than in tone.

"So, page, what happened to you? I expected you back here."

"Pearrenz!" I said, fired by my desire to tell what had happened. "She insisted on following Wissagalos' footsteps. And look what happened! She got a tooth! Although it may have been better for her if she had not. I'm afraid the experience there has disordered her mind."

Only then did Dahazendtre seem to notice the jagged triangle of bone in Pearrenz's hand.

"You too, child?" she said. "And what hidden truth did you see in those ancient eyes when you reached out for that terrible fang?"

And Dahazendtre's cloak fell open where she had it gathered, and it was my turn to notice that she also had such a tooth in her belt.

"Master!" I gasped. "You went on without me!"

"What? Oh, that. Well, of course I did. Knights don't turn for home when their pages quit, you know. I do remember how to dress myself."

"Then we've won, Master. As the knight with a tooth you can become queen!"

Dahazendtre smiled a tired, crooked, bitter smile. "Oh, could I? Yes, I know I could, but what I realize now is that that is not the point. I could become Queen of Daerkeveid, yes, I know that for certain, just as I also know, having seen it in the dragon's eyes, *that I would not be a good queen at all.* So many people have whispered into my ears that I should become queen because I am loyal, because I have been devoted, because I have followed orders so well, because I've always tried to align myself with just causes—but these things alone . . ."

"Loyal?" a small voice croaked. "Devoted? Justice?"

Dahazendtre and I looked around us in a full circle before we realized that Pearrenz had broken her muteness, and was now staring at us with fire in her eyes.

"Can you be loyal, knight?" she hissed at Dahazendtre. "Do you have courage enough? Are you at all afraid to fight and kill and die?"

Dahazendtre stared back at the little girl. "What did *you* learn from the dragon, child?" she whispered. "What did *you* see in its eyes?"

As my master spoke she reached blindly for my arm, found it, and pulled me to the ground beside her, kneeling before Pearrenz.

"Then take up your weapons, knight!" Pearrenz growled, looking over us, holding her dragon's tooth aloft and pointing it toward the wide distance, in the direction of the Castle Glaurrensterrn.

"They killed my family ten years ago, on the road to Tyrrannia, but I was rescued. Wissagalos and her allies kept me safe, but were waiting to tell me the truth. Now I've seen the truth in the dragon's eyes, and I know who I am, and I would have the crown that is rightfully mine. Are you with me, warriors?"

Her eyes blazed and her voice rang like the clang of steel on steel.

Dahazendtre looked up into the young girl's face, and gone from my master's visage was the gloom, the doubt, the loss, the dejection of a few minutes before.

"Let it begin here," Dahazendtre whispered.

SHEN'S DAUGHTER

Mary Soon Lee

Mary Soon Lee has sold stories to MZB for *Sword and Sorceress XIV* and *XVIII*, to *The Magazine of Fantasy and Science Fiction,* and to various small press publications.
This is a story about a choice that is truly life changing.

This story came down the river with the rice boats, eighteen years ago. It began with the shape of a stranger sitting in the lotus position in the front of Eldest Uncle's boat.

Because of the way the stranger sat and because he wore a black robe despite the noonday heat, I took him for a monk. But he was the oddest looking monk I'd ever seen. His limbs were scrawny as a starving dog's, and he had thick white eyebrows that ran together. Strangest of all, he had two daggers strapped to his waist, one in a curved scabbard, one in a straight scabbard, both with plain iron hilts. The monks of the Long Way school study self defense, but they shun weapons and fight only with their bare hands.

I was so caught up by this mystery that I let slip the reed basket I was weaving.

"Eyes down, Wai Suan!" hissed my mother.

Ashamed, I looked down at my lap. My sister always behaved properly and dressed immaculately. I spoke when I was meant to be silent. No matter how tightly I coiled it, my hair wriggled free. My sarong and my shoes seemed to be magnets that called to any stray mud.

My sister had made a very favorable marriage at the last spring equinox. I was two years older than she, and so should have married first, but no family had ever inquired about my dowry. Even if I had been twice as decorous, twice as neat as my sister, it wouldn't have helped. My right heel turned inward so that I limped. Not even the poorest family wants a daughter-in-law like that.

I heard the men laughing as they approached the jetty, just a dozen yards away from where my mother and I sat beneath a willow. The water splashed noisily against the wood as the boats drew up.

"Who is the man in black?" I asked quietly.

"That doesn't concern you," said my mother.

"Will he be at the feast tonight?"

"Shush," said my mother, and then, softening, "I expect so."

Intriguing noises came from the jetty: men running back and forth, packages being loaded and unloaded. I worked at my reed basket, but bit by bit my head crept upward until I could see part of the jetty. The stranger was coming toward us! "Mother!"

"Shush!" said my mother, but I saw her look sideways to see who was approaching.

The man gave a deep bow to my mother. "Do I have the honor of addressing the widow of Mr. Shen?"

"I am his widow," said my mother.

"I knew your husband many years ago, may his soul eat the ghosts of his enemies."

What a strange thing to say! I wondered how he had known my father, who died when I was nine years old. I remembered playing Go with my father every night, how he would ruffle my hair before we started, how he treated our games as seriously as those he played against Eldest Uncle. I remembered the deep bass sound as he chanted the morning invocations, and how he loved the sweet dumplings my mother made. But I didn't know what my father had done outside

our home. Once I had questioned my mother about
him, but she grew so sad I never asked again.

"And you must be Shen's daughter." The man in
black dipped his head to me. "There is a matter I
need to discuss with you both."

The boatmen had paused in their work to stare at
the three of us under the willow. The stranger moved
his left hand in a curious gesture and the boatmen
returned to their work. Had that gesture been a prear-
ranged signal, or something more? Maybe the man
wasn't a monk: maybe he was a sorcerer, or a
demon, or—

"I am one of the emperor's advisors," said the
stranger. He sat down on the ground facing us. "The
war in the Eastlands is proving very costly for both
sides. Last month the enemy sent a delegation propos-
ing a new treaty, and the emperor, may his descen-
dants be many and wise, agreed. The treaty will be
sealed by the marriage of the emperor's second daughter to an enemy prince."

"Poor girl," I said before I thought. My mother
glared at me. One does not interrupt an advisor to
the emperor, even if the advisor has just told you that
an imperial princess is to marry a monster. Because
although the advisor discreetly called them the enemy,
even rice growers on the far side of the empire knew
that vile beasts with horns and claws and scabrous skin
inhabited the Eastlands.

"The second princess is spoiled." A hint of disapproval entered the advisor's voice. "The princess said
she would sooner live in a pigpen than agree to the
marriage. And the emperor, whose wisdom is without
question, though at times his reasoning is obscure to
one such as myself, promised his daughter she need
not proceed with the marriage."

My mother covered her mouth with one hand. If
the emperor had already agreed to the treaty and the

marriage, how could he go back on his word without dishonor?

"There is a way to redeem the situation, though regrettably it requires both deception and sacrifice," said the advisor. He held my gaze as he spoke. "I have some skill in the Art Magic. I could exchange the princess' soul with someone else's, transferring their essences into each other's bodies. The two would then live out their lives in each other's place. The emperor has consented to this proposal, and has left me to find a suitable subject. Wai Suan, daughter of Shen, will you exchange your soul with the princess'?"

For an endless moment the world held stationary, the sun stopped in the sky, the breath stopped in my chest. I waited, waited for the moment to pass, for time to come back. And then the pulse throbbed in the old man's temple. A breeze sang through the willow leaves. And I, Wai Suan, the cripple-girl who had never been more than four leagues from my village, I found myself with something altogether unexpected: a choice. Not a small everyday choice, not a matter of which sarong to wear, or which dipping sauce to taste. But a choice that would alter the balance of my life.

If I said yes, I would no longer be Wai Suan of the village, but an imperial princess. My clothes would be made of silk and satin. I would live in a great castle. And my right foot would be whole—I could walk without a limp, could jump, leap, run.

If I said yes, I would have to marry a monster vile and ugly. His rancid breath would mark my days, his claws would mark my nights.

And I might never see my mother again. When she grew too old to support herself, she would have to live at her son-in-law's, dependent on his generosity, always taking second place to his own mother. "Will the emperor punish my family if I refuse?" I asked.

"No," said the advisor.

Perhaps I should have agreed out of loyalty to the emperor, but though our village was close enough to the imperial capital for me to fear the emperor, it was not close enough for me to love him. So I held my head up high, and said no.

My mother said nothing, but her hand stole across the gap between us and squeezed my fingers gently.

"A pity," said the advisor. "I needed someone trustworthy, someone who would keep this matter secret."

"Neither Wai Suan nor I will tell anyone else," said my mother.

"I know," said the advisor. He turned to me again. "Is there anything I can offer that would change your mind?"

I almost said no immediately, but the steady way the advisor looked at me reminded me of my father. *Don't rush,* my father had told me when we played Go. *A move that initially appears unpromising may hold merit when given careful consideration.* So I sat in silence for a while, thinking, before I said, "Gold. Enough gold to make my mother wealthy, arranged to seem like an inheritance from a distant relative. And your promise that my mother and I can write to each other as often as we wish."

"The gold is simple. The letter-writing poses a challenge. Why would a princess write to Shen's widow?" He paused, then nodded. "Difficult, but not insoluble. So let it be."

He held out both hands, palm up, and I laid my hands down on his to show my agreement.

"Be ready tomorrow morning an hour after dawn." The advisor stood up, bowed to each of us in turn, then walked away toward the village.

My mother folded me in her arms. Neither of us spoke. Even in the shade of the willow it was hot, hotter still when we clasped each other, and the boat-

men on the jetty were watching us again, but we clung
to each other for a long time.

I had thought the advisor meant to take me away
on a boat the next morning, but instead he cast the
spell within my mother's house. The distance between
the palace and the village, he said, was much less than
the distance between the princess' soul and mine. I
limped across a white chalk mark on the bedroom
floor, through a sheet of cold and dark, and out into
the princess' bedroom.

Let us pass quickly over my stay in the imperial palace. Though the princess' aide, who knew about the
spell, coached me in how to behave, still I found it difficult to play my part. True, the princess was so spoiled
that I didn't have to feign demure politeness. But I had
to learn names and faces and the layout of the palace,
how to scold the servants, how to titter instead of laughing properly, how to pick at my food like a sparrow
though it tasted so delicious I could have emptied the
table. Hardest of all, I had to treat the emperor himself
as if he were my father, as if I loved him.

The monsters insisted that the wedding take place
at the height of the monsoon season. Rain filled the
streets of the capital, drenched the crowds who gathered outside the Imperial Temple. I marched up the
broad stone steps of the temple behind the emperor.
A canopy stretched above us, but rain dripped through,
spattering my silk wedding jacket.

Inside, the reek of the monsters overpowered the
incense. The beasts smelled like putrefying meat. They
squatted on the left side of the temple, dark lumbering
shapes somewhere between oxen and giant dogs, but
uglier than either, and with clawed hands in addition
to four hoofed feet. As I walked toward the altar, the
monsters clicked their claws together as if preparing
to gut their prey.

I knelt on the mat before the altar, pressing my hands together to stop them shaking. The beast I was to marry squatted beside me, but I did not, could not look at him. Instead I stared at the red tassels bordering the mat while the priest chanted above us. *My marriage will end a war,* I told myself, but the cold heaviness in my stomach remained. *My marriage will bring my mother wealth,* I told myself, and for a moment I felt better.

The silvery chime of cymbals sounded the end of the first part of the wedding rites. The priest lowered the gold marriage bowl onto a stand between myself and the beast. Calling me by the princess' name, he bid me place my hands on the bowl to mark my consent. I laid my hands on the gold bowl.

The priest called on the beast beside me to place his hands over mine. The beast knocked the bowl from its stand with a clawed swipe. Frozen, I clutched the empty space where the bowl had been. Metal clanged on tile. Roaring, the beast swung round toward the king of the monsters. Over the screams of the imperial guests, the beast shouted, "No! I will not marry this puny, puling, witless creature!"

Many times I had overheard people in the village refer to me as the cripple-girl or Lame Foot, but no one called me those names to my face. At the beast's words, the heaviness in my stomach lifted and a hot madness seized me. I stood up in front of the crowds, in front of the emperor and the monster king and the raging beast, and I said, "Witless? You are the one who is witless! If you didn't want to marry me, you should have said so months ago! Now your stupidity is likely to start the war all over again."

The monster king reared upright. "You dare call my son witless, you scentless offspring of a degenerate line of a degenerate race—"

The emperor's guards drew their swords. The imperial guests screamed as the monsters surged forward.

"Wait," said a calm voice, and the word, though softly spoken, carried throughout the temple. People and monsters alike stood still as an old man in a black robe walked over to the altar. I hadn't known the emperor's advisor was back in the city.

"This matter of wits or the lack thereof can be settled simply," said the old man. "True, our two peoples share a common history of war, and we could shed more blood here today to celebrate that. But we share other customs too, ones better suited to determining mental superiority. I propose a game of Go, called Wei-ch'i by the traditionalists, between these two young people."

He clapped his hands and a Go board and pieces appeared before me on the mat. He looked at my bridegroom. "You do, I take it, know the rules of Go."

"Of course," snarled the beast. He snatched a black stone, thereby claiming the advantage of the first move, and placed it near the center of the board.

I picked up a white stone and laid it on the board, and it was as if I were a child again, sitting on the floor playing Go with my father, nothing else in the world but the two of us and the game. Yes, I heard the monsters' rumbles, the whispers of the imperial guests, but they had no place in the patterns of black and white stones, in the battle of boundaries and the waiting expanses.

Once, midway through the game, a dry cough sounded above me. I glanced up to see the old advisor's thick white eyebrows drawn into a frown. I looked down at the board again, and saw that I was winning, so why did the old man frown? Ah, yes, belatedly I recalled the broader implications of this match: best to win, but not to win too easily.

So I beat the beast by three points. When the pieces were all cleared away, I looked up from the board. Night had fallen. Candles lit the temple.

"Well played," said the beast opposite me. He picked up the gold marriage bowl and set it back on its stand. "I will marry you."

I laid my hands on the gold bowl, and he placed his hands, clammy and rough, over mine, his claws sheathed.

Before I left for the Eastlands with my husband, I spoke to the emperor's advisor. "It's lucky I know how to play Go."

"Luck had nothing to do with it," he said. "Your father was a master of Go. Did you not know that?"

I shook my head. I knew my father beat the other villagers, but that was all.

"Shen wrote to me once," said the advisor, "and mentioned you showed promise at the game." He paused. "I am sorry for manipulating you into this marriage. May it turn out better than you expect."

And so it has. My husband is quick-tempered, moody, and hideous to look at, but he is also fair-minded, even kind. We have no children of our own, of course, but we adopted two, one of my race and one of my husband's. While the children were home they made the great castle less lonely.

And every night of our marriage, my husband and I have played Go together. Each time as he squats down by the board, my husband announces, "Tonight I will win."

But he never has.

THE ROBBER GIRL, THE STRANGERS, AND OLE LUKOIE

Phyllis Ann Karr

Phyllis Ann Karr was born in Oakland, California. After a fair amount of moving around she ended up in Wisconsin, where, with "the bookmobile librarians serving as matchmaker," she met and married her soul-mate, Clifton A. Hoyt. Phyllis and her husband live in Barnes, Wisconsin, a small town that does not even have a traffic light. She is seeking to achieve a hermit's life by staying off the Internet as long as she can.

Her characters Frostflower and Thorn have been bouncing around in alternate worlds for about a decade and a half. Phyllis says that the present installment "doesn't necessarily end the series forever, because not all their adventures have yet been written, and some of the ones that exist in manuscript have yet to see print. Nevertheless, I judged it time to reveal how they eventually get home, even at the risk of losing any semblance of proper sequence."

What a jolly nightmare the Old Man with the Umbrellas brought me the night after we murdered the farmer and gave the little girl to Hulda Doublechin! Not just a plain old bad dream, either, as things fell out. Listen a while, and you may hear something.

I said, "we" out of loyalty, but how can it hurt poor old Half-Ear if I tell it all the way it happened? We called him "Half-Ear" because I had bitten off the other half of his ear myself when I was still a brat riding around most of the day in a bag on my old dam's back—but that was just sport between comrades. And if I wasn't exactly tickled out of my skin to meet him again by chance in Copenhagen—after all, I had ridden out of that backwoods life and left it as far behind me as I could—still, I wasn't really all that sorry, either, to sit down and drink a mug or two with him. One always likes to hear how things are going with the people one used to know.

Not that Half-Ear had much to tell me about them, seeing he'd struck out not long after me, and been on his own long enough that he was eager to talk me into going partners with him.

He knew for a fact, he swore up and down and on his mother's skeleton, that such and such a farmer near Glostrup had found a fortune in old Danish gold buried in his fields, and on such and such a day he was going to bring it in to the bankers of the great city, hidden in his cart beneath the hay and turnips. Well and good. So there we sat on our horses, waiting in the cold and rain of the summer's dreariest day, until the farmer came rumbling up along the road in his creaky old cart drawn by a creaky old mule. Then out we rode at him, waving our pistols, looking, I suppose, as fine and brave as the weather allowed us.

At this point, any sensible Christian out traveling alone ought to have spread his hands and let two such gallants of the road have their way with his mere earthly pelf, as the preachers call it. Instead of which, he ups with a creaky old blunderbuss and returns our aim. Whereupon what should my old comrade Half-Ear do, but shoot him through the heart, so that he toppled down dead.

"You booby!" I shouted at Half-Ear. My anger took even me by surprise. Truth to tell, making friends with gentle little Gerda had done something, even all those years ago, to dull my edge for killing; and my little chat with Captain Death face to face had done more.

Since being out in the wide world on my own I had hardly killed anybody at all, except a few who tried too hard to kill me first—and I didn't judge that counted poor fools like this bumpkin of a farmer with his poor old blunderbuss. "He could have told us where to find his treasure," I added, because I had to say something to cover what Half-Ear might think was tenderheartedness, when all it really was, was the feeling that we had enough victims waiting for us in the Gray Castle of Death already.

"We know where to find his treasure," said Half-Ear. "All we need to do is look beneath the sacks of turnips he was pretending to take to market. Help me get this cart off the road before somebody else comes along."

"If it's as easy to find as all that," I returned, still angry, "why work any harder than we absolutely have to?" With that, I jumped into the cart and started throwing bags of turnips right onto the road.

And there, among the turnips, I found not old Danish gold but a little golden-haired girl, shivering in her fright, with both eyes wide open and both hands to her mouth to keep from crying out aloud.

She looked about the age my old friend Gerda was when first we met, so I told her the most comforting things I could think of, took her up in front of me on my pretty white horse, and started off with her. When Half-Ear shouted after me I shouted back that he could have the Danish gold all to himself for the finding.

Not that I wanted the little girl for myself, but I could guess how much her life would be worth if my old comrade had any chance at it. She had a silver locket around her neck with the portraits of her father and mother inside, as she told me when her fright grew less. They were rich people, she said, and had been sending her back to her boarding school in the big city after a holiday at home. The thought of ransom money crossed my mind; but if they were as rich as my little darling supposed, why was her locket silver instead of gold, and why was she riding with a neighbor in his creaky old cart, instead of in a fine coach and four?

My chum Hulda Doublechin lived not too very far from there, in a secluded spot less than a winter day's ride away. I had made her acquaintance while searching out a remedy for something we won't go into now. She was one of your motherly old half-witches with a garden full of flowers, a cupboard full of dried herbs, and a heart full of longing for a child to mother. I think that last was why she filled her garden up with so many statues, mostly of children. I took the little girl to Hulda, silver locket and all.

That was the night, as I started out to say, that the Old Man with the Umbrellas brought me one of the jolliest nightmares I have ever enjoyed, and, as it came out, one of the very strangest.

I thought I was in a dark wood, fighting hobgoblins. Every tree was a hobgoblin, tall or twisted, sapling or huge fat oldster, with leaves like sharp-edged knives or needles like small, barbed arrows. Whenever I finally killed one, its leaves or needles would all fall off and show a sick, bright space in the hoary sky for just an instant before two more goblin trees squeezed in to take the dead one's place.

There was quite a bit more, and some I forget and some would make my story too long in the telling. But eventually I found other people beside me. There was a tall, robust woman with short straw-colored hair, who dressed like a man in trousers and tunic, the way I usually dress myself, only her clothes looked a lot more old-fashioned, like the clothes folk wear in picture books, with a vest of hardened leather. And there was a short, thin, pretty woman with long black hair and skin white as vellum, who wore a long black robe.

And also a blurry, middle-aged man with long, shaggy hair and beard, who wore an odd length of cloth.

The tall woman had a sword in one hand and a knife in the other, and knew how to use them, too, as well as I do or maybe even a little better. I was glad, if surprised, that the dream had us fighting together like old friends, and not against each other. The short woman had no weapons, only a long bag for carrying her things around in. But she had her uses, too— whenever one of us got a wound, this woman put her fingers on it, closed her eyes, and hey, presto! it healed up in a second or two. The man never did much of anything except hold his cloth wrapping on with a fair degree of awkwardness, and a few times reach up one hand as if it was a paw and try to bat a tree limb away.

He was the one who explained matters to me, though, when at last we broke clear of the hobgoblin trees and threw ourselves down to rest on the grass beside a swamp. The swamp was rank and smelly, the grass sparse and gray, but we were too tired to care anything about that. Besides, it isn't often that a nightmare gives me any chance to rest at all, so when I got it, I took it.

The tall woman was up again almost at once, prowling back and forth like a palace guard between the trees and the strip of grass, while her black-robed friend started getting things out of her bag, and the man turned, panting, to me.

"I am really a dog," he said.

It didn't surprise me, somehow. And, after all, anything can happen in a dream. Just to be polite, I asked him, "What are you doing going around looking like a man, then?"

"I amn't sure," he confessed unhappily. "It was in one of these worlds . . . We have been wandering around in all these strange worlds for a long, long time. My friend and her friend and me. That is my

friend, my dearest friend." He held one hand up
toward the woman in black. "She is Frostflower. I love
her. She has the most wonderful scent, soft and kind
and . . . I amn't sure what other words to use for it
in human-talk . . . and I can't even smell it any more.
Not like this." Tears welled up in his big, brown eyes
and rolled down his cheeks into his shaggy beard. I
longed to tickle his skin with the point of my knife,
for the pure teasing love of it, but I let him talk on
instead. I wanted to hear the rest of his story.

"Frostflower's friend is Thorn," he went on. "I like
her a lot. I don't mind it so much that I can't smell
Thorn now, but her scent is worth smelling, too, when
I am . . . right. It happened to me in one of these
strange worlds. Maybe this one. Maybe the last one.
I can't remember too well. Not like this."

"I would guess you haven't been a man very long,"
I said, "or you'd be more used to it. You'd be finding
out it has compensations. But how well can you remember things in your right form?"

"All my life. That is what we do, when we lie
around with our paws in front of us. We are remembering. I remember the first strange world. I was still
in my right form, then. We were in a boat, and a fog
came down over the water—it didn't come up, it came
down—and when it went away, we were in Dathru's
world."

"Never heard of it," I said. "Where is it from
here?"

His brows puckered helplessly. "I don't know.
Dathru was a wicked sorcery-man. He hurt Frostflower. So Thorn killed him, and Frostflower took his
sorcery things, and ever since then she has been trying
to get us home to our own world. I am sorry he was
wicked. Or I would have liked him."

"What do you think about me?" I asked in
curiosity.

"I like you. I wish I could get your scent."

"I thought so! You must be one of those silly creatures who like everyone."

"I think that must be true," he confessed sadly. "I have gotten my dearest friend in trouble, liking people I should not have liked."

"It is not your fault, Dowl," said Frostflower. "Nor would we have you other than what you are."

One of her eyes was blue and the other one brown, but she was still very pretty for all of that, in her pale, delicate way. She had taken a hoop out of her bag, stood it up on edge, and tapped it until it grew as big as a doorway. "But come, now," she went on, "and let us try again to reach home."

"Yes," I said, "or, anyway, you'd better get out of here before I wake up. I don't know what might happen to you otherwise."

"You!" the tall woman with the sword—Thorn—said, talking to me. "You mean you aren't native to this place?"

"Of course not!" I drew myself up proudly. "This is the nightmare the Old Man with the Umbrellas brought me tonight."

Thorn made a sound between a laugh and a grunt. "That's a new one! But it explains why this is such a hellbog of a world. All right, Frost, get us out of here. The quicker, the better."

"Wait," Frostflower said, frowning. "If we have indeed, somehow, come inside the world of a dream, our safest step might be into the dreamer's own everyday world. Can you tell us when you see it?" she asked me.

Well, for myself, I didn't see that it could make any great difference either way. But one might as well humor pleasant people whenever one meets up with them, especially in nightmares. So I stepped up to the portal she had made and watched it, like a picture that kept changing, until I saw the Round Tower of Copenhagen.

"There it is!" I exclaimed, stepped through, and found myself right where I'd gone to sleep the night before, in a snug little bed in the best inn I could afford. I got just a glimpse of the Old Man closing up his umbrella before he melted away with the rest of the dream.

Except.

That there the three of them stood in a row beside my bed: Thorn, Frostflower, and Dowl, looking down at me—or, in Dowl's case, looking up, because he was a dog again, although I think I'd have known it was him even if he hadn't told me all that while we were still in the nightmare.

He nuzzled close, looking for my scent, and I gave him a minute or two to whiff it in before slapping him away and playfully starting to tie his long ears together.

But Frostflower let out a cry. "Thorn! Ah, Thorn, it was a mistake! It was a terrible mistake! The Circle— Dathru's Circle—it is gone!"

Thorn said, "Hellbog and demonstink!"

"Be quiet," I told them both. "This is a respectable inn."

Meanwhile, Frostflower had sat down on the floor to pull things out of her bag . . . this and that and whatnot, not a thing I noticed that might have interested me unless on the leanest of lean days. "Dathru's book is gone as well, and his pendant," she mourned. "Indeed, Thorn—it has all disappeared, everything save what we had already in our own world, that day the fog came over us and these wanderings began!"

"Snip, snap, snurre!" I remarked, snapping my fingers. "What did you expect of dreamstuff? I'm surprised you came out with anything at all, you own skins included!"

"Has it *all* been a dream?" Frostflower wondered. "Can we be dreaming still?"

"Assume we aren't and it hasn't," said Thorn. "And

I don't see what else we can do, unless we want to curl up and turn into piles of dust." Thorn was a woman after my own heart. I liked her at once, and a good thing for her, too, or I might have taken it in bad part, the way she pointed at me when she said, "We've brought one thing along with us, anyway. Unless she's really talking our own Tanglelands tongue, which I doubt."

"Yes," Frostflower said slowly, closing her eyes the better to concentrate. "Yes, it is still here in our minds, all that we have seen and learned, and all the sorceries, as it would seem, that affect our minds and tongues alone. But, if we are trapped here forever in a strange world not our own . . ."

Tears trembled out from beneath her eyelids. Her dog snuggled his nose into her lap and whined, trying to comfort her.

"Well!" said I. "It's a wide world, full of wonderful sights. Maybe it isn't your own world, but you might like it even better, once you get used to it. If you don't fade away like the other scraps of dreamstuff first."

"How would you like it," Thorn demanded, "being stuck away from all your family and friends, everyone and everything you know, for the rest of your life?"

The way she glared at me, it was a very good thing for us both that I liked her well enough to answer with a simple shrug and leave things at that. If I could have ridden away from my first home into a different world entirely, it probably wouldn't have made that much difference. The only childhood chum I'd met again was Half-Ear, and look what had come of that! The only person from my old life for whom I cared more than two snips was Gerda, and whether or not I ever saw her again was a matter of pure chance. But I guessed that Thorn was too much like me not to land on her feet wherever luck bounced her, good or bad, and that meant she had been talking more about Frostflower's friends and family than about her own.

So all I said was, "Well, then, let's go to the university and catch a scholar who can tell us something about the Old Man with the Umbrellas."

To the university we went, where Frostflower might have been willing to search all the books herself, page by page, no matter how long it took to find the answers she and her friends needed—and I would have left them then and there and been done with it—but, by good luck or bad, we found that she couldn't read a word, not even one letter, except a few whose names she said all wrong—"T" as "O," and so on. Thorn guessed that they could talk our language but not read it because I had come and joined them in Nightmare Land, but none of our books or newspapers had. Frostflower feared, however, that they might already have started to lose all the things they'd learned in their travels, and that would mean their time was more limited than we had thought.

So we caught a scholar, which is easier than catching a bird. In case you'd like to try it yourself someday, here is how: you look for the poorest old scholars because as a rule they know the most, being too busy chasing knowledge all their lives to stop for money. When you find the kind of scholar you want, you offer him a meal in the nearest good eating-place, along with your willing ears to spout his erudition into. Then you have him fast for the evening, whether you like it or not.

One who could talk about nothing but fractions and angles, or frogs' livers and gnats' tongues, wouldn't have been any great use to us. I spelled out gilt letters and inked labels on leather backs until we found the right books for the kind of scholar we wanted, and there we waited until a gentle-looking, bespectacled old graybeard in a patched and shabby gown came along to browse. Half an hour later, we had him snug over his meal, lecturing us eagerly between bites.

"The Old Man," he told us, after just as much priming as we needed to get him onto the right subject, "is undoubtedly the entity nowadays popularly called 'Ole Lukoie,' but known to the classical ancients as Somnus—Sleep—brother to Thanatos or Death, and father to Morpheus and Phantasus, the Oneiropomists or Bringers of Dreams, who have obviously metamorphosed in our day into his twin umbrellas. Although I have heard it vulgarly opined that, while Old Lukoie's brightly painted umbrella produces good dreams, the other and plainer one produces no dreams whatever, but only a dreamless if curiously restless slumber."

"Well!" said I. "You're the scholar, old man. I only know that he mostly brings me jolly, rousing nightmares."

Our scholar cleared his throat and ordered coffee. So did the rest of us. Then he went on, "Your account might imply three umbrellas. And, indeed, a third son—Phobetor—has sometimes been assigned to old Somnus. But surely all three of his sons were said to be Oneiropomists. On the other hand, good dreams and bad coming both from the same umbrella would seem to substantiate the theory, espoused if I remember aright by Asclepius and others, that all dreams have healing power and even the least pleasant of them are preferable to none at all. The one thing worse than the nightmare is insomnia, or the inability to sleep at all. Or so I have heard it opined by one who left money on the windowsill in an attempt to buy the favors of Ole Lukoie. But Ole Lukoie cannot be bought. Not with money."

"With what, then?" Thorn wanted to know.

"With nothing that I know of, unless it be a clear conscience, or else one so deadened that its possessor has given worrying up as a hopeless cause."

Our coffee had come. Frostflower took one sip and pushed her cup away. Thorn made a face, but drank hers down, after adding a lot of sugar. That surprised me, because the brew was excellent. Maybe they weren't used to it, but I had taken to it the first time I ever had any to drink, and I would have finished Frostflower's for her, if the scholar hadn't beaten me to it.

First, though, sipping out of his own china cup, he looked at me and went on, "What I find surprising, my generous friend, is your claim still to see Old Lukoie. This ability, rare enough in children, has hitherto gone virtually unknown, or at least unrecorded, among members of the adult population."

"I don't see him often," said I.

"Even occasionally," said the scholar.

" 'Occasionally' won't work," said Thorn. "We don't have time for 'occasionally.' What can we do to see him right away, tonight?"

Our scholar rubbed his chin and drank more coffee before he answered. "Well, you might try the experiment of rubbing your eyes with sweet milk. It is generally opined that Ole Lukoie sprinkles sweet milk into the eyes of children so as to hold them shut from seeing him; but, as they who report the milk seem to be largely the same individuals as those who report glimpsing him in childhood, the converse might conceivably represent the truer or more accurate state of things. Does he sprinkle sweet milk into your eyes?" he asked me.

"He tried to," I replied. "I usually manage to catch it in my mouth, instead."

That being all this scholar could tell us—all that fit our own purposes, anyway—we bought him a candle, left him in his garret poring over his studies as contentedly as a cow chewing her cud, and found a dairy where they still had enough of the day's sweet milk left for the experiment.

We all three rubbed our eyes with it, and the dog's eyes, too. But Dowl and Frostflower seemed to nod off almost before the Old Man popped up from behind them and started spreading his colored umbrella.

I stayed awake long enough to hear Thorn shout, "Hey, you! Ole Lukoie, if that's your name! Roll dice with me!"

He looked amused, even a little flattered. "People are always challenging my brother to games of chance or skill, but no one has ever until now challenged me. Very well, let's see what it is like."

That was all before I fell asleep and dreamed about blue rats and flying hedgehogs.

When we all woke up next morning, Frostflower said she had dreamed about Thorn's little son growing up back in their home in the Tanglelands, and nothing else that she could remember. As for the dog, he whined and kept his dreams to himself. But Thorn, looking tired and angry, said, "I sat right here and threw dice with him all night. And won every damned game I could teach him! But the bogbreath just laughed and said, 'It's only for sport. No, you can't have her things back, I've got them safe where they won't cause anybody any further mischief.' Hellbog and demonstink!"

She gave the table a good, hard kick. The noise brought the landlady up. She was a sour, fierce old dear, and after one look she demanded payment for all four of us in the room, asking as much for the dog as if he was still a person.

Well! One can't always settle accounts in respectable cities the same way one does it in robbers' dens in the woods. And, besides that, she wouldn't have made such a bad robber queen herself, that landlady. So I paid her. By now, what with this and that, my purse was getting uncomfortably thin, which gave me my own sense of urgency to see my strange new friends on their way.

I don't know how far we can believe Thorn's story, because if Ole Lukoie sat there throwing dice with her the whole night through, when did he put anyone else to sleep? Although it's true that I seemed to notice a lot more people than usual yawning the next day.

Did I mention that, while I was off taking that little girl to Hulda Doublechin, old Half-Ear had been caught in the cart with the farmer's body? And served him right, I can almost hear you think. But, flick, flack! Those are the chances all of us take, some of us more often than others. And what had he done, after all, so much worse than what that soldier did who murdered the old witch for her tinder box, and came out of it the hero of his own tale. Poor old Half-Ear had already been sentenced and was due for hanging that very day, as I learned at the coffeehouse.

"Well and good," I said to Thorn. "You've had your chance. Now maybe I can have mine. Our scholar told us, didn't he, that Ole Lukoie is Death's brother, and I was on speaking terms with Captain Death, face to face, once upon a time. If only I still had the charm for it I had then!"

Frostflower got very excited. "A charm to make the senses come more fully alive? I learned the making of some such charm, four worlds ago. Perhaps much the same technique would work here?"

That was how I learned that in her own world, and in most of the others they had visited, our friend with the one brown and the one blue eye was a sorceress—"and a very good one, too," Thorn said proudly—and that sometimes the sorcery that worked in one world worked in others as well. Not always, but often enough to make it worth the try.

So Frostflower went to work, and wove two loose patches out of sweet meadowgrasses. What she did next, I don't know and could never repeat, since she went into a kind of trance to do it. But when she woke up out of it to tie one patch over my left ear and the other over my right eye, I could hear things and see them as sharply and deeply as back when I had had that ruby with the little diamond inside it.

Frostflower took no further part in my turn after that. She and her dog came along with us to the hanging-field, but she held back on the outer edge of the crowd with her hands over her eyes most of the time, and Thorn said to let her be, we'd call her if and when I won them safe passage home straight from there.

They were still hanging folk the old-fashioned way, rolling the cart out from beneath the gallows and letting any friends the soon-to-be-deceased might have in the crowd run over and haul down on his legs to help him leave this world a little faster. So nobody thought anything about it when Thorn and I ran up to old Half-Ear, and the rest of the crowd was too busy pelting us along with him to notice or care that our intention was a little different. Being a stranger in those parts himself, he didn't have any other friends in the crowd that day, which was handy for us because they would have gotten in our way. But it seemed the people blamed him for the disappearance of the little girl as well as the death of the farmer, so he was not exactly what you might call a popular or romantic figure of an outlaw, and that made it a sloppy job for us to stand under him. I was glad we hadn't seen any need for the sorceress to make charms for my senses of smelling and touch!

The ones for my sight and hearing worked to perfection. "Hello again, Captain Death!" I greeted him as he stepped up to collect Half-Ear . . . only Thorn knew her job, even if she didn't have any patches to see and hear Ole Lukoie's brother, and she was really holding my one-time crony up to keep him alive longer, though the crowd naturally assumed otherwise, and the poor old robber was too badly choked up to say anything about it.

"Have a care, young woman," Captain Death returned, "or you won't be so cheerful to greet me when I come for you in your own time." Only he sounded

so dapper about it that to this day I don't know how
much in earnest his warning might have been. "What
rule do you want to bend or break this time?" he
added.

"None you didn't break first. Or your brother did,
anyway, and it's the same thing."

"I might question that," said he, "but for the sake
of curiosity, I will listen a moment longer."

"Then listen! Your brother Ole Lukoie let these two
women—this one here with me and her friend over
there in the crowd, and their dog, slip into our world
through one of his umbrellas. But he kept the things
they need to find their way home, so they're stuck here."

"And what am I to do about that?" he asked with
a smile.

"Make him give those things back, of course!"

He shook his head. "Brothers we may be, but each
of us has his own work and his own way of doing it.
The only thing I could do for these three would take
them into my Gray Castle right away. Now it is your
turn to listen to me. I know the sorceress over yonder.
If she could, she would help this poor fool to come
with me faster, and when I come for her, in her own
time and in whatever world I find her, I will treat her
courteously. And also the dog. That is more than I
can promise either her swordswoman friend or you
yourself, especially finding you prolong your unfortu-
nate old comrade's pain in this way, after he loyally
told the authorities nothing about your part in the
crime."

Without even giving me a chance to point out that
that particular robbery had been Half-Ear's idea and
the killing his work entirely, Death shoved Thorn and
me aside, snatched him away in the black cloud of his
own last, choking breath, and was gone.

Thorn grunted. "I should've had her make me a set
of those patches, too. Well, from what I heard of your

side of it, that didn't work any better than my dice games with his brother."

I had to admit she was right. We made our way back to Frostflower and Dowl. When the sorceress heard what Captain Death had said about her, she only replied, "His warning was meant for both of you. Had he been speaking directly to me, it would have been the other way around." Then we all returned to my room at the inn to clean ourselves and think what else we might try.

"They said he stole a child," Frostflower worried as she washed both our clothes in the china basin. "Her parents were there in the crowd, watching sadly but doing nothing."

"Nothing to stop the crowd jeering," I remarked, "or pelting old Half-Ear to say what he did with that little girl. Poor fellow, he couldn't have said anything. He didn't know."

"And *you* do?" Thorn asked suspiciously.

I hadn't told them until now of my earlier connections to Half-Ear or my part in that robbery. But now, seeing how I'd put my foot in it and aroused their suspicions, I made the best job I could and explained everything. I supposed that, being a sort of witch and loving children herself, Frostflower would be happy for poor old Hulda Doublechin. But instead of that, she shook her head and insisted mournfully that nothing else would do except getting the child back to her parents.

"How do we know," I protested, "that Hulda Doublechin won't be a better family to her than all your respectable, sermon-listening people put together?"

"I know what I saw and sensed of those good parents," Frostflower argued. "Yet already I grieve for Hulda Doublechin, too. But I learned something in one of the worlds we have visited that we might use to help her, if it can be made to work here."

Well, that was that. Frostflower refused to say anything more about her own troubles until she saw the little girl safe with her parents again, and Thorn sided with her old friend. So there was nothing for it but to hire a cart and take them all to Hulda Doublechin.

We found them both in her garden, Hulda pulling weeds while she watched her new little girl on the other side of the herb beds, weaving flower garlands for the statues of a pretty pair of children, probably brother and sister, dimple-cheeked and lifesized.

"Oh, no! Oh, no!" the poor old woman cried softly, in dismay, when we explained why we had come. "She is my own dear little Ingrid now. I have given her only just the one little spell—the one to make her forget her old home and family—and as long as nothing reminds her of them, we will be as happy together as two swallows in summer. But if you take her away again, I will be as lonely and sorrowful as the emperor who lost his nightingale."

"Believe me," said Frostflower, "I know well what you must feel. But do you not see that the grief you fear is the same that her own parents feel now? No, theirs is even worse, for they have no idea where she is, while you will at least know that she is safe again with others who love her. But in one land we visited I learned something that may help you, if we can make it work."

Then the witch and the sorceress went together into the house, leaving the three of us—Thorn, me, and the dog—to watch little Ingrid. I went over now and then to peek in at the window and see them opening up the drawers of Hulda's herb cabinet, putting their heads together over pinches of this and dabs of that before stirring them into a pot on the stove. The last time I looked, they had set a saucer of brew right on the open window ledge, where yellow butterflies fanned it with their wings as they perched to sip drops of sugary syrup of the saucer's rim.

When the brew was cool, they brought it out to the garden, where Hulda sprinkled it on the twin statues Ingrid had been garlanding, while Frostflower stood with a hand on each of their stone heads and sang strange words over them in a soft, low chant.

And they came to life.

Little Ingrid laughed and clapped in delight, then joined hands with the two new children and all three danced in rings while Frostflower and old Mother Doublechin went back into the house. When they came outside again, Frostflower was wearing one of Hulda Doublechin's dresses and shawls, along with a pair of smoked spectacles, and Hulda was carrying the little girl's silver locket, that she had been keeping locked in a drawer.

On getting it back into her own chubby hands, the little girl opened it to look at the portraits inside, and her eyes filled up with tears. "Oh, Mama! Oh, Papa! Why, I forgot all about you!"

Hulda proceeded to give her another spell so that, by the time Frostflower had driven her back to town, she would have forgotten all about her time with the pleasant old witch and would truly believe the mild sorceress had only just found her wandering in the woods. She didn't know her rescuer was a sorceress, of course. With luck, nobody at all would recognize Frostflower in her disguise as the same person Thorn and I had joined after pulling on Half-Ear's legs.

Thorn didn't like letting Frostflower run the errand alone. As for the dog, he watched the cart off without a single bark of protest, but then spent the afternoon moping and whining, when he could get a minute's peace from the pretty pair who had been statuary until that same day but now were as lively as any children who had been real flesh and blood for their whole existence.

Frostflower returned, smiling, in time for supper, to report that Ingrid was safe with her parents. "It happened that they were both at the school, talking with her teachers, when we arrived."

"Did they recognize you from the hanging?" I wanted to know.

She shook her head. "I think they never so much as saw me there, at the back of the crowd as I was."

"All right, as far as it goes," said Thorn. "What next?"

"Have you forgotten," Frostflower replied, fondling her dog's ears, "that here are two new children, about to fall asleep for the very first time?"

That was true enough. New and full of energy as they were, we hadn't even had the heart to make them try to take a nap their first afternoon of life, so already over supper they were both yawning at every bite and asking what it meant to yawn.

We grown folks, including Hulda Doublechin, rubbed our eyes with milk again, and Dowl's eyes as well. This time, Thorn and I both having taken our turns, we agreed to leave the bargaining to Frostflower. But we stationed ourselves on all four sides of the children's bed to keep watch.

Sure enough, after a minute or two, here came the Old Man with his umbrellas in hand, all ready to spread the big, bright one over the two children, whose eyes were shut fast, and—as it appeared—over all the rest of us with them.

But Frostflower held up her hand and cried, "Good Ole Lukoie! Wait, please, and hear me!"

He paused and chuckled. "Yes? What is it now?"

"To you, I hope, a small thing. But we were trapped against our knowledge or desire into this round of strange worlds, and we have tried so long and desperately to find our own again . . ."

"Ah, is that all?" Ole Lukoie said with another chuckle. "Why didn't you say that in the first place, instead of all this nonsense of rolling dice with me and trying to strike bargains with my brother? Just hop into my umbrella, you Tanglelanders, and I'll see to it you wake up back in your own world."

"That's all?" I exclaimed. "All we ever had to do was just *ask* you?"

"That was all," said Ole Lukoie, "from someone with the soul of a sage and the heart of a child."

"Meaning someone like Frost," Thorn remarked to me. "Not a couple of bloody outsmarters like the pair of us." Then she turned, caught her friend's hand—because Frostflower was already leading Dowl into the umbrella as Ole Lukoie opened it—and scrambled up beside them.

From the picture in the panel, Frostflower looked back at me. "Ingrid's parents insisted on giving a reward," she called happily. "I judged that refusing it would have caused too much comment, and I thought we might need money if we had to stay in your world. I am glad, now, that I can offer it to you in thanks for your help."

With that, she tossed a little purse back out of the umbrella. To my surprise, Ole Lukoie let her get away even with that: I found it on the floor beside me when we all woke up next morning, Hulda and her new children and I.

So I got my ransom for the little girl, after all. Not a huge sum, and most of it in silver or copper rather than gold. But enough, anyway, to cover expenses, with a little left over for a meal and a drink and a fine new pair of boots.

I've visited with them once or twice, in their own world, as Ole Lukoie's special gift to Frostflower. They seem to be doing all right. It isn't exactly the safest world, but it has its own pleasures and excitements. Just like ours.

TOO IN THE MORNING

George Barr

For nearly forty years, while George Barr has made his living as an illustrator of science fiction and fantasy, he has been writing as well. Although he wrote primarily for his own amusement, he kept writing, and rewriting, and revising earlier efforts. MZB bought his first story for issue 4 of *Marion Zimmer Bradley's Fantasy Magazine* (she was already buying his artwork; he had done the cover art for issues 1 and 2), and she continued to buy his stories for other issues.

In addition to his short story sales, George has an illustrated novella, *The Lost One,* awaiting publication, and several novels making the rounds of prospective publishers.

"Zanita can't spell worth Sower apples."

It was true.

Dame Magda would go to the orchard each morning and pay Farmer Sower a few coppers for a basket of his beautiful red apples, then use them during the day as rewards for good work from her pupils. They were only apples—cool and delicious, but nothing a student couldn't have obtained on her own. They were symbolic. And they were coveted.

Zanita was just not a very apt pupil.

An incantation that was intended to produce the smell of roses to perfume a room once materialized an entire chamberfull of flowers, all but smothering the class in petals, leaves, thorns . . . and *aphids*. Dame Magda had managed to reverse it in moments, but not without receiving several nasty scratches in the process.

The second attempt—with the rest of the class prudently watching from outside—called up an odor well enough. And roses were involved. It was, however, a sweetish stench the like of which none had ever experienced.

"If flowers could break wind," Dame Magda had said, her eyes watering, her nose wrinkling in disgust, "this is certainly the smell they'd produce."

Zanita had hoped to become a sorceress. But it never quite seemed to work for her. A simple effort to use magic to frost a cake—something Dame Magda could do with a word and a wave—inundated a tabletop with dripping globs of gooey sweetness that drew every fly and ant in the countryside before it could be cleaned out of the cracks in the wood and tiles.

Dame Magda stopped her mid-incantation while Zanita was attempting to bring a little rain to water the garden.

"No, my girl," the teacher admonished her. "Just fetch a pailful from the well. With your usual luck at spells, the kingdom could suffer a repeat of the Great Flood. You must resign yourself, my dear. Sorcery is not your field."

"Then what *is?*" Zanita asked. "I know the words. I know the passes. I have a good memory. Why doesn't it work?"

"It does, Zanita," Magda replied with a sad shake of her regal gray head. "It always works . . . only too well. And that is your problem.

"It has nothing to do with the words . . . or the passes. It's *talent*. Sensitivity. Restraint. You have none of that.

"Something in you—deep within your innermost being—made you from the beginning a creature of . . . excess, I guess I would call it. You are *too much* of everything that you are."

"I don't understand," the girl said, her voice catching in an almost-sob. She saw the future she'd so desired dwindling like a dream.

"My dear," Dame Magda soothed, drawing her into the garden, "that your spells go so awry is just about all that keeps the rest of the girls from hating you.

"You're not just pretty; you're *gorgeous* to such a degreee that it's almost indecent. Your eyes are too blue, your lips too red, your hair too golden, your skin *too* fair. A form like yours has thus far existed only in the dreams of lonely and lustful men. As I said, you are *too much* of everything that you are.

"With you every movement is a gesture, every position a pose, every spoken word a declamation.

"You wear the same wimple and robe as the other novices; on you it looks like a coronation gown. Even that smudge of dirt on your cheek only points up what a *perfect* cheek it is.

"You will be a *queen,* perhaps . . . someday. But never, I think, a sorceress."

Dame Magda's prediction came true . . . to a degree. Zanita, as was inevitable, caught the eye of the king and did become Her Royal Highness, Queen Zanita. And there was no one, even among those who'd hoped the king would choose otherwise, who could question *why* he'd made his decision. No more queenly queen had ever existed; it was as though the title, in all its previous usage, had been quite undeserved. And Zanita made of it a title that any future holder would assume with trepidation, wondering if she could ever really measure up to what it required.

Zanita was a *good* queen. Even her kindness was to excess and her subjects loved her.

But she did not totally give up her dream of being—also—a sorceress.

* * *

Dame Magda knew it. When, one year, the bluebirds came in such numbers that they threatened the
crops, Magda knew that Queen Zanita had decided
she really *liked* bluebirds, and that there were too few
of them in her garden.

Likewise the summer when the swallowtail butterflies grew to a span across and turned iridescent green,
Magda knew one of the queen's spells had again
proven too much.

Zanita had no great ambition to be *powerful*. As
queen she had as much power as she'd ever needed.
What she envied was the ease with which a good sorceress could make nice things happen when there was
no practical way to bring them about. It wasn't gran-
deur she sought, but the pleasantness of little things,
pretty things, the kind of things which made an otherwise dreary day bearable: sweet perfumes, bright flowers, birdsong, and sunsets, the subtleties of which she
was, apparently, incapable.

Dame Magda saw the queen often, feeling a sense
of responsibility for having been unable to curb the
girl's natural excess, and for having taught her just
enough of the processes of sorcery to make her genu-
inely dangerous. Their visits consisted mostly of the
tutor's grim warnings of the possible results of unre-
strained magic, and impassioned pleas that the queen
rein in her impulsive creativity.

The time came, however, when the headmistress of
the Academy of Arts and Sorceries had to admit that
excess occasionally had its uses.

The kingdom to the north—traditional enemy of the
realm of Queen Zanita's homeland—began making
forays into the border territories. Not yet an all-out
invasion, it seemed the king was being tested: his defenses, his temper, and to what lengths he would go
to avenge minor incursions.

Something else was being tested also: the powers of

sorcery. Dame Magda suspected it when word came
of how spears and arrows seemed somehow to be
turned aside, prevented from reaching their targets
when those targets were the raiders advancing into the
farms and border towns. Magic was being used, but
only defensively, so far. It was not spectacularly powerful magic: the kind of simple spells any first-year
sorcery student could have managed, and managed to
defeat, had any first year sorcery students been in
those areas when they were needed.

Magda couldn't tell *what* was being tested, if the
simplicity of the magic was because of the limitations
of the enemy's abilities, or if attempts were being made
to induce the defenders to reveal the extent of their
own abilities.

The sorceress might have foreseen what was to
come if she had been present while the possibility of
war was discussed. But she wasn't, so even she was
surprised.

"How bad is it likely to get?" Zanita asked her
husband. "Are we going to have to call all the young
men in from the fields and farms to build an army
strong enough to defend our homes?"

"I don't know, my dear," the king replied grimly.
"I don't know what has prompted our neighbor to this
action. I'd thought we were well enough matched that
he'd see no advantage in attempting an invasion. He's
got some new grievance, or some new weapon, I don't
know which. He's got *some* kind of a bug up his
tunic."

That was the phrase which set Queen Zanita to
thinking. *A bug up his tunic.*

What, she thought, *would our neighbor to the north
do if I sent him a* real *bug to crawl up his tunic and
take a little bite out of his . . . ambition?*

She knew that an ant or a flea couldn't do much to
deter their enemy. No matter how painful the bite, it
was unlikely he'd interpret it as an aggressive retalia-

tion by the kingdom he'd invaded. He'd see it merely as a *pest*—something to hunt down and squash between a thumb and forefinger—not as a reason to discontinue his campaign. But Zanita had good reason to expect that her sorcery would produce something a little more than the troublesome flea she intended to conjure and send against their foe.

By this time she'd realized some of her own limitations; she knew her spells always produced results far beyond their design. She wasn't sure if it was that her gestures were too broad, too theatrical, or if the words were spoken—as most everything she said was—with too much vehemence, or too much enthusiasm and hope. She was sincerely trying to learn to hold back.

It was a little past midnight when she began to spell. She spoke the words in barely a whisper, and moved only one finger on each hand.

It was three days later that one of their spies returned with the news of how effective Zanita had been, though none but she and Dame Magda had any idea it was the queen's doing.

The man looked like the victim of some awful disease. Red lumps spread like a fierce rash across his face, his hands, and arms. He'd been scratching at those lumps, and his pebbled skin was raw and bleeding.

Dame Magda, in attendance at court, spoke a quiet spell to relieve the poor soul's itching, and he stood more easily before the king—who exercised every iota of kingly self-control to avoid shrinking away from what appeared to be something highly contagious.

Zanita fretted nervously, certain that his discomfort was her fault. Despite her precautions and her conscious and deliberate effort to tone everything down to near insignificance, in her heart she'd known that what she'd really *wanted* was not just a flea. She'd sincerely hoped her magic might produce a flea to match the enormity of their neighbor's offense. Her imagination envisioned a great, black-shelled, hungry monstrosity which, with one savage bite, might leave the invading armies without a head—literally and figuratively—and a far more serious opponent upon which to expend their energies than the defenseless farmers they'd thus far attacked.

"The *intent*," Dame Magda had told her class repeatedly, "is equally as important as the incantation."

"It was about midnight," the messenger said, "three days ago, when their army prepared for an attack upon the village of Wayside under cover of darkness. It was their plan, from what I heard being spoken about the camp, to burn the entire town simply to see if the inhabitants possessed any effective means of fighting the fire.

"They carried tinder, but no burning torches, not wanting anyone to see them coming. Thus they themselves did not see what it was that sent their horses— every one of them—into absolute panic. They reared, snorted, whinnied, bucked, and—no matter how viciously they were spurred and goaded—would not cross the border.

"Many threw their riders. And those men, as had the horses, screamed and leaped. They swatted at their faces, clawed at their hair, scratched their arms and legs . . . and retreated.

"Back in the camp, with lanterns and torches lit, we could see that both men and horses had been bitten and stung, but by what, no one could say. *Insects,* it seemed. But, as the men had retreated, whatever it was that had bedeviled them had dropped off or flown away. There was nothing but the bites, the welts, the stings, and the scratches to prove there'd been anything at all.

"Some were in such agony that they were useless. The swelling had closed their eyes, and some were even having trouble breathing. But those who could regrouped and charged again toward the town.

"Again they were stopped, this time some distance *before* they'd reached the border. Whatever had repelled the first foray was moving toward the camp.

"Their king himself took a torch and walked slowly forward peering into the darkness to see what had attacked his army. Those who walked a few paces behind saw him all but disappear into a dense cloud that boiled up from the dirt at his feet. He shrieked and fell, clawing at his body, his face, his hair.

"His men dragged him back. And by the light of his fallen torch they could see the very earth alive and moving—dust motes whirling forward like windblown ripples on a seashore.

"I know not what it was. Magic, I suppose. What else could it have been? Whatever it was, it sent the entire army scattering in terror. Even the king's own men fell back, leaving their lord to his fate.

"I've never seen a man move so fast. Though the others had run before him, he soon outdistanced them and led the retreat himself, though I doubt *leading* was much in his mind. I suspect his thought was simply to get as far from our border as possible. He may well be half across the wild lands to the north by now.

"I, myself, thought only of getting home, getting back here to tell what I could of what had occurred. I started at a hilltop, so steep that I knew, that once running I'd be unable to stop, and I raced as fast as I could.

"It felt like needles were being jabbed into my skin—envenomed needles that burned where they pierced until I feared I would die of the sting. But I could not stop. I dared not. My only hope was to get through that infestation.

"And I did.

"Suddenly it was no more. I had crossed the border, and the pestilence fell from me like grains of sand. I was fearfully bitten and stung, as you can see, but there were no vermin upon me, in my hair, nor in the folds of my clothing. At the border they'd disappeared. Whatever sent them, they move only against our enemies; they do not plague *our* land."

As the discussion and speculation raged on and on, with no one able even to suggest a source of their salvation, Dame Magda approached the young queen who stood apart looking like she didn't know whether to be disappointed at another spell gone so strangely awry, or proud of having bested a foe. Without a word, the Mistress of Arts and Sorceries drew from her sleeve a large, firm, beautifully ripe apple and set it firmly into Zanita's palm. She smiled her approval.

THE SONG OF THE STONES

Diana L. Paxson

Diana's story for this volume arrived late, as usual.

Diana L. Paxson was the only person exempt from the strict deadline imposed on the rest of the writers for *Sword and Sorceress*—Marion used to call her "the late Miss Paxson." But Diana does good work, and Marion always bought a story for *Sword and Sorceress* from her, usually sight unseen. Every year she would do the final line-up the day after the deadline, and every year she would leave a space for Diana's story. By now, it counts as a tradition.

The pack-pony ahead reared, squealing, a black-feathered arrow quivering in its neck. Bera clutched at the mane of her own mount as it came to a plunging halt, hind legs scrabbling for purchase on the narrow trail. From the cliff above came the harsh ululation of a war cry and more arrows. She saw one of the men who was supposed to guard the caravan fall.

Scots raiders! Bera realized, fighting to keep her horse under control. They had chosen the perfect place to ambush the plodding line of traders and ponies; just past the village, where the trail wound along the edge of the gorge.

Another arrow snicked past, grazing the flank of Alfhelm's pony and sending it snorting across the slope. She could see the boy still hanging on as the animal crashed through a stand of broom and disappeared. The traders were fighting back now. As their arrows flew, a body wrapped in tattered plaid tumbled down the slope and into the gorge.

Bera's horse lurched forward as the beasts scattered across the more level ground ahead. Only the traders had managed to stay together, shooting back when they glimpsed a foe. She saw Devorgilla with Alfhild on the saddle before her heading into the trees. Achtlan followed, and Bera booted her own mount after them.

"The northern trail will be safer," the traders had told them. *"If raiders come so late in the season, they'll not look for us there!"*

And I believed them, Bera thought grimly. *A fine seeress I am, not to have seen what could go wrong!* But even a Voelva trained in Norway could not answer the question no one had thought to ask.

"Are you all right?" she called as she came up with the others. Behind her, swords clanged as three of the attackers held the traders at bay while the others began to round up the laden ponies.

"I am, but they've got our chest!" exclaimed Achtlan, her eyes blazing with the passion of Ireland's warrior queens. Bera could feel the great brown bear who was her inner ally snarling with rage, but the kinds of magic she and Achtlan had been trained to use could not help them now.

Bera grabbed for the Irishwoman's rein. "Never mind our baggage—we're carrying our silver, and even if these wretches don't take slaves, they'll strip us bare!"

"But Alfhelm's gone—" cried Devorgilla.

"We cannot help him if we're raped and robbed here! Come on!" She was the smallest and youngest of the three women, and all of them were strangers in this land, but Bera had brought them here, and they were her responsibility. She forced her way past and the other horses caught the panic and followed.

They did not stop until the sounds of conflict had faded behind them. Beyond the edge of the forest lifted the bare shoulders of the moors, dappled with pockets of last night's snow. This was an altogether wilder land than the rich lowlands around Jorvik that might tolerate, but would rarely welcome, human settlement. The snow was moving—no, it was sheep, whose bleating came to them on the wind. From somewhere farther down the slope, smoke was rising. Standing in her stirrups, Bera saw the curve of a thatched roof.

"We'll go there—" she pointed, and the others followed her.

"And you say that none came after you?" asked the farm's master when the women, shaking now with reaction, had been settled with bowls of hot soup around the fire. White hair straggled around shoulders that were still broad, though they were bowed now with age.

"Why should they?" Bera asked bitterly. "They have all the plunder of the caravan." She spoke in Norse, for the man was one of those who had taken land under Eirik Bloodaxe when he was king here. Thorstein Hvitr was his name and the altar of heaped stones she had seen beyond the holly hedge as they rode in told her he followed the old ways.

"If they do, will you fight?" asked the thrall Bolli, a skinny youngster with ginger hair.

"Better still if they pass us by—" said his master. "Tell Samson to drive the sheep across the meadow to confuse the trail."

He may have been a wolf when he served Eirik, thought Bera, *but now he keeps to his den.* The rushes that covered the floor needed changing, and there were other small signs to tell her that if Thorstein had ever had a wife, she was long gone.

"But my son is still out there!" exclaimed Devorgilla, pushing a strand of hair darkened by the damp to carnelian back from her brow . . . "We must find him before night falls!"

"He'll have to take his chances. Perhaps tomorrow I can spare a man to look for the boy, after the Scots have gone."

Bera laid a warning hand on Devorgilla's arm as she opened her mouth to protest once more. The night before they had slept in thick blankets, and even then they had all huddled together to keep warm, and these hills were colder.

"I will go after him," she said quietly. Achtlan looked up at this, but her features were drawn with exhaustion, and she had not even the strength to protest.

"You?" Thorstein's amazement was clear.

"When I was a girl I tracked my father's cattle, and I know the prints of Alfhelm's pony. I should be able to pick up the trail . . ."

"No doubt!" Thorstein let out a short bark of laughter. "And then the Scots will pick up you!"

Bera drew herself up, gathering around her the glamour of a wisewoman. "I do not think so—" she said softly. His eyes widened, and she knew that he was no longer seeing a small, travel-worn woman with tangled brown hair, but the commanding figure of the Voelva, a seeress who in former days could have commanded kings. "I have the old magic, and know how to pass unseen."

"And do you know how to find your way through the fells and dales of this country?" he asked, though most of the challenge had faded from his tone. "This can be a chancy land to wander, where strange powers dwell."

"Then send one of your men to guide me—" Bera replied.

"And be captured with you?" Thorstein's tone turned querulous. "I need every man I've got on the farm!"

"I will stand surety!" exclaimed Devorgilla. "My life and my labor to serve you if your man is lost seeking

my son! The powers above know you need a woman's
work in this hall!"

Now it was Bera's turn to stare, knowing how the
young Irishwoman had hated the thralldom from which
Bera had rescued her. She was willing to risk her life
to search for the boy, but she did not think she would
have possibly condemned herself to servitude.

"Is it so?" Thorstein looked from one woman to
the other, and his gaze sharpened in appreciation of
Devorgilla's fair skin and the curving line of her
bosom and thigh.

A fine warm armful for a winter night, he was thinking, and a good trade for any of the unwashed men
who were goggling at their unexpected guests. That
was no surprise. Devorgilla had been the favorite of
Halvor Skjalgson, who captured her in Ireland, and
had borne him Alfhild and her twin Alfhelm, who
now was lost.

*But I did not risk my soul to win their freedom only
to lose them now,* Bera told herself. *I will find the boy
and come safe back again!* her considering gaze
stopped at Bolli.

"That one—" she pointed. "He looks as if he can
keep up with me."

Thorstein snorted with laughter as Bolli paled.

"Please mistress—I've no skill with weapons!" Bolli
stammered. "Take a man who can protect you!"

Thorstein turned to Bera. "He's better at hiding
than facing a foe, but if it comes to fighting, no single
man, were it Sigurd himself, could save you. You've
chosen well. Bolli is the man I send when a sheep
goes astray, and he knows every footpath in these
hills. Go—" he nodded to Bolli, "and may the gods
watch over you!"

There was no time to lose. *In this country,* said
Thorstein, *two legs would go as swiftly as four, and be*

easier to hide, so they did not take horses. But Bera did accept the loan of a pair of stout boots and a rough sheepskin coat with the wool inside.

The rough spikes of broom were crushed and broken where Alfhelm's pony had crashed through them. The trail led off at an angle after that, through broken country, but the boy had let his mount make its own way, the animal's prints showing clearly where it chose the softer ground.

And after the wide-spaced prints of the first, frantic rush the tracks came closer together as the exhausted pony slowed, and by then Alfhelm must have been weighing the dangers of being lost against those of capture, and would be looking for refuge.

Perhaps, thought Bera, *the horse will find its own way to Thorstein's farm, and Alfhelm will be waiting for us when we return!*

But as they continued, that began to look less likely. The pony had headed due north, where the ground folded downward towards the river Nidd. And when, as the pale winter sun was beginning to sink toward the hills, the pony's track was crossed by those of many laden horses, her heart sank.

Bolli had seen them as well. He offered her a conciliatory smile. "The Scots scum came for plunder, not slaves, but they will not pass up a likely lad if he falls in their way. Come, lady, there is no point in exhausting ourselves when we cannot save the boy . . ."

"We do not know that he is a captive," Bera said stubbornly. "They might have missed him. I will not go back to face his mother until I am sure."

They went on, but more carefully, in case the raiders had set someone to watch their rear. In these high fells a few trees clung to hollows; on the slopes, gorse and heather and short grass struggled for life in the thin soil. It was a wide and empty land, open to the sky, and the wind was cold.

By now, thought Bera as she trudged upward, the mountains of Norway would be covered with pure white. Wind had swept most of what had fallen the night before from these fells. Why, she wondered, did this land feel so much colder than she remembered ever being at home?

But if she had been in Norway, Bera thought then, she would not have been walking the hills. By now she would have been the guest of one of the king's lords or some prosperous farmer who would boast of having a wisewoman at his disposal for the winter, and assure her of an honored place at the feasting table or the fire. A stone turned beneath her foot and only her staff saved her from going down. *I don't belong here!* she thought grimly. *I should never have left the Norse lands. . . .*

In Norway there were places where Ymir's bones thrust strongly through the soil, reminding the wanderer of the jotun from whose body the gods had fashioned the world. But this was a kingdom of stone. She paused, closing her eyes, and quested outward with other senses. She had been wrong, she thought then. This land might seem empty, but there were forces moving all about her, whispering on the wind, shifting among the stones.

"Jotun country . . ." she whispered, wondering if even the elemental powers in this rugged land were the same as the ones she knew.

Bolli nodded, looking over his shoulder as if he expected one of the giantkind to come looming over the hill.

"How does your master deal with them? He is a stranger in this land—"

Like me—she added silently.

"My master accepted the white robe and the head washing when King Eirik took the new faith," he said. "But here in the hills he calls on Thor to keep the balance between the wild powers and humankind. He says that Thor is the same as Thunor, who the Saxons called."

"And what of you?"

"My mother followed the White Christ, and had me christened when I was a babe. They say that he listens to the prayers of slaves," for a moment the mask of truculence was gone. "But I do not think that he can hear me here."

Can Thor hear me? Bera wondered then. *Thorstein lives here and makes his offerings. He will give his bones to this land. But I am rootless as the wind. . . .*

The tracks of the raiders were fresh now. Bera and the thrall ranged out to either side of the trail, hoping to find that Alfhelm's pony had taken another way, but this was the best route down to the river, and the boy would have seen no reason to hide his trail. The sun flared suddenly as it touched the rim of the hills, then disappeared, leaving only an angry glow in the western sky.

Once more Bera paused, peering through the gathering gloom.

"Lady, without light we will not be able to find the boy, and without shelter, both he and we will die here on the moor," said Bolli. With the approach of nightfall the thrall's fears had returned. He cleared his throat. "Whether the child be taken or still wanders, he is lost. *Please,* lady, let us start back now."

Bera did not answer him. Across the river the skyline grew jagged. In the dimming light, it was not rocks, but distorted forms she saw standing there, a tall figure with a lumpy cap wrapped in a shawl, and a smaller being crouched beside her. Beyond her, others were taking shape from the stones. And below them—

"What is that?" she asked, pointing.

"The sun must have touched some hidden pool," he answered nervously. "Lady, we must go!"

"No. The sun has set. I think it is a fire."

"All the more reason to avoid it," Bolli said frantically. "That place has an uncanny reputation. No friend to us would dare take shelter among those stones."

"I am curious to know what manner of wight has done so. With Thor's help I mean to go there and see."

"You'll go alone, then!" glowered Bolli.

For a moment she considered him. "Very well," she said softly. "If you will not come with me then wait here until dawn. A bird of ill-luck like you would only hinder me, and someone should carry the tale back to my people if I do not return."

The thrall stiffened. "What makes you call me a luck-bane? It is I who will have the luck if I stay safe here, it seems to me!"

Bera shrugged. She knew well that it was not always lack of worth that brought a man to thralldom, and Bolli's station in life was no reason of itself to discount his warnings. And yet luck was a factor too, the ability to sense how the energy in a situation was flowing and move with the current. The lucky man did it instinctively; the wise-folk by intention. Which should she trust here, she wondered, Bolli's luck or her own wisdom?

"Bolli, tell me truthfully how you came to be a thrall."

He turned his back on her, and for a moment she thought he would refuse to reply.

"My father was one of Eirik's men," he said when a moment had passed. "He got me on a Saxon woman of the town. He gave her six children, but never married her. When he was killed she could not feed us all. She sold me as a servant to Thorstein when I was ten years old. It has not been so bad for me—I have enough to eat, and Thorstein treats his servants decently. I count myself lucky to be here!" he added suddenly. "I wager my brothers and sisters have not fared so well!"

"Then I take back my word," Bera said softly. "Is your luck strong enough to follow me up that hill?"

Bolli straightened, and she saw that there was manhood in him after all. "You mean that . . . you really think I can . . ."

"Bless yourself with the Cross, and I will sign myself with the Hammer, and we will see . . ."

Clumsily, as if he were trying to remember the movements, Bolli touched his fingers to brow and breast and then from one shoulder to the other, while Bera motioned with her fist across and down, smiling a little as she realized how similar the motions were.

"Remember that I have weapons you cannot see," she said boldly, hoping that it was true. Without looking back to see if he was coming, she started down the hill.

Bera chafed her feet, still numbed by the chill water, and pulled on her stockings and shoes once more. The river Nidd ran chuckling behind her. There was a voice in that water, and she wished she had something to offer the nixie of the stream. She stilled, listening, and for a moment, she thought she understood the words—

"By rock and rill . . . swift and chill . . .
blood of stones . . . Ymir's bones . . ."

No sweet and gentle spirit of spring lived here, but something far colder, far removed from the hot blood that ran beneath her own skin. Bolli's teeth were chattering. He stamped his feet to warm them, then looked apprehensively up the hill. He was still afraid, but seemed determined not to flee.

"Strength upwelling . . . power swelling . . .
ever flowing . . . eons knowing . . ."

Bera gazed upward, where the hill loomed against the early stars, wondering from what hidden crack that water sprang. As she started up the hill, Bera could still hear the river's song.

Bolli was a dim figure beside her, feeling his way carefully forward in the dark. From time to time he would pause and point to some obstacle. When he put out a hand to help her, she could feel him trembling. Wonder grew in her as she realized how much courage he had found.

And what about my *courage?* she wondered then. With every step she grew more aware of the power in this mountain. There was more than fear in the imagination that made a figure out of every outcrop or pile of stone.

But now, from above, she could hear the sound of singing, hoarse, and sometimes incoherent—she grinned suddenly, remembering that some of the beasts in the caravan had been carrying casks of wine. Were they drinking to dispel a sense of unease they could not name? The spirit of the vine would not banish those other spirits that were gathering, she thought with grim amusement, only dull the senses by which they might have perceived them.

Now they were near enough to glimpse the flicker of firelight. Bolli laid a hand on her arm.

"What are you going to do?" his voice was a breath against her ear.

"We must find out if they have the boy—get above them and look down. These vermin have raided the dales before. Do they post guards?"

"Out here?" Bolli shook his head. "Who would be so stupid as to follow? But they have their own magic," he added, "even drunk, there may be some who sense what moves after dark in this land."

The climb around the enemy camp seemed to take as long as the rest of the journey, but when Bera glanced upward, the stars had scarcely moved. She scrambled a few more steps and stopped short, staring. The rock formation that fancy had given a human

form from across the valley was above her, the shape
less familiar and more menacing against the dim sky.

Only after she had stopped Bolli with a tug at his
sleeve did she realize it was because she sensed that
they had been about to step onto forbidden ground.
By day, perhaps, those might be no more than stone,
but now they were something more. Painfully aware
of the pulse that thudded in her ears, she chose a
slanting course that would bring them above the fire.

"Is that the boy?" breathed Bolli as they peered
around a boulder.

Bera stretched enough to look down. The wind had
come up, and patterns of light and shadow danced
around the fire. At first glance all she could discern
was arms and legs emerging from a tangle of striped
and checkered woolens. The Scots had made good use
of the wine. But not all of them were drunk, or not
drunk enough, at any rate. Two men, their arms across
each others' shoulders, were singing. Several others
were dicing by the light of the fire. And one, a big,
red-headed fellow who seemed quite sober, sat by the
pile of booty from the caravan, which included the
sleeping child.

Bera sat back with a silent sigh. Alfhelm seemed to
be unharmed. He had always been able to fall asleep
no matter what was going on around him, and he
seemed quite comfortable despite his bonds.

"If I were to attract their attention, you might be
able to steal the boy away while they were chasing
me . . ." whispered Bolli.

"That's a fine plan for one who not so long ago
counseled running away!" She heard him swallow.

"I complain about my fate, but I see now that there
are worse things than being Thorstein's thrall. I can
run like a hare, and I'm willing to take a risk to save
that child from the life those savages would give him!"

"A thrown knife goes faster than a man. I mean to
bring you both safely home again!" And not only for

the sake of Devorgilla's freedom, Bera thought then. Now she cared about Bolli, too.

She shivered as a new gust of wind probed the weave of her cloak. In that moment of attention she realized that just as there had been in the river, there were voices in the air—

"Flying high, soar the sky, so-ooh . . .
Scour the land, stone to sand, go-ooh . . ."

Was it the wind that had shaped the masses of rock above them so fantastically? Flying grit stung her cheek and she ducked back behind her boulder as a clatter of falling pebbles brought the guard upright, staring into the darkness.

The windspirits sounded uneasy. Were they angered at these strangers who had dared to invade their land? Yet Bera herself was even more of an alien in this country than they.

The difference was that she could hear the voices.

"Whisk and whirl, sweep and swirl, blow-ooh . . .
Ymir's breath, Ymir's death, woe-ooh . . ."

Wind and water spoke of Ymir, or at least that was how she heard their song. Here, as in the Norse lands, the Shining Powers had wrested from their elder kin the raw stuff from which Midgard was made. But though the wind might frighten their foes, it would not move them. What she needed now was the might of Earth herself.

Bera dug her fingers into the gritty soil. Surely it was not her own racing pulse that she felt throbbing there—this was a tremor so slow as to be almost beyond perception, but it was there. Once, long ago, she had been trapped in a deep cave and learned to sing the dwarf-runes that released the song of the stone. The Stone Giants themselves had their home on the top of this hill. Could she find a song to call them to her aid, and having done so, survive their assistance?

She took a shaking breath and then turned to the thrall.

"Bolli, I want you to go back down the hill. Get down on your belly and worm your way as close as you can to the pile of plunder. When the guard moves, be ready to snatch the child."

The moon was rising. His eyes gleamed as he faced her. "What are you going to do?"

"I was a singer to spirits in my own land," she said softly. "I am going to see if the spirits of this hill can hear my song."

As Bera approached the hilltop, the wind died. She felt the fine hairs on her forearms rising and knew the sensation did not come from the cold. Instinctively she slowed. Had Bolli been right to beg her not to try this? It had taken some minutes of argument to persuade him to play the part she had assigned him, the intensity in their voices covered by the wind. She would have been gratified by the completeness with which he had abandoned his fears if she had not, she admitted it now, been afraid.

When she sang the dwarf-runes long ago, the choice had been between one death and another, and she had had a companion whose skills equaled her own. Now she was alone. If she awakened the Stone Giants, her flesh might be destroyed. But if she did not, she would lose her honor.

"*Men die and cattle die,*" she remembered the old saying with a grim smile, "*but a fair name dies never.*"

She took another step, bent forward as if she faced a strong wind. But there was no wind. It was the air itself that stopped her, more dense than the stuff that filled human lungs, and by that she knew that she had reached the border of the Jotun world.

At the top of the hill there was a slight depression, as if the earth had been compressed by the weight of the stones that stood in a rough circle around it. In the moonlight the air within had a faint glow. The rock formations wavered as if seen through water. Or were they really moving?

Less from reverence than because her legs would no longer support her, Bera laid down her staff and sank to her knees, hands flat against the bare stone. The rock quivered beneath her palms, once, and again, as if some huge foot struck the ground. Her attention sharpened as she realized the tremors were coming in rhythm.

She closed her eyes, questing outward with other senses, and as she had heard the sounds of wind and water, heard the song of the stones:

"Crack, rock, crack—round and back!
Through wind and rain, we remain!
Stamp and stump! Clap and bump!
This is sure, we endure!"

When she looked up again, the rocks were moving.

Bera blinked. She could still see the shapes of the rock formations that had been there before, but in the moonlight they were translucent images through which the horizon could be dimly seen. Before them moved distorted forms shot through with sparkles of light. The spirits of the stones were dancing.

For a moment Bera knew only wonder. Few indeed were the mortals who could say they had seen such a thing and lived to tell the tale. With one touch, one look even, she knew they could flatten her—there were reasons why the gods acted as intermediaries between men and the Elder Powers in the old tales.

"Sithi Thor," she whispered, "grant me the magic I will need. Speak to your mother, Son of Earth, and get me Her blessing . . ."

She knelt without moving, striving for the inner stillness that would allow her to hear a reply. If even the voice of a god could be heard above the song of the stone spirits that throbbed in her bones.

The answer, when it came, was not in words but in

a breath of wind that lifted the hair from her brow, and a tingle of power down her right arm. Slowly she lifted it, fist clenched as if she held a hammer in her hand. Her muscles trembled, braced against the weight of it, and her lips drew back in a grin.

"Jotnar, Mountain-alfs, Rock-alfs, in the name of the Son of Earth I summon you. Enemies are here. They have taken a child of my kin. They hurt the people of this place."

She waited, sensed the rhythm faltering, felt her shoulders bow beneath the weight of their regard. The answer, when it came, rumbled up from the depths of the earth.

"Why should we care? The ones who dwell here now do not care for us. It has been long since mortals came with offerings."

Bera's mind whirled. She had no beast to sacrifice. They had eaten all the food, and she had left her valuables with Achtlan. Yet what such beings desired was not the thing itself, but its energy. Biting her lip with determination, she drew her knife with her left hand, pushed up her other sleeve, and slashed the sharp blade across the inside of her forearm.

For a moment the cut stung, then she felt the warmth as blood filled it and began to drip onto the stone.

"I offer the life in my blood to feed you, as a pledge that I will teach those who dwell in these lands to honor you."

She waited for the chill that would tell her she had lost too much blood, but it was warmth she felt, and an easing of that oppressive weight, as the atmosphere of the stone circle expanded to encompass her and the forces were equalized.

"Sing your spell . . ."

Bera staggered to her feet, swinging the hammer around her head so that black drops of blood spattered across the stones.

"Crack, rock, crack—round and back!
Down the hill, foes to kill!
Stamp and stump! Clap and bump!
Shatter and shake those who take!"

Three times the hammer whirled, until she faced the Scots' fire, and then she brought it down. In the sky, lightning flared, but the echoing rumble came from the rock, a tremor that spread outward through the hill, releasing an avalanche of boulders.

The shadow shapes of the rock formations trembled, but their spirits rolled downward with the boulders, shouting like children at play. In another moment cries from mortal throats echoed them.

Dizzied, Bera stared at the column of dust illuminated by the fire. Her arm had almost ceased to bleed. She tore a strip from the hem of her shift to bind it. Presently the screaming gave way to moans, and the sounds men made as they frantically scrabbled across stone.

When Bera started back down the hill, the moon was sinking and the eastern sky had the gray pallor of approaching dawn. She had waited until the Stone Spirits returned to their circle. They were quiet now— inert lumps of rock to ordinary eyes. Weariness dragged at every limb, but a great peace was in her soul.

Beside the river she found Bolli and Alfhelm, bruised and grimed from their flight, but whole, and fearing more for her safety than she had feared for theirs, after this night of miracles. Bolli crossed himself as she approached, but Alfhelm came running up to hug her.

"You see—I am not a spirit—" she smiled.

"Bera, you missed all the fun!" exclaimed the boy. "You should have seen them go!"

She laughed a little at that, and shook her head. "I heard them, and I think they will not soon return." She turned to Bolli.

"The Stone Giants rule this land, and they will protect you if you honor them. Give whatever name you will to the god who made this world, but do not deny the elder kindreds who are its life. Will you come here at Midsummer to make the offering? In ordinary times they require nothing to disturb your faith—a horn of mead or a few flowers."

"I will." Shyly, he touched her hand. "Until this night I have felt a stranger in this country, never belonging, though I knew it so well. But now it does not matter whether Thorstein Hvitr calls himself my master. I have only to step out onto the moors to be free."

"I'm hungry!" exclaimed Alfhelm, "Please can we go now?"

By the time they reached Thorstein's steading the short day was drawing to an end. And by the time they heard the farm dogs barking and the folk came out from the house to meet them Bera was so tired she could scarcely speak. It was Achtlan, whose own training in the use of power told her what Bolli had left unsaid, who half-carried Bera inside and began to spoon-feed her the nourishing soup she had kept simmering over the fire.

"I brought both of them home . . ." Bera whispered presently. "Devorgilla is still free."

"Thorstein is not—" said Achtlan with a snort that might have been derision or laughter. "One day has shown him the advantages of having a woman here, and he wants to marry her."

Bera sat up at that, her gaze turning to the high seat, where Devorgilla was watching Thorstein eat his soup with an already possessive eye.

"I have advised her to accept him," said Achtlan. "Even if she has kin alive in Ireland, there's no telling if they would welcome her back, and Thorstein will make a good foster-father for the twins."

"I will miss them," Bera said after a time, but there was no disputing that she and Achtlan would make their way more easily on their own. She realized then that so long as she had her companions she had carried Norway with her.

But she need do so no longer.

My gods go with me, she thought then, *and in every land, the powers behind wind and earth and water are the same. So long as I can touch them I will be at home.*

HOMILY

The Rev. C. Robbins Clark

Robbin Clark is the Rector at Saint Mark's Episcopal Church
in Berkeley, the church Marion attended. She was called to
the post in 1993; one of her first homilies there was preached
at the memorial service for Marion's husband Walter Breen.
It must have been a challenge—she had never met the man
and knew very little about him. But Robbin has a genius for
homilies. Marion recognized this; Robbin appears as a character in *Tiger Burning Bright* with the same talent for producing
brilliant sermons on very short notice.

For those of you who don't recognize the Gospel reading
referred to in Robbin's homily, it's Luke 7:36–50. Marion
chose it beforehand. The story is of an incident that occurred
while Jesus was having dinner at the house of a Pharisee.
A woman came into the house, washed Jesus' feet with her
tears, dried them with her hair, and anointed them with oint-
ment from an alabaster box. The Pharisee was smugly thinking that Jesus wasn't so smart, or he would know that this
woman was a sinner and wouldn't let her near him. Jesus,
of course, saw the woman truly, and to enlighten him Jesus
asked the Pharisee, "Do you see this woman?"

Normally we end each volume of *Sword and Sorceress*
with a short, funny story. But this is the last volume Marion
herself edited, so it seemed appropriate to end it with these
words about Marion's life from Robbin's homily at her
funeral.

"Do you see this woman?"
What a question! Of course he saw her. It
was his house. He'd watched her enter and wondered

what the hell was she, or anyone like her, doing there. He'd been transfixed by her "outrageous performance" and was muttering derisively to himself about her when Jesus broke in with his story about debtors and creditors. He saw her all right.

Or did he? Perhaps he just saw what she represented to him. Perhaps he just saw that which he feared and despised and didn't really see her at all. And he certainly did not see the beauty and poignancy of her lavish outpouring of contrition and gratitude. Jesus saw it. Jesus saw her. He saw and understood what she was doing. What's more, he valued it, valued her, and raised her up to be an example to his smug, self-righteous host. And he spoke to her directly and granted her heart's desire.

I love it that Marion chose this Gospel reading for her funeral, as she chose all the readings and music for this service. (Think of them as a sort of final story outline.) Except for the Hebrew Scripture portions, these are not "designated" funeral readings. But then, what did Marion ever do in the "designated" manner? The Hymn to Love from First Corinthians is most often heard at weddings. And the Gospel: it just takes its turn once every three years with so many other Gospel passages. It has long been one of my favorites. Especially as a long-haired and earnest seminary student, I fancied myself in the role, throwing myself at the feet of Jesus in total devotion, heedless of the shock waves it would send through the established order. I think Marion was deeply sensitive to and appreciative of both the extravagance and sensuality of the woman's act and its importance as a statement against an establishment which had lost both heart and humor and even its ability to discern the truth which was before its eyes. And she knew first-hand the complex interweavings of passion and compassion, fear and hope, sin and forgiveness. She spent most of her life on or over the edge in one way or another, even amid her great success as an author. I cannot even pretend to have understood all she was about.

"Do you see this woman?"
Perhaps the question should be addressed to us. Many from Saint Mark's would be surprised to know that the woman of increasing physical frailty, so lovingly attended by Raul and Elisabeth, whom they saw at church each week was a famous author. Her fans might be equally surprised to know she was a long-standing communicant of the Episcopal Church. Those who revere her as a science-fiction/fantasy guru might never imagine her down-to-earth matter-of-factness or her puckish sense of humor. Of course, most of us have not been privileged to see and know her fully. Indeed, which of us ever knows another's being completely?

But that is no excuse for not trying to see the full reality of another and, even more, extending our hearts in affection and forgiveness. If we do not, we show ourselves one with the blind-eyed self-absorbed host in the story. The famous are particularly vulnerable to having their unique humanity obscured by the projections of others. We lionize or vilify according to our own needs, heedless of the wholeness of the one who has made such an impression on us.

Thanks be to God for Jesus' clear and loving eye. As he saw, knew, and appreciated the woman in the story, so he sees, knows, and appreciates each one of us. So he has seen, known, and appreciated Marion and now does so face to face. Though we weep here, and weep we must for the pain of our loss, let us not weep for her. She is whole and well in ways she would never be this side of death. Her pen and plots have ceased, but her spirit lives on in love. Her work is her memorial and will continue to inspire. We will dry our eyes and go on living. But we will also remember. Let us do so with honesty and affection. In our hearts and minds let us truly "see this woman" whom we gather here today to celebrate: loving lavishly, if not always wisely or adeptly, a brilliantly inventive groundbreaker and also a practical, if not totally resigned, bearer of life's burdens.

Her families, both biological and "adopted," were many and varied and extend outward to include all her fans and her brothers and sisters in Christ. Today, as we celebrate this "Easter" service of the resurrection, we share a foretaste of the heavenly banquet where Marion now feasts with the whole communion of saints. As Jesus said to the woman in the Gospel, so we now say to Marion, "Your faith has saved you, go in peace."

DARKOVER

Marion Zimmer Bradley's
Classic Series

Now Collected in New Omnibus Editions!

Heritage and Exile
0-7564-0065-1
The Heritage of Hastur & Sharra's Exile

The Ages of Chaos
0-7564-0072-4
Stormqueen! & Hawkmistress!

The Saga of the Renunciates
0-7564-0092-9
The Shattered Chain, Thendara House
& City of Sorcery

The Forbidden Circle
0-7564-0094-5
The Spell Sword & The Forbidden Tower

"Darkover is the essence, the quintessence, my most
personal and best-loved work."
—Marion Zimmer Bradley

To Order Call: 1-800-788-6262

MERCEDES LACKEY

The Novels of Valdemar

To Order Call: 1-800-788-6262

OTHERLAND

TAD WILLIAMS

*"The Otherland books are a
major accomplishment."*
−Publishers Weekly

"It will captivate you."
−Cinescape

*In many ways it is humankind's most stunning
achievement. This most exclusive of places is also
one of the world's best-kept secrets, but somehow,
bit by bit, it is claiming Earth's most valuable
resource: its children.*

CITY OF GOLDEN SHADOW (Vol. One)
0-88677-763-1

RIVER OF BLUE FIRE (Vol. Two)
0-88677-844-1

MOUNTAIN OF BLACK GLASS (Vol. Three)
0-88677-906-5

SEA OF SILVER LIGHT (Vol. Four)
0-75640-030-9

To Order Call: 1-800-788-6262

Kristen Britain

GREEN RIDER

"The gifted Ms. Britain writes with ease and grace as she creates a mesmerizing fantasy ambiance and an appealing heroine quite free of normal clichés."
—*Romantic Times*

Karigan G'ladheon has fled from school following a fight that would surely lead to her expulsion. As she makes her way through the deep forest, a galloping horse plunges out of the brush, its rider impaled by two black arrows. With his dying breath, he tells her he is a Green Rider, one of the legendary messengers of the King. Giving her his green coat with its symbolic brooch of office, he makes Karigan swear to deliver the message he was carrying. Pursued by unknown assassins, following a path only the horse seems to know, she unwittingly finds herself in a world of deadly danger and complex magic, compelled by forces she does not yet understand....

0-88677-858-1

To Order Call: 1-800-788-6262

DAW 7

Melanie Rawn

"Rawn's talent for lush descriptions and complex characterizations provides a broad range of drama, intrigue, romance and adventure."
—*Library Journal*

To Order Call: 1-800-788-6262